One of the best feelings
in the world is knowing
that your presence and
absence both mean something
to someone
All My Love —

To: Colleen –

A Perfect Match

A Young Man's Life Journey and Triumph

Barbee Kinnison
12-2015

Barbee Kinnison

authorHOUSE

AuthorHouse™
1663 Liberty Drive
Bloomington, IN 47403
www.authorhouse.com
Phone: 1 (800) 839-8640

© 2015 Barbee Kinnison. All rights reserved.

No part of this book may be reproduced, stored in a retrieval system, or transmitted by any means without the written permission of the author.

Published by AuthorHouse   11/24/2015

ISBN: 978-1-5049-5739-7 (sc)
ISBN: 978-1-5049-5737-3 (hc)
ISBN: 978-1-5049-5738-0 (e)

Library of Congress Control Number: 2015917423

Print information available on the last page.

Any people depicted in stock imagery provided by Thinkstock are models, and such images are being used for illustrative purposes only.
Certain stock imagery © Thinkstock.

This book is printed on acid-free paper.

Because of the dynamic nature of the Internet, any web addresses or links contained in this book may have changed since publication and may no longer be valid. The views expressed in this work are solely those of the author and do not necessarily reflect the views of the publisher, and the publisher hereby disclaims any responsibility for them.

Disclaimer

A Perfect Match is a work of fiction. Apart from the well-known actual people, events, and locales that figure in the narrative, all names, characters, places, and incidents are the products of the author's imagination or are used fictitiously. Any resemblance to current events or locales, or to living persons, is entirely coincidental.

Acknowledgments

My special thanks to Dr. Charles Carlini for his contributions and involvement with this book in the initial talking stages. He broke six ribs on Thanksgiving morning enduring excruciating pain that put him out of the picture before we were even able to dream about a project. Breathing life into what started out as a few thoughts and sentences, then seeing it evolve into a novel before my very eyes, was exciting and mystifying. I enjoyed every moment of it.

I wish to thank my husband who was my constant sounding board and reader of each chapter as it progressed. He is so full of patience. He was exceptional with his "keep it going" prompting. He also gave me the full support that any writer needs to keep their fingers on the keyboard.

And, to my two computers, who were my constant companions... I cannot thank you enough!

Ronald Reagan was once asked to review a book when he was President. He described the book as, "The perfect yarn."

Barbee Kinnson's book is the perfect story.
-Judson Phillips

Prologue

The BABE and the Legacy

There are young boys born every day that dream of growing up to become a professional baseball player. Their next dream, if they achieve the first, is to break the gold standard of "60 home runs," hit in 1927 by George Herman (Babe Ruth) in a full season, which was 154 games at that time. It's the one constantly coveted and most relished record of all time to defeat.

Babe Ruth's record was broke by Roger Maris, of the 'New York Yankees' in 1961. Roger Maris was under intense pressure as he defied the odds and chased the ghost of Babe Ruth and his season home run record. The fans were not supportive or very happy to have their legend's record broke just yet, and this weighed heavily upon Maris' shoulders. His inner desire weighed just as heavy.

Maris did achieve the feat of "61 home runs in one year," through raw determination and focus. Unfortunately, it was accomplished in more than 154 games, still falling short of the "ne plus ultra" of baseball. While some count this as a new home run record, others do not. "The Babe" could have hit more than 60 home runs had he played another eight games.

Then the steroid era rolled in. Mark McGuire and Barry Bonds were able to hit more home runs in 162 games than Roger Maris did. Unfortunately, these two ball players were not voted into the Baseball Hall of Fame because their accomplishments were achieved with the help of PED (performance-enhancing drugs), such as HGH (human growth hormones) and anabolic steroids. Few armchair experts make the successful argument that these are legitimate records. The United States Congress and the Department of Justice do not. Their prosecutions involving Barry Bonds and Roger Clements examples of how they view artificial enhancements involved in sports.

Since 1927, fans of Major League Baseball – and there are many, have been waiting for someone to hit 61 home runs in 154 games. It seems to be the ever elusive gold standard set by The Babe in a New York Yankee pinstripe uniform, that is always just out of reach.

Mickey Mantle made a gallant attempt in his best year of 1961, also in a New York Yankee pinstripe uniform. He hit 54 home runs, but failed to meet the Babe's benchmark. Sixty home runs in 154 games is the perfect or most extreme example one could give. It is the ultimate in personal achievement for a serious baseball player.

Any young boy growing up in America – even those with only a passing interest in Baseball, realize a new home-run king has to surpass the Babe's record in all of its natural splendor and glory. Nothing else will constitute a true achievement, no matter who jumps into the arguments.

When Justin Edge walks on to the Fenway Park field and feels the inner connection with The Babe, his inner, younger self, the all American young boy who was now a grown up, yet, still coveting and willing to grab the dream like a kite by the tail. He silently vowed and dared to dream about his abilities to challenge the most famous record in all of sports. The ever so often unrealistic world when a baseball player is looking for the promise in his home run performance to excel to heights unknown. It is when the sports writers and announcers let the words occasionally emanate from their mouths. This is all called "normal," but this savoring of one's ability to surpass The Babe only serves to make Baseball all the more interesting and exhilarating. Justin's thought process was no stranger to this endeavor, or any other hurdle that came in his path.

The tide begins to shift when Justin's fourth season of Major League Baseball arrives. He finds himself situated at a Major League game, leading 58 home runs after 153 games.

Over the past week, he had pressed very hard for the final three home runs, but it was not to be as his strikeouts increased, as they usually and normally do when one swings for the fences. Justin was robbed of many home runs. No pitcher wanted to go into the record books as the "goat" that gave up the homer that beat the Babe's record. These pitchers and their manager's, were more than complicating his quest as they dug in deeper and found inner strength or just threw the ball outside of the strike zone for an intentional ball so as to deprive Justin of his goal.

The sports writers felt compelled to explain that the long season was coming to an end. The Boston Red Sox players had been exposed to a very hot and humid July and August, and the everyday team players may have been feeling the effects of the "Dog Days of the Baseball Summers," a good and believable theory that still sold papers.

Justin did not buy into any of these excuses and was relieved that his manager had not rested him as he chased" *The Babe's record."* Justin's destiny was in his own hands now

Chapter 1

"Hello Ladies and Gentlemen, distinguished guests. Welcome to Cooperstown, New York, home of the world renowned Baseball Hall of Fame where memories of the most impressive players in baseball history reside in perpetuity," said Wanda Sue Helms, Chairman of the Cooperstown Hall of Fame. I would like to introduce the current Commissioner of Baseball for today's presentation, Commissioner Frederick Chesterfield.

Hello Ladies and gentlemen, and thank you for being here with us today as we begin our induction ceremony. Though most names within these walls are from the past, there are many who are with us still, and some of those are here today to celebrate with us as we have a new inductee that you will meet in a very short time, as we recognize another one of Baseball's most impressive champions who have helped make the game magical, thrilling and everlasting.

We will place his name among the most prominent and immortal names in all of baseball history to live as long as the world exists and as long as people love the game of Baseball

No one man is responsible for Baseball's legends, but one man at a time forged it through hard work and a spirit that imitated his highest personal standards. These men were and are the vanguards to whom we pay homage.

Today, we are honoring a man who never lost his determination to be the best of the best. His hope was always covered in a blanket of determination and optimism. Justin Edge overcame obstacles of enormous proportions to become a standard anybody could set as an example for his own life. Justin has, and always will be, a man of peace, loyalty and unparalleled determination to succeed.

He lives in our hearts to this day as an American bittersweet success story that finally came to fruition through raw determination and a belief in God that kept him going when others would have fallen apart. His humility and his dignity are what gave him a very long career that provided Boston fans, and baseball fans everywhere, with a competitive and decent hero to admire during his playing days and long after, as attested by the ceremony today.

Therefore, Justin Edge, today we are honored and proud to add your name to be enshrined with other Baseball heroes. So ladies and gentlemen, please help me welcome Justin Edge, our newest inductee into the Cooperstown, New York "Baseball Hall of Fame."

Justin arose, walked to the podium and shook the Commissioner's hand. He then accepted the beautiful plaque presented by the Commissioner of Baseball. They posed for pictures and he read the inscription.

As the crowd cheered and applauded Justin Edge, he paused, with eyes closed, and held the plaque next to his heart. His mind was filled with thoughts, as the crowd continued its standing ovation.

He listened to the applause, savoring every moment because he knew this would probably be the last time he would hear the all-adoring enthusiasm of a crowd. It brought back so many memories. He couldn't help but smile as he looked at all the people across the front of the building, spilling out down the steps and out onto the street, far from the podium, and further than he could see in the bright sunlight.

Justin stepped up to the microphone and began his speech.

"This is without a doubt, one of the proudest moments in my entire life. I would be remiss if I didn't say that my proudest moment was the birth of my son, Bradley," he added, waving to his son. *"I can't imagine my son's not being part of my life. A lot of people don't get the honor to share such a joy.*

The second proudest moment in my life was breaking the home run record set by the immortal Babe Ruth in 1927. That perfect record had held for almost 88 years.

Some players have broken the record before me in more games, but my goal was to beat this record in his same number of games, or less, and in one season. This would be an authentic and undisputed record in my mind. The record of home runs in one season by Babe Ruth was 60 in 154 games. Those numbers are forever ingrained in my mind.

I have many more monumental moments that stand out in my mind, enough to fill Fenway Park, including our World Series victory over the Los Angeles Dodgers. But for the sake of time, I'll be much briefer than that. The sun needs to set at some time today." He said smiling.

During the time he spoke to the crowd, he recalled how amazing and mystifying it is that tragedies, sadness and pain are such an intertwining and inexorable part of life, something he learned from birth forward.

Chapter 2

Justin's early life was hard and cruel. By the time he turned ten, he had some serious self-esteem, abandonment and insecurity issues. He was left for days and parts of days on end to fend for himself, ignored by his prostitute and drug-addicted mother, Suzanna. She was all he had in his young life. Every time she walked out the door, he begged her not to leave, or quizzed her relentlessly on when she would return. Then, deserted, he would retreat into his singular world, to read and be taken away from this world. He loved school, his sanctuary, and he was an excellent student.

It was amazing how well he fared, as he rarely had more to eat than potato chips and corn chips, until his mother would sometimes bring home cereal and milk. His dirty clothes stank and he began taking home the school's hand soap to use as laundry soap. He could only hope that his underclothes would be dry by the next morning.

Strange feelings of panic welled up inside him on the occasions when his mother didn't return by the second day. Then, when she did, and was a wreck in need of sleep, he always took care to cover her as she slept on the sofa. After school, as money would allow, they would then go to the market together and shop for groceries.

Overcome by feelings of loneliness and isolation, Justin sometimes wondered if the man who fathered him would ever return, and if his mother would ever straighten herself up. Dwelling on these intense thoughts sometimes brought him to near hysteria, and he would turn to his books for escape, and how he would read!

His favorite subject was baseball stories. He followed newspaper articles about baseball from the outdated newspapers given him by the barber down the street. He was given free haircuts because he swept the

Barber Shop three times a week and mopped the floor. He was even able to catch a few games on the television when the World Series was on. The stories in the newspaper and magazines calmed him and he was able to sleep. He continued to earn excellent grades, as school and the school library was all he had.

His mother once told him that she had a mother who lived about a hundred miles away, but that they couldn't visit her because they did not, and would never, get along.

She told him that her father was a white man who deeply loved and married a black woman. He had worked in a lumberyard until one day the ties around a stack of lumber broke. The load collapsed, killing him instantly, with a hard blow to the head. It was after her father's death, that she and her mother began having arguments about her boyfriends and failing schoolwork. She never mentioned her drug use. "No matter, we don't need her." Suzanna told her son. "We're doing just fine."

Justin guessed this was fine enough for now, but not for his future. He was going to make something of himself. He was going to be a professional baseball player and then maybe become a doctor and help people.

He must have fallen asleep somewhere between the grandmother story and his self-uplifting thoughts. He heard the door close heavily and his mother stumbling around. He hopped out of bed and went to help her as usual.

"You are such a good son, Justin," his mother always said as he tucked her into bed. "Can we go to the store tomorrow, Mama?" he asked. "We are out of everything!"

"Sure, baby," she said. "Just wake me up when you get home from school, and I'll be rested up and we'll go."

Reassured by her words, Justin slipped back into bed and slept deeply until he heard the usual alarm clock from the next apartment, a bonus provided by the thin walls.

School was good today. The lunch of tomato soup and grilled cheese satisfied a mighty hungry, young, growing boy. Justin scurried home after the last bell rang and informed his friends that he wouldn't be at the baseball field today because he and his mom had shopping to do. He couldn't wait to speak of his mom this way – it almost bordered on normalcy.

As he entered the shabby apartment, he called out, "Mama, I'm home. Time to wake up." His mother was not on the sofa, and she wasn't on his bed. He looked at the bathroom door; it was shut. Knocking gently, he called, "Mama, I'm home, are you ready to go?" No answer. "Mama, are you in there?"

Justin opened the door and peeked in only to see his mother under the water in the bathtub! He ran in and raised her limp, lifeless body. He panicked and ran to the next apartment door and banged on it while yelling to please call an ambulance, his mom was drowning.

One of the neighbors stuck his head out and looked at the frightened young boy, but by this time, an unknown man down the hall had come running and took Justin by the hand. Together they entered the apartment. The man said, "Son, you stay here and I'll check to see if your mom's okay and try to help her. I called for an ambulance. You watch for them and guide them in, okay?" Justin nodded his head yes, unable to speak.

Willie was the name of the man who'd come to Justin's aid. His heart sank to his feet as he saw Justin's mother submerged in the water. Reacting swiftly, he heaved her body out of the tub and on to the floor. He tried to perform mouth-to-mouth resuscitation. He tried CPR, he pounded her chest with repeated thrusts to try and start her heartbeat, but there was no response. The medics arrived and, after checking her vital signs, pronounced her dead. They still needed to remove her body and transport it to a trauma center for the doctors on staff to determine the time and cause of death, and other related details.

Willie never left Justin all the while this was going on. He held him in his arms and on his lap away from the activity he felt was too dramatic for such a young boy. "Do you have a father, son?" he asked. Justin nodded no. "I had no one but my mama." Willie pulled Justin in closer to him and tears formed in his eyes. "Do you have anyone, anyone at all, son? Any grandparents, aunts or uncles?"

"I have a grandma who lives near Mobile and her phone number is on a matchbox in a kitchen drawer. I think my mama forgot about it, because we never see her. Mama said she is a crazy person."

Willie felt he should call this woman and tell her about her daughter. Child Welfare Services could figure out the rest. He told the paramedics who were preparing to put the body of Suzanna in a body bag for transportation to the hospital morgue, "I'm taking her son with me, two doors down, to call his grandma, her mom, pointing at Suzanna's lifeless body. "Don't leave without us." They promised to let him know when they were ready to leave.

"Son, how about you show me that matchbox and I'll make a call so you don't have to." Justin retrieved the matchbox out of the back of the drawer. He was the one who hid it from his mama because he was always curious what made the woman so crazy and thought some day when he was older, he would find out about his grandmother on his own and maybe when he was a doctor, he could help her.

"Here you go, sir."

"Son, my name is Willie Johnson, what is your name?"

"I'm Justin Edge."

"Ok, Justin. Come with me while I make that call and we'll be back before the paramedics are ready to leave so we know what to do from here."

"OK." He uttered mindlessly.

Justin didn't know what to expect now, and didn't have the foggiest idea where to go or what to do, so he held on to Willie's hand and followed him two doors down from his own. Willie left his door open so he could hear what was going on outside and dialed the number on the matchbox.

"Hello, this is Ruby." Said the soft voice on the other end.

"Ms. Ruby, this is Willie Johnson a neighbor of your daughter Suzanna." Waiting to hear if she denied knowing a Suzanna,

"Yes, that is my daughter. What's wrong? Why are you calling me?" Ruby could feel her heart beat pacing out of her chest and somehow inherently knew it was not going to be good news.

"I'm with your grandson Justin, and I wanted to let you know the paramedics are taking your daughter to the hospital emergency room in a few minutes as she has passed away. Your grandson said he doesn't know you and we aren't sure what to do right now other than let the child services take him over."

"Mr. Willie, I'll be there as soon as I can get a suitcase together. Please, please, Mr. Willie, don't let them do anything with my grandson!" Her voice sounded hysterical and pleading, but with such soft undertones.

"I'll tell you what, I'm off of work today by some strange reason, so I'll take your grandson to the hospital following the ambulance and you can meet us in the emergency waiting area. I'm Willie Johnson and we will be at the University Medical Center."

"I'll be no more than three hours or less. Please wait for me as I will meet you at the hospital!" The phone went silent.

Willie was a man of his word, a rare thing in the Projects.

"Son, I just promised your Grandma I won't leave you or let anyone else take you until she arrives at the hospital. So for right now, I'm a distant cousin…OK?"

Justin just nodded yes again as his dry throat could offer no sounds.

Willie held his hand and offered him a drink of water which he took and drank all of it. Willie thought Justin was going to faint and thought it would be best if the emergency medical staff did a check-up on the boy. Off they went as quickly as Willie could follow the ambulance in his truck.

By the time they arrived at the emergency room, Justin's eyes were glassed over and Willie knew from his days in the army that this was not a good sign. He wrapped the spare coat he always carried in his truck around Justin and picked him up like a baby surprised at how light the boy was, and carried him into the emergency room. He was a tall and big husky looking man, with a gentleness that was noticeable. The nurses' eyes at the desk were on him the moment his large, but, pleading and emerging presence entered through the emergency room doors.

In his deep and compassionate voice he said, "I've got a very sick little boy here who is not doing well. His mother just died and he was the one who found her." With that statement, nurses came running with a wheelchair and a gurney.

They placed his little body on the gurney as they could see he was out of it mentally, completely by now.

They wheeled the boy into one of the private emergency rooms and began an I.V. while calling for a doctor that was preceded and succeeded, by the word "STAT" that meant urgent.

This is serious now thought Willie beginning to be afraid for the boy's welfare even more. "Oh dear Lord, help this little boy, please!" Willie had quickly developed a bond for Justin in the short time he was in his care. How could a little guy like this be so polite and quiet with a life he was living? Something didn't measure up right. He was different from his mother as daylight was to darkness. How could she have abused the love of such a precious little boy like this? If only I had paid attention and not been so cautious and careful about minding my own business, he felt so remorseful for his past insensitivities. Now it was too late to change how he had conducted his private life for the last two plus years since living in the apartment complex. This little guy could have probably used a friend.

"Oh me, oh my, I'm a marked man." He said out loud for no reason other than his own thoughts coming out unintentionally. More thoughts were flooding his mind and he needed them to so he didn't think about Justin's health predicament so much right now. He paced the floor and talked to the nurses, and they would bring him coffee, as he waited for Justin's Grandmother to arrive or hear anything about Justin's condition.

All of a sudden an out of breath, voice came booming from the entrance doors of the emergency waiting room. "I'm Ruby Edge and I'm looking for my grandson, Justin Edge and his deceased mother, I presume, Suzanna Edge."

Willie immediately bolted over to Ms. Ruby, "Hello Ms. Ruby, I'm Willie Johnson, the man who called you and I have been waiting for you to arrive."

"I got here as quickly as I could Mr. Willie and I thank you so very much for phoning me today. I just am so thankful and grateful for you."

"Ms. Ruby, The Doctor's have Justin in the emergency room here now because he went into some kind of shock after all that's happened, and there has been too much happening for this little guy in my opinion." Said a sad and remorseful Willie Johnson.

"Willie will you please help me get to my grandson?" Her eyes were so pleading and there was something in the way she looked at him so helplessly, that he turned and walked quickly over to the nurses' desk.

They had come to know Willie and befriend him during the last three or four hours and treated him as Justin's only relative until someone else came forward with documentation to prove their self as a bone fide relative. Willie was the one who carried Justin in and he was their name on record for Justin. The nurses and Doctor's had kept Willie abreast of Justin's condition as they could.

"This is Justin's blood grandmother, Ruby Edge. Please let her see her grandson now."

"Oh! Yes, of course, come with me please this way." The head nurse made no delay in attending to the wishes of Willie. While Ruby followed the nurse, Willie was following at her heels. Just let them try and stop me, he thought to himself, but they didn't.

There lay the grandson she had never seen until today. Ruby began to weep silently. Willie had to turn his head as he began to silently fight off the tears welling up in his eyes. He was afraid he might weep for her and the boy. He knew the drug addicted prostitute he had as a mother was wrong about her own mother; her terrible life caused this little guy suffer for it. It was all too evident. This well dressed, clean and mannerly little Christian, black lady, to his astonishment, was now stroking Justin's little head and kissing his forehead and hands, dirty and all and praying for him aloud.

Willie gathered his composure and walked over to Ms. Ruby. "I would like to give you my full name, phone number and address so I can be kept abreast of little Justin's condition and future. I have become very fond of him in the last five hours, which is not hard to believe after you get to know him, Ms. Ruby. He is a mighty special little guy."

"Thank you Mr. Johnson. I will be ever so grateful God placed you where you were today to help and I'll be happy to repay your kindness somehow. I will be happy to give you a progress report everyday, and it will be a progress report--I'm trusting God!"

"I am too Ms. Ruby, I am too." Said Willie softly as he walked out of the room glancing back once more at Justin and his adoring grandmother. He felt at peace leaving him in her care. That was good enough for him.

Justin's Grandma Ruby continued to stay at his side, stroking his hair and rubbing his hand. She was praying and reading her Bible every day, all day, asking God to spare and heal this beautiful young boy she just saw for the first time in his and her life. She loved him instantly when she saw him lying in the hospital bed.

Tears streamed down her face when Dr. Kamps told her the young boy "would be fine in just a matter of time. He said Justin was dehydrated and malnourished, which caused him to easily slip into a coma to counter the shock of his mother's death." He continued to assure Ruby that nothing showed up on his CT scan regarding brain damage or any bodily damage. "He is a strong young man, and no doubt a real survivor." Said a very amazed Dr. Kamps.

"The brain can decrease its metabolic activity and induce healing sleep," Ma'am, said Dr. Kamps.

"The human body is an amazing machine." "An amazing creation of God," Ruby said.

"Yes. A creation of God, but for now, we are his caretakers and we are going to keep him on the drip so his body does not dehydrate and he gets some nutrition until he awakens and can eat, which by the looks of him he could use." Dr. Kamps said all this with the sentiment of a caring father and then he departed. His words were very touching and comforting to Ruby, and Lord knows she needed comforting right now.

Chapter 3

The death of her daughter took little toll on her because she had known of her addiction problems for many years. Ruby had been unable to help her or be a part of her life. When Ruby found out Suzanna had a little boy, she begged Suzanna to let her raise him. Suzanna wanted to punish her mother for not sending her money. She wouldn't even let her see the baby from birth forward. Terribly cruel, and Ruby couldn't drive it from her mind. What would this young boy be like? Whatever he was, he was her responsibility now. Justine was her flesh and blood, and that was all that mattered to her.

For now, this beautiful grandson was her main priority. She was going to take very good care of him and give him the love and support she knew he had not received. Willie had taken her a couple of days ago to the horrible apartment they lived in to retrieve Justin's belongings. She entered in the door took one look around and walked right back out. What a rat's nest. How could her daughter sink so low into this abyss when she had been raised in a clean, Christian home that was full of love, singing and laughter. Suzanna was so bright in school. She was pretty and popular with the other students and even the teachers thought she would aspire to do great things. Suzanna loved her life. "That's what happens when you're weak and let others influence you in the wrong direction." Ruby said out loud while shaking her head at the shame of it all.

"It is what it is." Ruby quickly reminded herself, careful not to let this drag her down too low.

It didn't take long for Ruby to realize that her grandson didn't have anything of value or worth other than his books and magazines she scooped up quickly so she could get out of this filthy dump that was unfit for human living.

"Justin doesn't have anything of worth Willie! I'll buy him new clothes, ones that fit and don't have holes in them and shoes that don't look like they are from trash cans. Please take me back to the hospital if you don't mind, and they can burn everything in this pigpen for all I care! Nothing more can be done here."

Willie totally agreed, appalled at the filth himself. They talked the whole way back to the hospital and Willie had a much better understanding of Ms. Ruby. She was going to be a wonderful grandparent for little Justin and this made him feel so much better. He said his good-bye to Ms. Ruby and gave her his address and phone number so she could keep him informed of Justin's condition and anticipated progress.

"Ms. Ruby, if you need anything while you are here, please call me and I'll do whatever I can at anytime."

"Thank you so much, Mr. Johnson and I shall keep you informed. Your kindness has been above and beyond anything I could have ever asked for. Thank you so much for everything!" She gave him her phone number and address in Alabama where Justin would be living with her, and gave him a hug as a gesture of her thankfulness and the bond she felt he and Justin would have for the rest of their lives. Mr. Willie Johnson had saved her Grandson's life and she would forever be thankful to him for this.

"I will take care of this wonderful grandson of mine!" She said aloud in Justin's hospital room, hoping perhaps he would hear her down deep and feel comforted.

She felt he would have a hard time with sudden change and the death of his mother, the only person in the world he had as family by Suzanna's hand and her hand alone. She started to cry thinking of what this little guy's life must have been like.

"He's going to have a fighting chance at life now." She enjoyed saying with a matronly arrogance and motherly pride, but with a tinge of deprecation for her daughter's lifestyle.

She decided to cremate her daughter's remains and pick up the ashes when the crematory called. This way Justin, if he wanted, could say a final farewell - just in case he needed closure as the hospital chaplain had explained to her.

Ruby would be taking Justin back home with her to Mobile, Alabama to the 'Theodore' neighborhood. It was a middle-class neighborhood and full of potential and a good place to start a new life. Good Morals. Good churches. Good people. Good schools. Ruby was so drawn into her thoughts and rubbing Justin's arms, she jumped when he flinched!

By the time the nurses came running in after Ruby hit the call button, Justin had opened one eye, and then, both eyes. He was looking straight at Ruby with a quizzical look.

"What happened?"

"Where am I?"

"Where is my mom and who are you?" He said faintly, yet clearly remembering what had happened, or so it seemed to Ruby.

"Now, now, sweetheart, we have plenty of time for questions once the Doctors say you have the strength to talk." Trying to buy time, and allow the boy to gain some strength and mental stability.

Right now an answer of any kind would only be a bullet of truth. Additional hurt and pain were not on the docket for today. Ruby was setting her own therapeutic rules.

However, she did say, "I'm your grandmother dear. And, I'm not leaving your side for one minute. You just rest and I'll be here until you're all better. Does that sound ok to you?"

It must have, because he closed his eyes, and drifted off to sleep again.

"Oh Dear me." Ruby said.

"How am I going to handle this one?"

She called the hospital psychologist, Dr. Yamil Portello, for an immediate hospital appointment, because her word was her word to Justin. I might as well start off on the right foot of trust.

"Ruby, tell the boy the whole truth. From what you've told me of his mother and his living conditions, it sounds like he is already well matured beyond his years. He was the adult so to speak, in cases such as this. The child becomes the parent of the parent. It's doubtful he has had much of a childhood thus far. You'll need to find out what his interests and passions are fairly soon, and get him involved in them…therapy!" He said with a wink.

"It is a known medical and psychological fact that neglected, abandoned, or mistreated children in any way, often try harder to obtain their parents love and attention when they are young. If it goes on too long, these are the children that end up in criminal court. You can be thankful for some intervention of some higher order here, Mrs. Edge. Justin is definitely a case of neglect and poverty. He is young and the young can forget to a certain degree.

I must warn you to be careful though because his memories and fears could re-surface subconsciously, when you or he, least expect them to. Example: When he feels moments of anxiousness or extreme abandonment issues arising. You will know what it is and why. Get him immediately into counseling if it happens and give him all the love and reassurance you can and you will be fine, I know you will be." Dr. Portello said with cheer and assurance for Ruby.

"By the way, the protective services have sent a case-worker, over to talk to you after we have finished. They want proof of relationship and how you can afford to care for him."

"Stupid people. Where were they for the last ten years while this young boy was alone and unattended for?" Said a very disgruntled Ruby Edge.

"I agree with you Ruby."

"Anyway, on with the analysis. This is perhaps the reason your grandson never tried to contact you himself. He might have once he got older, one never knows. I strongly believe he will respect you far more for the blunt truth than a tap dance, or even a cover-up story. Suzanna, left you, and wouldn't allow you around so she didn't have to feel guilty about being a prostitute on drugs and neglecting this beautiful son of hers. It's your open door into his life now. He will need time to adjust and heal, but he will come around, just be patient."

"I'm a very patient woman, Dr. Portello. You have no idea how patient I am. For this boy, I can have the patience of Job if need be."

Dr. Portello responded. "I suspect he will be shocked at what a new and wonderful world you have to offer him, quietness may be his response, so don't take it the wrong way. If what he has come from is all you say, he will be in a whole new world. Let him evolve into it gradually. Your reward will be his love, and trust. I suspect that will be ample for you, Ruby." Smiling and giving her hand a warm embrace, the psychiatrist was happy to of been of service to such a lovely lady willing to raise a young boy all on her own.

"Call me anytime if you need me, Ruby."

"Please bless her in this effort God, she may need a miracle." He said as he was walking down the hallway back to his office in another part of the hospital. Not all of his patients had a chance to have a happy ending as Justin and his grandmother may have. He hoped so anyway.

"Willie?"

"Yes, this is Willie. Is this Ms. Ruby?"

"It is, Willie and I'm calling to let you know I'll be taking Justin home with me tomorrow to Mobile on the 1pm bus. I wanted to thank you again for everything you did."

"It was my happiness to help that young man in his distress and know I did something good, Ms. Ruby. Thank you for keeping your promise to keep me abreast of his progress. I hope you have a safe trip home. Can I take you and Justin to the bus station tomorrow? This would allow me to see Justin once more before he leaves."

"Well, I certainly don't want to impose, I can take a taxi very easily."

"It's no hardship at all and I would love to shake that little guy's hand once more. He is such a good kid and I know he will be so happy with you, Ms. Ruby."

"Okay then, that would be lovely. Can you be here at the hospital around 11am? I like to be early." Chuckled Ruby.

"I certainly will be."

Right on time the next morning, Willie was in the hospital lobby waiting for Ms. Ruby and Justin.

When Justin saw Willie, he ran over to him and gave him a big hug, which surprised everyone.

"My goodness son, you are all well and looking good. You have a wonderful Grandma now to live with little man." Willie was so happy for Justin.

"I'm thankful for you Mr. Johnson and how you helped me. I think I would have died if you hadn't been around." Said a very young and mature sounding 10 year old, Justin.

"I will never forget you, Mr. Johnson. I hope you will never forget me and maybe even see me someday when I become a baseball star." Willie and Ruby chuckled and winked at each other with Justin's new vitality.

"You are already a hero and a star to me, Justin. I promise I will never forget you either. My promises are my word and my words are my honor."

Willie dropped them off at the bus depot and carried in the two pieces of luggage they had.

"Thank you so much Willie and I will keep you posted of my boy's progress often and then, once a year at least, via a Christmas card if you would like that."

"I would enjoy it more than words can express, Ms. Ruby!"

"Okay, you will get one then because I am very diligent about sending out Christmas cards to my small list of recipients, of which you are now a part of."

Willie kneeled to Justin's height and gave him a hug and then said, "now you mind your Grandma, give her lot's of love and respect, and eat everything she says is good for you. This will all help you grow up to be the best baseball star ever." Justin looked intently into Willie's eyes and promised he would do what he just advised. Willie then left them and knew in his heart, Justin was in good hands and God would definitely be with that boy because of his Grandma.

Chapter 4

It did take a bit of time for Justin to accept his new life and in such comfortable and clean surroundings, as it was all so wonderful, he couldn't help but wonder when it would end.

Grandma Ruby had plenty of good food around and even cooked and baked for him. He had clean clothes, clean sheets for his very own bed, and new shoes that fit! Time went by and they grew closer and closer the more they got to know each other.

Justin was in his new school. He blended in beautifully with his schoolmates who seemed to be very smart. The common ground led the way to some very natural and authentic friendships.

He was tested via an entrance exam, and was placed in accelerated classes. Ruby was not one bit surprised because his mother was always in accelerated classes when she was younger, and she was a college graduate as was his natural Grandfather.

Justin would be just as capable as anyone else to go to college, she would make sure of that and would start planning on it early. Her boy would never suffer from neglect again as long as she was alive.

The environment Justin was experiencing was very much different from the project housing and school he had come from.

He loved learning and being given the chance to learn at an appropriate pace that better suited his intellectual skills.

Many of his classmates in the old school experienced failure at lower academic skill levels and their history of poor attendance and behavior problems only compounded the lack of time spent in actual learning. He appreciated this environment so much more. Time was passing and so was the trauma of his previous life.

He actually said to one of his teachers one day, for no apparent reason, "life is beautiful, isn't it?" She smiled and said, "Yes, it is, Justin. It's all in the way we look at it, and make of it." Grandma heard at every single parent teacher conference what a bright and wonderful child Justin is, and she just beamed.

"Grandma, are you going to let me stay here forever?"
"Why Justin, I would be so happy to have you live with me forever. But I have this knowledge about life that it's highly probable you will one day find a woman to love and get married. I doubt that you would want to move in with your grandma?"

They both laughed together for the first time since Justin came home with her. They were definitely bonding and Justin was relaxing and even enjoying his life with Grandma Ruby.

Grandma took time to tell him stories of everything his mind could think of asking or comprehending.

Their whole world was all within walking distance and Grandma Ruby thought it fitting for a growing young man to learn to like to walk.

They walked to church every Sunday, with their Bibles in their hands, wearing their Sunday best clothing.

Ruby walked Justin to school, and was always waiting for him after school by the gates. They walked to the grocery store and he helped her carry the groceries that didn't fit in her little cart on wheels. This was much different than going to the grocery store with his deceased mother!

They walked together to the pharmacy if one of them were sick and needed the pharmacist's recommendations for the ailment. They walked to the barbershop when Justin needed a haircut. Grandma always walked to the beauty shop for her needs while Justin was in school. He would not like sitting in a beauty shop so no sense in making a young boy go through that.

They walked to the park together where he could play baseball with the other boys and sometimes men. She waited for him and watched the games and the great athlete her boy was swiftly becoming.

In her heart, and in her mind, she saw something very unusual about this boy. He was a natural athlete and he loved baseball more than any other sport. It's all he talked about in his spare time. He checked books out of the library every week, mostly about baseball and some on medical interests. The signs were very telling where his passions were.

Thankfully, the memories of his former anxiety-filled life that was full of filth, hunger and abandonment were dissipating into a vague memory, mostly because Justin wanted it that way! Justin had accepted his mother's death as being for the better, even if he never verbalized it, and he never cried one tear over her passing. This concerned Ruby, but the hospital psychologist said this might happen.

"Thank-you, Lord, for huge miracles." Justin prayed before tucking himself into a clean bed on a full stomach.

Justin grew quicker than Grandma wished him to. She enjoyed every day with this bright, energetic, and ever so active young boy.

The holidays were more joyful to share with a young loved one, and his company was more enjoyable than she could have ever imagined.

In the summer time, Justin mowed lawns for neighbors for extra money. He ran errands such as picking up a few groceries, or washing their cars, picking weeds; whatever they asked him to do, it was hastily answered with a yes sir, or ma'am right away.

He was adored by all of Ruby's neighbors and friends.

They walked everywhere they went because Grandma thought a car was too expensive of a possession. She sold the one car she and her husband had owned when he died. He did all the driving and navigating. Grandma thought it too dangerous and actually boring to drive. She enjoyed walking and taking in the scenery outside whenever she could. Her work kept her inside and this was a welcome treat to be outside.

"All the maintenance, gas cost, insurance, replacing tires, and so on, I'd rather ride the bus or walk. It's good for your health and you'll get good exercise this way." Justin always thought whatever grandma said must be gospel.

"You always make sure your Sunday shoes are shined, Justin. You show respect to the congregation and mostly to God when you are clean and dressed as best as you can be."

"Yes, Grandma."

She showed him how to shine them properly from his Grandfather's old shoeshine kit.

"Justin I am going to always be teaching you something, but this time, it's table manners, such as: when someone asks you for the salt, you pass the pepper and the salt together, just because it's proper etiquette."

She taught him how to hold his fork and knife when cutting a piece of meat, and to place the fork at the top of the plate cross-wise if there is no side dish for bread. Justin learned the place setting of flat wear and how to work from the outside in on forks and spoons for a formal dinner affair. The flat-wear, or silverware, at the top was for desserts. Stemware, also known as crystal goblets, was for red wine, white wine, dessert cordials and of course water. Justin memorized all the placements and what they were designated for. He hoped Grandma was right when she said, "you will need to know all of this someday, my boy."

"You place a napkin on the chair if you're coming back to you seat, if you leave for a moment. On the other hand, if you leave your seat and are finished, you leave the napkin on the table next to your plate. Most fine restaurants will ask you if you need a white or black napkin and the reason for that is the color of clothing you are wearing. If you have black trousers on, you don't want white cotton lint all over them and visa versa for light colors.

She raised her eyebrows and this always made her eyes look larger when she said something of real importance.

"How did you learn all of this fine dining stuff, Grandma?" Justin loved learning how to be mannerly and know how to act in the finer circles of people if he ever had the opportunity to be in such a place.

"Honey, I wanted to raise my standards all my life. It's something all people should just want to do for themselves if for no other reason." Justin knew she was right.

"It's not hard to have good table manners; it actually takes less work than being a low class hog at a table. Why, those people should just have an apple stuffed in their mouth and lay on top of the table if they don't know how to sit at a table and use good table manners." This made them both laugh.

"That's quite a visual, Grandma!"

It was a subject I studied at the library and was able to use in my work when we would go to Christmas dinners with my company.

"Oh, how I loved dressing up and being proper and full of social graces. Your Grandpa and I always felt extra special on those occasions." She pursed her lips as she smiled feeling the fond memories.

"We even danced on many occasion!" Grandma laughed as she remembered those fun filled times with her husband. Justin was mesmerized with her stories and of a Grandfather he would never know.

"I want you to experience that feeling many more times than I was able to. I just have the feeling you're going to amount to something big some day, and I'm getting you prepared for it in every way I can, with everything I know. You will be able to teach me new things some day, you just wait and see!" Grandma raised her hand and pointed her finger in the air as if to make her point more valid.

"Now, etiquette and social skills are two different things but work hand in hand. You are going to be able to mix with the finest of people in the finest of restaurants or homes when I'm finished with you. You just never know where life is going to take you, so it's a good idea to always be prepared. You might be the President of a huge corporation someday and need to have refined skills, like being a great conversationalist." She was visualizing Justin speaking before a corporate meeting at this point.

"I'll have to work on the 'being a great conversationalist part." Justin said, and Grandma just smiled at him.

"Did you know that there is a huge mansion in California, sitting high up on a mountain, called the Hearst Castle? It was a home and a show place, built by Randolph Hearst, the son of a very wealthy silver mining man. It is a fact that he only invited people who were fun and great conversationalists to come and stay with him for a week. If they didn't prove to be interesting, they were never invited back. You see what I mean?"

"Yes ma'am."

"You love to read Justin, so, read about everything you can on various subjects so you can be interesting and a contribution to a discussion, or the instigation of a great conversation from your expansive knowledge of things. It's fun too! Of course, I'll be sitting with you when that happens." Grandma laughed so loud when she enjoyed her own jokes. Justin had to laugh with her. Her laughter was infectious.

"You sure will be, and no one better ever say different."

"It's good for the soul to laugh, my boy. Laugh as much as you can and as often as you can. There's a time for tears and a time for laughter. One is better than the other, but you don't always get to choose your own situations."

(She was speaking of her husband's death and of course his mother's).

"Happiness is a choice. I choose to be happy and I feel the good Lord gives me much to be happy about. How about you?"

"Oh, yes ma'am, I prefer to laugh any day!" He meant that with his whole heart.

"Yeah, me too." Her voice trailing off with thought.

Chapter 5

When Justin turned 16 he applied for, and was granted, a summer job with the City Parks and Recreation Department. This meant he had to mow the parks lawns nearby his home. He had to empty trashcans of their plastic liners and put new ones in then empty all of those into a main dumpster and do general trash patrol around the areas. He also had to maintain his normal grass cutting customers he had acquired over the years. Justin was a very happy young man and loved to work.

"Grandma, I made a hundred and fifty dollars this week!" Exclaimed a surprised and proud, grandson of hers.

"Can I take us to lunch after church Sunday, please Grandma?"

Noticing how proud he was of his new ability to earn money, Grandma thought it best to accept her Grandson's generous offer to take her to lunch and show him respect for earning his money.

"Why, I'd be honored to accompany my grandson to lunch on Sunday. Where shall we go my boy?" Hoping he would not pick an expensive restaurant or she would have to give him another lesson in the value of money.

"I'd like to take you to the café by the church where a lot of the people seem to go after church on Sunday's. Is that suitable for you Grandma? I know it's your Birthday this next week and I'll be busy mowing lawns and hauling trash, so I'd like to make it special for you."

"You're making me cry, Justin. I wasn't going to make a big to-do over my birthday and here you go and surprise me. I'd love to try that café out, since you recommended it for my birthday treat. Thank you, honey so very much. Your thoughtfulness is so sweet."

Sunday was one of the best days of Grandma Ruby's life. She dressed in her Sunday finest complete with a hat and her gloves. She was going to lunch with her grandson at a sit down restaurant.

"Order anything you want, Grandma, I really mean it."

"Okay, my boy, I'll order the hot turkey sandwich with extra gravy, mashed potatoes and cranberry sauce. It's one of my favorite meals."

"I'll order that too, it sounds so delicious and I'm starving!"

"You're so cute, Justin. I just adore you. Thank you for making my day so special."

"Oh, Grandma, I have a card for you too."

"What? You had time to do that in between all your work?"

"I sure did. Here you go." He slid it across the table.

When Grandma opened the card, a ten-dollar bill fell out of the card and Justin giggled with sheer pride and delight.

"I'm going to cry again, Justin. Right here in public you ornery boy making me do this." She pulled out a tissue and wiped her eyes and nose.

"This was one of the best days of my life, Grandma. I was able to do something really fun and nice for you. You always do nice things for me and for a lot of other people without ever expecting anything in return. I love you and appreciate you. This was the only way I knew how to properly thank you and honor you with respect."

They hugged each other so tight right in the middle of the block before their house. It was a memory never to be forgotten by either one of them. Justin had learned how to be grateful and generous. Grandma had learned how much Justin loved her and how generous he would forever be with her. He hadn't cared if he spent his whole paycheck on her. She cried tears of joy in bed as she said her prayers. This miracle in the form of a little boy that had been given to her to watch over as he grew up was more than she ever dreamed for. After a little reminiscing of the day, she was fast asleep with a smile on her face. Happy and proud of her darling boy she loved with all of her heart.

Justin was on the High School varsity team for Baseball and he was only a sophomore. An honor not bestowed that easily to high school boys. He was growing bigger, stronger, and more handsome and his skills and talents were astounding the coaches of the High School. He made them look good. They were winning games basically because of Justin's homerun hits most every time he was up to bat. The opposing teams had no equal match for him no matter who they put up against him. The High School

Principal gave them the extra money they needed to travel and defeat the higher division schools because they could defeat them easily and eventually bring home trophies.

They had no idea what they had in their midst. They just knew they had a work horse that produced results and the other boys played better to keep up with him. Small potatoes for a player like Justin, but he knew he was destined for much more and this was his play time and learning time. The coaches gave him extra coaching and brought in a professional to work with him who was a retired baseball player just to keep him ever excelling.

Excellence breed's excellence, Coach Iverson said to the boys in a meeting after winning another State Championship. They were probably happier than the young boys were because this meant bigger school offers, maybe even colleges, and bigger salaries to go with them.

This is how High School Coaches careers take off, and they were going to milk it for what they could. Thank you, Justin Edge whispered Head Coach Sam Iverson with a huge smile after every win.

By the time Justin was a senior in High School he had played every position on the team except catching and he refused the offers to catch because Grandma said that's a good way to ruin your knees. You are going to need those knees to be a power player and your Grandpa used to tell me about baseball catchers and how their careers were the shortest because their knees were always a problem. I just think you should concentrate on other positions.

The coaches didn't argue with Justin, when he said that he would prefer not to play a catcher's position. His reason being, they already had a couple of really great catchers. He was good at pitching, very precise and very fast. His specialty however was batting and bringing in players on base. Home runs were a dime a dozen for him in high school games. His name was everywhere in the local papers every high school baseball season. Grandma and he would read the paper together and then go over the game as she saw it from the bleachers, and how Justin saw it from the field.

There were many nights he didn't get home until dark and went straight to the kitchen table to eat and do his homework. Grandma didn't worry because she knew her boy was going to be a great baseball player or maybe a Doctor. She just surmised that all of this was great training for his adult life. She just really missed seeing him earlier in the day.

Justin listened to his Grandma and they discussed everything he did in his life. She was totally devoted to this young boy of hers and took raising him very seriously at every level and every turn.

Grandma never missed a game if she could help it. The only time she missed a game was because she had the flu and she just couldn't get out of bed. So the pastor of their church went in her place and gave her a detailed report of the game after when he and Justin returned home. She thanked him gratefully for doing her the favor. Not a problem Ruby, anytime as he was leaving, he turned around and said, "oh! I left some chicken noodle soup in your refrigerator my wife made for you and Justin for your dinner."

Chapter 6

Justin was in college now and loved it. He had graduated from High School with honors. He had excelled in baseball during high school. It was only fitting that he should receive a full baseball scholarship. He could have also qualified for an academic scholarship, but baseball was his first passion. This was a celebratory moment for he and Grandma.

"Grandma, this will really help us out and you won't have to dip into your savings." Justin said with pride and jubilance, not knowing that ever since he came to live with her she had started a small 529-college fund for him.

He seemed so grown up already and they had just gone to his graduation and here he is thinking about taking care of their financial concerns.

"I'm so proud of you my boy. I knew you were destined for great things. A college degree will mean you will get a good job and be a contribution to society. Keep your grades up and you will reach the moon someday. God has placed great favor upon your head." Grandma Ruby usually referred anything of significance to scripture, or that it came from the hand of God. Justin felt he needed to talk to God every day, just like Grandma, and pray often. It was a good, peaceful and very stable life with Grandma Ruby.

"Oh! I plan on it Grandma, I plan on it. I'm going to study hard and make you proud of me, you'll see."

"I'm already proud of you, Justin Edge! What do you mean--you'll make me proud." Ruby said this through a fun little prod with the boy she loved more than life.

Justin was 18 and would be 19 in a few weeks. He had great plans--plans to make a name for himself in college baseball and one day be drafted into professional baseball. He wondered if it would happen before or after he earned a degree.

The first year of college went smoothly and provided Justin with a whole new world of knowledge and opportunity. He met friends from all over the state and outside the state.

The Head Coach saw tremendous talent in Justin and took him very serious. He placed him in the varsity team halfway through the season because he was over-powering and over-shadowing the other young men on the baseball team. It was time to move him up and he did it. Ironically, Justin excelled to the level he was now in as if he mirrored any level he was placed in. During his second year of college and on an away game they had chartered a bus for the two and a half hour trip to Montgomery, Alabama. The Coach made it a point to seat Justin next to him for the ride over because he wanted to talk to him.

"Justin what is your internal feeling and future expectations out of baseball?"

"Baseball is my passion and my addiction, Coach. I can't imagine me being in a world of not playing baseball. My Grandma has always made sure I was able to be in baseball teams in our neighborhoods, and some of them were adult leagues because they said I was good enough to play with them. I know there are a lot of guys who spend a lot of time dreaming of becoming a baseball player in the Majors, but I don't feel like I'm dreaming. I feel like it can be a reality and Grandma says that's where it all starts--in your mind."

His coach had wanted to quiz Justin and find his level of dedication and plans for his future. Were they baseball oriented or were they medical oriented. He excelled in both areas. The answer was crystal clear that Justin just gave.

"I can see it in you, Justin. I can see it, but I just wanted to hear it from you." His Coach chose his words carefully.

"You see, we have a couple of scouts that have been watching you play and they are showing interest in you for their minor league ball clubs. The Boston Red Sox have had their scout here three times to watch you and you were completely unaware by his design.

"Really, Coach?" Sounding mystified. "I mean, that's great news! It's something I've dreamed about, without really giving it a definitive time frame, but I've definitely dreamed of hearing those words someday."

"With your skills and intellect, Justin, you're going to be hearing a lot of those words now," chuckling as he said it. Coach Miller was a jovial man, even though he was hard pressed to win, and expected nothing but hard work and commitment from his players. He never had to doubt Justin's drive…ever!

He was a natural, and the real deal. Coach Miller was just happy to know that someday, he would be privileged to say, "I coached that boy in college!"

The only concern he had was how much longer did he have with Justin?

The young boy had become a young man just in the short time he had been with him, now going on 2 plus years. Justin was destined for the Majors, and Coach Miller knew it down to the tips of his toes and it was right around the corner. He knew this young man was destined for the major leagues and he felt good inside to know he was a part of it when it did come true. The Boston Red Sox were the first who were sending a scout. First Responders, he mumbled to himself.

The Coach asked him many more questions and they talked about baseball non-stop and before they knew it, they were in Mobile. Coach Miller enjoyed talking to such an intelligent and mature young man and could only imagine what great things Justin was going to accomplish. Never in his wildest dreams would he have imagined how far he would go. Justin never forgot people who were and integral part of his life.

Chapter 7

An unexpected and pleasant surprise happened one day in Justin's biology class, during his second year of college. It was springtime and everything was blooming. The sun was starting to warm the earth, including Justin's emotions and hormones.

It was on a Tuesday morning during his first class when a pretty, smart, dark haired, girl with big gorgeous green eyes, caught his attention. Besides all of those startling assets, she was a perfect height, probably about 5' 7" and she seemed to be very athletic from her beautifully formed body. She was assigned to Justin's group for a group project on "Endosymbiosis," otherwise known as organisms living together, one inside the other, or, interdependent on each other.

The professor wanted a detailed paper written with electron and microscopic comparisons between cyanobacteria and chloroplasts. They were allowed to use the words and examples drawn and exuded from the studies of Hans Ris. (A little hint if they were paying attention, and Bree Wilkes was). She sat down next to Justin and smiled.

"Hi! I'm Bree Wilkes." She said as she tossed her long silky dark hair to one side of her shoulders. She put her face on her hand while looking at Justin with those huge brown eyes, and the longest lashes he had ever seen. He even noticed how the red sweater she was wearing made her glow and made her hair look even more beautiful. He felt his insides acting very strange. His heart rate went up, he was short of breath and he finally gathered his senses about him.

"Hi, I'm Justin Edge."

He hadn't made it much of a practice to talk to girls since his life was engulfed with baseball, school studies, helping Grandma Ruby around the house, and tending his yard jobs in his spare time when he was home.

"Yes, I know who you are, and I also figured you didn't know me, but that's ok, because we know each other now."

She gave him her charming smile again, with her head tilted slightly. He felt a tingle of nervousness as this conversation was breaking new ground for him.

"What year are you in?" asked Justin.

"I'm a sophomore, same as you."

"Oh, cool."

"Cool! That's the best word you can come up with, you dunce," he berated himself while pretending to read the book for the project. That will really impress her! Hey, wait a minute, why would I care about impressing her?

Because, Dumbo, there is something different, beautiful and wonderful about this girl, that's why. Was he actually having a conversation with himself? Had Grandma Ruby gotten into his head? This is crazy! I think I need to see a shrink! There I go again, talking to myself!

Bree broke the silence first. "Well, I suggest we take the professor's advice and study Hans Ris research and then draw a diagram and do a 3-D diagram which explains a step-by-step evolution, and another diagram showing another example such as how certain living things exist off of and because of each other."

She shuffled her papers together and looked at the other three people in the group and then focused back on Justin who had just been staring at her.

"Absolutely, that is a fabulous and creative idea," exclaimed one of the other classmates. "Who does what now, Bree?" She had already set herself as the lead of the group. Justin would have but she was too beautiful to compete with. He felt a sort of "love paralysis" for the first time in his life and he didn't know what else to call it. He knew his feelings and Bree had taken them over. She knew she had too, and liked it.

It took a few weeks to finish the group project and, by this time, Bree and Justin were talking to each other as though they had always been old friends, eating lunch together outside on the lawn and enjoying each other's company.

Justin thought to himself, Bree obviously likes me or she wouldn't be spending all her available time with me. I'm not too dense to see that, and I really like her too.

What's the connection here anyway? All my life, all I have basically thought about is baseball, friends – even girls as friends, work and school. What makes this so different is I feel special when she comes near me. I feel comfortable when we're alone together, even if we talk about nothing in particular. Get your head back into your studies, Justin, he mumbled as his senses brought him back to reality. Still, his mind would revert to thoughts of Bree now and then. It felt good and even better when she was near.

"Why do you keep your distance from me?" Bree asked one day at their grassy lunch spot.

"What do you mean?" Asked Justin

"I'm wondering why you never try to come closer to me to kiss me?"

Justin's cheeks felt like they were burning.

"Ahhh, you're blushing, Justin. I never realized you were so shy."

"Do you have any feelings for me, Justin? I know this is a bit forward and I'm making a pass at you, but I'm a smart girl and I know what I like when I see it, so I usually go after it. I don't think that makes me any less of a lady, do you?"

Justin was used to springing into action with quick reflexes from his baseball training, and he was thankful for the trait right now, but he didn't want to blow it. Grandma was so right when she said ages ago to learn to be a good conversationalist.

"I didn't think it would be proper for me to let my feelings be known, especially if you didn't feel the same way. I'm not very good at reading a woman's emotions, and I knew we were very close friends, just didn't know how good. I haven't had extensive training in that field yet and I am certainly not looking for rejection." They both laughed and felt the butterflies as they confessed their feelings to each other.

Their faces moved closer to each other slowly, until their lips touched, and it was the most passionate kiss on the planet. It had to be. It was the kiss that rocked Justin's world.

There is definitely a difference between hugs and kisses from your grandma and a first kiss with a girlfriend! Justin thought comically to himself.

"Is there a term for this kind of kiss?" Justin asked Bree.

"That's too deep, Justin. We'll be kissing a whole lot more so just enjoy it with me, okay?"

"Okay, you got me hooked!" Justin replied, and again they laughed. He felt as though he were drifting on a cloud.

Many more days were spent together at lunch and some evenings studying at the library together, slipping in a few of those glorious kisses now and then.

"Grandma, I met a beautiful and smart girl in my Biology class, and I've been studying with her for the last two months when I go to the library in the evenings." He had to tell Grandma Ruby, she was his world.

"Really? Now, why haven't you told me about this sooner young man? And what is her name?" She asked with interest.

"I don't know, it was just sort of special keeping her just to myself until I knew I really had strong feelings for her. Her name is Bree Wilkes. The feelings I have and the relationship we've developed, I guess I just wanted to wait and see if it lasted first."

"That makes perfect sense to me, honey. You are a very wise young man to test the waters first."

"Let me tell you a little something about love. Love can sometimes be magic. But magic can sometimes be just an illusion. You can only be hurt by love if you give it to the wrong person. Apparently you have tested the waters and found you like the temperature. That is all I need to hear from you, my boy. I trust your judgment." Grandma meant that.

"So, how about we invite this young lady, Bree Wilkes, over for church and lunch next Sunday. That is, if you'd like to." Grandma was coy about finding out if this young lady was as good a girl for her grandson as he thought she was.

"That would be wonderful, Grandma. I'll ask her tomorrow."

Justin extended the invitation the next day and Bree immediately accepted church and lunch.

"I just want to tell you, Bree, that my grandma raised me since I was ten years old, after my mother died. She's a loving, gentle, Christian Black lady." He waited to see how Bree would take that information.

"So how come your skin is so light?" Bree asked without flinching over the color issue.

"Well, it's her husband was a white man – he was killed in an work accident – and my mother conceived me from a white man – a long story

I don't want to go into right now." He really didn't want to get into the trashy mess his mom was, as that would for sure embarrass him.

"That makes sense Justin. You have a story to tell, but just not yet. I understand." Bree didn't care about the rest. She knew she loved Justin as he was. He had to have a wonderful grandma for him to be the way he is, which was perfect to her. She couldn't wait for Sunday and to meet Grandma Ruby.

Sunday came quickly due to the exhaustive overload of studying he had to do for finals. Justin met Bree at the school and walked her to his house a few blocks away.

"Why did we meet at school, Bree?"

"Because I live on campus with my family." Bree said.

"Justin stopped in his tracks and asked, "Bree Wilkes, as in Dean Wilkes?"

"Yes." Bree answered pulling her head back and to the side.

"Why didn't you tell me this sooner?" asked Justin.

"You never asked or caught on and I was a little afraid it would intimidate you a bit. I'm not sure." Bree replied as though she were considering her reasons.

"Do they know about us? I know I just told my Grandma, I'm thinking that you may not have said anything yet either." He was probing.

"No, I haven't told my parents anything yet, but I did tell my brother, Nathan, and he's interested in meeting you. He is one year younger than me and we're very close – especially close because we've been left alone a lot with our nanny when we were younger. And now, it's just the two of us at home most of the time because we're older. We're glad to have each other. With our parents always busy, going to functions, parties, we usually go to the movies or something by ourselves. That stuff goes with being a university dean and his wife. The daughter and son are not part of that life." She sounded a bit sad or bitter. It was hard to tell which, maybe both.

"I understand. All in the right time." Justin truly did understand. They had to make sure they were their own primary focus and if they lasted, the parents would be told eventually. On the other side of the coin, Justin was thoroughly excited to meet Bree's brother, because he never had a sibling and envisioned great joy now that he knew Nathan was just as eager to meet him.

He also knew the day would come because he had such deep feelings inside for Bree. He knew they were for real. He didn't know why, but he felt blessed with intuition, like a woman.

Oh for God's sake! I'm going out of my comfort zone now; I'm getting in touch with my feminine side! He laughed at himself and thought he was pretty funny for thinking of that one.

"Ok, when can I meet Nathan? I am already looking forward to this introduction. I never had a brother or sister, or even a best friend for that matter – just a lot of friends. My circumstances didn't permit it."

Bree sensed another one of Justin's deep, dark, forlorn secrets that would eventually come out when he was ready to talk about them.

"How about we invite Nathan to go to church with us, Sunday?" Bree quickly suggested.

"That would really be awesome! Grandma can set an extra place setting for him for lunch, too." She always had dinner baking slowly in the oven for a delicious feast after. Many times in church, Justin thought more about the dinner after the sermon than he concentrated on the message.

"If it's okay with Grandma Ruby, I'm sure my brother would be super excited, more so, knowing there will be a home-cooked meal afterwards. We don't get much of that these days, neither one of us is a great cook, unfortunately."

Sunday came and so did Bree and Nathan. It was so much fun to have a house full of young people, Grandma Ruby thought to her self.

"Mercy, I haven't laughed or cooked this much in a while. You boys sure do eat good."

She was in her heyday with the young people eating and loving everything she'd made.

"I never knew a pot roast could make kids so happy. I would have been making one every day when I was a young girl If I'd only known."

Justin bellowed out a laugh so loud it caught everyone's attention and they looked at him laughing.

"I'm sorry, it's just that I never thought about Grandma's being young and interested in boys. It just struck me as being hilarious, my little grandma, who's always taken care of big ole selfish me."

A Perfect Match

Everyone joined in the laughter, even Ruby with a twinkle in her eye as she winked at Justin and enjoyed his happiness. If he was happy, she was happier. Today, however, she was truly happy.

"We will do this again kiddos, anytime. You just give me the word. I certainly loved being helped with the clean up! It went so fast and easy. I'll be happy to cook any time like this! You be safe and God Bless you, both."

Ruby was tired and so content with the day's results. What a delightful young boy and girl this Nathan and Bree are, she thought to herself as they were leaving, Justin with them. He wanted to walk Bree and Nathan down the street toward the campus.

"I'll be right back, Grandma."

When he returned, Grandma Ruby said, "I'm so happy you found two delightful and good friends. I know full well Bree is your girlfriend, but it's important to be friends first in any relationship. Never forget that, and you'll do well with people and future relationships of any kind. Last Grandma advice of the day. We have a walk to get in before it gets dark."

"I really liked Nathan, Grandma," Justin offered on their walk. He has the same genuine warmth that Bree has.

"That's because they have been close and share the same traits." Grandma said. Her comment surprised Justin, since she didn't know their background like he did. She really was a wise lady.

During the weeks to follow, Nathan would sometimes join them at church. Since their first acquaintance, Nathan had taken an internship and it occupied his Sundays once in a while to compensate for school days he couldn't work. He loved going to a real home full of love and laughter, good home-cooked food, eaten in the company of a great guy like Justin. He seemed to be so self-confident, athletic, smart, clever, funny and Grandma Ruby was the *Sine qua non* of their Sunday social events after church. What a great lady she was, he commented to Justin. Nathan truly loved her. He even teased her one Sunday dinner about luring him in with her cooking.

"If I didn't know better, I would think you're trying to lasso me with your cooking."

Grandma Ruby laughed so hard she doubled over and covered her mouth.

"You might have been right 30 years ago." She gasped between laughs.

It had been a long time since she had ever been teased so much and she loved every minute of it, and Nathan knew it. Every time she was told that Nathan was coming for Sunday dinner, she cooked some extra special dishes, so it was only natural for Justin and Bree to beg him to forget his other plans and come to Sunday church and dinner with Grandma Ruby.

"Great times and great people seem to find each other," Grandma Ruby commented on one such occasion. "And through time, they tend to stay with each other too," winking at her boy, something she usually did when she was making a point for him.

With all the concern for a college degree or baseball career, the decision was going to be made for him soon enough, and Justin didn't even know it was coming right around the corner.

Chapter 8

The school year flew by and a summer full of activities and work kept Justin and Bree from seeing each other as often as they wanted to, but they talked on the phone at least once a day.

Justin was in summer baseball leagues to keep sharp and the scouts were contacting him left and right. His coach was talking to him on the phone daily as Justin kept him abreast of what was going on.

A new school year had started and he and Bree would both be juniors. Nathan had graduated and was working full time.

Months passed that seemed like weeks, with their heavy schedules. There had been several, passionate sexual encounters with the now, more than ever, love of his life, Bree. Justin didn't mean for it to happen, but it felt just as natural as kissing her, only more. He felt so guilty at first, no matter how hard he tried to rationalize the fact that this was the woman he wanted to marry. They seemed hopelessly inept at controlling their passion with each other.

Justin and Bree knew beyond any doubt they wanted to be married and they were talking about it more and more. They had quite a few passionate forays because neither one could contain their emotions when they were together. They let their love flow between them as if it were a completely natural and normal thing to do, planning a marriage in between.

Their discussion was wound around the subject of: do they wait for her to graduate or not. If they did, she would be separated from Justin if he went with a baseball career that was quickly coming towards him. It was actually a definite now. The Red Sox Baseball Club was sending a baseball scout this weekend to talk to him.

Bree's studies were in Biological Sciences. She hoped to be a medical chemist and find cures for diseases.

Justin realized he would be the responsible provider once they were married, so they both agreed the best thing to do was wait until things stabilized. They would get engaged after Justin knew how his baseball career was going.

Justin knew by now that Bree's parents were not interested in meeting him because no mention was ever made by she or Nathan. They always wanted to come to his and Grandma's house. So he just left it at that until it was time to ask her Dad for her hand in marriage. He felt he needed to have something substantial going for him before he asked the Dean of the College if he could marry his daughter. He needed to meet him first!

Grandma, Bree, Nathan and Justin's baseball coach were the only ones, outside of the church pastor, who knew he was talking with the Red Sox scout this weekend and the Oakland Scout next weekend. Everyone was so excited and eager to hear wonderful things they expected to hear.

Justin was early, rather than just on time, for his Interview. The MLB Scout would be in the Hilton Hotel conference room. This was where he had been directed to go via a personal phone call last night from Mr. DeMarco, the Scout from Boston. It was Saturday morning, about 8 a.m.

"Good morning, young man. I believe you are Justin Edge, am I correct?" said the husky voice coming up on his side.

"Yes sir, I am."

"I'm Frank DeMarco with the Major League Scouting Bureau."

DeMarco was all Boston Italian and it showed. He loved his heritage and Boston surrounding areas. He was a jovial and forthright man. Not a stranger to laughter and fun but could just as easily, become a terror on the negotiation tables, as Justin would expect of him. He was very sincere in his talking mannerism and didn't make Justin feel like he was in a hurry to get on to the next guy for an appointment. There was a human element about him Justin liked and felt comfortable with. If it were a reflection on the Red Sox, that would be most interesting to see.

"I have observed you for the last two years, Justin. During these last two years of college ball, you have become so impressive, you have become a stand alone player in dire need of being in the big leagues – if that appeals to you, you are in front of the right man."

"Yes sir, it sure does."

"Great. You see, my role is to provide as much information as possible about potential baseball players to the ball club I represent. Management is then able to make more educated selections in selecting players." He was explaining the procedure in detail for Justin's sake.

"The owners of teams and the top brass are really busy people believe it or not, running these Baseball Organizations as huge corporations. There is tons of money being spent to keep up the beautiful parks, players, memorabilia, and a whole host of ancillary things that keep these organizations running. It's not just what you see on television. There is 98% going on behind the scenes, and you and I being here today is 25% of it, in my books and I can argue that point with anyone." Justin was beginning to like DeMarco more and more as he listened to him.

"There is a group of us who scan the whole United States, Canada, Mexico and Puerto Rico, looking for the best of the best. That's why you're here today. I think YOU are one of the best in the world. I don't waste my time on so-so, types, son."

"I thank you for this meeting, sir. I'm looking for an open window to jump through, and use my talents that I feel are pretty much kicking their way out of me at present. I know I have much more to give."

"I like your attitude son." The scout stared at Justin for a bit, letting his mind percolate, and then continued.

"Our system has basic and generic applications we base and grade players with. We use a scale of 2 to 8 in each category to grade our players, and eventually come up with an overall future potential (we call it OFP), a way of grading a player.

Let me explain it further. He picked up his pen and began drawing on a sheet of paper.

"To give you an idea of where you stand, a total range of 40 to 80 covers Major League prospects. Forty is the minimum for a Major League Prospect. Anything in between these numbers has our attention. We send in a different scout to be sure, and if we have a potential prospect that scores an 80, he then becomes a definite prospect of a particular category. The higher the number gets, the better the prospect. Are you following me here son?"

"Yes sir, I certainly am." Justin was as involved with this information as DeMarco was in giving it…wholeheartedly.

"The generic qualities we look for in all our potential prospects of position players, such as pitchers, catchers and batters, are things like aggressiveness, instinct, dedication, work ethic and personal traits that are not on the chart, but are on our personal charts."

He looked over at Justin with a single eyebrow raised, just as Grandma does when she's making a point.

"I get it, sir." Justin answered

"If a player is great but can't get along with anyone, he won't get along with a team he lives with, and we don't believe in being babysitters or referee's. This is the wrong business for those traits. You follow me?"

"Yes sir." Justin was intrigued with the way this conversation was handled. Professional Baseball was a world all of its own.

"You can put a radar gun on a guy's arm strength and get a reading, but you can't put a radar gun to a player's heart or head. Do you get my meaning?"

"Yes sir."

"Well Justin, you have scored 80-plus in all areas with all scouts!" He stopped to assess Justin's response at this time.

Justin sat intent and upright in his chair, looked the scout in the eye and said, "I'm still getting better and better too, sir. It's in my whole being and I feel it." One thing about Justin was his honesty and it wasn't bragging. DeMarco knew bragging and bogus talk from honesty.

"You're not surprising me at all, Justin. I actually expected this type of a response from you after watching you for two years. I've watched you progress and mature to where you are now. I began seeing your name in the newspapers continuously. When you were awarded State Champions in High School, and when you were voted MVP. I saw it all. It's kind of like having a secret pal or a little angel over your shoulder." He laughed heartily – with the robust laugh he had, and what a great analogy, thought Justin.

"I've told the Boston Red Sox all about you and placed my own reputation on the line with a full recommendation for them to sign you up now and not wait for the draft.

I'm all in for you, Justin, and they trust my instincts as much as they trust my proven skills over these many years. You have a quick, super strong, wrist, bat speed, and precision by obviously having a very quick eye and can make a split-second decision – that shows me, you're smart. Those are just a few of your traits and attributes that I love about you.

You have plate discipline as well as deep focus and concentration abilities. I haven't seen a batter like that since Babe Ruth. You in Boston, with the Red Sox, equals, a perfect match!"

Those words ran through Justin's whole body, and he repeated them aloud to himself. "A perfect match with the Boston Red Sox."

DeMarco noticed the comment and saw Justin seriously visualizing himself with the Red Sox, which was exactly what he wanted.

This would give more credence to his future recommendations once they saw how great a player Justin Edge actually was. This was only the beginning; he would further evolve with age and Big League, professional training. This one young man was a golden player, he reflected, and maybe even one of those "once-in-a-lifetime finds." He had to make certain Boston got him.

"You have not once turned your eyes away from me, neither did you give me a limp handshake. You give the first impressions I look further for – self-confidence and sincerity. You're not shy. You have manners and diplomacy. You are certainly in command when you're up to bat. I like the way your whole body has flexibility and freedom of movement with great agility. You keep on doing what you're doing. You will just get better and better, my man, and you'll have yourself a professional baseball career in no time. I'm still on a quest for the best player in history. Make me proud!"

DeMarco burst into another robust round of laughter, but Justin knew the man was just as serious as he was in wanting to be one of the best of the best.

Chapter 9

"Justin," he began again, "If you feel like you need an agent, the best man for you to sign up with is Vince Calloway. He will take a percentage of your money of course, and agent's fees vary." DeMarco felt he should give Justin the simple advice he needed with total honesty to build a bond of trust. "His family owns the Calloway golf clubs company. He is an avid baseball fan and enjoys rounds of golf off-season. He can be trusted, and he is already rich, so no need to worry about a greedy agent at this point in time." DeMarco played golf with him often and knew Calloway personally. He felt confident in recommending him as an agent if Justin felt insecure in dealing with the Red Sox inner office people and the contract on his own.

"You can interview others, of course, and if you have any questions on accountability, give me a call at this number on my business card."

"There is one more thing, Mr. DeMarco. I have another appointment with a scout from Oakland later this week." Justin planned to finish his comment but was interrupted.

"Forget about them son. I've been watching you longer than they have and they only found out about you through me in the first place through the MLSB. That means they're not on top of the talent pool like I am." DeMarco felt in his heart and his head, he was the best talent scout out there and had little to no reservations in saying so.

"Listen Justin, you could get stuck with a bunch of lazy players who are happy enough to win the division title, but not the World Series." There went the raised eyebrow again. Justin trusted that trait because his Grandma did it too.

"The Red Sox are eyeing the World Series every year even in the bad years. They always say, 'next year', no matter how bad a season they have, because that's the mentality and the drive they have." He was on a roll, selling the Red Sox like a snake oil salesman.

A Perfect Match

"You can interview with any team you want to, but they have too many hot shots that will keep you in the triple-A ball club earning a lousy $1,500 a month if you're lucky. They'll overlook you because all of their overpaid, older, players are proven ball players. They don't take chances on young players because they are hot on the trail of winning. Winning means big money. They want winners every year and they're not looking to build. They're not that concerned with building a ball club for the future. They figure they'll just buy free agents." This information completely made sense to Justin. He was interested and captivated by DeMarco's knowledge of every aspect of the way things ran, plus, his straight, forward way of talking.

"You'll be sorry you didn't take my advice if that's what you want to do. One thing about us Bostonians, our word is our honor *and* our character. If you lose one of those, you have no reputation left. We are full of American history and heritage."

"I can agree fully with that comment, sir."

"Who has been around longer? Fenway Park, established in 1912 or the Philadelphia A's who left for California in 1968? So who's more loyal? Who has more Hall of Famers? Who has more legends to their namesake? Who is more famous outside of the Yankee's -- who is already full of huge names on their roster? Who has a better rapport with their players than the Red Sox?

You give me the answers and you'll have your decision made." DeMarco said without batting an eyelash and looking Justin straight in the eyes.

He was extremely professional and good at what he did, that was for sure, Justin reasoned in his mind.

He knew the history of the Oakland A's but let DeMarco leave out a few relevant details out of respect and an inner desire to be with the famous Boston Red Sox. He rather liked the idea of being a Red Sox but dared not act too overly excited for fear of looking desperate and grabbing at the first offering.

"I have been instructed personally by the owner himself, Mr. Duncan, to offer you an unprecedented signing bonus of $5,000 and a two-year contract of $120,000 a year. That's one whale of a generous offer for a rookie! Usually rookies get about $1,500 a month at best, and a one-year contract. Based on my recommendations and predictions, Mr. Duncan expects you to be in the Boston Red Sox camp in one week. That's something to brag about young man." DeMarco deliberately pointed out.

"I'll make my decision right now to go with the Boston Red Sox, if you are that convinced that they're a perfect match for me and I'm a perfect match for them. I am going with my gut feeling. I trust you, Mr. DeMarco." Justin's statement hit a tender spot in DeMarco's heart.

They shook hands and DeMarco gave Justin a good hug, too, which surprised Justin. "I'm proud of you for making the right call Justin," he said with sincerity.

"Kid, I know all about you, and your past. I may know things you never even knew about yourself. I know what you are, and I know what you can strive to be with the Red Sox. You deserve a good break, and you're an achiever." His voice was soft and genuine, and Justin's gut was nudging him to go ahead and trust that what had been placed in his path was by divine intervention.

"Yes sir," replied Justin. "I'm going to play for the Boston Red Sox. I'm going to totally trust you, and my intuition on this one." Demarco jumped for joy.

"Then, get ready, son, you're on your way. See you in Boston next week. Management will get the publicity and contracts worked out before you arrive. They'll be calling you with the details on how to proceed and anything else you want to know. Prepare a list of questions so you won't forget anything. They are all honest and upfront people. You'll really like them.

Baseball has the largest fan count in the nation for a national pastime sport for a very good reason. We're America's game! And now you're part of it. Congratulations Justin."

Deciding to go professional in his baseball career instead of entering his third year of college felt positively right to Justin. He, Grandma and Reverend Matthews prayed over this meeting, that Justin would make the right decision, but he was as sure as he'd ever been that this was the right decision. He felt good inside.

The exciting and wonderful part of this situation was that Justin didn't have to wait for the draft next June. The Red Sox had already determined to bring him on as a free agent. The Boston Red Sox organization was taking Justin on two recommendations: DeMarco, and the other one being his college Head Coach. Each one guaranteeing this kid was a winner, and a one-of-a-kind baseball player.

DeMarco, made the call to the Red Sox management. "Justin Edge is signing up with the Red Sox over all the other teams that are becoming interested and courting him. The early bird gets the worm." He said with some braggadocio. He reiterated how Justin would be a perfect match for them, and he would stake his career on this one. I tell you, this kid is the object of my attention and my affection. DeMarco didn't feel he could emphasize this enough. "The great part of all this is," he further explained, "I snatched him up before the other teams did, and you're very welcome for that because this young man is going to become a national spotlight player. Mark my words!

I told him you would have the contract and publicity going before he got there next week. See you all tomorrow."

DeMarco hung up the phone and felt quite satisfied with his performance and victory in persuading Justin to sign with the Boston Red Sox.

Providence was about to lift her finger and point the golden boy out. Further proving this to be a very valuable asset in just a short amount of time. A clarion call had been made. Made by a needy ball club. A needy and desperate ball club, that was in a rut, to be more exact.

Unbeknownst to Justin at that moment, the Boston Red Sox were rebuilding a perfect team for a formidable future. Justin Edge would be the most important first step they would take.

Durie Duncan, the Boston Red Sox Owner, was set on his heart's desire being fulfilled, a World Series Championship. Little did he know that by signing Justin Edge on, it would be the first step in making that dream become an eventual reality!

Chapter 10

Grandma Ruby, Bree and Nathan went wild when they heard the good news from Justin.

"I am on my way to Boston next week as a Professional Baseball player. I'm a proud American Leaguer right now, I think." He said with a proud but nervous laugh.

"I have to start out in their Farm Club in Pawtucket, Rhode Island for a year of training first, and I am to await the management's phone call for details this week, and that's about all I know other than this is a big thing for us. I'm going to make sure it is."

Bree clapped her hands and laughed in agreement.

"I leave one week from today and there is so much to get ready and to do. I have to work out too. I must be in peak condition in case I have to do a performance of some kind." Everyone got a kick out of that one. He was already in peak condition.

Grandma went and called Reverend Matthews to tell him of the good news and thank him for his prayers. Nathan left to go back to work and Bree took Justin outside to talk to him alone.

"What is it Bree? Is everything okay?"

"It will be now Justin. I waited for the right time to tell you, I'm pregnant. I was so scared and out of my senses before all this happened with the Scout and all that I sort of freaked out considering what I had done to us. Like, your Baseball career or your college education and my college education. I prayed so hard and just left it between God and me. Well, everything is going to work out now and we will be together as we wanted to, just much sooner than we planned." She laughed nervously and then stopped and looked at Justin who hadn't said anything up to this point.

"Are you upset?" She asked almost despondently.

A Perfect Match

"All I can say right now is Praise God! I am so shocked, and happy. I feel so blessed to have you and knowing we will be a family is huger than the great news of my Baseball meeting today."

Bree sighed a sigh of relief and let out a happy laugh. She ran into his arms. He swung her around and they kissed like the loving couple they really were. They were on a high of life right now and no artificial enhancements were ever needed for their happiness. They both seized the moment and said their thanks for such a blessing that was inside of her growing.

"I would like to ask for your hand in marriage now so when I return, if you'll have me, we can be married. I love you Bree, one thing I do know for sure. I'll ask Nathan for his blessings and permission since I can't ask your father if you wish." Justin offered.

"Yes, yes Justin. I would love to be Mrs. Breanna Edge!" She was jubilant with his proposal. "I love you with all my heart! Nathan already knows everything and is happier than I've ever seen him. All hush, hush right now like he doesn't know, of course." Justin smiled and rolled his eyes.

"Oh my gosh! I never imagined such a great thing as this happening so quickly for us Justin. I will marry you, and I do understand your strict schedule. If it weren't so strict, I would marry you tomorrow!" She said and meant it.

"Go for it my love. Go with the Baseball offering and we will begin our life from this point." Bree was so inspiring and optimistic about Justin's career and her ability to go forward with him. He felt they had made a wonderful decision together.

"Grandma, Nathan, Reverend and Mrs. Matthews will help me plan the small wedding ceremony for us when you return. Just let me know when that will be as soon as you can." She said it with a smile and a little girlish shrug.

They both laughed and kept talking to each other like magpies, as they were busy getting everything readied for Justin to leave.

"What a pair we are, my gosh!" Exclaimed Bree.

"Do you think Grandma Ruby will let me live here with her while you are gone? I can take care of her and make sure she's ok too, you know." She was testing the waters with Justin first. If he didn't think so, she would move in with Nathan.

"Grandma already offered." Justin said.

"When were you going to tell me?" Bree inquired with glee. Gosh! This is great news.

"I can't live in my home after I tell my parents tomorrow, and I can hardly wait to do. And trust me, I have no fear." Her voice was as stern as Justin had ever heard it.

"I'll go with you." Declared Justin embarrassed he hadn't thought of that sooner.

"No! Please." She said quickly in response to Justin's offer. "I already know how they are going to act, react, behave and treat me. It might be worse if you were there. I don't want you to see or be a part of the mental disorder that will occur tomorrow. I already see it unfolding in my mind. Nathan will be there, in the shadows anyway. I told him about us, and he is so excited. He is more excited for himself to be an Uncle. He is in love with the thought of us being a family. Can you imagine that?" Bree just shook her head and smiled thinking beautiful thoughts now.

"Back to your parents…if that is how you want it to be, then that is how it shall be. It's against my better thoughts as being the man in your life however."

"Let's go tell Grandma Ruby now. Then, will you ask her for me if I can live here while you are gone? And then, will you please call Nathan personally? It would mean the world to him to hear it from you, Justin. He loves you so much." Bree pleaded.

"I'd be delighted to tell my new brother in law all the wonderful news." He said as he was smiling from ear to ear.

"First, Grandma."

The news electrified Grandma Ruby. She was a bit shocked at first with everything that was happening around her so fast, but after she gathered her wits, she was happier than she could express. She gave Justin and Bree a big loving hug and congratulated them both. She was truly happy for them. She loved Bree and Nathan. Now there was someone else coming into this family she was going to share her love with. What an exciting time.

"So much to prepare for and I must get busy!" Grandma Ruby acted as if it were her duty to get everything in order and be the one in control. She had done the role quite well for a very long time. Justin and Bree looked at each other and smiled a big, huge, happy smile. Life was full of activity already she thought to herself as she imagined the changes about to occur.

The Red Sox Management office called and gave Justin exact details of what to bring, where to get his first class boarding ticket and the private room to go to while he waited for his flight. There would be a chauffer waiting for him with his name printed on a piece of paper to bring him to the Corporate Headquarters and all the other details he needed to know to get there.

He had quickly gotten a complete medical physical and an eye exam. He would have all of his medical records in hand for the Management when he attended the first meeting in Boston. Grandma Ruby kept meticulous files and records, since she had been a bookkeeper in her working years, so she had all of Justin's personal information they asked for.

"Bree, we'll open a joint checking account tomorrow for the sign up bonus to go into. Then, I'll be able to direct deposit the money into the account however and whenever I'm paid. You'll have plenty to live on." Justin was already taking care of his beloved Bree. "Just think Justin, the sign up bonus and the salary is huge to us considering we had nothing between us except a paltry sum of money from our dual savings this morning! Nathan would have had to chip in if this hadn't of come along." They enjoyed their little laugh together. "The sign up bonus is like a brick of gold to us right now. Someday we will look back at today, and laugh at ourselves." They laughed, kissed, and hugged each other a lot.

"This is all so *big time*, I can hardly believe I'm in real time and not in a dream." Bree knew exactly what Justin was experiencing because she was feeling that way too.

Chapter 11

As Justin, put his hands on the podium to speak, the crowd fell silent. Those in the back leaned forward, straining to hear every word he had to say. The atmosphere was electric. He spoke, with carefully chosen words that flew like swift arrows finding their mark. He had already captivated his audience. They were spellbound listening to a baseball legend of historical proportions.

"I'll give you a bit of my own observations I have discovered along the path of life. I've discovered and come to understand, 'we don't control circumstances. Circumstances control us.

It's like you're going through a valley of clouds and you only see parts of a tree here and there through the mist. You can't see the complete valley because of the misty circumstances.

In spite of these circumstances we are controlled by, we do have the ability, and are required as thinking human beings to make decisions within those circumstances when needed to survive or to keep going forward to the goal.

If you are a young person here today, and you don't quite understand what that meant, give yourself time, eventually you will. The older people here get it."

This prompted a rousing round of applause much to his surprise.

Chapter 12

"Grandma, everything is going to be all right. You've taught me well."
"We'll plan the wedding my boy, you just get back here to be a part of it, or, I'll be marrying her if you don't!" Grandma said in her little laughing voice he adored.

Justin let his train of though focus on his little Grandma as he watched her scurry about. He looked at her with love and ultra respect. The adoration he had for this wonderful lady who had saved him from a horrible life that was filled with the gnawing pain of emptiness and insecurity was beyond words. He went over and picked her up and hugged her with all his might. She didn't know what to think of her big grandson, and all his strength picking her up to hug her. She realized quickly the bond they shared. It was his appreciation for his life with her. He was expressing the love he had for her in a much larger and different way this time. She hugged him back tightly in response, and Justin knew she felt the same as he did.

"Grandma this home has always been warm, and full of plenty. Plenty of everything... love, clean clothes, food, education as a priority, and you made sure my baseball was no less important in our lives. They had always shared his interests. Whatever he was interested in, Grandma was interested in. I just want to thank you and tell you how much I love you." Grandma had tears in her eyes as he whispered in her ear, "thank you God again and again for my Grandma."

"Grandma, tomorrow Bree is going to tell her parents about us and I think you know why she has never told them anything before without me having to tell you as wise as you are. I'm just asking you to pray for her. She won't let me go with her because she said she doesn't want me to see how they will treat her because of us and doesn't want me treated badly by them. I feel terrible she won't let me go with her. Nathan is going to be with her however. That is reassuring in a little way. I feel less of a man like this, but I have to respect her wishes. I believe she doesn't want to be fully embarrassed in front of me either." Justin was pouring his heart out to his Grandma and wanted her to know how much Bree was protecting both of them. Her only salvation from her parents was living with Justin's beloved Grandma Ruby. Grandma was looking so forward to Bree living with her as well. She was already making room and cleaning out closets.

"You know, my boy, growing up and coming from the South, at my age, I know what Bree has in front of her with the part about your Grandma being a Black Woman. I'm fine with it as things have changed with time, and God has changed me. Some people still haven't changed from the old ways of the South son. I want you to understand that fact, and I'm okay with it. It's not our fault. It's not even their fault as they are a product of their parent's bondage. Let's just wait and see how this turns out tomorrow. I love you, Justin! I love you deeply, and with all my soul. I think Bree is very special too. I'm comforted in knowing Nathan will be with her."

"I want you to have a soul mate, and a family someday, Justin. I won't be around forever and your life must continue and expand. I know you don't like to hear this kind of talk but it's just the facts of life."

"I know Grandma, I accept the fact that you're right and no, I don't like to hear it. Good night, and thank you for everything." Justin winked at her and went to his room.

"Good night my boy."

Chapter 13

"Mom and Dad, I have something very important to talk to you about, this evening," Bree began, as her parents entered through the doorway from one of their cocktail parties.

"Oh dear, I was so looking forward to a nice hot bath and relaxing Bree." her mother said. "Let it wait until tomorrow."

Bree's father was thumbing through the mail and only grunted an inaudible sound.

"Please," insisted Bree. I can say it in three minutes."

"Go ahead then. Tell us what it's about while I hang up my jacket and put my purse down, that should be about three minutes," her mother replied with the demeaning half smile she used when speaking to those beneath her.

"Fine. I have met a young man and have been seeing him for about a year now and we are going to be married."

Her mother lifted her eyebrows, "Do go on, Sugar." She said in a condescending tone.

"I am in love with him and we enjoy the same things in life. I would like you to meet him very soon. Nathan already has met him and absolutely adores him and his grandmother who raised him."

Her mother looked at husband, who was still going through his mail, and said, "His grandmother raised him?" What kind of family does he come from with no parents, nanny, or other family members you failed to mention?"

"His father died in an accident when he was very young and his mother died when he was ten, and he's lived with his grandmother ever since." Here, Bree hesitated, and then said what she knew would blow the roof off the house.

"She is a black lady who was married to a white man, and his father was a white man. He looks like a normal white man, not that it should be a factor in this conversation, but for your sake, I'm telling you the whole lineage up front. He is a very handsome man. He is smart and very talented in baseball." Her mother cut her off.

"My God! What on earth are you doing with your life, you stupid little girl!" Her mother was quick to insert her disdain in rapid fire.

Dean Wilkes looked up and said, "However did you meet this scallywag?"

"He is not a scallywag, as you put it, father. You haven't even met him, whose name just so happens to be Justin Edge, and he plays baseball for your University. Don't you even go to the games or know the sports teams?

"Well he is leaving in one week to play professional baseball. He is in love with me and I am in love with him. We would like to be married soon and receive your good wishes."

"Oh, splendid! This is just great!" said her mother. "You got yourself a wannabe professional baseball player, who are, by-the-way, a dime a dozen. They make about fifteen thousand dollars a year while you're making two hundred thousand or more a year when you finish your Doctorate degree. I can just see the details in this relationship already." Bree expected her mother to think in terms of finances.

"He will be a professional baseball player, Mother!" Bree jumped to Justin's defense.

"Can you just meet him and accept him as the man he is and the man I love and am going to marry?"

"And what is wrong with a good man from an Ivy League college with a great family line behind him?" Her mother was insufferable when it came to status. "I would love to meet one of those young men when you tell us about him. As for this one, don't mention him again to us." She was becoming very angry and went for a drink.

Dean Wilkes put down his paper, ready to interject his thoughts now. He spoke calmly, "It's clear that this young man you think you're so in love with is behind in achievements and in academics because I've never heard of him. I don't really like baseball so this could possibly be the reason I never heard of him.

"His name does sound somewhat familiar passing across my desk for academic scholarship and sports awards, but all names sound the same in those areas.

"I only put up with baseball because it's part of the university curriculum, to be completely honest." He rarely was. "Furthermore, you'll not be seeing this young man anymore because he is not of our status in life and it would be a horrible mismatch if I let it continue. I absolutely cannot allow, nor WILL I allow, your personal mistake to continue. This conversation and lovely crush-affair of yours is over. Now go to your room young lady and think about what you have done."

"By your own provocation, Bree, and your incessant need to tell us this insane tangent of yours tonight, you obviously felt the need to try and make us feel sorry, guilty, pity, what? Whatever it is, it is completely useless and insane. He has no parents to set him up in life, or to leave a legacy to your offspring. It is a horrid thought for your father and me to try and live with, so it just cannot continue." With her father gone to the parlor to get himself another Scotch before retiring, her mother thought her own input would put an end to the conversation.

"Mother, I'm not going to stop seeing Justin. You can't just cut out your heart and put a new one in. He is forever in my heart. I'm not a child and I know what is right for me."

"You stupid little girl. Do you realize what mischief you will bring upon yourself if word gets out you're damaged goods?

There is not an Ivy League man in the world with good family roots or background who would want to lower his standards and court someone who has no higher standards than yours are right now.

People should stay in their own strata and marry within their own ranks. Come out of it, Bree! I thought you were a very smart girl and you wanted a college degree, a good husband to provide the best in life for you, give you a family and carry on good family traditions and a good blood line."

Her mother was standing firm without even meeting the man she told them she loved. How cold and self-centered could two people be?

"Take two aspirin and go to bed, and you'll feel better in the morning." Her mother said sarcastically as though she were a physician, prescribing for a headache.

"I will not succumb to you and Father's ridiculous demands, and I won't devalue myself based on your assessments of what my social status should be. My social status happens to be wrapped around a Godly man who treats me very well. You and Father are the ones who have it backwards. Will those friends and Ivy Leaguers be around if you went belly-up broke? Lost the Dean position? Didn't live in this fabulous house provided by the University? Have you a back-up plan of your own, if your world went upside down? "You think all of this will last forever. I have news for you: nothing stays the same. Nothing!"

"We have lived like this for 23 years now. I don't see the problem you forecast, you little bitch."

"I'm actually thankful to God that Nathan and I have had to raise ourselves. We are better people for it, clearly."

Her mother wheeled around and raised her hand to slap her face, but before she could, Bree grabbed her arm and said, "I'll break that calcium deposit of yours in half, if you even come close to striking me!"

Her mother acted as though she were horrified and shocked, a complete drama act. "I'll call the police on you, you little monster," she screamed.

Bree was beyond angry that her mother would want to hit her instead of extending her arms to hold her and tell her she loved her. Bree had never heard her mother tell her she loved her, so that was a useless thought.

"You do not hit a respectful daughter who tried to talk to her mother and father about something so very important. This is my life! I had hoped you would be happy for me, wish me joy, and ask to meet my future husband. Instead, you pontificated! You leave me no choice, but to leave this house! You're not my parents! You're – you're social climbers!"

Bree turned to walk up the stairs to her room, and added, "You two are the poster children for the 'nouveau riche' and why they shouldn't have children. You have no time for them with all the bootlicking you do. How can you forget that you both came from humble backgrounds? You've been accepted and absorbed into the wealthy lifestyles because of Dad's position only. How shocking and embarrassing it will be for you, if your house of cards were to topple down on your ostentatious, over-inflated, heads."

Her mother was quick to retort, "You'll see we are right when you are living in squalor and have to come back asking for money, or help to find a good-blooded family to take your cheap hide in."

Her mother apparently had too much to drink at this last function she'd attended. With yet another drink in her hand, she yelled, "Get yourself out of this house before you dirty our good name." She plopped herself down on a nearby sofa and just lay there. Her mother then took off her shoes and threw them at Bree, missing her, but managing to dent the wall.

Bree began crying before she reached her room and Nathan met her at her door.

"I heard everything, Bree. I was about to come down when she was going to strike you, but you handled yourself well. I abided by your wishes and stayed out of sight. They don't know that I'm here. I did tape record them so if they hurt you or called the police we would have proof of your good behavior. I'm so glad you didn't disrespect or hit them."

"Yeah, me too. They're not worth it, Nathan."

"I can't believe our mother is such a venomous and hateful woman. You know, they are stupid and ill-bred drunks. It is so pitiful and embarrassing to think how they must act in public. We're the one's with dirtied names!" Nathan was angry because Bree was hurting.

"They'll be sober tomorrow and won't even remember a bit of this. They never even know where we are anyway," Said Nathan.

"You know I love you, Nathan. Thank you for being here for me."

"I love you too, Sis. Anything for you."

As she gathered her clothes, she thought of a favorite Voltaire quote, "It is difficult to free fools from the chains they revere." No further description was needed, just a heavy sigh. She blew her nose and shook off the horrible feeling of what had just happened. This was the very ugly part of her parents she never wanted Justin to see. She never wanted to see it again either! She left the house she hoped to never return to again. Grandma Ruby's house already felt like home.

As she drove up in the driveway, Justin came out immediately and took her into his arms as she sobbed. Nothing needed to be said.

Grandma Ruby got Bree's bed covers folded back and put out fresh towels for her and a glass of water by her bedside and a box of Kleenex, just in case she needed them. Then, she said good night to the two of them with a loving kiss and hug. She thought it best to let them be alone to sort their own life out together. Ruby went to her room and got her Bible out.

Chapter 14

Grandma Ruby was ever so full of sound advice. After listening to Justin, she finally said, "Son, God made you into a tremendous athlete. Why is it wrong to glorify Him, by acknowledging the gift you have? You should feel no guilt for leaving to pursue a baseball career when it has been offered to you." Her eyes were steadfast on Justin.

"There's no need to call what you did with Bree a mistake, because how do you know it was? When did God start talking to you directly? I'm feeling a little left out here," she added with a smile.

"And, what's with this 'IF' business? God doesn't deal in If's, He deals in Go forth's." That one brought the eyebrow up.

"As for Bree, I'll keep an eye on her and help her along with her doctor's appointments, and make sure she has what she needs until you can get yourself home to get married, which will hopefully be very soon, and way before the baby is born. That is, if I have my druthers."

"You have always guided me so straight, and right, Grandma. You're my guiding light and I need your truthfulness, and your candidness." He said with such tenderness, Ruby grabbed him and hugged him. She would never stop hugging her boy, even if he had disappointed her by engaging in sex and getting this young girl pregnant. She would never tell him this because she knew he already knew this deep inside and what was done was done.

"We go forward from here, my boy. You just keep your eye on the goal." Grandma knew that's what Justin needed to do for his new little family.

She had done her very best to raise Justin in church and by the word of the Bible. He was a good Christian boy, but Ruby knew that even young Christian boy's hormones wore party hats. She also knew God was always quick to forgive.

No one is perfect and far be it from me to shame this grandson of mine who is making life-changing decisions to better his family's life and even mine. Somehow, God would make it all good. She had the faith and she never looked back once she knew the word of God was on her side.

"You're a very wise woman Grandma, and I would not be where I am had God not put us together." Said Justin most appreciatively.

"I'm going to go for the gold!" The confidence in his voice convinced Ruby instantly. Her grandson, her pride and joy, was regaining his senses and confidence. He was well on his way to making things happen. She would continue with her prayers for him as always.

"Justin, I want you to know I am comforted in knowing Bree's parents will not be able to hold money and power over you two young people and make you cower and grovel as I know in my heart they would do because it seems to be in their DNA." Ruby wasn't usually one for mincing words when things were serious. Justin appreciated Grandma's keen senses and realized what she just said was more truth than thoughts.

The week of preparation sped by and it was time for Justin to leave his family and his home and head to the unknown territory of Boston.

They were all up and sitting around the kitchen table by 7:30 a.m., having piping hot coffee and warm cinnamon rolls straight out of the oven, Justin's favorite. Grandma had baked for them before Bree would be taking Justin to the airport. One last little breakfast together for a little while. Grandma Ruby had already adjusted the television to the weather station and she informed Bree and Justin the weather was clear and looked like there would be no bad weather for flying today.

From my lips to God's ears, Ruby said to herself.

"We always have decent weather here in Alabama," remarked Grandma Ruby, "but it's Boston that worries me. I hear about their unpredictable weather there!"

"Don't worry Grandma, I'll call as soon as I land and I'm sure everything will be fine." He knew the airlines were about safety first.

"Do you have your heavy coat, rain coat, ear muffs, gloves, neck scarf…"

"Grandma! I'm all set and yes, I do have it all. You are such a worrier." Justin walked over to give her a big hug and they both felt so much more relaxed hugging each other.

"Ok, I had better get my suitcase put in the car and Bree, are you ready to take me to the airport my love?"

"No, but I will." She said with a little smile and pouty look of misery from already missing him.

Ruby walked them out to the car and hugged Justin one more time, and left them to go to the airport together.

She had never been away from her grandson like this since he came to live with her about ten years ago now. She was already feeling lonely without him.

Bree and Justin talked all the way to the airport and they seemed to get there entirely too fast. Bree took him to the passenger drop off area to make it easy to get in and out of the airport. Justin unloaded his suitcase and said very endearingly, as he pulled her close to him,

"I'll call you every day, Bree. Take care of yourself for me. I love you more than words could ever say."

The separation felt so strange for Justin, Ruby, and Bree as reality set in. He was now actually on his way.

Back at the house, Bree was happy to see Nathan sitting at the table with Grandma Ruby.

Ruby was also the first to speak. "Well, a new course has now been put into motion. Godspeed, my boy!" Bree and Nathan both cheered a hip, hip hooray, lifting their cups as a cheer to the notion of Justin's new path of life.

Nathan said, "I'm buying lunch for any takers as a celebration for our boy's new adventure."

Grandma and Bree looked at each other with smiles, and said they're both in. They nearly ran for their sweaters so excited to go out with Nathan and leave a bad feeling behind.

"It felt good to be out of the house with Nathan since Justin had just left an empty space in their home.

He made them laugh and they talked about a lot of different things, which helped greatly. They didn't rush to leave either. He paid the check and they walked to the car.

Thank you my sweet love, Nathan," said Grandma Ruby gratefully, giving him a hug and a kiss on the cheek.

""Yes, thank you, my dear brother." Bree said as she also gave him a huge hug and big kiss on his cheek.

"You're both welcome. It was my pleasure, of course. I didn't feel like leaving the two of you just yet either, to be completely honest. Now, I can go and get some things done." He paused, and winked at Bree and said, "I do believe you have some unpacking to do."

"Yes! I do. And I'm eager to get settled into my lovely and loving new home," she added, smiling at Grandma Ruby.

"Ok, then, we're off." Nathan said with a smile. "You two do realize I will be coming by quite a bit when I can, don't you?" He winked and drove off yelling, "I like all of your food Grandma Ruby!"

Ruby bent over laughing so hard. She apparently had a new adopted son in Nathan. Bree just shook her head, smiled, and walked into the house saying, "That Nathan can make anyone smile and laugh. I love that brother of mine."

Chapter 15

Justin arrived in Boston on time. His driver was standing exactly where he knew to expect him to be standing and he was holding a sign with "Justin Edge" in large letters.

"Hello, I'm Justin Edge," he said as he approached the driver.

"Good Afternoon Mr. Edge! I'm Daniel, your driver." The man was burly, good natured and eager to pick Justin up and deliver him to downtown Boston.

"I see that you've picked up your luggage already. I'll take them from here. I'm parked out front. It's about a half hour to the Boston Red Sox corporate headquarters in downtown Boston." Said Daniel.

"That sounds wonderful." Replied Justin.

Justin enjoyed the drive and the scenery, particularly the unexpected luxury of being driven by a chauffeur. This gave Justin ample time to take in the views as much as he could. He would always remember this monumental day in his life. He could see the views of modern buildings intertwining with historic buildings in perfect symmetry and out of place historical buildings with a brass plate on the front of it signifying its place in history.

Justin was admiring the limousine and the unparalleled opulence of being in this magnificent automobile that stretched longer than his whole body. The car was beautiful and loaded with every type of beverage he could imagine. Starting with water, to ice in a bin for soft drinks or cocktails. Napkins with the "Red Sox" logo on each one were available in a tray. The plush and soft leather seats were worthy of sleeping on. Soft music was playing for ambiance and the drivers' window was up for his personal privacy. He decided to make the most of the opportunity at hand and called Bree and Grandma Ruby.

"Hello my love!" He called Bree's cell phone to let them know he had arrived and was on his way to the corporate offices. They were so pleased to hear from him. By the time he had hung up, he had arrived at the Corporate Headquarters of the Boston Red Sox. Justin got out of the limo and stood there looking at the ominous looking building that stood so tall and beautiful in the heart of downtown Boston. History was surrounding him right now, and to he was standing in the middle of what seemed to be a dream.

Daniel walked him to the elevator and punched the up button and told him to walk through the huge wooden doors which were the Boston Red Sox Corporate Offices and he would be back after taking his luggage to his hotel and waiting for him in the same spot. No thinking on his part, at least yet. Everyone had taken care of all the details of his necessities for now. How nice is this, he said to himself riding up the elevator to the top floor.

The office receptionist looked up when the door opened and immediately welcomed "Welcome to the Boston Red Sox corporate offices, Mr. Edge. I'm Angela Rivera and I'm the Office Receptionist." She walked from around her desk and she extended her hand to shake Justin's and he extended his hand in response.

"Thank you. I'm happy to be here." Justin responded.

Rivera was dressed in a beautiful dark blue suit that was very nicely tailored to her slender body and her shoulder length blonde hair looked beautiful against the color and bounced as they walked down the hall together. Her Heels clicked softly on the marble floors as she talked with him and led him into a conference room with food and beverages on the massive cherry wood table with oversized chairs all around it. They were just as comfortable to sit in and the upholstery was red velvet with splashes of gold and green in a beautiful pattern that went well with the décor of the room.

"Please Mr. Edge, pick and choose what you want to eat. The plates, silverware, cups and stemware, are all here for you. If you need or prefer anything else, please let me know and I'll get it right away." Rivera said in a happy and very energetic voice that flowed as smooth as silk and was as natural as she was relaxed with his arrival.

Three well suited men, and one woman, equally well dressed, but no high-heels, soon filed into the room. Each person showed a genuinely warm eagerness to welcome him to the organization.

They introduced themselves, and each one shook his hand beginning with Mr. Kevin Cubinati. He was the Vice President of Operations, was the first to shake Justin's hand and then hand him his business card. He was a tall and middle-aged man of imposing dignity. When he stood by himself, he stood so straight he could be mistaken for a nutcracker ornament. Cubinati had a thick Bostonian accent and when he walked he had a quickstep with a very firm handshake, definitely a man always on the move. It was no wonder he was so thin and in great looking shape. He was extremely handsome for an older man. Justin thought to himself. Justin noticed Cubinati also had the thickest head of jet black, hair he had ever seen, well manicured and coifed, which suited him perfectly.

The next man to step forward and hand his business card to Justin and shake his hand was Mr. Sam Frost. He was the Chief Financial Officer (CFO). The bean counter, moneyman, and probably the one man who had to make sure money was spent wisely.

Frost was in excellent shape too. He was of a medium height and suitable body frame for his size and age. He seemed to be the eldest of all the men and women so far. He was bald and very gentle in his talking mannerism and his movements. He kept his eyes on Justin the whole time. His demeanor could be very misleading if you were not on your toes with this man. That was a gift he obviously possessed for his position. Justin observed him likewise, with the same caution he was being observed with. This seemed to make Mr. Frost uneasy and he looked away. Justin definitely was intimidating and he knew it but never abused it.

Mr. Lakes handed Justin his business card after they shook hands and his handshake was just as enthusiastic and firm as Mr. Cubinati's. His title was the V.P. of media affairs and he was definitely the different thinker in this meeting. He had a personality that would definitely fit in the world of media to keep him ahead of the pack. Energetic and charismatic made him a conversationalist and extremely full of charm. Justin liked him.

Mrs. Tanya Argona, shook Justin's hand, handed him a card and seemed to be a very feminine and articulate woman. She was definitely in her late thirties or younger. Her auburn hair was pulled into a tight ponytail with a beautiful silver band around it, and she had an exact matching silver broach on her jacket lapel. It was an emblem he recognized on the wall of the room they were in. It would have to be Scottish, he though to himself, he had already heard about the background of Mr. Duncan being Scottish and proud of it.

Argona was a petite, and seemingly soft lady in her demeanor. That was until Justin read her business card. "President of the Boston Red Sox, Inner Office Operations." What a surprise. That just changed his whole perspective of her. Justin didn't see that one coming at all with her being the youngest of the staff. Now he could see clearly the class, sophistication and professionalism she exuded in her speaking style and her body language, walking and sitting. When she looked at the other staff members, they took notice instantly. He noticed everything now.

Noticing his facial looks, she said, "In other words I run the entire Red Sox inner office operations and then report directly to my father, Mr. Duncan, every Thursday morning." She smiled the biggest smile and winked at him. Seeing his eyes enlarge hearing these words, Argona said, "Don't worry, I'm not a spy and I'm not a spoiled child, nor was I just given a position or a job in this organization. I have an MBA from the 'Wharton's School of Business and Finance' in Philadelphia." She seemed to look taller and much more exquisite, as she explained herself to him.

"I had to work my way from the bottom up. Trust me," she was still smiling, "I know what it is like to clean the restrooms!"

She then went about her business as usual. She was very cordial in spite of her position as President, and offered to get a beverage for him. He already had one, but thanked her anyway.

Justin found them all to be very friendly and accommodating.

Angela proceeded to uncover the catered lunch and then left the room.

Cubinati then began to explain the restructuring plans and expectations to assemble a greater team that was capable of winning the World Series in three to five years. "This year, preferably, if miracles are being handed out." He said with a smile to break the seriousness up of the talking points.

"In the meanwhile, we want you to train with specialized coaches to perfect the skills we know you already possess. Justin was definitely in agreement there. He hoped to hone his skills to perfection as quickly as possible for everybody concerned.

Justin knew he was accepted on a trial basis to see how well he could work in the majors. DeMarco had already explained this to him. Some great athletes have come and fallen apart under the intense pressure of being in the big leagues.

"We want to see how well you cope with intense pressure and a rigorous schedule that is a third or less of what the majors go through, Justin." Cubinati explained again.

Justin shook his head in agreement although he wasn't worried. He knew he was built 'double tough'. Grandma had been telling him this throughout his life.

Cubinati did most of the talking, explaining many details during the lunch meeting. Argona explained the next final steps Justin would be experiencing from this moment forward and the itinerary set for him.

"Justin, you will be taken to your hotel for the night, and then one of our corporate helicopter's will pick you up at 8 a.m. to take you straight to Pawtucket. Breakfast is served in the coffee shop beginning at 6 a.m. I suggest you eat. Pawtucket is just a short flight away, and you will be there for the remainder of the spring training and games. This should be a great experience for you, and a wonderful observation for us to see how well you perform in a semi-professional league. Good luck to you, and please contact us if you need anything, or any further information. We are all here to make sure this ball club is a success. We all thank you for being a Boston Red Sox teammate." They all lifted their water glasses and toasted Justin, and he smiled and did the same.

"Thank you for this opportunity," he added. "I'm looking forward to everything and expecting to have a great career in Pawtucket and then here in Boston." He smiled with them all and then another round of toasts ensued.

Frost passed over the contract to him from across the table and explained a few paragraphs in case Justin needed further explanation or it was just a habit of his either way, Justin read it quickly and signed it. He didn't need an attorney to explain this one to him. He was bright enough to understand that you don't stay if you can't perform. Justin scanned the contract to make sure its stipulations were as agreed upon. It was for a two-year stint, and all the money previously agreed upon with their scout, Mr. DeMarco was written in. It was a simple contract with no gimmicks. Just the way he was told Mr. Duncan does business. He liked the owner's style.

"The signing bonus will be wired into your account today and be available by tomorrow morning," said Frost, the CFO.

"Thank you, Sir." Justin replied courteously.

"I'm eager to get some rest and head out tomorrow to Pawtucket. I'm ready to get things moving for our organization. It was a pleasure meeting every one of you. I certainly thank you for the food. It really hit an empty spot."

They laughed at his remark and Angela came back into the room. She packed up some fruit and cookies in case he wanted to snack on them later. "I noticed you liked a certain cookie so, they're are all in there." She added with a very motherly smile.

"Thank you, Angela. I can assure you they won't be there tomorrow morning." Justin said with a big smile on his face. Angela smiled and felt like she had just done something very nice for a really nice man.

After Justin left, the team reassembled in the conference room and Mr. Cubinati spoke first. "I am deeply impressed with our new Justin Edge. He is exactly as Frank DeMarco described him… athletically built, handsome, polite, quick in reaction and very intelligent. He looks wonderful so far. Comments?"

The entire conversation was focused and traversed around Justin and his abilities, the records he holds from high school, college, and their high hopes that he'll be able to stay the course they wanted him for.

Chapter 16

The helicopter ride was less than 30 minutes to Pawtucket training camp. As they arrived, he thanked the pilot for the ride and explanation of the scenery as they flew over. He took his headphones off, shook hands, and off he went towards the main office. Before he reached it, The Coach and a few other players came over to greet him personally.

"Hello Justin, I'm Coach Bricket."

"Hello to you, Sir, I'm Justin, just as you said." It seemed a little funny to hear and made them all laugh. There was an instant fondness that seemed to overcome them all. Justin was much more friendly than they thought he would be. This new guy just might be nice and fun after all. They had been hearing so much about him and his expected arrival, they were a bit dubious as to what kind of person he would be. Their minds were at ease now.

Justin was surprised to see one of the Red Sox Major league catchers, Tim Hines, working out with them and soon found out he was rehabilitating from a knee surgery. There's that knee problem with catchers he said to himself. Grandma was right. He told Justin he hoped to be ready to go back up to Boston within two months of the new season starting.

The Red Sox management had sent word already that they wanted him groomed and readied as quickly as possible. They wanted an initial showing to see what he had to offer with the 'Pawtucket' ball club first on the list.

They also had high hopes for a better season this coming year than the previous last three for both ball clubs. The Inner office Management and especially, Mr. Duncan hoped to bring him up when he was physically and mentally ready. The sooner the better was the word to Coach Bricket. They needed their rising star to rise early.

His starting position was center out fielder, even though he could pitch or play third base. His talent could have given him just about any position, but the coaches concurred this was a great place for Justin to save that valuable batting arm.

What they really wanted to see from him was some home runs!

The Management and coaches went over the game statistics every week. They were especially interested in their great new hope they had just signed -- Justin Edge.

Their eyebrows lifted when they saw his stats. He had the raw talent and it was being honed to perfection in all areas with the personal coaches assigned to him. They made the strategy for the team, but as always, singled him out for some additional training with his own batting, fielding and base Coaches.

Justin was a fresh breath of air coming in and his light-hearted and humorous demeanor made him instantly likeable. He was a natural all around. His energy alone could be the fresh blood the other men on the team would be inspired with and cause them to rise to their full potential. The last four years of a losing streak had done nothing to help boost their morale.

Justin's coach in Pawtucket, Coach Bricket, briefed Coach Chambers weekly on his minor league team and Justin Edge. His remarks about Justin were: "What is amazing about this young man, is that not only is he a remarkable and promising ball player, but also the life style he leads. He doesn't go out drinking, or swearing. He doesn't talk filth and smack talk. He's not a womanizer, he isn't a spend thrift, or a materialistic junkie. The guy is completely disciplined! He says Yes Sir, does his workouts systematically and without being guided. He's always well groomed and respectful of his fellow teammates and the employees at the ballpark. He has a tremendous sense of humor, he always has the guys smiling or laughing. I'm telling you, this man is an all-around good person. He's almost unbelievable!" Coach Bricket was so excited he was talking faster than Chambers had ever heard him speak. It took Chambers a few seconds to digest what was said and fully take it all in.

"On top of all that Coach, he has a brilliant mind that has a tremendous retention capacity. They discovered quickly, he was all about baseball his soon to be wife, and his Grandma who raised him. "You just don't get a whole package like this," Coach Bricket said.

"Someone like this doesn't come around the corner every day. I'm telling you, his skills have gone into warp-speed with the individual and personalized coaching. He's a serious and dedicated player, intent on being in the Major League and by George, he will make it, trust me on this one!"

Coach Chambers said, "Let's keep him low keyed for now. Don't compliment him too much, or he'll get a big head early." He said with deep concern and maybe a hint of superstition. He remembered what happened to Babe Ruth starting out at such a young age, and many others too. "We're going down a lot of blind alley's here, and we're only six games into the Spring Training Games. Let's keep watching for now."

"If we could compare Justin to a previous player, it would have to be Lou Gehrig." Said the club Psychologist. He had to report into Boston on the new ball players as part of the Ball Club's program. He smiles, loves his mama who is his grandma, and his soon to be, wife. That's all he has or really wants to talk about when you talk to him about his personal life.

Mr. Duncan was quite pleased with the report. He had paid top dollar for a sign up bonus to obtain this man, and wanted him to produce. He wanted him brought up fast as possible too. Heads were going to roll if they did as poorly as they had the previous year in Pawtucket.

"By the way, Coach Chambers, Justin is going home on Thursday, making it a long weekend so as to get married. Wild horses can't stop him, so I figured it's only a weekend. It's ok, isn't it? He says he'll be back Monday night."

"A quickie wedding? Hmmm…sounds like a need to be there type thing to me. Let him go, and don't disrupt his momentum. Keep him happy!"

Chapter 17

Justin was leaving Pawtucket for one long weekend. He had decided on the date and weekend during training, and that was relayed to Bree so they could make the wedding arrangements as she had requested before he left. He was so excited to get married to this woman he was floating on a cloud. He had told the coaches and teammates he was going home to Alabama a single man and would return a married man. This brought him quite a bit of attention and some heckling as was expected.

All his teammates congratulated him, and wished him well in all sincerity, as they had really grown close with Justin. Some kidded him that he was single and had it made, why ruin it? They were all married of course. Still, the joking was a team sport and pastime for the last evening before Justin left. He went along like the good-natured man he was. Justin seemed to glow with happiness some of his teammates noticed, even with a bit of envy. Justin had a goal and he knew he was on his way to achieving it. The first step was to marry his beloved Bree!

Pike, whom he had grown the closest relation with, told him, "The best way to ruin a romance is a wedding Cake! So, make sure you don't have one, and if you do, don't eat any of it!" Everyone laughed and scolded him for such a lousy joke, but Justin was so excited and happy, he didn't care about lousy or good jokes, it was all smiles and chuckles for him no matter what anybody said or did.

Everyone from the teammates to the coaches wanted him back and happy. "Tell us all about it when you return." The guys were yelling as his taxi drove off.

Once inside the taxi Justin switched his thinking and began to think about his time away from home. He had been at practice in Pawtucket for one month and although it felt like it had been a very quick month, it had also seemed like an eternity since he had seen Bree and Grandma.

He would be a married man within days, and way before the baby was born, which was what they both had wanted, and Grandma did especially.

The Church had been beautifully decorated with the help of the Ministers wife, Grandma Ruby, and her friends. Justin was so surprised and impressed. Bree had a beautiful cream-colored wedding dress with beautiful brown sash coming down from one shoulder draping to the hips. She looked ravishing! The church pews had ribbons and flowers in the same colors. She held in her hand a bouquet of yellow roses and a few Cymbidium Orchids in them. Everything was beautiful and perfect.

Candles illuminated the church and the feeling was so touching Justin felt his throat choke up a bit.

Grandma Ruby and her friends were dabbing the tears in their eyes with their kerchiefs, so everything was a typical wedding from that standpoint.

It was a short and very small ceremony with Reverend Matthews from their church presiding over the wedding ceremony. Grandma Ruby, her friends, some from the church, some of their neighbors Justin had grown up mowing their lawns and Nathan, were the other attendees. They had all brought a wedding gift for Bree and Justin and wished them the all the best in their life together.

Afterwards, the Reverend and his wife and all the other parishioners who attended the wedding, took them to dinner to celebrate. They were all surprised when a small wedding cake was brought out by a group of servers. Mrs. Matthews had made it her self. She was a baker in a bakery and this was her gift to them.

"I wasn't even expecting such a wonderful surprise as this, did you know about it Justin?"

"No, I didn't either, I thought we would order cake for dessert," he said with a funny gesture, mainly because he remembered what Pike had warned him about, but he dared not mention that bit of information. Everyone laughed and admired the beautiful cake that was a gift of love. Reverend and Mrs. Matthews were wonderful friends to share their happiness with.

"It's too beautiful to cut," said Bree

"I'll make another one for your first anniversary if you promise to invite us to celebrate with you," said Mrs. Matthews jokingly.

"Oh, we will, we will," promised Nathan. Laughter erupted after his statement.

Justin so enjoyed Nathan and knew in his heart, this was now his brother too. Both he and Nathan felt this special bond, it was something each seemed to need and want. No effort had to be poured into this brotherly love that was coming so naturally.

Justin ended his first season of Spring Training Games in the minor leagues playing for the Boston Red Sox Triple-A team, the Pawtucket's with 24 home runs, 79 runs batted in, and all in 42 games. That's about the number of games a minor league team plays per season compared to the minimum of 162 games played by those on a Major League team. The season had absolutely flown by.

Justin already had his ticket to go home. Bree had called what seemed months ago to inform him after the ultra sound came in with the wonderful news the baby was going to be a boy. He would be home just in the nick of time for his son's birth. Great rejoicing and hooraying was the major subject of that particular phone call. He was as happy as a kid in a candy shop, going home to Bree, and a baby boy soon to be born

Justin was beginning to catch the attention of the local media through his outstanding plays, good looks, amazing physique and his stats that made it look all pretty and tied up with a bow. As he entered the airport, he was astonished over the entourage of journalists trying to get a comment or two from him. He had been sequestered in Pawtucket and away from the direct media. They are brutal, he thought to himself.

"Look, I'm on my way home, and I am in a rush. Please excuse me for not taking time with you, but it's more pressing for me to make my flight right now." Winked at them and ran to the security checkpoint.

Every Major League team now wanted a good look at this promising young rookie. They only wished their own rookies would move up to the coveted position of Majors in as little time as possible just like Justin was doing. Just like politics, nothing is a secret in baseball. Rumors flew around like leaves on a brisk, windy fall day.

Unfortunately, for Tim Hines, the catcher who was rehabilitating later discovered his knee wouldn't rehabilitate quickly enough and he was replaced with a fantastic catcher bought outright from a Mexico team. Justin looked forward to meeting this Buddy Montaño fellow someday.

Chapter 18

Head Coach, Harvey Chambers, was the first to speak in the end of the Spring Training Season corporate meeting in Boston at the Corporate Headquarters.

"Ladies and Gentlemen, I'm impressed with our record this year. For the first time in the four years that I have been here as Head Coach, I'm impressed with our progress and performance not only in the Red Sox ballclub, but also in Pawtucket." A few claps went a long way among the management.

"The Team has really crystallized and come together. For a change, they played ball." He was relieved and beaming with joy. "Our Minor League Team is doing quite well with several players who were there last year as new comers, and our new rookie, Justin Edge. He is beginning to look as promising as was promised by Mr. DeMarco. He's definitely one heck of a home run hitter and a great 'go-to' guy to bring runners in on base. I am proud to say, it is befitting and a tribute to the Red Sox Ball Club, that our Rookie, Justin Edge is being awarded the title of International League Rookie of the Year this year. Now that's the kind of progress we're looking for!"

With this news, the upper office staff, who, had first met with Justin and Mr. Duncan, applauded and even let out a few whistles upon hearing all this great news together at one time. This was their opportunity to let off a little pressure and have some fun. It was their team, their rookie, and they had a great season in both the Majors and the Minors Spring Training Games. Things were definitely looking up, and that was something to celebrate.

They didn't fully understand Justin's total potential at this point, but this would soon change. Very soon!

Continuing on, Chambers said, "Attendance for Pawtucket was a sell out every game. The curiosity of this new rookie player being drafted in the first round, and the fact that he was in their own back yard, the people came to see a good game of baseball, and they got it. The team as a whole is playing like a team. Our other new guys who were here last year are performing beyond our expectations at this point. I personally feel, Justin has been the glue that we needed to make them all bond. He's quite a unique personality. He plays ball and gives a great performance. All eyes everywhere, are on this new Rookie next year. Even our competition, sad to say!"

Mr. Duncan was no novice in this baseball world. He knew that was to be expected and the wheels in his mind were already turning. It agitated him for others to go after what he discovered and made. He would fix that problem very soon.

"Oh!" "And our concession sales were double from last year!"

That comment roused a hearty hooray from everyone, laughter ensued and joyful comments how *everyone* loves to eat at the ballpark!

The owner of the Boston Red Sox, Mr. Durie Duncan, had earned his way up the ladder through shipping, and buying his own boats one at a time. He was no dummy when it came to a keen eye on good investments. He kept this news of his new Rookie close to his vest. He silently thought he would do a little prospecting on his own, and keep a close eye on what the coaches are and are not doing or seeing. But for now, this was a time of reports and the news was very positive so far. He didn't mind a little celebrating over this last year's report. They had earned it.

Justin endeavored to be a respectable and responsible husband to Bree and father to their son. Being with Bree was like heaven on earth.

When Bree had given birth to their son he was a typical father-to-be sitting by her side in the labor suite. After a long, laborious 7 hours, Dr. Spencer was able to deliver a 7.6 pound baby boy as healthy as anyone could imagine."

Grandma Ruby responded with delight and approval, clapping her hands and laughing. Nathan was there as the ever admiring Uncle he would always be. Justin hugged and kissed Bree after viewing their new, beautiful miracle of a son for the hundredth time.

"Justin would you approve of naming our son Bradley Justin Edge?" Bree asked softly. "We could even call him BJ as a nickname, wouldn't that be cute?"

Justin was elated with the name and thought that it was loving of Bree to want to include his name in their son's name. He said, "I couldn't think of a better name for such a distinguished young man."

So, they named him Bradley Justin Edge. He was a beautiful bouncing baby boy. weighing in at 7 pounds and 8 ounces. He had a little bit of brown hair and Bree's big brown eyes and he already had long lashes. He was beautiful, his parents both agreed as expected and laughed with pride and joy.

Grandma Ruby said, "He is going to be a gorgeous boy. We'll have to fight the girls off of him at an early age. I'll keep my broom handy."

Bree said, "I know now, where Justin gets his sense of humor from! It just dawned on me. Grandma Ruby, you are so funny at times." Everyone enjoyed the laughter and love going around.

"No doubt he will be a fierce and mighty baseball player like his father," Bree interjected in between all the fondling and admiring from Justin, Nathan and Grandma Ruby.

The head nurse came in and suggested, "You all might want to let your new mommy get some rest. She is exhausted and in dire need of some sleep after being up and in hard labor for a long time." The family agreed and began to file out.

"Bree, I am the happiest man on earth right now, and I'll leave so you can rest, but I'll be back after a shower and chow. I'll check in on our little guy and you, while you sleep, Ok?"

"No worries, I'm here." Justin assured her.

"I'm exhausted," said Nathan. "Please don't count on me for anything right now, I just don't think I can take any more stress, I'd be worthless." Bree gave a big smile to her brother who was always at her side and finally let out a laugh as everyone else did.

"You get some of that much needed rest, you sure do deserve after producing the beautiful baby boy you just delivered to all of us." Said Grandma Ruby chuckling as usual, as she was walking out of Bree's room. She joined Nathan in walking down the hall to the exit doors.

"I do think I deserve some credit. After all," said Justin. "Bradley looks a lot like me!" Justin smirked knowing full well Bree would giggle at him and she did. Bree tried to keep awake for a little while, but could only smile and drifted off to sleep with the heaviness of exhaustion that was rapidly setting in.

Justin stayed with Bree and Bradley a couple of weeks, tending to their every need or whim.

"I'm going to miss you so much when you have to leave, Justin. I could really get used to having you around 24/7."

"You're such a brilliant, charming and beautiful woman. In all truthfulness, I can't stop looking at you and Bradley. I am in awe. I actually feel like I have an inflated chest right now." He said it with a great big smile. "I have a beautiful family to love with all my heart." He was expressing his happiness of being a husband and a new father.

Justin did most of the up-at-night feeding's for baby Bradley, so Bree could get some rest, and mostly because Justin wanted to be a father and share in this experience he was enjoying fully.

After another week had passed, and Bree was feeling so much better and healthier, she asked Justin to sit and talk with her for a bit. This talk would be different from the many others they had while the baby was sleeping.

"Justin, I realize you have work to do, and you need to make preparations for the upcoming season. Grandma Ruby, Nathan and I will be fine taking care of Bradley and each other."

"I only wish we could be there for the games when you are playing so we could see you in action and share our lives completely with you in your would. I'm uplifted though, Justin, because I know that will come very soon. There is no doubt in my mind because I have great confidence in you. For now, you must go! You must make it happen for us as a family. The cream always rises to the top! You're the cream, my love!" Bree smiled and let the words sink in that it was ok to leave.

She knew he was eager and wanting to get busy making their future happen she could tell he had been thinking about it because she had come to learn to read his feelings and what drove him inside.

"Justin, you are a champion in the making and it requires hard work and uninterrupted, dedicated practice right now. This is a critical time for you. You have a Baseball career in the making. We moved me into Grandma Ruby's house. You and I had a marriage, and then we had a baby. Justin, It's imperative that you pave the way and make it to the big leagues with a steady contract. Afterwards, we begin a very stable life." She said it while fluttering those long lashes on those big, brown eyes at him. How could he resist her?

"You are my man, and I love you, sweetheart. I can't make it any clearer or more relative than what I just said to you." She put her hand over his heart and said, "Your heart beat is my heart beat." Justin was moved by Bree's love and selflessness.

He was thinking intently and didn't speak.

"Besides, practice makes perfect." Bree was smiling as she said it, so Justin knew it was his signal to go do what he had to do.

"Thank you, Bree. I don't want to leave and you know this. But, I don't want to let any of you down either. Something inside of me is saying, I'm not going to be in Pawtucket much longer." He gave her a look she knew so well when he meant business. She preferred seeing this look most of all.

"I'm your wife, and best fan. Surprise me my love, if that is possible." They kissed and held each other for the longest time while Justin set his brain in motion. He knew the course he would be setting for himself and it was going to be rigid and full. He felt less pressure with them together as a family living at Grandma's house and Nathan near by. This security would allow him to work relentlessly and guilt free.

"Bree, I vow to you that I am going to make this a year to remember."

"Okay! And I'm going to hold you to that Mr. Edge." Bree's eyes were sparkling and happy. This was Justin's time to shine and get results, Bree expected it of him and that was all the stimulation he needed. He was a self-starter anyway, but his love for her drove him harder. The results he wanted, was a position on the Boston Red Sox team as a permanent player. For that, he had to focus and excel at his God given skills and talent.

"One day, Bree we will have a nice home of our own. It's a dream I expect to become a reality." His voice was confident as he spoke with an uncanny and inexplicable tone.

"I'm determined to give it only one more go this year if they insist on keeping me in Pawtucket. I'm going to excel above and beyond my normal and I'm also a free agent after this year. I have teams coming to me like I'm a magnet now.

Since you are sending me off with good blessings and expectations, I'll go with the first and best offer if Boston doesn't come through." She kept smiling because her husband was the man she always dreamed of having. He was her protective Prince Charming named Justin Edge.

Justin was raising the bar because his contract was expiring after this year and he would be a free agent. Everyone in the world of Baseball knew it too.

This year the positioning was definitely in his favor. Hopefully, it would have a happing ending with a win-win situation for everyone. His future was definitely in the pipeline as of now.

Justin knew he needed to completely impress the coaching staff with his abilities and earn his way to Fenway Stadium in Boston, as quickly as humanly possible! He had slightly expected, instant results, but in reality, he knew he had to pay his dues. He was doing what was necessary to polish the rough edges and learn how to make his desire to be a professional Major League player into a reality – his heart and head were set on being with the Boston Red Sox. He never deviated in his thinking and focus after that day with Bree.

"Please God; help me to help myself, and as always, I will praise your name no matter what." Grandma Ruby raised him to talk to God every day about everything. She also said, "God placed you where you are, it's important to praise Him." How could he not thank God? He agreed with his Grandma wholeheartedly.

He had gone home to see Bree, Bradley and Grandma Ruby for a few weeks after the first season was over and now it was time, and sad, he had to leave. Justin promised himself, "This will not be much longer. I'm working it out in my mind and in my performance on how to make changes for the better. I'm going to be out of Pawtucket, and on to Fenway Field next year, if not sooner!"

He was moving into his mental zone too quickly. He had to slow it down so he could say good-bye to his family. Then he would move back into his mental zone again.

Grandma Ruby bid her farewell to Justin again just as she had done before.

"Justin, I know you'll give it you're all my boy." Grandma felt it was a good time for a pep talk about now. "I see the changes in you and your abilities. You're gaining more confidence. You're not confused in your focus or your decisions. Your workouts are forming your body into a beautiful and muscular form! Your brain is maturing. You even look like so much more of a man. She relished telling him these truths. It was a proud moment for her.

"I feel all of that too, Grandma. I have power and abilities I can feel, developing inside and outside of me. I want you to know that I do recognize them. I have a powerful God on my side and I value it greatly. Not all people have been fortunate to be raised the way I was by a loving grandmother!"

"That's right, my boy! Your Grandma didn't raise just a pretty face." They both smiled.

With Bree, it was a different separation and good-bye. "Bradley is just a baby and too young to know it will be a few months until your return, and that's a good thing. But for me, I'm older and know. It makes me sad to be away from you, but I'm the one who is in essence sending you off." They both smiled and Justin loved the way Bree brought her mouth up to one side to express disgust.

"As we have discussed, it's for the best. I am fully pledging my full support for you because I know it's going to be our year."

"That's right and I'm already planning on making a huge impact, Bree. I feel it down inside of me and I know when that feeling is so strong, it means God has gone before me, I'm doing what I'm supposed to be doing."

"I know. I've come to learn to trust it too." Bree said.

"How could I have won the heart of such a decent perfect woman?"

"You must have been studying magic, became a prestidigitator, and put a spell on me, I guess," joked Bree.

"Seriously, I've been blessed with a great husband. How could I say anything different? I love you so much, my life has constant sunshine in it because of you."

They kissed and held on to each other as long as they could, but each knew it was time for Justin to go. "I'll call every day go give you an update and tell you how much I love you." Justin said with a torn heart.

"Yes! You do that for me. I want to hear your voice if I can't see you."

Chapter 19

Justin had plans to make this his last season and his last year, in Pawtucket, Rhode Island. It was too far away from his little family. The cost of living was too expensive to have them with him on his meager salary for the time being. The cost of airline tickets twice a season to go home for a couple of days in between games was less expensive but harder on the heart being away from his family for such long intervals.

"Change things. Focus and change things Justin." Aye, aye, captain he replied to himself as he awaited his flight for Pawtucket.

Everyone but Justin had cleared their lockers out and packed their duffel bags to head home until pre-season came around again. Justin didn't because he knew he would be back.

Before the guys had left, he remembered they were in good spirits because they had a winning season. He knew he had fared well with management. Each man had high hopes of being moved up to the majors or at the very least, be given a decent monetary contract for another year with a nice signing bonus. Justin hoped the best for each of them, as he had grown close with his teammates quickly.

This year was definitely destined to be different for Justin. His initial two-year contract was going to expire this year, and the Red Sox Corporate offices wanted to negotiate with him very soon for a long-term contract just in case he was entertaining other ball clubs offers. "One never knows." said Mr. Duncan to himself. "I didn't get where I am by waiting on fair weather!" This he said aloud as if to someone else in the room, but he was the only one there. He was a determined man himself. He recognized determination when he saw it and he was looking determination in the face every time he saw Justin Edge!

Justin had already sent word with his Coach that this was to be his last year in Pawtucket, one way or another. He preferred to not be there at all this season to put it into plain English. Nonetheless, he but would carry out whatever their wishes were, because his contract was not fully fulfilled yet and he was theirs to do with as they pleased. Then they could take his meaning however they wished. He let them know and then, if he had to call an Agent, he would.

A free agent was worth a lot of money these days, especially of his caliber.

His confidence had strengthened and increased with his performance this past season. There had been swarms of new agents coming around giving him their business cards or wanting a meeting to talk about their firms representing him, or the teams who wanted to pick him up, and other such spur of the moment ideas bouncing off of their heads to get an audience with him.

One team's manager did come personally to meet with Justin in Boston. He was from the Yankees. They had quite a long talk about a lot of nothing getting to know each other and to try and develop a friendship, the usual tactic. Finally, the Manager said,

"We would love to talk to you when your contract is up with Boston. Here is my card and my number, call us and we will set up a meeting."

"Thank you, Sir." Said Justin not giving any indication of his full intentions or interest one way or another.

Some of the other offers were lucrative (or at least the Agents were saying they were), but Justin's heart was still set on Boston. He wanted to stay there and move his entire family there, including Grandma Ruby, so they could attend every one of his games. He desired this more than any other teams offer. He loved Boston, the people, and its history. The proximity to other interesting places that were nearby was a big plus for short trips with his family. The water and the air were almost Jurassic in smell, mixed with foods in the air when he went to the North End. Italian food was heavy in the air. Everything about it was good. Boston had given him his start, the most important element to value. The Red Sox brought in specialists to work with him. He had met the upper management. Justin felt a very strong bond with the Red Sox organization, case in point!

Chapter 20

Justin finally arrived in Rhode Island and it was cold! It went straight through his clothes to his bones with cold. Good thing he had the right clothing in his locker. He couldn't wait to get to it and get into the clothing.

Upon his arrival at the field in Pawtucket, Justin was greeted by the head Grounds keeper, José Gallegos. José was a jovial and friendly man. He had a robust personality that matched his fast moving body. He zipped all over the place with a lot of energy, probably to stay warm, Justin figured. He was talkative, hard working and on the job every day. He had a lot of responsibilities to keep the place in shape and manage the employees that were much larger in the regular season. Minimal employees kept the place up with him in the winter months.

José was actually younger than he looked. Probably from being outside everyday, and almost all day in the weather, rain or shine, freezing or hot and humid, José was out there. He most definitely had a weathered look on him but it suited him. He was happy with what he did and went about his business routinely.

"Hello José!"

"Hello Mr. Justin. What brings you here at this time of the year?"

"José, I would like to work out anonymously here during the winter off-season months, so I can be more than just ready come spring training. I want to be super ready, if you get my meaning."

"I read you loud and clear my friend. You are to be commended for such an attitude." José truly was impressed. Never had he seen this happen before.

"I really don't want any newspaper journalists or media people, poking and snooping around watching me or reporting about me. It's imperative to me personally, that I do this under the radar. I really want to progress and improve my abilities without interruptions. I would like to concentrate and give it my all, for my family's sake number one and for the Boston Red Sox number two. Can I stay here and work-out?" Justin asked José.

José smiled and said, "It would be so nice to have another pretty looking face around here besides mine. My regular winter workers who don't want to be here have hang-dog looking faces all the time." He laughed and then said,

"Follow me, Joven. I will put you into your lovely suite and no one will have access to you but me."

It was anything but a suite. It was sort of under the tunnel leading to the field, but most importantly, it was tucked away from the road traffic, away from any views from walkers and the ball field. It was just outside the tunnel facing the ball field, out of the weather, and the book/film room and weight rooms were very near as well.

The food hall is at the end of the tunnel and to the left José told him. "We eat breakfast at 7:30 a.m. in the cafeteria, lunch at noon and dinner at 6 p.m. everyday. Mr. Duncan likes his employees to be happy and healthy. You may join us for feasting, or, fasting whichever you prefer to call it my friend."

"This is so perfect José. Thank you so much. You knew exactly what I wanted when I didn't even know really what it was I was looking for. I didn't even know this area was here. I owe you José. "Thank you with all of my heart. I will never forget your kindness Sir."

"I'm proud of you for showing such a burning desire to do your best. I will be rooting for you all the way. We are all Boston Red Sox fans around here." José was laughing heartily and the laughter was trailing off into the distance as Jose walked off to return to his work, jumping into his little Rhino full of yard equipment and mending junk.

He did turn back to tell Justin one more thing. "I left my cell phone number on your bed so you can get hold of me for anything. I do mean anything, okay?"

"You're the best, José. A million thanks are really not enough!"

José just waved to him and was soon out of sight.

Justin used the remaining day light to get himself settled in, then watch a few past Yankee and Red Sox game videos to begin memorizing the players moves and quirks. He would watch all of them in a matter of a few evenings. Then start on the other contending leagues the Red Sox might be contending with for the Pennant or Division Title after he did a bit of research.

"Tomorrow is a brand new day, and the beginning of my brand new life. I have planned, I have strategized and I'm ready to rumble, but first, the basics. I have to crawl before I walk. Maybe I'll skip the crawling part and just start walking and go on to running!" He allowed himself a laugh, as there would be plenty of time to be serious after tonight. He was getting a bit tired from the long trip today. He ate a lot of fruit he had gotten from the cafeteria as a bedtime snack because he got hungry. The cold makes you hungrier. "I'll bring some cheese with my fruit tomorrow," he said to himself.

The Red Sox owner, Mr. Durie Duncan knew all about Justin's arrival for training because his 'Grounds Foreman' José Gallegos had informed him. Needless to say, he was impressed beyond words. José had been reporting in to him as instructed on every thing new or ordinary that happened at the ball park during regular and off seasons for his full fifteen years of employment with Mr. Duncan in Pawtucket. Mr. Duncan had given José his personal cell phone number and told him he expected him to use it. José was a great man and did exactly as he had been asked to do. Mr. Duncan knew everyone who worked for him by first name, and that always made his employees feel important and special. Mr. Duncan knew they were special, or they wouldn't be working for him in the first place.

It was easy for José to report all activities of their guest because he and Justin were always outside during the day. José doing his routine grounds checks and maintenance, and Justin in the batter's box with the machine throwing every conceivable ball it was programmed to do. Every night Justin read and watched game videos of various teams, and studied the players, the coaches and their ballparks. He had a photographic memory so it wasn't hard to retain what he saw. He made notes, so he knew what film clip to grab if he ever needed it.

Mr. Duncan had his pilot take him and the President of the Red Sox, his daughter, Tanya Argona, in his helicopter over the field the next day after José had called him and sent him a copy of one of the batting videos Justin had shared with him that evening as they watched the first set together. Justin had set up a tripod and filmed himself to study his posture, swing, stance and positioning over the plate in different spots and variable positions.

As his helicopter flew by close but not directly over, he had brought the team videographer with his high-powered, zoom lens to film Justin batting. He wanted to see this first hand. Just one of the traits that made Mr. Duncan so successful, he was in the driver's seat on all situations that concerned him or his empire he had built. His daughter, Tanya, was learning from the master and she knew it, valued it and glowed over her Father. He always included her, and he made her look smart and on top of things more so than what she already was. That was their little secret.

Justin had no idea because small planes and helicopters were always flying around on clear sunny days. The reports to Mr. Duncan from José were the same as the lead scout had originally told him, but more. Justin was maturing and was going on two years older than he was when DeMarco was watching him. There was quite a bit of difference with age and practice, even if it was just going on the second year. This made it all the more alluring.

Duncan settled back in his soft lamb's leather seat and waited to land on top of his down town office building, where he and the passengers would disembark. Now he and Tanya would wait and see if their managers were on top of things as he expected them to be. It was important for the minor league coach to be in touch with the major league coach so everything moved smoothly. If they were not, and he didn't hear something soon, he had the wrong coaches.

"Tick, tock, tick, tock. Time will tell us everything," he mused between the two of them once they were alone, and out of earshot of anyone.

Tanya adored her father and thought he was the most remarkable man she had ever met, until she met and married her husband. He still wasn't the man her father was, but she loved him dearly for his other wonderful qualities that made him unique in his own way and unlike any other man she had ever dated. They had been married for two years now and they were still happy and in love. She savored the feeling of his love.

One day while the sun was shining and there were no winds to speak of, Justin needed Jose's help to move the machine to the pitcher's mound, which Jose thought was weird but unique.

"Jose." Yelled Justin. "Can you give me a hand here? I need to move this batting machine to the pitcher's mound for batting practice."

"Of course I can, Joven." I'm not as young and strong as you, but together we can manage it alright."

It wasn't as difficult as either of them thought it would be when they lifted the machine up into Jose's little Rhino trailer bed he used for tootling around the property in.

"Hey thanks, José."

"No hay problema for the future home run king of America." Smiling through his sun weathered face. His eyes sparkled at Justin. "I just want to be there to see you in real action doing your spectacular thing Muchacho! Viva la campeon!" José expressed with upraised arm and fist.

Justin accepted Jose's compliments with a huge smile and said, "I'm giving it all I've got amigo."

Three hours later, Justin yelled for José again. "José, can you do me a favor and film me? I want to see how I'm positioning my stance, and how I'm swinging so I can review myself and tweak where I might need some tweaking." By now, Justin was a master of body moves, stances, positions and swings.

"You bet I can. I need a break, or I'll be an old man before my time. You're helping 'me' out compadre."

José was one of the most fun people Justin knew outside of his teammates. As the first ball was on its way out of the field, José was doing his own color commentating. "Out of the Park, Home Run, Bases Loaded! Dios mío, you're killing 'em in this game and it's only the bottom of the fourth inning.

Almost every ball went out of the park and most of them were clean, clear cinches, out of the park, home runs. For every obvious home run, José had a little victory dance he would perform. One was with his right hand up and his finger pointing to the sky he did a little circular and swivel bit with his hips in a circle kind of a dance singing, uh huh, uh huh, I like it by K.C. and the Sunshine band. Justin laughed so hard because that was an oldie but a goodie. José was giving away his age.

The next ball was flying out of the park with more air under it and after José was sure it was going over the fence, he started doing the running man dance singing, "I'm coming out, I want the world to see."

Next hit, the Hammer Dance with the wrong words, I've got a batter (instead of a hammer).

Another home run on film and José did the twist, Chubby Checker style. What a cut up José was. He was funny to the bones naturally.

The next home run, José did the moonwalk with some semblance to Michael Jackson's with just the expression, "ee, ee." and waving his hands in a fluid, waving-motion in front of him. He definitely had the moves, and Justin found himself enjoying José's company and humorous special effects, but never had a hard time concentrating on his mission at hand.

They both enjoyed laughing, and taking a break from their two jobs in the late afternoon of the day. "Hey, thanks José. For the filming, AND the side effects show. I'd pay to see you on stage any day!"

"Maybe I should think of a career change, huh?

"Maybe you should keep your day job just in case you run out of material... you know, as a back-up." Justin winked his eye at José.

"Thanks again, José, this will really help me and I'll never forget your most colorful antics!" They both slapped each other's backs and laughed some more before departing company until dinner.

José went directly into his office and called Mr. Duncan on his private cell phone. "Hello Mr. Duncan! You should have seen what I just saw today with my very own eyes!"

"What did you see, José?"

Chapter 21

When the coaching staff and team showed up for the pre-season training and Spring Training games in Pawtucket, they were more than a bit surprised to see that Justin was already there. They were even more surprised to learn that he had been working out for all but two weeks of the off-season.

It had been cold and snowy and still raining when they arrived. How in tarnation had he done it? Wondered Coach Bricket. How had he managed to work out during the notoriously miserable weather of the east coast? The winters in Rhode Island are cold, snowy, rainy, windy – severe and unmerciful. Yet, Justin did it. He had practiced every day and watched videos in the evenings or when severe weather hit with high winds.

Their teammate, Justin, was in beautiful physical and mental condition, minus a tan, but he looked as though he could tackle a bear. Fortunately, this was not football.

Is this guy crazy or just focused and determined? The coaches discussed him among themselves. "I think he is one determined young man salivating to go to the Major Leagues at warp speed!" said Coach Bricket.

"How many times were you up to bat in the batting cage, Junior?" asked Pike, his good friend by now.

"Oh, about 10,000 times is all. I kept running out of balls and had to go pick them up behind the fence. I was kind of slowed down when I had to hunt for them in the snow," Justin replied.

"Besides, I thought I'd save some of the balls for you all. They're out over the back fence waiting for you girls to pick them up." He was acting as if he were joking, whereas in reality, he was as serious as a thoroughbred racehorse heading for the finish line. He was bred and trained for this.

He had developed steel in his blood over this autumn and winter break. His wife and son were his inspiration. He had never known such determination and sheer will. He'd never had a reason to until now.

Justin had kicked into overdrive and was now in granny gear going down a steep cliff. He had all the bases covered in his mind and his strategy firmly in place.

"Ya know, spending some time watching movies is so relaxing and quite beneficial." He just had to throw that in and keep the ribbing up.

"Oh yeah? Which ones did you watch that were good? Any action movies in that pile?" Pike fell for it hook, line and sinker.

"Yeah, I loved ALL the action movies of the Yankee games with Boston. I see why they're bitter rivals now," he added, with a wide grin.

"They'll be waving the white flag, or screaming 'Uncle' by the time I'm finished with them."

"You little delbert!" Pike spewed at him.

"You know, they have a page in Psychology Today for people like you!"

The rest of the team laughed at Pike for letting Justin get the better of him. They enjoyed getting in on the joke.

"You were watching baseball games? Atta Boy!" said Bobby McFinch, the second baseman. He was as impressed as Pike was with Justin and his tenacity to be an excellent baseball player. He also wished he had been smarter and come a few weeks earlier and practiced with Justin.

Pawtucket Coach Ronald Bricket couldn't help but overhear their little jabs going on in the next room. "Whoa! That's impressive," he said to himself in astonishment.

He curiously took a long stroll around to the back of the outfield, and let out a thunderous, "Holy Mary Mother of God!" There were baseballs everywhere. He had never seen so many on the ground at one time behind the fence to boot.

Justin had been so busy practicing hitting that he hadn't had time to go out to collect all the batted balls – just the ones he needed to keep replenishing the batting machine. Besides, hunting for them in snow was hard and time consuming. Sometimes, José helped him when he was caught up with his work.

Justin also knew he was in his second and last year of his contract. He expected some reciprocation for all his hard work and performance. He knew the ticket and concession sales had skyrocketed and now his excelling talents were going to skyrocket once he showed his stuff to the world. The newspapers would take care of the rest.

Being gifted as an athlete wasn't his only talent. He had a keen sense of awareness and business savvy. It was human nature to want to make money and be successful

"Lord, I would really like to play ball for the Boston Red Sox Major League Team. However, if you have a better option, like another team for me, I'm in your hands and thy will be done, Amen."

Justin was tired of working himself to the bones before the normal season arrived. He decided to turn in early and read until he fell asleep – his reward now that everyone was here and his alone time was over. As he was slipping into bed earlier than usual, even the sun wasn't completely down yet. He happened to glance out of his window just in time to catch Coach Bricket running from behind the walls of center field all the way into his office. He had been checking the balls out behind center field for himself. Justin laughed so hard. He now knew Coach Bricket was eavesdropping on the guys razzing him. He was happy his hard efforts were noticed. He knew Bricket would be calling Coach Chambers about now.

"Thy will be done Lord, I'm in your hands." Somehow, he knew that was exactly what was happening at this moment. He then drifted off to sleep in a heavy exhaustion.

Coach Bricket was indeed running back to his office to call Head Coach Harvey Chambers in Boston just as Justin had predicted.

On his way, he stopped to tell the grounds men, "Will you guys go collect the balls in the back behind the outfield wall right now? I want to know how many there are out there, and hurry before it gets dark. I want EVERY one of them!"

"Hello, Coach Chambers? This is Coach Bricket over in Pawtucket.

"We have our season Home Run King, Sir." He said half out of breath from running.

"No, it's not Pike." He exclaimed.

"No, it's not McFinch either."

Impatient with the guessing game, he blurted it out, "it's Justin Edge, Sir."

"No, I'm not blowing wind at you. The guy has been here all winter working out and practicing on his own, I'm telling you! That's Right, all by himself. The groundskeeper, José concurred it. Helped him on occasion too, so he says. Even the other various workers around here have said it's true."

"They said Justin had told them he had made a personal vow that he would knock the threading off these balls with the pitching machine speed up to 95 mph, non-stop. About 1,000 of those balls are still over the outfield fence. I just checked it out myself. José, said he's been here all off-season working out and practicing everything from batting to reviewing himself, and watching films of other minor and major league team games. Justin has a photographic memory and I say we are going to see some heavy JuJu this year!" Coach Bricket would have gone on and on, but Coach Chambers interrupted and said, "Slow down. Let me process all of this, will ya?"

"That's not all. He studied every one of the past Yankee, Oakland and Dodger games with the Red Sox and some others of importance to him personally, to get to the playoffs. I'll guarantee you he has their names, moves, gestures and signals memorized. I've seen this kid perform. I know how his head works. He is a mind machine. He goes after what it is he wants with everything he's got, and he stays with it until he gets it! He's the most powerful and persistent man I've seen in my lifetime. I've read about the other greats, but I'm witnessing this one in real time, on our own team! If he weren't so nice and kind and determined to play baseball for the Red Sox, I would be afraid of him! I'm telling you Coach," Coach Chambers halted Bricket in midsentence, I'll be there tomorrow!

"Oh, ok, Yes sir, great, you bet. See you tomorrow."

Chapter 22

Over the next two days of practice, Justin continued his impressive display of batting and hitting the balls out of the ballpark. His practice was paying off. He was a honed machine in every form. He performed with grace and ease, like a walk in the park.

The coaches noticed the huge difference and his teammates did too. He was batting runs in, and his fielding was like newly polished steel. He was now methodical and mythical in his mammoth abilities. The team was proud and at the same time, upset with themselves that they hadn't had the same drive as Justin did. They vowed to change.

His teammates were not jealous, they were proud to be associated with Justin and play with him on the same team. They had a better shot at the much dreamed of hope of playing in a major league. Justin was paying the price for all of them to enjoy a sweet taste of success and they realized it. They vowed to help out to the best of their abilities. This was indeed the shot of adrenaline the coaches had dreamed of. Here it was standing and performing right in front of them.

Justin was goodhearted and not phony. He was the kind of guy who had talents and abilities so perfect, that it was hard to tire of watching him. The others endeavored to meet his standards. This was the epidemic the team needed; the shot in the arm to cure what ails you; the shot heard around the world. If words could describe it, it was beyond the men's ability to express.

Justin was often funny, but always genuine. There was a deep side to him that was felt by everyone and they knew they couldn't pierce that area. They knew he was a scholar and the epitome of an athlete at the beginning of a promising career. His own enthusiasm and faith in himself and in his God carried him like wings of an angel to heights unknown until now.

"Highly unusual, yet a very unique individual." one of the pitchers said to another as they discussed Justin.

Justin defined himself with a quote from one of his favorite books by Bruce Barton, an American author born August 5,1886.

"The fire of their faith burns away all obstacles. The determined abandon themselves utterly to their tasks and the tasks mold them into greatness. These are the most fortunate, and the most valuable people on earth."

He dared not say this to anyone lest they consider him a braggart. Grandma would occasionally say, "Conceit is God's gift to little men." He chuckled at her wit once again. She also quoted the Bible and said, "Don't brag on yourself; let others do it for you!" Still, he didn't see any harm in reading this and claiming it for himself. God made him what he was and he was thanking Him above all else!

Truly, Justin's real asset was his batting. He could adjust to any type of pitcher and pitch. His hand and eye coordination was becoming supernatural. He could switch hit as needed and never skip a beat. Pitchers had no advantage over him. One teammate had commented, "There is no fooling that wizard of round ball and stick! He is like something out of Marvel Comics or the X-Men. He is a mix of Babe Ruth and Mickey Mantle, all without the wild lifestyles." His colleagues knew that statement to be true and not mythical.

The guys concocted a slogan and had a banner made just for Justin. It was meant to be both a gag and a bit of bragging. They taped it up in the cafeteria so he would be sure to see it when he came in. He never missed anything. He would see it.

"We have the 'COMPETITIVE EDGE."

Justin just stood and looked at it in humility and astonishment. He thanked the guys for doing this, and told them he would do everything in his power to not let them down. He really liked the slogan. He knew it to be true, thereby making him feel a bit egotistical, but mostly because he knew his teammates liked him and meant it as a meaningful gesture and gag, of course to prove their bravado. However, he knew they respected him and counted on his performance to get them into the big leagues and anything else possible. He was giving it all he had so they could reach their dreams too.

All they needed was the pitchers to do their part, so they could do their parts. It was a team effort of magnificent proportions. They knew what lay ahead of them, and they knew it was going to be a tough season. Team 'Red Paws' needed a great season as that meant payoff in their minds. Justin just hoped he and most of the other guys would be a part of it.

Coach Chambers had witnessed all of Justin's attributes while watching practice one day and quickly reported back to Mr. Duncan – who was already aware, unbeknownst to Chambers.

Mr. Duncan was happy to hear the great news, but acted very busy at the same time. Chambers noticed the difference in Duncan's voice. He wondered what that was all about. Mr. Duncan was actually disappointed that Chambers hadn't discovered this sooner and had reported into him sooner.

"This is very unlike him, Tanya. I know he heard it from Coach Bricket first. That concerns me and we'll have to keep an eye on him to make sure he is on top of everything below him. Tanya, keep an eye on him to see if he has lost his zeal. If anything will perk it back up, it will be seeing Edge in action as we witnessed firsthand. If it doesn't, he is gone. She totally agreed with her father.

"Still, what is his problem?" He asked his daughter, being the over achiever he was. He couldn't help but be concerned about Chambers lethargy.

"I personally feel he is more involved with the upper leagues to perform than Pawtucket. He is making a huge mistake with a player like Edge over there. He isn't seeing the whole picture we are painting here. He is relying too heavily on reports from Bricket instead of traveling and checking it out personally. That tells me he has gotten fat and lazy and I don't like that!" Said Tanya. "I'll be watching him alright." Duncan loved it when his daughter took control and got steamed up. She was absolutely correct in her assumptions too. Papa wanted to give a little test for the President of his ballclub and she passed with flying colors.

Nevertheless, he and Tanya had personally gone up to Pawtucket to see it firsthand, which was better than sitting on his hands and depending on others for instant information he knew would never come. José was the better informant of them all. His gut feelings always prevailed to be the best course of action. He and his daughter, Tanya, the President of the Red Sox Ball Club, were the only ones in on this meeting in his office.

Chapter 23

"I want that kid given a new and binding contract and I want him here in Boston for this season, and I want it NOW." Duncan was telling Cubinati and Tanya the next morning after their private meeting. They went into action quickly, to make it happen. "We'll see if he holds up to the pressure of the big leagues, OK?" Duncan only said things once and things just happened.

"Justin, Coach Chambers needs to take you to Boston for a meeting at the corporate offices. He will be accompanying you on the company chopper out of here tomorrow. Dress clean and neat for travelling, not for playing ball, OK?" Said Coach Bricket on Thursday afternoon.

"Yes Sir." Justin replied.

So, after just four days of spring training, Bricket and Chambers saw all they needed to see. They were both convinced he was a rising star, or better yet, an exploding meteor. A firecracker and a reckoning force the Red Sox needed on their team right now! Coach Chambers was jumping for joy for a couple of reasons. He knew he was going to be accompanying Justin to the Caribbean. A total surprise for Justin. His job was going to be made easier having Justin in Boston with him. He had been fearful to this point he would lose his job with a non-performing ball club.

Until they were actually in the air, Justin didn't know he would be experiencing the first class treatment that Duncan provided for his top-notch players or business associates. First, he would be taken by helicopter from Pawtucket, R.I. to Boston. From there, Mr. Duncan's private jet was on standby, awaiting Justin and Coach Chambers, ready to take them to the Caribbean where his yacht was moored in "Nanny Cay Marina" in the fabulous Caribbean yacht charter destination Club. The waters were like crystal. They were a turquoise blue and warm to the touch. Perfect for viewing the coral reefs and white sand 35 feet below – perfect for snorkeling and skin diving too. All the equipment was stored in the yacht's lower level, along with a mini speed-racing boat, known in luxury circles as the Cigarette. The Caribbean was beckoning for anyone to jump in just as Sirens of Greek Mythology enticed the sailors. Duncan had planned every detail of this meeting. He was self confident it was perfect.

Justin was hours away from seeing all of this for himself. Mr. Duncan was using his yacht in the perfect ambiance of the beautiful and serene Caribbean as a means of luring Justin to the Red Sox Ball Club on a long-term and most anticipated contract that would satisfy all the parties. He was getting Justin away from the mundane that could sidetrack his normal thinking patterns.

Durie Duncan knew that, at the moment, Justin was a slippery fish with his two-year rookie contract expiring. He knew the other ball clubs were courting his rookie and that made him even more competitive to sign on his best home-run hitter and fielder. What Durie Duncan didn't know for a fact, was that Justin Edge wanted to stay In Boston more than anything in the world. This made for interesting maneuvering that kept Duncan in peak performance. He thrived on these types of situations. Out-smarting his opponents, out-performing his adversaries and out-witting his competition.

Mr. Duncan was not a multi-Billionaire by mistake. He had more extra sensory perception than most men when it came to business and actions of human nature.

He could read people within seconds and, if he so desired, talk them into just about anything. But Justin Edge was not your average man. He had to strategize his opponents every movement and gesture. Every surrounding feature had been planned and was there for a reason. He was in his element. Duncan thrived on rivals of great intellect. He felt he had everything in order and eagerly awaited Mr. Edge's arrival.

"I'm in the people business Tanya, and you have to know how to treat them and what makes them tick. Everyone wants something. I just need to find out what and how much it will take to keep this man, and I will."

Duncan was already deep in thought preparing for the meeting. "I will call you tonight and brief you on the days outcome. Love you my darling."

"Night Dad, I love you, and I want you to know that you always make me so proud to be your daughter!" Tanya loved her father and had a deep respect for him because he made her feel so involved and important in his self imposed, sheltered life." He did with all of his very small family of two girls and a wonderful supportive wife.

"I'll wait up no matter how late, ok Dad?"

"You got it my dear."

"Gabriel," he asked, do you have the menu printed and ready for the dinner tonight? Is everything ready?"

"Yes, Sir, just as you and Hans had specified. Everything was available and fresh when I went to the market this morning. I was very pleased, Sir."

"Fine. I think I'll take a swim and you wait at the foot of the boat to help me back in. I'm a little stiff from the long and cold New England winter. I only moor my yacht in summer months in the Rowes Wharf in Boston. It's convenient and close to my office.

Justin was sitting in the corporate jet, now very aware of where he was headed and why. Satisfied that his efforts were paying off, he quickly called Bree to tell her and Grandma where he was and why. Bree was happier because she felt right for having sent him off to prepare and proud of him because he had done it so spectacularly.

"That's my guy!" she said to him. "I'm more than proud of you at this moment. I just have one request. Please Justin, take the time to relax and enjoy yourself, please, my love. You have worked so hard for this. Take a vacation and don't feel an ounce of guilt or I will be so mad at you. Promise me."

"Wow, I will since you insist. The next vacation is with you, promise me that."

"I'm not crazy, Justin. Of course I'll take you up on that. Call me when you can, we'll all be on alert for the phone to ring, we want to hear every detail, but enjoy yourself. You can let it all out, my love. Enjoy yourself."

"Thanks for your love and support. I'll call as soon as I can." Justin hung up feeling so blessed and comforted just from hearing his lovely wife's voice and reassurance.

Chapter 24

Coach Chambers informed him of the surprise. Justin smiled and rather enjoyed the comforts of his first luxurious corporate jet flight. The flight attendant came around constantly with fresh sliced fruit and apples in the shape of birds and wedges of cheese.

A light, pleasing Caribbean meal and beverage were served on fine bone China and Waterford crystal stemware. Silver flatware and fine linen napkins were used with every course.

He took it all in and didn't mind one bit in letting Coach Chambers know that he was feeling pretty special with all this opulence and attention. Coach Chambers admitted he did too, and thanked Justin for creating the opportunity for both of them. They clinked their Waterford water glasses and enjoyed a light-hearted laugh together.

Inside, however, Justin's thoughts were going wild. This was living! He wished Bree were with him – and Grandma. Grandma might not like this; she was too humble and modest.

Coach Chambers noticed Justin's interest and intake of everything. He was so happy for Justin to experience all of this luxury. This young man already meant the world to him inside his heart, not just inside the personal business side of him. This young man came from hardship they never discussed, but he knew about, to this. He was overjoyed for the wonderful human being on this jet with him.

After dinner service, Justin decided to lie down on the beautiful leather sofa and take a short nap. A fluffy pillow soon was under his head and a very soft blanket was covering him. It would not take long to doze off with such luxurious accommodations.

A five-and-a-half-hour flight and then they would be taken by helicopter from the airport to the yacht, minutes away. It was time for some relaxation after a scrumptious meal that had been lavished with all the fine details fit for a king.

Both he and Coach Chambers were sliding into this luxury quite nicely. They laughed at their pampered setting and decided they could learn to like this. He was loosening up, as directed by his wife.

"See you when I wake up, sir."

"Likewise, Justin. I'm tired myself."

He had a hard time drifting off because his mind kept recalling the events of the day. It was beyond magical.

Justin knew what he had aspired to in baseball, and what he had to offer in terms of talent, intellect, leadership and skill. Otherwise, why would Mr. Duncan be going to such great lengths to impress him and wine and dine him?

He pleasantly remembered the helipad atop the building that took him to the airport last night.

He remembered the walls and chairs in Mr. Duncan's personal office were decorated in the beautiful red, green tartan pattern of his heritage. It all came to a clear meaning now. Mr. Duncan had no idea he wanted to stay in Boston more than anything else. This was all to his advantage and he would play it cool and calm.

The battle of the wits, were about to begin. Justin was not one bit worried; he felt quite able to think and answer whatever was thrown at him.

Justin knew the upper management and Mr. Dunkin had to be aware he knew what was going on by now.

Who could predict the outcome?

Grandma had said she and Bree had said a nice prayer for him. They had him covered. That was all he needed to hear. He said a little prayer for himself and was soon fast asleep.

Chapter 25

The Owner of the Red Sox made his money through the shipping industry. He was a shipping magnate who had brought himself up on his own from a rented boat, to his very own first personally owned boat, then moved up to ships, one ship at a time. Now he had his own 153-foot luxury yacht, with a crew of 14 to attend to every need, and countless commuter ships and barges for commercial use.

He proudly wears his name, Durie Duncan, his Gaelic roots and Scottish ancestry that harkens back to a King of Scotland. He felt bona fide. He had his authenticated lineage hanging in his luxurious downtown high-rise office complex that Justin had seen when he was there for his meeting with the upper management and they had showed him around. He remembered it well because he was impressed anyone could trace their lineage so far back and be so proud of their roots.

Justin also knew why his daughter, Tanya Argona, the President of the Corporation had a hair clip and broach with the same clan insignia and crest on them. They were all proud Scottish people.

Duncan often bragged that his name was an Anglicized form of the Gaelic Donnchadh, meaning, "Brown Warrior." The name was traced as far back as 1606, perhaps to the Scottish King featured in Shakespeare's Macbeth. He knew his legacy from the Clansmen, Scottish family and their crest that bore the words, "On waves of the Sea."

"Was that my appropriate destiny or what?" he would respond to those who inquired about the phrase on his heritage banners. He felt that the ancient Clansmen who preceded him had prepared him for his destiny.

His Christian name, also from the 1609 era, originated from the entourage of Queen Margaret of Scotland.

His particular Clan's motto, "Savor the Moment," became the reason for serving the fine stout, dark and light Scottish beer every managers meeting, and on very special occasions he brought his adored Scottish Whiskey straight in from Scotland.

Although Duncan had one of those famous Scottish tempers when it was called out, he was usually a happy, generous man, known to take his family and other distinguished businessmen and their families to the Military Tattoo in Edinburgh, Scotland, every August. This was a coveted invitation because of the traditions and values laced on this pageant by the Scots themselves.

Chambers joked with Bricket about Duncan's being Scottish to the bones, in an Irish Town! Go figure. They both enjoyed the comment and novelty of humor.

After another corporate meeting in the "Irish Castle", as Duncan's office was known, Head Coach Harvey Chambers quipped to another pitching coach, Ben Raker, "Guess that's why they're called the United Kingdom, and they're still united in the United States."

Chapter 26

Justin felt poised and confident about meeting "The" Mr. Duncan on his fabulous yacht in the Caribbean. He reasoned that Mr. Duncan needed him as badly as he needed Mr. Duncan to bring him to Boston. He figured it could be a win-win for both sides if all the details worked out according to plan.

On his way from the airport to the yacht, Justin sat looking out the window, thinking of Bradley, Grandma Ruby, and Nathan – which energized him even more. With all of his being, he wanted to be a good father to his son a good husband to his wife and take extra good care of his grandmother who raised him.

No one had wanted a father more than he had when he was growing up, and his mind was determined that his son would never have that feeling.

"I can be a great father, and I will be!"

Now it was time to see Mr. Duncan.

"Let's take what flows, and go with it, Justin, he was talking to himself as he was looking out the back window of the helicopter. He had his microphone turned off so he could think alone." He was used to thinking out loud, or talking to himself, as others might say, but what the heck, he enjoyed talking and thinking to himself. The thought of it all made him chuckle. "I guess I'm my own best friend. What a thought!" He mused aloud once more.

When the helicopter landed on the yacht with such precision, Justin was surprised and impressed, with the size of Mr. Duncan's yacht. Actually, it took his breath away. He felt as though he were in the land of OZ or some epic fairy tail. Imagine a helicopter landing on the bow of a yacht and still having enough room to jog around it if one desired. Super amazing.

"Hello, Justin and Harvey!" said an exuberant Mr. Duncan.

He approached them with a spry step, shaking each of their extended hands with a firm grip as he welcomed them aboard the R.S. Boston.

"Abbreviations for Red Sox, Boston. Clever name, huh?" He asked Justin.

"It is a very clever and appropriate name I think, Sir. Stately and dignified, Exactly what the Red Sox are."

"That's a great explanation son!" Said Mr. Duncan, "I really like the choice of words...Stately and dignified!" His laugh was a serious one. More like a thinking laugh Justin thought.

They walked down one level to where a table had been setup prepared with freshly made smoothies and cold bottles of water on silver trays. The smoothies had beautiful fresh fruit skewered on long silver picks hanging on the sides of each glass.

The beverages had been promptly brought out by an on board stewardess as soon as they came down stairs. She was dressed in a marine-tailored white and blue short-sleeved shirt, navy blue skirt, and treaded rubber-soled semi-high-heeled shoes.

The Caribbean flair clothing suited her and her lovely tan. Her hair was secured loosely, but perfectly, on her head so that she looked fresh at all times. Justin observed and took in every detail of this experience. Everything intrigued him and everything caught his attention. He noticed the same hair clip with the Scottish emblem the President of the Boston Red Sox Ball Club, Tanya Argona, Mr. Duncan's daughter, had worn. This made him wonder if she were Scottish of the same clan, or, was it was just something Mr. Duncan liked his attendants to wear in commemoration of his heritage he was so proud of. Maybe she was related to Mr. Duncan. Nothing would surprise him at this point. He would have pondered this puzzle further but Mr. Duncan broke his concentration.

"Justin, I'm eager to show you the beauty of life on the water in the sunny Caribbean. I love spending as much of the winter months here where I can stock up on Vitamin D, notoriously hard to find in food, but supplied amply by Nature."

Moving along, Mr. Duncan offered, "You know, Justin, Vitamin D is important for healthy bones. Those who are nutritionally savvy have reached a fever pitch level in the world of nutrition recently, thanks to the mounting medical research in the unveiling of nutrition. It has become quite tangible in today's world of serious people's mounting interest in good natural health.

"There is now evidence that it may play a key role in preventing illnesses, including cancer, heart disease, diabetes, arthritis, multiple sclerosis and dementia. Therefore, I maintain a steady diet of Caribbean 'Vitamin D' to ensure that I am well cared for, to the best of my ability anyway, with natural health." He was on a natural health roll now and quite serious about it Justin noticed, who couldn't have?

"I've been doing quite a bit of studying in the nutrition and exercise areas. Power walking through the white sandy beaches, and the unstable surfaces, bring resistance into play, and these workouts can be challenging as they increase anaerobic capacity while improving your maximal oxygen consumption.

"As a matter-of-fact, anaerobic exercise is intense enough to trigger lactic acid formation and it's used by athletes to promote strength, speed and power, especially in body builders to build muscle mass.

"It's much different from aerobic exercise," he went on, "because it gets the whole body's metabolic energy operating in less than two minutes. I find it quite fascinating since it is such a short strain on my body and easy for me to indulge in on a daily basis this way. I don't want to become a stud muffin at my age." Everyone laughed heartily at Mr. Duncan's sincere humor that made him so real and easy to warm up to.

He was a genuine icebreaker conversationalist. And to add to the fun, he enjoyed doing it for their entertainment. He honestly loved to converse with people and even to make people laugh.

Justin was reading Mr. Duncan faster than he was reading Justin, because Justin wasn't talking yet. What a blessing this man is, Justin felt deeply. He is not going to be a hard whip on my back full of do this, and don't do this kind of controlling. What a relief.

"No wheezing from me in my old age, by Jove! Fresh fruit, vegetables, fish and spices! What more could you possibly need?

"Well there is one more thing and here it is! My Scottish roots are showing through now. It's called, Liquid Gold. The water of life – whiskey."

Laughing again with a beautiful, leisurely grace about him, he was the Scotsman to his core.

"The Water of Life has been distilled in Scotland since the fifteenth century and there can be few finer ways of getting to know this wondrous spirit than by cruising the waters of western Scotland, which I've done, through the islands of Mull, Islay, Arran and Skye. There you can drop anchor before a rugged, but exquisite, backdrop of scenery the eyes have never beheld. I've toured the distilleries and I've discovered first-hand how my ancestors made the whiskey taste so divine while using the simplest of ingredients. To some, it is an acquired taste, but for me, it's in my blood to like it and be proud of it. I'm not going to offer you more than one shot because you're my star athlete," he said with a twinkling wink.

Justin thought this was the first bite for the meeting.

He found Mr. Duncan amusing and very conversant. Justin was the perfect guest, listening intently and with genuine interest. They were well paired.

Duncan seemed to be a warm and jovial man, but he wasn't about to put his guard down. Justin was wondering how and when they they'd be getting around to talking hard-core business. He did realize that this was the primer for the big event. Just when it would occur, he didn't know, but as Bree had instructed, he was enjoying it all.

Justin had studied foreign diplomacy in college. He reasoned that if he couldn't succeed in baseball, he'd enter the medical field and consider work abroad, where he'd be dealing with different cultures.

The Japanese feel personal relationships are the cornerstone of all business relationships. They prefer to become friendly before conducting business, and it appeared that Mr. Duncan felt the same. He is a well-traveled businessman in the shipbuilding business, which takes him all over the world. It only makes sense.

"Gentlemen please, first refresh yourselves with something cool to drink. I'm sure you are thirsty and a bit jet weary after the long flight from Boston.

"After you have relaxed a bit, the chief stewardess will show you to your rooms. Your closets are stocked with Caribbean-style clothing - linen slacks, loose shirts and flip-flops for daytime; espadrilles and lightweight jackets for evening. Nothing has been overlooked, hopefully." he said with a hardy, confident, but very inviting smile and uplifted finger making his point very valid.

"After you have showered and feel refreshed, I'll give you a tour of the ship. Then the chef will have a wonderful dinner for us as the beautiful sun sets for our enjoyment."

"Sounds wonderful, Sir. I would enjoy a shower. Thank you for bringing me here and providing the clothing. That will really come in handy." Justin smiled at Mr. Duncan and then followed the stewardess.

Yes, indeed, Mr. Duncan," said Coach Chambers, "And it was very nice of you to invite me to come along."

"My pleasure, Harvey. Gentlemen, I'll see you back here, at your leisure."

Justin showered quickly and shaved. He found the clothing to fit and felt like an islander, or a tourist instantly. Everything was new and of the best quality. The labels were Italian, the best he could tell.

"Hmm, these garments must be very expensive because I can't pronounce the names," Justin surmised.

There in the closet was a Brunello Cucinelli, light brown, marine-style, tailored Cashmere cardigan, in case the evening were to become a little chilly, he suspected.

There was a pair of fitted trousers in a different material that looked like dinner-wear, luxe. A suede belt looped over the hanger clip likely meant they went together along with a polo shirt with a lightweight pullover next to them.

"Very chic and sporty with a hint of whimsical panache," said Justin as he performed as if he were a fashion designer talking to a crowd of spectators.

After he showered, he certainly felt refreshed. When he saw his reflection in the mirror, he playfully articulated to himself, "Lubby, you look ravishing in your new outerwear. I guess that's how Thurston Howell the Third, would have said it in Gilligan's Island." Justin recalled watching the re-runs of Gilligan's Island with Grandma Ruby.

He then used the Lizard Marine to initiate a video call by tapping Coach Chambers' cabin. The chief stewardess, Tristen, had shown both of them how to operate it for instant communication. It also provided them access to movies, an iTunes library of music, and a host of other up-to-the-minute features he knew he would not use.

"Are you ready to go?" he asked Coach Chambers' image on the screen.

"Oh, you bet I am. I'm eager to see this beauty and then eat one of Mr. Duncan's fabulous meals his chef is creating for us. He really puts out a beautiful and tasty spread, so be hungry, young man." Coach Chambers was giving him a heads up just in case.

"I'm looking pretty dapper in my new threads, how about you sonny?" Chambers asked.

"I look quite the Caribbean Islander myself – and I'm starving right now."

"Both smiled and clicked off their devices. They met outside their cabin doors and headed to the stateroom for appetizers and some cool tropical fruit drinks before joining Duncan for his grand tour of the beautiful yacht they were on.

Chapter 27

"Hello gentlemen," Duncan greeted. "I dare say you two look relaxed, as well as in tune with the local social mode. I don't feel so out of place now in your presence." He was quite the statesman at all times.

Justin offered, "I think it's the other way around, I don't feel so out of fashion now in your presence and in this tropical paradise." Duncan laughed heartily.

"Grab something to eat and drink over here men. The chef prepared some fruit, and cheeses and meats to hold us off until dinnertime. Dinner is in a few hours, usually as the sunsets. It's just too captivating to miss while eating one of Han's creative and delicious presentations.

"Then, let me know when you're ready and we'll take a tour of the R.S. Boston."

At those words, Justin said, "I'm ready right now. I'm thoroughly intrigued and can wait for dinner now that I've had a few pieces of cheese and fruit," still holding a handful of nuts, "if you are, Coach."

"I hate to waste Hans's talents, but I'll make up for it at dinner. I'm ready to go."

Duncan joked, "don't worry Harvey, it will be your breakfast."

The yacht had three levels plus a top viewing deck for the captain and his first officer.

"Gentlemen, I would like you to meet Captain Matthew Dillon of the R.S. Boston, and his first officer, Captain Craig Carlton. We refer to the Captain as "Marshal Dillon," he said with a mischievous smile.

Marshal Dillon smiled back and he put his hand out to shake both men's hands.

"Don't mess with Marshal Dillon." said Duncan teasing his ship's captain.

"That's right, I'm watching everything at all times, and I run a tight ship." He produced an elegant smile with teeth so white they matched his perfectly white uniform of tailored, knee-length shorts and a tailored captain's shirt topped off of course with the traditional Captain's hat. He had a very happy face that made everyone feel welcome.

By the way, Captain, will you join us for dinner tonight? You know what a great Chef Hans is and it would please him to have you as one of his guests.

"I will honor Hans and be present Mr. Duncan. Thank you for the coveted invitation." Smiling again even larger.

"Hans food is fabulous gentlemen, you will see why I'm so happy later!"

Everyone laughed and Justin said, "I'm drooling for his food right now."

Lighthearted and fun, these men were all in the same mood. It was a very pleasant start and Justin couldn't help but notice the ambiance of calm and happiness. He relaxed and enjoyed himself fully.

"Gentlemen, I think we'll take the lift and go all the way down to the engine room and then wind our way the up the ship to our dinner in the dining room. Allow me to lead the way," as he walked over to a beautiful pair of doors. They descended down to the engine rooms where generators and pollution prevention systems and sanitary systems work their mechanical magic. "This room is cleaner than many hospitals I've been told." Said Mr. Duncan proudly.

This ship is operated by two Caterpillar 3512c engines, and could propel the ship speed to max cruising up to 15 or 17 knots. The generators are Caterpillar 2x125kW C4.4, and the fuel capacity is 57,916 liters. Freshwater capacity is 13,627 liters.

Justin found this to be fascinating as he had never been on or much less thought about such a yacht. He was taking it all in and loved learning about new interesting things. He had an inquisitive mind and this was feeding it quite nicely.

The next floor up was the lower deck, where there were cabins for guests, enough to sleep twelve. The men were impressed to discover there were a Far Infrared Therapy spa, a spa pool tub with Jacuzzi, and a workout area. Coach Chambers commented, this was his favorite room because of the Jacuzzi. Justin could understand that as an athlete.

The next level was the main deck, with the formal dining room suite and entertaining areas. Soft, plush sofas, wet bars, TVs, and soft music could be heard everywhere. The rooms were done in rich dark wood, trimmed with glistening brass rails, and highly polished marble floors in certain areas for accent purposes, with beautiful dark wood framing them. The floors were polished to a mirror-like sheen.

The rooms were banked by beautiful drapes. The removable glass windows allowed for a soft breeze but were replaceable if the wind kicked up. The staff was well trained and performed this task before being asked to if the wind did pick up. They were invisible and fast in their tasks.

"The Upper Deck has a foredeck lounge as you discovered today while having cold drinks and appetizers," explained Duncan. The two guests were surprised to see that the sofa beds used for sun tanning and lounging during the day had been converted into a table for use for the next morning's breakfast. The conversions and clean up had been done quietly by the staff while the trio was touring the yacht levels. It amazed Justin how he never saw anyone performing these duties and yet they were done so cleanly and perfectly.

"Gentlemen, there are two hydraulic tenders in the bow behind the glass walls," Duncan continued. "There are swim platforms built on the aft and the starboard sides of the boat with ladders that submerse all the way into the water. The balconies are let out by hydraulics from bedrooms and staterooms for a very open and breezy ambiance." Mr. Duncan was a detailed man, Justin was observing more and more just how much so. This was speaking volumes about the man.

"The wave runners are in side compartments with the ship's other smaller boat for tendering to shore or going about in the water. There are so many varieties of watercraft and diving equipment to keep anybody happy at anytime aboard this ship." He said with a smile and a twinkle I his eyes.

Mr. Duncan was a stickler for all the latest and greatest equipment and used this boat as a example for potential customers of what all he could incorporate and build in his ship building business. It was also a great write off for his ship building business. Always the businessman, Justin thought to himself.

This was one half of Mr. Duncan and the Red Sox were the other half. Justin saw this very clearly.

Justin was well aware of what a cigarette boat was. Mr. Duncan gave more details of the ship as he knew far more about the luxurious side of boats than Justin ever would. He had been in this business for many years it was very apparent.

"The Cigarette brand has outlived wars, recessions, oil and gas shortages, inflation, and recessions, and will more than likely out-live all of us! This puppy can move in the water when it's even slightly powered up, then on to full speed…. Oh My! This baby roars like a beast.

Coach Chambers who had said little during the tour because he felt this tour was mainly for Justin, interjected, "you should see this man on the open water, Justin. When he is in that cigarette boat, he is quite an impressive watercraft aficionado."

"I am extremely cautious about water safety, especially in the open waters. What seems calm one minute can turn drastic the next minute. You only have fun if you are being safe." His face showed that he was very serious about this subject.

"This is an amazing ship, Sir. If I were your father you would be my favorite child!"

"I like your sense of humor, Justin! He said pointing his finger at Justin.

"Just how many boats do you have inside this ship, Mr. Duncan?" queried Justin.

"Two boats, and two tenders, each with their own lift. Three wave runners on sliding hydraulic chocks that are able to put them out over, and in the water. And four inflatable rafts that are powered by human calories." He smiled, his eyes sparkled and Justin couldn't help but smile back and let out a hearty laugh.

"Wow, Mr. Duncan I thoroughly understand your love of ships now. You know how to not only build the best but also how to have some serious fun and life on the open water." Justin shook his head in complete awe. Mr. Duncan liked his observations deeply.

"I have learned how to have this kind of fun from taking a bit of all my clients' ideas and incorporated them into this craft, son. I was born poor, but near the water, and my idea of a yacht back then was a rubber tire insert." He laughed at his own description, and so did the other two men.

"I'm in the ship building business and I am very good at what I do because I take it as serious as I do my own family's life. They are the one's that make this all fun for me. Otherwise, it would be just a business and I'm a very serious businessman, Justin." Mr. Duncan wasn't joking at this moment.

Hint number two: he knew what he was doing and he was setting the stage again. Justin observed every detail of Mr. Duncan's words and body language. Even to the squinted eyes when he was extremely serious In making a point.

I wanted this ship built to last, built to be a testament of what I and my company are able to build, while bringing happiness to my family and friends."

This was Mr. Duncan's way of letting Justin know how his head, heart and detailed brain worked. Justin liked what he was hearing and seeing so far. He knew they were both reading each other at every opportunity.

"Well, Gentlemen, this concludes our tour and now we are ready to sit and enjoy one of Hans's relaxing and exquisite dinners with some of the most wonderful personalities in the Caribbean. The sun is about to set, so let's go and partake of nature's creation and of Hans's creations. I hope you'll enjoy his meals as much as the my family, and I do."

"Thank you, Mr. Duncan, for the most impressive tour of your ship. You have something here that most people will never even dream about. I wouldn't have, if not for seeing it and being a part of it. I really thank you for this monumental experience with your masterfully detailed and descriptive tour. Coming from the master makes all the difference in the world, Sir."

"Thank you, Justin. That was very courteous and I am happy you enjoyed it. I can over do sometimes because it is my passion. Forgive me if I did." Said a very humble Durie Duncan.

"Not at all, Sir. It was exactly as I said." Justin was honest and sincere with his interest of the beautiful yacht.

Coach Chambers said, "I have seen this ship once before and I could enjoy seeing this magnificent ship over and over. I too thank you, Mr. Duncan for another wonderful tour.

"You're most welcome gentlemen and I am honored and pleased you enjoyed seeing what I can put out onto the sea."

"Now, Let's feast!"

"Sounds wonderful and I am more than ready." said Justin eagerly. He was starving by now.

After enjoying a dinner of appetizers, salad, seafood dinner and desserts to dream about, Justin enjoyed a most interesting conversation among the four men at dinner.

The Ship's Captain excused him self from the table after a break in the conversation and told them he enjoyed their honorable presence and now he needed to prepare the ship for the night and the early morning readings. This would ensure everyone's safety and enjoyment for the remainder of the trip.

They all said, "good night, and thank you for joining us for dinner with your delightful knowledge and stories fit for Physicists!" They all laughed because the wine made everyone but Justin, a bit tipsy and happy. Mr. Duncan had plenty on hand. Still, Justin abstained for his athletic reasons. Mr. Duncan appreciated that very much.

Mr. Duncan turned to Justin and asked, "Justin if you would participate with me, I would like very much to begin our talks tomorrow morning, beginning with breakfast, regarding your future with the Boston Red Sox Ball Club and your contract." There was no soft toe, tap dance here. Exactly how Justin liked it.

"Mr. Duncan, I've been waiting for this opportunity all my life." Justin said with a smile emitting such calmness, his self-confidence was radiating. His eagerness to get on with business was most evident. This pleased Duncan greatly.

"That's what I like to hear! Tomorrow then. I hope you'll enjoy a good night's sleep. I'm older than you and I'm quite tired, so if you'd like to stay up, the crew will attend to any needs."

"Oh, no, Sir, I'm ready to turn in, too. Besides, my bed looked like it was going to wrap me up in it as soon as I could get to it. Thank you for all of your gracious hospitality, Sir. It is most appreciated."

Justin was thankful at this point for all of Grandma Ruby's past table etiquette lessons, proper sitting and napkin placement, flatware usage and stemware usage. Thank you, again, God, for Grandma! I know I passed this part of the test because of her, he reflected. He fell asleep as soon as his head hit the luxurious pillow.

Justin awoke early in the morning, ready to get to breakfast and business. He showered and shaved and put on another new shirt and pants. Using the Lizzard he called Coach Chambers to waken him.

"Go on ahead of me and I'll join you two as soon as I'm able. Thank you for the call or who knows how long I would have slept in this fabulous bed. Wow! I went to dream town and enjoyed all of it." Justin laughed at the Coach's expressions.

"Ok Coach, see you in a while."

Chapter 28

"Good Morning, Mr. Duncan. What a beautiful sunrise!" Said Justin as he stood for a moment to take in the beauty of a new dawning day. Duncan shoved his newspaper to his lap surprised to hear the sound of Justin's perky and nice sounding voice so early in the morning. He saw that Justin was completely showered and dressed, ready for action obviously. Good thing he had risen extra early himself this particular morning and was ready for action.

Duncan responded to Justin's good morning. "And a wonderful good morning to you too, Justin. Did you sleep well?"

"I did, Sir. It was one of the best nights rest I believe I've had in a long time. Guess it has something to do with this Caribbean air and sleeping on the water in the most luxurious ship probably known to mortal men."

"Ah, probably not entirely true, but I'll take the compliment anyway. I'm happy you enjoyed it, very happy."

"Coach Chambers is getting ready and will join us in a while, I woke him up. He was sleeping very well." Justin smiled at Mr. Duncan.

"Good for him. He works hard and deserves to sleep in. If he slept well, that means he got some great rest. That's what this is supposed to do for all of us. And, it helps clear the mind so we can think clearly and intelligently. I feel a little smarter in the mornings." He belted out a great laugh at his whimsical statement. So did Justin.

"Yes, I know what you mean, I do too most mornings come to think of it." Smiling with a half chuckle.

Mr. Duncan looked to the Stewardess standing by and said, "Tristen, will you please start bringing out some fruit, pastries and yogurt?" All the while, he was waving his hands in the air as if he were Italian and not Scottish. Everything Duncan did, amused Justin.

"Right away, Sir." Replied the perky and refreshed looking and always-attentive Head Stewardess, Tristen.

"And we'll give your our breakfast order when Justin is ready."

"Coffee or tea, sir"

I'll have coffee, please, with no cream or sugar."

Justin loved the pampering. He knew it would end tonight and decided to indulge himself completely in the realm of the royal domain he was in the middle of. There would be plenty of time to work him self back to reality next week and forward.

"Mr. Duncan I have taken to the City of Boston like a duck in water. Boston has a passion for baseball that matches my own passion. I love Boston and could call it home for my whole life if given the right circumstances." Mr. Duncan took off his reading glasses and was looking directly at Justin and leaning his body into him now. Justin read body language like a second language.

"I believe Boston will take to you as if you are its very own son, Justin. I can already hear the fans roar when you walk out onto the field for the first time."

This made Justin smile. He could visualize what Mr. Duncan was saying without saying a word.

Tristen brought the juices, coffee and pastries with a beautiful dish of yogurt and a side dish of fresh fruit.

"Hans was on shore at 5 a.m. gathering fresh fruit for you this morning, sir. He loves to go shopping when we are here, like a kid in a candy shop only full of fruit and fish instead of candy." Tristen was so happy to report of Han's happiness in shopping for food.

"I think the best way to thank him is eating almost all of what he worked hard to gather and prepare for us." Said an appreciative Justin. "I know I have a huge appetite and can put a dent in it."

"Yeah, me too, why not." Agreed Mr. Duncan.

"The first sip of coffee is the best for some reason, and I love to savor the first sip, so just excuse me as I enjoy this, Mr. Duncan, it's a personal tradition."

"By all means, indulge. I think I'll do the same and truly enjoy the first sip. Never thought of it to be so sensory. I like that type of simple appreciation of the little things in life. You seem to have a lot of those types of interesting quirks. You're a very interesting young man. I'm glad we've had the opportunity to get to know each other on a more personal basis, Justin. These two days were meant for just this." Mr. Duncan took another sip and savored it just as much as the first. "I'm learning from you, Justin and I'm feeling very…. savant!" They both smiled and laughed.

"I would like to jump right in to the contract talks and our future if you don't mind, Mr. Duncan."

He about burned his mouth from listening to Justin and not paying attention to the amount of hot coffee going into his mouth.

"You're ready? Well then, I'm ready. I was born ready, let's get to it my man.

I'm an old hand at this Justin and I want you to hear my thoughts and I want to hear yours. Then, we meet in the middle somewhere. Unless you plan on your agent entering these talks that is, otherwise, it's between you and me right now, as you're about to be a free agent."

"Yes Sir, I realize that and I would like to make this simple and uncomplicated if at all possible because the MLB contracts make it necessary for attorneys to enter in on behalf of an agent, because the 300 pages of legalese in that big ole thick thing called a MLB contract is a tricky piece of work."

"I see you do understand better than the average player."

This young man, Justin Edge, impressed Duncan more and more. He is beyond my wildest imagination more intelligent than I originally figured, and I thought he was quite smart to begin with thought Mr. Duncan to himself. He had only somewhat read this in Justin's mannerisms. He was now completely intrigued by this young man.

"The Red Sox Ball Club has money, and plenty of it in reserves and investments. My best investments are in my players and my ball fields that bring in real meat and potato revenues."

"I have a question for you Justin."

"What is that, sir?"

"Do you want me to make my best offer up front, first and final, and be completely upfront and done with it, or, do you want to volley back and forth to try and get more out of me?"

"I'm a no nonsense kind of guy as you well know Mr. Duncan. I had to learn how to joke around believe it or not.

Therefore, first, best offer and no nonsense suits me just fine."

Mr. Duncan was quite aware of Justin's background and never even winced so as to give it away. It was his business to know everything he could about his business and associates.

"Okay, here it is; I have made a success out of what I call my devotion to homegrown players.

I try to stay away from the rat race and exercise of overpaying complementary players. I like my ball player's hand picked and homegrown from within the Red Sox Organization when possible. It has worked for me for well over 20 years now." Duncan explained.

"Most of the major ball clubs have enough money that they can and do prevent their best players from becoming a free agent, at least until their prime has past, which by then, the player is happy to stay on in management or move on in life to another vocation." He took a drink of water and continued.

"You are a major contribution to the Red Sox organization and I would like to keep you in Boston and keep you happy at the same time. I would be happy and the city of Boston would be happy. Heck, they might even forget the ghost of Babe Ruth always haunting us some day with your batting and fielding averages." Looking for the right words to say very carefully, Duncan proceeded.

"Here's the offer, Justin. Listen very closely because I feel it is generous and decent.

You've been to two All Star Games and you have won Rookie of the year, and I believe you will win MVP in one of our pennant races very soon. I believe in you Justin!

Therefore, I'm offering you a signing bonus of $7-million once the contract is signed, and I'm guaranteeing you $160 million by the Red Sox for the next 7 seasons with a first option clause for an additional 5 years, at my discretion. Cost of living adjustments included after the first contract.

That's my final and best offer." He stared at Justin, unable to read his poker face. Ten seconds went by but seemed like thirty seconds to Mr. Duncan.

Justin did this on purpose. It is a trait of the Japanese and works well in corporate negotiations to stress the one with the upper hand but wants something really bad. He didn't even blink. Then he said as he leaned in with his body towards Mr. Duncan,

"I'm your man, done deal. Give me a contract to read and sign."

"My God, I've never had a negotiation go so fast and so easy. Are you completely serious?"

"To be completely up front with you, Mr. Duncan, I was offered an unofficial, $5-million dollar sign up bonus by another premium ball club, and 170 million dollar contract for seven years. That would put me past my prime, and no offer of a first option for a second contract mentioned. I'm not even interested in any other ball club except the Red Sox. I want to be a Boston Red Sox Player with all my heart. It is a clean and honest organization with top-notch executives running the corporate offices, overseen by you, first and foremost. My relationship with you is a very serious one and I'm fully committed. Mr. Duncan you are being completely honest and generous, you're right on that one. I would like you to know. It's not all about money for me as much as where my family and I will be the happiest.

We will be very happy in Boston and I would love to call it home for the rest of my life. I have really bonded with the coaches, the guys, the organizations creed and the whole scenario encompassing the Red Sox Ball Club. I couldn't be more serious with you. The only additional favor I have to ask will be the determining factor to seal this deal."

"What's that?" Inquired a very serious and completely down to business, Mr. Duncan.

"I would like to bring my wife and son to this yacht in the Caribbean for a two week vacation next year during off season." Justin wondered if Mr. Duncan would wrinkle his nose at that request.

"My Gosh, man! You drive a hard wedge at the bargaining table don't you? If that's all you want, shake my hand before you change your mind. Consider it done; signed, sealed and delivered!" Justin shook Mr. Duncan's hand and they looked each other in the eye and studied each other intently, enjoying what each man saw.

Chapter 29

Coach Chambers came walking up to the two men at this point and asked, while popping a strawberry into his mouth, "what is the hand shake all about? Something new I should be aware of?"

"Why yes it is, Harvey." Mr. Duncan smiled at Justin and said, "We have our Home Run King and Center Out Fielder for the next seven years sitting here before us." He had a glow about his face that showed relief and happiness and he actually looked happier than he usually did which was extraordinary.

Chambers was overjoyed and gave Justin a hearty handshake and half hug, and congratulated both men for such a speedy and obviously agreeable conclusion. Mr. Duncan and Justin both shook their heads yes and thanked Chambers for the congratulations.

"The contract details will be drawn up this week, then you, your attorney, agent and family can discuss it and get back with me one week after you have received it. How does that suit you?"

"It suits me just fine, and I'm most appreciative for your generosity and faith in me, Mr. Duncan. I won't let you down." He knew Justin was a very sincere and serious young man when he was talking business and baseball.

"I know you won't Justin, or we wouldn't even be having this meeting. I've known this about you when I saw you in the cold wind and rain struggling in the mud and more often in the snow in Pawtucket, to practice during off-season, and make yourself a professional ball player. I flew over the field and saw what your were doing. I know all about you, I make it my business to know what and whom I'm dealing with. We all evolve over time, and I've watched you grow and never complain about your circumstances. I've watched with not only my eyes but with the help of other eyes who were with you and reported in to me. I've been with you everyday unbeknownst to you. I think you're one very special man. I know people very well, Justin. I've had to make a life out of it."

Coach Chambers was a bit embarrassed at this point and stood very stoic as he realized what Mr. Duncan had just said, and he knew before he or his coaching staff knew.

I know where you came from, how you've been raised, and I have talked to your high school and College coaches. I know the man I'm staking my return on investment in." Justin looked like a deer in the headlights for the first time. He never realized Mr. Duncan knew about his secretive workouts.

"That José, what a character." Justin said as he shook his head and smiled. He adored José.

Coach Chambers was surprised in a little sense, but he knew Mr. Duncan and that he did indeed operated a very tight organization. Mr. Duncan didn't become a self-made billionaire by waiting on information to come to him; he went after it himself.

"Congratulations, Justin." Coach Chambers extended his had to shake Justin's hand and he shook it quite enthusiastically because he knew great things were coming down the pipe very soon. He was happy to be a part of it and not on the outside looking in!

The rest of the day was spent relaxing and indulging in partaking of the water sports equipment with Coach Chambers. The Deck crew accommodated their every wish and operated the equipment they wanted to use, and they wanted to use everything!

Lot's of laughter and splashing was heard in Mr. Duncan's office, but being the hardcore businessman that he was, business first. Frolicking later with the guys would come and he would take them out on his baby, the Cigarette! The Cigarette boat is known for its speed in the water. It has a capacity to reach 80 knots in the water. This is why he was the only person who was allowed to drive the boat. He was a professional racer at one time, in his younger years, in his boat and ship building business. The two engines required to make the powerboat work give a sum of around 1000 horsepower. That is a lot of horses under one person's control! He usually took his Captain and First Officer with him while driving the boat as it takes three people to operate it to full efficiency.

These boats got their name from smuggling cigarettes and because of their speed the smugglers got away very quickly from the coast guard and other authorities. This always gave him a rush feeling. He guessed it was the aura surrounding the boat that appealed to his wilder side. The ability to own a boat that once lured smugglers added to its uniqueness of the boat. A very famous boat with history, and I love history.

"Boston is loaded with history, and I'm smack dab in the middle of making more history here today." Always the thinker, Duncan was deep in thought as he made this statement.

"That's why this boat is my darling." He amused himself with these glorious thoughts of his younger years when he was rambunctious and invincible.

Business first! Mr. Duncan was on the phone quickly talking with his attorney to get the ball moving ASAP on the contract. Tanya was the next to know everything and all the details. She was so excited and would let the upper management know immediately.

Vivian Jordan, Duncan's personal secretary and general at arms, was his next call. "I want you to schedule a full-fledged meeting this next Wednesday. I want all the key management, the regular staff, and all of the front-office people. I'm faxing you a list of the various minor league staff I want to be included right now. Can you get this done for me as quickly as possible?"

"Ok, I'll be back in the office tomorrow. We'll work out some additional details regarding the press releases I want sent out and I want to flood the news sources with this great news. Can you begin working on this right now with the agency and attorney's? Thanks a million!" He knew she would, but he liked to pose it as a question so she didn't get irritated with him barking orders. She was his best worker and also the most outspoken. Nonetheless, he didn't want to upset her. Women…I'm surrounded by them! Duncan said to himself thinking of his wife and two daughters and staff. Then he laughed thinking how he couldn't do it without them all.

This will alert the other teams to stop sending their blood hounds after one of my star players and trying to snatch him out right from under my nose. Nothing irritates me more, than one of my players being courted by another team. Although Justin showed great class and discernment in not mentioning who the other ball club was, he wondered if it were the Yankees or the Los Angeles Dodgers as they were the cream of the crop Clubs with the most money and best players. But Duncan was no body's fool. He acted like it didn't' matter. It was all about Justin, Duncan and the Red Sox.

"Some day, he will tell me, but for now, Justin is an official Boston Red Sox player! Just the sound of it made him swell with pride. The news will get out quickly, I'll make sure it is headline news every day of the coming weeks with something new leaked out each day. The scouts can go pick on somebody else's players now. It will be a cold day in hell before they outfox this ole Scotsman. After all, we were the first to ban fox hunting in 2002, that's how smart and civilized we are!

The day was fun, Mr. Duncan took them with his Captain and First Officer out in the Cigarette, and gave them a thrill they would never forget. He loved every moment of it. "What a great day this has been, boys. Let's go clean up and have a final, "Han's special dinner," shall we? And Captain will you please join us again tonight? It would be very special for you to get to know my newest, best paid and most promising Boston Red Sox Player even better now."

"How can I refuse? I love Han's cooking and the sheer thought of being in such wonderful company would be my great pleasure. Thank you, Mr. Duncan."

The evening was epic. It ended with a most satisfying ending to a perfect two-day meeting. Duncan had hired a small local Caribbean five-piece Band to play just a nice bit of background music Island style while they ate. The Tin drums intrigued Justin and Coach Chambers.

The two men would be leaving around 9 a.m. in the morning on the corporate helicopter, for the Caribbean airport and jet back to Boston. Imagine that! I'm an official Boston Red Sox player. Silently celebrating in his mind. He was already visualizing the awesome opportunity he was now deeply involved in.

Justin had so much to tell Bree and Grandma once he got home and before he left for Boston.

Chapter 30

As Justin walked into Fenway Park his first evening in Boston, he walked through the long and famous tunnel the teams used. With this his mind went racing. Since he was the only one there at the moment, he said his thoughts this time instead of just thinking them. It made it more powerful and real to him.

"Hello World. Here I am in the middle of Fenway Park Stadium, located in the heart of Boston in Kenmore Square. This has been the home of the Boston Red Sox since it opened in 1912. It is the oldest Ballpark in Major League History, and here I am in the middle of the baseball field where I will be playing ball tomorrow for the very first time in my new career as a Boston Red Sox player. I do love the sound of that." He continued as if he were talking to the world.

"You and I are going to become very good friends Mr. Fenway Stadium!" He softly chuckled because he felt like a school kid right now. Inner excitement was welling up inside of him and the pride he felt in saying he was a Red Sox professional ball player impacted him mentally as well as deeply in his heart. Justin was standing in the middle of his life long dream.

"It was here, where some of the most famous World Series Games have been won. This place has past legends fingerprints and footprints all over the place." Figments of his imagination were running all over the bleachers yelling, "peanuts, popcorn, water."

"This Field was where it all happened. Babe Ruth, Lou Gehrig, Ty Cobb, you name it, Red Sox legend's, they were here on this very dirt and grass, in the sunlight and under the lights. Who knows what all went on every second they were here. The place is loaded with history no matter what, and I love it. I love my predecessors and I love you Mr. Fenway Park!"

Justin was beginning to feel overwhelmed with the largeness and dignity of this place. He knew he would be a perfect match. He just needed to get comfortable with who he was now.

"Babe Ruth played here until he was sold to the New York Yankee's in 1918, thus igniting the more than intense, fierce and historical rivalry between the Boston Red Sox and the New York Yankee's. The greatest rivalry in Baseball history, imagine that. The Babe! Played here! I'm probably standing on the sacred ground he walked on." Justin looked down at his feet as if to see another pair of feet standing by his and he did see them in his imagination and the skinny legs that went in them. He gave himself a good laugh out of that visual.

"Over there," he pointed to another area of the field and said, "in 1946, Enos Slaughter's, 'Mad dash' occurred." He concentrated for a bit to visualize the event.

"And then, over there, in 1967 the "Impossible Dream" happened. That's when they broke their 9-year losing streak and went all the way to the World Series. Finally ending the season with one of the most memorable photo finishes in baseball history!" He was imitating in real life, the sports pages he had read and reread all of his life.

"Bostonians consider the 1967 season as the 're-invention' of the Boston Red Sox Ball Club. That's right! Boston went from the pretenders to the Contenders that year!" Giving out a continuous proud, soft laugh.

"That's right Mr. Fenway Park. That's when the Boston Red Sox became the 'Contenders' again, and no longer the 'pretenders'!"

In 1975 Carlton Fisk gave the Red Sox the winning home run over the towering Green Monster here in front of me, giving the Red Sox a 7-6 win to send the whole series into a deciding seventh game. Of course you knew the big Red Machine would clinch the first back-to-back World Series. This is where legends and history are made in the baseball world.

Justin loved this time alone on the field and no one around. He was able to just play around with whatever came to his mind, recalling all the highlights of the infamous Fenway Park and the Boston Red Sox in his photographic mind. He kept at it like a child enjoying his playtime. He never had much playtime as a child and never realized it anyway. This was perfect and acceptable behavior at any age he felt.

"You know Mr. Fenway Park, my Grandma Ruby told me a little history I'll bet you already know but you just keep it to yourself. She said the name Red Sox was first used by a "colored" team from Norfolk, Virginia back in 1888, when the Black people started their own baseball leagues. She knows all about it and told me the story I'm repeating it to you.

She even laughed as she told me how the name 'Boston Red Stockings' name, wouldn't fit on the front cover of newspapers, so they shortened it to Red Sox, just like the 'colored' team from Norfolk used.

She's proud of her heritage, and I'm proud of her, she worked hard all her life, and took care of me all of my life. I sure do thank God for that.

She had her ups and downs just like you, and she overcame them all, just like you." Justin paused for a little while to think of all the sacrifices, hardships and mostly the love and devotion, his Grandma had given to him.

"I'll be a proud man Mr. Fenway Park to play my utmost highest and best right here, for you, in my career. Just let me have the chance. I won't let you down. Be my friend and let the breezes be at the back for my baseballs so they will go out of the ballpark. He couldn't help but laugh a bit saying that one.

"Actually, I love to joke and I'm sure you've heard the best of them Mr. Fenway park. You can rest easy knowing I'll be back for more tomorrow. You and I will be best friend forever no matter what."

Justin turned around and jerked. He was surprised by the presence of Mr. Duncan, the Red Sox Owner. He had been standing there silently, listening to Justin talking and was almost speechless from his own shock of what he was hearing from this young man, and he was holding back a few tears of his own.

He stood in amazement with what he heard. Moved deeply by the sapient words of this new young man, and player of his precious Red Sox. He immediately felt kindness and love run through him that gave him a chill thinking this young man could love being here as much as he did, and a warm feeling of endearment in his heart for this young man that had been through so much as a young child.

This young man's brain could turn images over as fast as a pancake house could flip pancakes. They had a lot in common!

"Mr. Duncan, I hope you didn't hear me talking and acting like a mental case! It's that I'm just so thrilled to be here."

Quickly catching his wits, he walked up to Justin and patted him on the back, "If all you said makes you a mental case, I must be one too. I loved overhearing every bit of what you said and you taught me something to boot. This is all being said from one who has done the same thing as you just did, many times by him self at night. We have quite a bit in common young man; you just don't know me well enough yet to realize this." Mr. Duncan was a complicated man; yet he was also a down to earth man in terms of people skills and rationalization.

"Yes indeed, some mighty memorable people and some very historical events happened right here in this Stadium son. I've talked to this park so many times at night because its so magical feeling. Some things only Mr. Fenway Park and I know and will always be the only ones who know. I'm sure God over heard of course." They both chuckled together. This made Justin feel less goofy. Mr. Duncan had been up in the press box in a meeting with the press and watched Justin with the eyes of an Eagle during the conference.

He chose to end the conference early and ran down to the field curious what Justin was saying and who he was pointing to.

He loved this young man because he knew Justin loved being with the Boston Red Sox and playing in the Fenway Park Stadium. That showed Mr. Duncan volumes about this rising star.

"No wonder you are considered special by your teammates and coaches. You feel history and events with emotions. You see the invisible, well... so do I. That's what make or breaks a successful man, Justin."

"Tomorrow is a whole new chapter in history for not only Mr. Fenway Park, but also for Durie Duncan, Justin Edge and the Boston Red Sox. And I have a feeling you know that too."

"Yes, sir, I sure do!" They walked off the field together talking about nothing in particular but yet everything important to the two of them.

Chapter 31

The professional Baseball season took off fast. Justin learned quickly how the constant travel of a 162-game schedule can take its' toll on a man's body.

By the end of the of the road trips, his body was worn out and tired. He slept in a different bed so often, several times he jumped out of bed in a panic and rushed to look out the window to see what city he was in. He never knew what time of the night he would be eating dinner, so he kept power bars in his personal bag with him at all times. Some of the guys lost so much weight their regular clothes would hang on them when they were out of uniform.

A couple of his teammates complained of backaches and thought it was turning into more than a simple backache from chronic pain. He had to admit, some of the beds, even though their hotels were first class all the way, had some pretty bad beds that sagged, or were too soft, or were just downright awful bedding and pillows. There's nothing like your own bed and your own pillows, he thought to himself every night he got into bed in a different hotel. The 5a.m. check-ins, he thought they were a killer. Flying through the night even on first class seats, were hard because he wasn't lying down in a bed. He knew he had some issues he needed to get straightened out and others he had to just get used to.

He understood fully now when the guys who had been around a while would say, "Just give me a firm mattress without lumps and an air conditioner that actually cools the room, and I'll be happy."

Justin was getting tired of his usual, room service and a cheeseburger, something he thought would never happen in his life.

Some of the hotels didn't serve breakfast past 11 a.m. and there were more times than not, he wanted bacon and eggs so bad and he would get an, "I'm sorry sir, breakfast ends at 11 a.m." "Well I just got in at 4 a.m. this morning, can I pay extra?"

"Sorry sir, their rules, not mine."

He had walked to a breakfast café nearby a couple of times when he would see a sign that said breakfast all day. Not often, because sleep was more desirable, and now that people were getting to know him better, they would bother him for autographs, pictures or chit-chat, when all he wanted was to eat and sleep. Justin wasn't the rude type, so he just went with the hotel's policy. As Time progressed, he was catching on and getting smarter with every passing week. In the wee hours of the morning check-ins, he would order a breakfast right away if he felt like it. Eat it and go to bed. This seemed to satisfy that craving and if it worked out, he liked it.

He enjoyed getting out for a walk around the hotel, and would try to dress incognito. He carried sunglasses and a hat with a different color of hair sewn into it as a distraction. Goofy, but it did work. The other teammates made fun of him, but asked where he found it. Great laughter came when his eyes twinkled and he said they never knew what Santa Clause might bring them.

The real thrill was when the two beautiful Prevost Coaches would pull up for them on game day, and they were transported to the cities ball field. They always used two because the coaches and certain members of the media rode in the first one.

The entrances were secure, and they were out of sight from possible fans, or seekers with not such good intentions. The ball clubs were always about safety first. Their bus even had clearance to drive straight to the runway to make their exit from the bus and entrance onto the airplane safer, plus their baggage went right along side of the plane with them, therefore, never any lost or delayed baggage. Quite a difference from the normal, leisure family-style traveling.

The ramp they traveled up to the field in the bus would let them off within feet of their locker rooms and not visible from the street. He imagined how it must feel like a Presidential candidate using kitchen entrances he had seen in movies and suspected there were more truth to it than fiction.

The coaches always had them travel in their finest suits on travel day. It was the Red Sox Ball Club's personal dress code requirement. It didn't matter if they were traveling by bus or by aircraft. They had to look like a very professional ball club and they were representing the Red Sox Ball Team at all times. These were some of his proudest moments.

He heard the guys talking in the back of the plane that if they made the play off's, Mr. Duncan had promised to charter a luxurious Boeing 757 for them to travel in. Those are nice, Justin, said Pike. They have soft, luxurious first-class sized Leather seats with TV monitors and are wifi enabled with blue-tooth over every row of seats. We have a selection of in flight movies and you can even feel like a kid with the computerized games they've provided now days.

They have tables for card games, or reading and the same flight attendants for most of the flights so they get to know what you like on the flight and just bring it to you. This is a major reason for being in the majors with the Red Sox. Mr. Duncan takes excellent care of his players.

Their current aircraft was pretty, clean and nice, Justin thought. I am not spoiled yet! Well yes I am. I like the oversized seats, extra legroom, bathrooms with amenities the guys might need on board, unlimited beverage service and delicious snacks and fruit that is always available at our beckon call. Maybe they come from wealthy families, but for me, this is really nice, no complaints from this guy. Besides, sure beats a car or a bus ride across country!

Mr. Duncan also demanded they act like gentlemen and professional ball club players. He said, we are professionals and we represent him, so he would accept nothing less than pure professionalism.

There were some horror stories about other teams who had trashed airplanes from wild frat-like parties while in the air. So bad, the airline, refused to transport the teams.

"Not our team, though. We like our comfort and amenities too much to ruin that benefit." Pike went to recline as far back as possible, in his own seat after visiting with Justin for a while. They seemed to have the closest friendship, all beginning from Pawtucket.

It's good to have a close friend, Justin thought to himself. I really appreciate Pike for being outgoing and so thoughtful to take me under his wing and give me the in's and out's of the ball club details as he learns them.

Justin was one of the fortunate few who could sleep on an airplane. Not the entire flight, but long enough to help out a great deal, especially when he knew he wanted to order a breakfast before getting into bed and after his shower. He didn't mind the ribbing from those who couldn't sleep, even if they tickled his nose once in a while. It was all in good fun, and putrid jealousy! He made himself laugh and before he knew it, he was dozing off to sleep quite easily, and he smiled knowing they would be landing and transported to a hotel before he knew it.

Chapter 32

"Justin, I'm coming on the 3pm flight into Boston from Mobile on Thursday. Bradley and I are planning on being with you and are so excited to live as a family in the same time zone, imagine that."

I'll be there early on time, to pick you and Bradley up." Justin was so happy.

"I have sent boxes of items Bradley and I will need so they will be there before we arrive."

"Sounds good. What about Grandma?"

"Oh, Justin, Grandma Ruby is planning on coming out when we have a house and will spend the summers with us, and some of the holidays too. She's having a tough time with the thought of leaving her home, and us leaving her! We will need to let her make the gradual change to come and be with us, if she so desires." Justin could understand that about Grandma. She had lived in Mobile, Alabama all of her life, and the Theodore neighborhood more than half of her life. She raised his mom and him in that home. She had too many memories attached to that home, neighborhood, church and friends, to walk away from, without taking it one step at a time. Perhaps, that would come with time. He hoped it would anyway. The thought of living far away from his grandmother left a hole in his heart he didn't enjoy.

"Justin I'm just so excited to be with you again." Bree could feel her love so deeply for Justin, it was like a dream come true to be with him again, very soon, she had given it a good two years for him to have the freedom from worry about his family being alone at home in a strange city. Bree did not want to leave Grandma Ruby alone now, so she understood the relief this must have given Justin. Life was decent and perfect with her son and her husband on off-season and various other times he was able to be with them. Bradley was two years old now. Justin was on the road most of the time and when the season ended, he would be with his family in Alabama. Those were the perfect days in Bree and Justin's life. Things were going to change this year, Bree and Bradley were moving to Boston so they could be a family. The only unsettling aspect was Grandma Ruby would be staying behind with her brother Nathan. That would establish a void she was not totally comfortable with but it was more important to be with her husband. She missed him so badly the time had come.

Grandma Ruby had once made a comment to Bree stating, "You are such a special little lady. All the money you have at your fingertips and you chose to stay with me instead of in some big mansion in Boston." You certainly are a special gift to me my darling girl. Bree would respond with a simple statement that best described her feelings usually to the tune, "This is where we choose for us to be right now Grandma." Ruby would hug her or walk away smiling the biggest smile.

"The money Justin is making has made our life easier and I don't have to worry about social status and being alone in a big house by myself, Grandma. You won't move, so what's the hurry?" Bree would wink at her hoping to get her to break her steadfast decision to stay behind, but she never did. "Neither one of us need or want to be alone right now, Grandma Ruby. When Bradley and I do go to Boston, we stay in the finest of hotels and have limousines drive us everywhere, fines restaurants, who needs to clean and cook?" They both laughed so much because that made perfect sense. Grandma Ruby had gone with Bree and Bradley a few times to help out with the baby and enjoyed the lifestyle of both places.

The time had come though that things were settling down for Justin and he really wanted his family there so he could come home at night and see them when he was in town. He knew he was being a bit selfish, but he would talk Grandma into moving someday when he had the time to sit and talk with her seriously. There was no way he was living far away from that little lady that meant so much to him. This he vowed to himself.

"We can do this, Bree." Justin had said to his wife while they were making the decision that now was the time.

"Yes, and we will. I'm ready to be with you in Boston. I've grown rather fond of it myself from all of our visits and I know exactly where to look for a home for us. Not too big and a lot of yard." She sounded excited. He sighed a sigh of relief.

"Justin, I wanted to tell you, I'm going by my parents home before I leave to have one last attempt at talking to them and let them see our beautiful son." There was silence on Justin's end.

"He is their grandson, Justin and they have never seen him before. They haven't seen me and I feel I have changed so much for the better Depending on how I'm treated, will determine if I stay very long and if I see them ever again. It's a bit of closure one way or another for me. I want to do this, Justin." Bree waited for Justin's response.

"Bree, I want to show off our son too, but to people who care. They have never asked to see our son to this day. I'm agitated with them, not you."

Bree could definitely hear it in the tone of his voice. He didn't have to tell her.

"Justin, you know how my parents are. I felt it was the right thing to do as a person and a mother. I really want to leave on good terms, that's all I want, so I don't feel any remorse or guilt."

"Guilt? Oh, my gosh, that is unbelievable you could even feel or say such a thing!" Justin knew he couldn't protect Bree from her shameful parents. He was too far away to do anything about it either.

"Never mind what I think and feel, Bree. You do whatever you feel in your heart is the best thing to do. I for one don't feel the respect or obligation much less, guilt, you do, and that definitely makes you a better person than me. They have gone two years without asking to meet their grandson that lives in the same town as they do and I find that astoundingly inhumane. I know in my heart they are going to hurt you and I'm not there to protect you." Justin sighed and relented in his argument. He loved his wife and didn't want to see her get hurt when he wasn't there to protect her.

"Please don't worry about me my love. I have felt in my heart it is the right thing to do." She really didn't feel it was the right thing to do at all.

What she really wanted was to see if there were any feelings that were salvageable with her parents.

Justin had to give in to her and thought it will all be over with and she will feel justified by her actions. She deserves that much, as it is her bloodline she is thinking about after all. They don't act like it, but his wife is a very good and decent woman. He admired her ability to forgive and forget so easily.

"It's all well and good, Bree, like I said, do what you feel is right in your heart. You have always been such a good and forgiving person. I need to learn from you. Just be aware, I did warn you and I hope I'm wrong. I really do my beautiful wife." Justin had a tug in his heart yearning to see her and Bradley more than arguing about seeing her parents before she leaves. "I'll be waiting for you in Boston. Once you two are here the sooner we get on with our lives. I miss the two of you more than you can wildly imagine."

"Justin, I miss you and love you too. It will be wonderful to begin a new chapter in our long life together." Down deep she knew Justin was going to be right but she still wanted to do this one last effort to leave her parents on decent terms if possible.

"Ok Bree I will look forward to seeing you on Thursday. I love you!" He meant it with all of his heart.

"I love you more!" She teased him. Bree hung up the phone and finished packing her suitcase for the trip to Boston. She would finish Bradley's just before they left in case he needed anything that was going to be packed.

Her parents really should have seen the baby well before now! "Why am I so concerned with taking him to see them, when they did live in the same city? Why was it so beneath them to come over to our home because Justin and his Grandmother were not of their social status? Couldn't they have even met me halfway somewhere at a restaurant? Why do I have to prove anything to them? I'll just do it and see where I stand once and for all. People can change…. even my parents! God knows I've prayed for them, we'll see.

Bree called and left a message that she and their grandson would be there and it will be nice to see them once more before she left for Boston. "Lunch would be nice if you have time." She signed off with.

I know I'm an optimist because truly, I am hoping that they will see Bradley and soften up as most harsh parents do around grandchildren. I so want to show them we are just as much, if not more, than what their minds think we are. Actually, her reasoning was beginning to make less and less sense so she had to stop thinking about it. Her gut feeling was to cancel out, but she didn't.

The next morning came and Bree took special care to pick out the perfect clothes for Bradley. She bathed him and made him smell so wonderful, that she could have eaten him with hearty kisses. He giggled and smiled at his adoring mother.

"Ok, little man, into your car seat you go, and off we go to the other side of town." Grandma Ruby was out getting her haircut and didn't mind a bit Bree was going to visit her parents. It was a kind gesture, and full of humbleness on Bree's part to go to them, she had said the day before. Grandma Ruby was a devoted Christian lady and would have given her last penny to the Wilkes if they needed it as badly as they had treated her. That was just her good and always forgiving nature.

Chapter 33

Once inside the driveway to the house her parents still lived in on campus, Bree went around the back of the car to get Bradley out of his car seat. She wondered if her parents were there. If they had been watching, or waiting for her to arrive or would show any excitement whatsoever. That hope soon turned a bit sour when there was still no sign of them so far.

What a disappointment they are not outside to greet them, she thought. My beautiful son, and he gets the same treatment Nathan and I got growing up. We were invisible to them. She almost decided to leave, but being determined, and having driven all the way across town, she refused to act immature or like this bothered her. She wanted to act like a grown up woman who didn't let them get under her skin anymore. She took a deep breath and walked up the steps to the front door.

She rang the doorbell. In what seemed forever, her mother and father both finally met her at the door and invited her and Bradley in. There were no smiles or looks of kindness and softness on their faces. They looked at Bradley and studied him. His hair, his skin color etc., she saw it all too well.

She felt very awkward and uneasy, as there were few words spoken between them.

"Would you like to hold your grandson?" She asked her mother.

"Well, it's been a long time since I held a baby and it might be better if you just held on to him." Her mother said with a cloying casualness. Her father had barely looked at Bradley and said, "I certainly don't hold children; I only educate them." He had his usual alcoholic beverage of choice, scotch and water, in his hand. It was a crutch, something to hold on to Bree thought.

Bree felt her face stinging and her eyes felt strained as if they would tear up. This wasn't at all the reception she had expected, hoped for, dreamed of or wished for. After all, they had all been separated from each other for over two years and a lot of things had gone on in her life with Justin.

She had hoped they might have even remotely missed her. So much had gone on, as she tried to find the opening to tell them, still, they acted like they didn't care one iota. Her gorgeous little boy she brought with her, that she was so very proud of, wasn't even given a grandparents approval of any type. They could have bought him a gift for crying out loud. Her thoughts were running away with her by now. No mention of being offered a beverage or a cookie for Bradley, lunch was out of her thought mode now. This disheartened her even more. She had let her hopes go too far.

"What do you plan to do in Boston, Bree? Shop, socialize, join a club, start a charity or just be a rich housewife," her mother asked condescendingly.

"I plan on being as wonderful of a wife and mother that I can be, first and foremost. I will find a home for us we will enjoy living in and a church we feel comfortable in and then I'll worry about everything else as it comes along. I'm just excited to be with my husband in Boston."

"Oh, you mean your husband didn't have a home for you to come into already?" This time it was her father asking condescendingly.

"Justin, my husband, the wonderful man you have never met, wanted me to select the home. He is very respectful and considerate about things like that. He wants me to be completely happy first. I come first in his life. You wouldn't know or think about that would you?" She blurted it all out. She had enough of their stiff rudeness and making her feel like a stranger among her own parents. They didn't even want to hold her beautiful son when she asked them. That stung deep! They hadn't hugged her as she walked in. They hadn't offered her anything to drink or eat, or even to sit down, she just did. This was the limit of what she was able, or, going to take from them. It was giving them too much satisfaction to be rude to her and Bradley.

"Well...this party is over and I am leaving now" Bree said as she walked herself and Bradley to the door. They didn't ask her to please sit down and stay. That stung even more.

"You two are still just as mean spirited and selfish as you ever were. Your lack of hospitality shows me you haven't changed as I had so hoped. I'll be leaving tomorrow for Boston to live with the man of my dreams with our wonderful son. I guess you can just read about my husband, Justin in the newspapers and Time Magazine or see him on TV. He really is a wonderful and handsome man, it's too bad you didn't try to get to know him. He is so full of love and kindness, you're really missing out."

Her mother gasped and acted as if she would faint, her usual.

Her father went for another scotch acting untainted. Bree walked out the door with Bradley in her arms, not bothering to shut the door behind her. She had Bradley in his car seat in record time in the back seat.

By the time she had walked to the front driver's side of her car, Nathan came running up the drive. "I was coming over to have lunch with you all. What happened? You haven't even been here for ten minutes have you?" He asked inquisitively.

"Nathan, they treated me terribly and didn't even look at Bradley, much less hold him when I asked them to." Tears now coming forth fully upon seeing her brother who always was her only family. "There was no lunch or beverages either, I don't know what we were thinking. Nothing has changed at all with them, it is just so sad and unbearable."

"Oh Bree." Nathan sighed with disgust, disappointment and an anger swelling up Bree had never seen before.

"I'll be right back!" He wheeled around to go into the house, fuming.

"Nathan, No!" Bree quickly said loudly enough to let him know she was serious. "Leave them be. It has always been like this. I don't want you to say anything and give them anything to gossip about us with. Pay them no mind or attention. That's is the best revenge we can give right now. They are like street beggars begging for attention so they'll have something juicy to gossip about for their next cocktail party."

Her words seemed to make sense to Nathan and he said, "Then let me take you to lunch somewhere right now, with me. You shouldn't be driving in this condition anyway. We can talk like we used to and make both of ourselves feel better, like old times."

"I'm getting away from the old times, Nathan. The old times were too painful, except for you. That is the only pleasant thing about the old times. That life was a half life and it would have been a complete nothing life, if not for you."

"Thanks for that Sis. I feel the same way. That's the only reason I agreed to come over today when you asked me to come with you. I thought they were planning to have a lunch ready for us…guess not huh? I'm all worked up and ready for food. Come on! Let's go eat and be over this charade." He pleaded once more.

"I wonder if this 'pseudo family' meeting was a last stab in the back? You think that was their cruel motives, Nathan?"

"You got me there. We could never figure them out between us, you know that." He pursed his lips and put his hands on his hips in a lost thought.

"Please let me take you somewhere for lunch, you're all dressed up nice, and I'm looking clean and neat and I'm starving. Let's make it a good turn around before you leave, what do you say?"

"Thank you Nathan, but I think I'm going home, I'll feed Bradley, let him have his nap and then wait to leave tomorrow to be with my sweet and wonderfully loving husband, Justin." Bree seemed to be gathering herself and her composure and but Nathan still felt uneasy about her driving in her heartbroken condition. Nonetheless, she was a stubborn and determined woman when she had her mind set on something. He knew when he has lost a battle with Bree and this was definitely one of those times.

"Please Nathan, promise me you'll come to visit soon. I can't hardly bear the thought of leaving you, and being separated from you for the first time in our lives."

"I promise you, Bree, with all of my heart, I promise you. I can't stand the idea of not seeing you and little Bradley for very long stints of time either!"

This was a crazy moment for a brother and sister who had in all reality, raised each other. They knew each other knew well and their family bond was between just the two of them. That was before Justin and Grandma Ruby came into their lives. They counted them as their family now. They had the addition of Bradley, and they would remain the close-knit siblings they had always been. They promised each other they would. The world couldn't separate them! With a lingering hug and Nathan wiped her tear stained face with his handkerchief, he closed the car door as he told her to text him when she got home.

"Oh! And I will check on Grandma Ruby once a week, hopefully, on Sunday at dinner time," He winked hoping that would bring out a smile, but it didn't.

His sister just nodded, still suffering from complete humiliation and sadness for the snubbing of her beautiful baby boy, herself and her brother.

Bradley was securely tucked in his car seat and she wanted to get out of this place now.

"Ok, please call me when you get home and when you're at the airport tomorrow, ok? I love you, sis and I miss you already!"

"I love you too, bro." They waved to each other and Bree drove off slowly down the drive way and on to the college campus road she knew all so well.

Bree decided to call Justin and started crying when she heard his tender voice.

"Bree, try to shake it off. You had to suspect they were going to be like this after not seeing our baby for all these years." Justin wanted his wife to stop crying, it hurt him terribly.

"I wanted Bradley to have a full family, or at the least, have them look at him fondly and perhaps begin to feel something for him. Is that so wrong, Justin?" Justin tried to sooth his wife the best he could so she would be able to concentrate and get home safely. "Bree, please pull over if you're going to talk on the phone with me, or, call me when you're home. I would feel better if you were in better spirits while driving alone.

"Our child will have so much love and attention with all of us and his Uncle Nathan, Bree. He will have an aunt someday and cousins to play with, we have a wonderful future ahead of us. Just be positive, we will be together tomorrow, and it will all be good again. I love you two times around the world and back, Bree! Please don't talk on the phone and drive, and especially while you're crying. Please don't do this. I am in agony hearing you like this. I'll hold you, love you, do great things with you and more than make up for their lack of affection." Bree liked the thought; it was much more pleasant. Hang up and call me when you're home, ok? I want you to drive safely." The next sound was too loud and disturbing, Justin froze and panicked!

Chapter 34

"OH MY GOD!" Justin said after he heard a very loud crashing sound and the phone went dead.

"Bree! Bree, are you there?" Justin instantly called 911 for Mobile, Alabama and gave the approximate location of where Bree should be. He then called Nathan.

"Justin, I just left her not more than fifteen minutes ago." Answered a panicking Nathan now.

"I'll go the route she was taking and see if she pulled over to compose herself or what. I'll be right back with you."

"Please hurry, Nathan, I'm dying here right now."

"You bet I will, Justin."

When Nathan drove several miles up the main street speeding to get somewhere fast, he headed for the interstate. What he saw now was police cars and no ambulance yet. A couple of cars, one upside down and he fell to his knees as he got out of his car! It was Bree's car upside down!

He got up again with knees threatening to buckle under him again and ran to the car. The police were getting the baby out of the car, looking like a bloodied baby, and Bree was completely covered with blood, still in the car and unconscious.

The police asked him to step out of the way.

"I'm her brother and I was just with her. Is she alive? Her husband is panicking in Boston and he needs to know something!"

"We're not sure sir, she has a faint pulse, and the ambulance is just around the corner. They will have to get her out because her neck could be broken. We must be very careful. The baby is injured and we have him in his car seat still."

"Nathan, tell me you found her!"

"Yes, but Justin, it's a bad auto accident. There is blood everywhere and Bree is still in the car. She was cut off by another car that swerved in front of her that I don't think she saw in time. She was getting onto the freeway. Bree over-reacted, the police are surmising, her car rolled over, crushing the roof." Nathan hated to be the one to tell Justin this, but there was no one else who could.

"Justin, the ambulance just arrived and they are working to get her out."

"What about the baby?" Justin asked going from one fast subject to the next.

"They have him out and he is in his car seat with his head banded in place. One ambulance is rushing him to the trauma emergency unit at the University of South Alabama. Justin, this is horrible! I can't believe it." He began to cry even though he tried not to."

"Nathan, I'm chartering a plane and I'll be there in three or four hours. Keep me posted on any updates and where they are." Nathan heard Justin's voice break and he quickly said, "I'll pick you up Justin. Let me know when you land and where."

"Okay. And thanks. Call Grandma Ruby for me too please."
"Will do."

After the ambulance attendants had Bree secured on the gurney and into the ambulance, they then told Nathan they were heading to the hospital now and in a hurry! He knew it was not a good sign.

Nathan went over to Grandma Ruby's house to get her instead of calling. At her age, you don't surprise a sweet old lady with horrific news. She grabbed a coat, she was always cold when she was scared and nervous, then reached for her purse and out the door they flew to Nathan's car that was still running in her driveway.

Nathan picked up Justin, from the airport near the hospital where the private plane was able to land closer at a regional airport.

"How is Bree and Bradley now, Nathan?"

"They are both still in surgery, Justin. I've been pacing the floor waiting for you to get in and Grandma Ruby stayed at the hospital, she wouldn't leave in case a doctor came out. She said she would call with any news and I've heard nothing from her yet."

Justin could feel his throat tightening up and his insides being knotted and yanked out. He had been talking to himself and God the whole trip.

A Perfect Match

Quoting scripture to make himself think of anything but the images Nathan had described to him, and begging for his family to be fine.

As soon as they arrived in the emergency entrance one of the nurses let him and Nathan in. He explained that he was Bree Edge's husband and the baby's father. Just about five minutes later, the surgeon for Bree came out first. He was whitewashed and haggard looking. He had been working with Bree for four hours or better and he was exhausted.

His staff was busy going back and forth from room to room behind him.

"Dr. I'm Bree's husband how is she?"

"I'm Dr. Brashard, Chief surgeon. I'm on call tonight with Dr. Schmaltz for trauma and emergency calls." He looked at Justin and said, "Is all of your family here?"

"Yes, this is all we have, and we are all here. Why?"

"I want you to know, we did everything we could do to save the life of your wife. We just couldn't get her heart to stay beating."

Justin fell to his knees and began to sob. "Don't tell me she is dead. Please don't tell me that. Tell me she is in recovery and it's not over!" He began to hyperventilate and the doctor and his staff kicked into gear to get him stabilized.

Grandma Ruby and Nathan were holding each other crying in their own space. They didn't know how to comfort Justin, or themselves for that matter, particularly while the medical staff, were helping him. It was a nightmare for everyone.

"How is our baby? Bradley Edge?" Grandma Ruby asked softly, taking the lead to find out about Bradley.

Dr. Brashard said, "Dr. Rozabel is a Pediatric Specialist that was called in due to the child's neurological condition and more than likely he has 'Flaccid Paralysis' which effects the limbs, was the last prognosis. He'll be out momentarily to explain it all to you.

Flaccid Paralysis is when the anterior spinal artery is obstructed or severed which could have come from the trauma that your son just experienced. We don't know if he had physical damage or mental at this point. We are running every test to discover where the injuries are located." Explained the specialist, Dr. Rozabel.

Chapter 35

Mentally reminiscing about the death of Bree, but not actually dwelling on it, Justin continued with his outstanding speech and let the people see a little more and a little deeper inside of the legend.

"I can tell you first hand, that sadness caused by tragedies, if left unmonitored, will cause a person to spiral downward into a very deep depression.

Depression will rob us of our opportunities and moments in life that are purposeful and meant to be enjoyed, not wasted."

Men of greatness always share common attributes: Fear or failure, and sometimes both of them.

Look across time and history. It doesn't matter if it was George Washington, Abraham Lincoln, Babe Ruth, or even Mickey Mantle.

Take Mickey Mantle for example, Mickey started at age 19 with the New York Yankees. However, he was struggling and was sent down to their farm team in Kansas City. He went 0 for 22 and was in a terrible slump. So bad, he called his father and told him he didn't think he could play baseball anymore. His father came the next day, unannounced, to Mantle's hotel room and started tossing his clothes into a suitcase. Mantle's father told him he was going home and he was going to work in the mines with him. A very shocked Mickey Mantle did an about face and went back to the Yankees looking better than he had ever looked. Years later, he said, "That was the turning point in my life. His father didn't give him a pep talk, he kicked him in the butt and made him open his eyes and try harder. Look what that man accomplished, being a switch hitter, no less, when pain and failure, came to his door steps.

That's just one example of millions.

My pain and fear came with the death of my wife, Bree, and my son's paralysis, just when my career was taking off.

It sent me into such a downward spiral that my grandmother who raised me, had to kick my behind and shake me back to reality and open my eyes up again.

She made me realize I had a son to live for and a team that was depending on me to do my part to help win a world series that year. We had all worked so hard for this dream that was finally, within our reach. I reached down deep for the gumption to be the man they all needed through the grace of God.

Failure isn't a goal or an option; it's a nightmare. I was afraid. I had lost my compass in life and was on a collision course with failure. Fear is a physiological retardant that puts the brakes on, when you don't want them on. Fear triggers memories of more fear when a problem or challenge arises. Fear prevents us from taking risks and taking opportunities set before us that will make us successful in whatever we labor for or endeavor to do. Fear is our enemy; it is not our friend.

For you young people listening today, no one will ever tell you it's easy. No one will ever tell you, you'll never feel fear or you'll never fail. You will fail! You will feel fear! That is, if you want to be successful in anything. Remember what I'm telling you today and heed my words; there is always a light at the end of the tunnel to those who will search for it and reject fear.

I almost let fear ruin me and rob me of my blessings that were yet to be.

Failure and fear, to someone who has experienced them, turns out in the end to be nothing more than stepping stones to achieve something bigger or to become more than we dreamed we were capable of. It makes us what and who we are!"

He turned his face to face the sunlight and let the rays warm his soul. The people were completely captivated and drawn in to Justin's world. They looked as if they were watching a mighty drama actor on stage as the Commissioner looked over the crowd, not one person had their eyes off of Justin Edge. He is such a powerful and magnetic one of a kind, man among men, even to this very day. He was captivated by Justin Edge himself, he had to privately admit. He is such an honest and inspirational man. We are so honored to be hearing him he thought to himself as he watched the great orator on the stage in front of him.

Justin was pausing and doing this for his own emotional side and didn't realize the impact he was having on the crowd that was furthering immortalizing him. They were for the first time, allowed to see inside his soul.

Chapter 36

How do I make a three year old understand something that is beyond his comprehension? His mommy isn't here to hold him any more.

Justin couldn't talk, and he could hardly think. Instead of saying anything at the funeral, he would just have a piece printed up and passed out as his farewell thoughts from his heart about his love for his wife. His heart was bleeding to death. His mind was going blank. He determined that whatever he did, however it turned out, it would be fine in his soul. The other people were there to show respect and give him the support of their love.

He wrote a short poem of iambic pentameter style, or, was it iambic tetrameter style? Maybe it was neither! Right now he had forgotten everything he had learned in college, he was also shoving everything out of his mind that he could to keep away from reality.

This seemed to be the best way of expressing his feelings regarding the characteristics of their relationship and marriage. Their love knew no boundaries. Their bond was strong and so full of colors, plans for the future and dashed dreams. Justin harbored feelings of guilt and the loss of a mate that was beyond his own personal comprehension. He cried again. This is why he had to write and not speak.

He was finally able to finish his brief composition, a rare insight to the inner heart of Bree and Justin's love for each other. For the present time, he was completely vulnerable, heartbroken and lost. He asked the Minister to have this poem printed and passed out to everyone who attended the funeral instead of him speaking. It was his personal tribute and that was all he was able to do under the circumstances.

"It is perfect, Justin." Pastor Matthews said as he patted him on the back as a kind gesture of approval. This man had always been there for him and his family. He was a pillar of strength. Justin knew he could trust

Pastor Matthews to take care of anything he needed. "I'll have it printed beautifully on card stock for a keepsake."

Justin turned and walked away without another word that would have betrayed him yet again.

IF EVER TWO WERE ONE, CERTAINLY WE WERE

You captured all my dreams with one glimpse.

The air was clean and beautiful where ever you walked, even the trees turned as your beauty passed by.

Your scent will linger forever upon my pillow, too beautiful to forget.

You were a violin for all my songs, soft and graceful always perfectly tuned.

You were the drink of water for my soul that never thirsted when you were near me.

As I come to collect you in my arms today, there is nothing to hold on to, as if you are nothing but thin air.

My soul is crushed and my spirit is weak. I am a hollow man with nothing inside.

All I have left of you is memories that are painful, and your blood in our son, but for that, I am forever grateful.

Farewell, Bree, until we're together again.

-Justin

It was Grandma Ruby, who took Justin's hand into her own and said, "Justin, this is a day of great sorrow and I pray you never have to go through anything like this again in your life. You are allowed to withdraw all by yourself for Bree's sake, but only for a little while. Sweetheart, your beautiful poem expressed your feelings so eloquently. It was beautifully written and you made a powerful statement of the love you two shared." Grandma let it set with these words for now, but added, "Bradley needs you now more than ever, my boy!" Those raised eyebrows could still set him straight when nothing else could.

Justin did the best he could under the circumstances. The death of Bree coming at a critical time in the play off games was catastrophic. His team depended on him. He had struggled so hard to get to this point in life, and now, for what?

"I guess for Bradley." Justin said out loud to himself as he sat alone in a chair that night thinking to his self, unable to sleep and sinking further down into depression. "I must remain a father above all else now." Once things made sense to him in one area it was usually good, but not tonight, or for many more sleepless nights to come. He was letting himself slip by his own lack of self-discipline that could not be regenerated. Fully regretting he hadn't brought Bree and Bradley with him to Boston immediately, the list of regrets just wouldn't end. He was tormenting himself day and night. He was sinking into an unknown abyss. The funeral came and passed, and he put it behind him, or so he thought.

The post-season games were beginning, and Justin knew he had to play to the best of his abilities even under this severe, dark depression he felt closing in all around him. He had never known this emotion before now. He thought he was doing his best to overcome the dreadful feeling and knew it was going take time to heal a personal wound of this magnitude, yet he couldn't, or wouldn't, fully overcome this dark part of his life. He couldn't differentiate which power had control over him.

Finally, one day he said to himself, "Justin, it's Do or Die! I'm not dead, and I have a baby boy to raise and love. I shall overcome this and I will give myself time later to surrender to depression and therapy. I have a life to maintain and a vocation full of people who are counting on me!" This helped him get a grip for the time being and only suppressed his depression for the moment.

The fans were above and beyond kind. They were sympathetic and full of compassion. His fan mail was going through the roof with sympathy cards he never read. Many of the fans would rise from their seats in the stadium when he came on to the field for the opening of the game. Some fans would wave a white flag when his name was announced for the Red Sox Team. This made him feel like constantly crying. All this sympathy was a constant reminder of something he didn't want to be reminded about every moment of every waking day. This was a feeling and an emotion he had never remembered experiencing. He was hurting badly, and knew it was going to take time to heal, but how long? The sympathy of the fans helped, and hurt at the same time. Nothing could ease the pain in his heart except focusing and playing hard. He felt confused and out of sync, alone yet not alone. He tried and succeeded in covering it up in front of his teammates. Grandma Ruby saw through his cover-up though. No one knew him better than she did.

"Grandma, our games are going well and I'm able to stay afloat. I'm not at my peak performance though, and this is embarrassing and painful to me because I'm grieving over my wife, my son not living here with me as planned. Knowing you have all the weight of a little boy on your shoulders again. Everything in my life is up in the air… our intentions are to be heading for the World Series…

"Stop this, Justin. You are intentionally driving yourself crazy thinking about all this at night. Nighttime is for sleeping and praying, nothing else. Stop it right now." Grandma said again.

"You can't keep doing this to yourself or to me. Tomorrow morning will be better if you'll let it be." Grandma would have gone on but Justin blurted out an "Ok, you're right and I'm on it. Good night, Grandma." Grandma Ruby paused and knew he was pacifying her but said, "Goodnight my boy, I love you and I will talk to you tomorrow again. Bradley and I are just fine!" Justin just hung up without another word. Ruby was deeply concerned for her boy.

The next night brought forth a bright full moon, so Justin went for a walk outside. It was late, but he couldn't sleep anyway which had now become the usual. He was full of sad and lonely feelings. Knowing he could never call Bree ever again on nights such as these and just talk.

He began talking to himself as if he could give himself a pep talk. "What on earth am I doing? God do you hear me? Do you see me? I'm a wreck! I feel so many anxious and lonely feelings. I haven't felt these since I was a kid with my mom. Take this terrible feeling from me. I fear I'm falling apart." He thought of his Grandma Ruby and how he was leaning too hard on her at her age. Then he thought of his little boy, Bradley without a mother's love and a father to hold him instead. He began crying like a baby as he pulled out his cell phone and dialed his Grandma's phone number once again.

"Hello, Justin is this you my boy?" He woke her out of a deep sleep and she had only been able to go to sleep around midnight. She was staying up later every night reading her Bible for comfort and answers. She needed to help her boy. Something just didn't feel right inside of her no matter what he would tell her about himself.

Sobbing into the phone, it was Justin's voice, "Grandma, I'm falling apart, help me! I didn't know what else to do but to call you. I don't have anyone else, and I'm alone in this world again. I've lost my wife. I have a son and a grandmother that seem to be ten thousand miles away from me. I'm so disappointed with life." He kept crying as quietly as he could to not completely tear her apart.

Oh Dear Lord! Grandma Ruby thought to herself, she sat up in bed and then paced the floor as she thought quickly while he was talking to her.

"Dear Lord! He is living in the past in his mind. I've never heard my boy cry like this before, EVER!"

"Grandma are you there? I need you…I'm coming home." At this point Grandma Ruby cut him short and said, "No you are not! I'm coming to Boston with Bradley tomorrow. You just stay put. I'll pack our bags tonight and I'll call the travel agent to get us on a flight out there tomorrow. You hold on now, you hear?" All she could faintly hear was Justin crying and struggling to say an okay.

"Now Justin, you get a grip, you hear me?"

"Yes, I hear you, but I can't, Grandma."

"Justin, you get a hold of a tree, a wall, the ground, anything. You just pretend it's me you're holding on to and listen to me." She was in full command of her senses now and had to get a hold of her boy. She never let him down in the past and she certainly wasn't going to now!

Justin was leaning on a tree, so he turned around and hugged it even though it was rough and hurt his face, but he did it just as his Grandma had told him to do, and said, "OK, I've got a tree." His voice sounded like the little ten-year-old boy she brought home from the hospital, so many years ago.

"Justin, I raised you to be a man. You have a three-year-old son to take care of, to love and to nurture, as Bree stays alive inside of him. It's not fair for you to turn your back on him. He is a living miracle and I expect you to grieve, but I also expect you act like a man of God; a Samson! You have a quest set before you and I expect you to rise and meet it head on, if for no other reason than for Bradley." Grandma took a deep breath and a pause, to gather her thoughts and composure before continuing.

"I can't afford to coddle you and let you linger too long in this grieving and depression, and pit of despair lest you forget your son and your purpose in life. The demon of depression will put a grip on you and drag you down to failure and more pain than you have ever experienced in your life. I will never let you go down, I've got a hold of you. If you allow it to cling on to you, as you're doing, you will nullify my grip on you.

Justin, you're too strong for that. You're too gifted to let this happen and you have a huge responsibility with Bradley. I know I sound harsh, and I am! But don't forget, you're all I have in this world too!" She almost let her voice break but refused in the power of the Lord. She was a mighty woman of God and she was showing it right now, but would never admit her own strength for fear of sounding too proud.

"I realize that Grandma, and I'm sorry to do this to you in the middle of the night, but I have so many pressures on me and my head is about to explode."

"Justin, I'm a realist and I rely on God's strength just like we are all supposed to do. You get your self to reading the Bible and get on your knees until I get there. Play those baseball games you have to play and don't let your son, or me, down. Don't let your team down! Don't let Mr. Duncan and his Ball Club down! Don't let the fans down! I've seen on the television how they honor you in every game. You stand like a man and return the honor. Justin, people are trying to reach out to you and to help you in their own way. You accept that kindness and let the God given power inside of you perform for them." She was doing all the talking and Justin was listening with all of his might to this mighty woman he loved so much. He heard every word she said, especially the ones she said the loudest.

"Your team would be devastated without you, and Mr. Duncan believes in you enough to give you that handsome signing bonus and generous contract. You've got to do something of value with what you've been given! Do you hear me?"

"Yes ma'am."

"Justin, you get a grip on yourself. Get some joy going again, somehow. You just remember, time marches on; the sands of time keep dropping; the clock keeps ticking; the pendulum keeps swinging; the sun will come up tomorrow and it will set just like it does every day since creation. Even the moon will rise and set as normal. Another day and another opportunity to make sure life keeps functioning normally. You are just a grain of sand in the cycle of life's natural occurrences. Does this mean anything to you?" She waited for an answer this time.

"You always make sense to me, Grandma. That's why I lean too heavy on you." He was at least honest. We've gotten this far, so this was at least a start Ruby thought to herself.

"I'll take care of Bradley, so that you may continue your career's fulfillment, for his sake if for no other reason. We'll just get ourselves a home in Boston so we can be a family." She paused to think about more, but Justin spoke up before she had a chance to.

"Grandma, you'll do this for me?" He wasn't crying anymore, thank God for that Ruby thought to her self.

"Of course I will. I will help you back into your normal life my boy, as I have always done. It's not too hard for me to do. I am a survivor as well as your Grandmother by the Grace of God! She then toned her voice down and continued softly.

"I have come to like Boston anyway, mostly because I don't want to live far away from you since I'm being totally honest here. I didn't want to interfere with your life before. That has all changed now. I have decided I can live anywhere, if you and my grandson are there with me. You can't wait too long to help yourself son, or it will be too hard for you to do even with my help. Do you understand what I'm saying?"

"Yes, I do, Grandma. I'll be waiting for you and Bradley tomorrow. Thank you!"

She made a kissing sound into the phone and said, "Get some rest, or you'll get worse. Sounds like you're sleep deprived to me anyway." He truly was.

"I will, Grandma. I promise."

"Ok, I've got some packing to do and you need to sleep. We will be there tomorrow, Justin. I love you with all my heart I want you to know. We'll make it through this together, I promise you."

"I'll be here Grandma. Thank you, and I love you too. It will be better tomorrow, once you and Bradley are here. I know It will be. Thank you, thank you!"

They each hung up their phones. Justin walked back into his room to get some sleep and Grandma walked out of her room to get suitcases out of the garage and start packing just essentials. He could buy her everything else she needed. She just needed to get to him.

Chapter 37

"I will not allow that boy of mine to expect any pity from me tonight. His dependence on my pity could spiral too far down for his own good.

I lost a husband when I was a young, working, woman. I managed to raise a daughter by myself while I worked. No one came to my rescue!" Grandma was talking to herself to keep herself awake.

"If I let him sink deeper in self pity, he will be completely worn down with all this horrid grief he has had in his life. I just know he will.

Still nursing her own wounds she said, "No one ever said to me, grieve as long as you need to and I'll take care of your little baby girl. I'm a woman and I had to get out there and continue to make a living for me, and my little baby girl. What happened to Suzanna that she went so far off of the deep end? I have no idea. I did all I knew to do. She was smart, pretty and had a future. Well, whatever it was that happened to her will not happen to Justin, or I'll kick his behind all the way to the ballpark and back home every night!"

She was getting herself agitated and all worked up now which was a good thing because she needed to be wide awake to pack in spite of being very tired.

Ruby stopped in her tracks on her way to the garage for more luggage and it was as if she had a sudden epiphany! It was the words of Dr. Yamil Portello ringing in her ears as if it were yesterday. He had told her years ago in the hospital that Justin could have a relapse of abandonment issues or anxiety attacks when you least expected it. She had forgotten all about that because it was so long ago and there had never been an issue arise until now.

"Oh my goodness! My precious boy, what he must be going through. He never even cried over his mother's death. It's all coming out now!"

She hurried to the garage for the luggage, as quickly as she could.

"I have no choice but to do what I've always done, go to him. I won't stop now. That boy is my life and I love him." She stopped in her tracks and shook her head at her own vacillating at 2am in the morning.

She was talking to God as she always did, "Lord you know despair and heartache does crazy things to people. It hurts so bad you just don't know what you're going to do or say. I better get back in line myself real fast like. Lord, I need your help too! I'm sinking along with Peter on the water…I'm looking at the ferocious waters and not at you. I guess I'm just tired, Lord. My heart hurts for my family."

"Nathan?"
"Grandma Ruby, what's going on?" Nathan never dreamed of receiving a call from Grandma Ruby at 2a.m. in the morning. He was almost hysterical immediately.

"Nathan, I wanted to let you know I'm headed to Boston with Bradley to be with Justin. For how long, I'm not sure and I could sure use a ride to the airport if you can do that for me around 10:30 am. Otherwise honey, I'll call a taxi."
"I'll take you no problem. What's going on with Justin though? Is he not good?" At this time of the morning and a phone call from Grandma Ruby, something serious had to be going on.
"No, Nathan, he's not good. He is falling apart and I've got to get to him and be with him. I feel his childhood nightmares are surfacing and I've got to get to him. I'm the only one who knows that boy and his full life, if you get what I mean."
"Okay, Grandma Ruby, whatever I can do for you, Justin, Bradley you have it. Anything at all, and I do get what you're saying."
"Honey please watch my house and I'll be talking to you by phone about everything for a while, if you don't mind."
"Not a problem and you know it. I'll be happy to do anything for you. What about me? I just hate the thought of me being without all of you guys now."
"Oh Lordy. Don't start this on me now sweetheart. One son at a time is enough. You know we all love you very much, don't you?"

"Yes, I do, and visa versa. I'll be there by 10:00 a.m. for you to help with the luggage and anything else. I'll just take a half of a day off from work. It's not a problem, trust me."

"Thank you, precious boy. I'll see you around 10:00 then. Bye-bye for now and I love you."

"I Love you too, Grandma Ruby."

That was a relief for Ruby, now, to make sure all was done around the house.

Keys for Nathan, written instructions for different things like trash day, water, electric, sewer and house keys. She gathered together the names and phone numbers for the lawn company, her Minister and the next-door neighbors. She would take care of disconnecting the cable company herself. Ok, now I can rest for a few hours. She fell fast asleep before her head hit the pillow on the sofa. She awoke before the alarm clock went off. Fully bathed, dressed and even had Bradley cleaned, fed and ready to go long before Nathan arrived.

Chapter 38

Wow! Justin thought after he had hung up the phone. Grandma never has minced her words. She is a strong woman!

Quickly changing emotions, for reasons unknown to him, he shifted into a realm of stability and calmness. Then he shifted into anger almost as quickly.

"I almost resent her for demanding anything of me right now! This is the first time I have ever fallen apart in front of her." He said with resentment in his audible voice. He instantly regretted what he just let slip in his mind with words. He quickly acquiesced with deep remorse and said out loud again, "I'm so sorry Lord, I didn't mean that. I'm just so lost and forlorn. I feel anger, bitterness, sorrow, guilt and like I'm all alone. Am I going crazy?"

He cried just a little more, and then made himself stop. "Enough! Grandma and Bradley are coming. Why am I crying? And who am I talking to anyway?" He was talking out loud and realized it finally. He walked briskly back to his hotel room. He wanted to end this frenzy he was creating immediately.

When Justin returned to his room, his eyes were puffy from crying, but he did feel as if he had cried all the tears he had left to cry. He was exhausted and fell asleep but not before one last grateful thought. "Grandma, you're a hard woman, but you're a woman of great strength. You're the one who's double tough!" He said as he silently said good night to her in his bed and thanked God for her and her unselfishness.

Grandma and Bradley arrived about 4 p.m. into Boston. Justin was there to pick them up with hugs and huge smiles. He took them to the hotel he had already checked them in and food was being set up in the room on a beautiful table as they walked in. It was a three bedroom, suite, a full kitchen and a Butler assigned to her every whim. There was an adjoining room for a live in nanny assigned to help Grandma Ruby with Bradley for bathing and feeding and carrying or putting him in a stroller or anything she asked for. A car and driver was at her disposal to get to the games and anything else she wanted it for. He had been busy all day getting this part of their life in order.

"This will be home for a bit, Grandma." Justin said.

"Also, Grandma, I have done nothing but think about what you said, and as you know, I've gone through every emotion possible. Please forgive me for falling apart. Mostly, thank you for giving everything up for me, and for Bradley, by coming out here and leaving your home. I'm going to do what you demanded of me, and get myself together for all of our sakes. Its' always been just you and me and now its Bradley too. I apologize for doing this to you, but Grandma I need you so desperately right now." His voice was pleading for forgiveness.

"You always have been and you will always will be my boy. I don't know any other life now." She was as serious as he had ever seen her.

"We will all do what needs to be done, and we will get through this together, just like we have always done Justin. I am torn up inside, but I know you are worse off than me. I'll do anything I can to help you because you are my boy. I love you and I'm happy I am able to be here for you. I don't know what else to say right now honey. I'm tired from the long night and day of travel. Let me be alone for a bit and rest up." Justin stepped aside and opened her door for her. Kissed her cheek and went and sat down on a big cozy chair in the living room, feeling more at ease than he had in recent weeks that seemed like years.

Grandma let the nanny take Bradley to his bed sing him to sleep. The Butler unpacked her and the baby's luggage, cleaned up the table of food and then left quietly after explaining to Justin how the push button and intercom worked for his assistance for anything and at anytime.

Justin was now able to think about the task before him. I want to live beyond my recent self-imposed constraints. I'm going back with more verve and vigor than ever before. I'll take all my vented up emotions, frustrations and grief and bury it in my gift to play ball. That will be for Grandma. He then got on his knees and said a little thanksgiving prayer for them being there with him and asked God to forgive him for his weakness in his faith.

"Dear God, I wanted to die, but in reality, I really do want to live. Please forgive me, and help me. You have given me so many abilities now you have brought my family to me, and now I really do have the determination that will drive a locomotive up a mountain, but I can only do it with your help. Please be with me."

The tears started to rise again, but Justin stopped them instantly. It was time to go forward for the living and for the rest of their lives now and to stop the free flow of tears. He had to regain control of his faculties.

A couple of days later, and after Grandma and Bradley had a chance to rest up and get acquainted with Boston, Justin said, "Grandma will you let the driver take you to this Real Estate company where I have already set an appointment with a Realtor to go shopping with you to find a home for us?" Justin was really serious about this home business, Grandma thought.

"Okay, let me get myself together and get that nanny readied to watch Bradley and I'll be off shopping for us a home in the wink of an eye." She was actually excited and it was visible to Justin. This pleased him greatly.

"They already know the areas I've asked for and the price range. You have up to 50 million to spend on a house."

"Good Lord, son!" Grandma exclaimed. "Is that what a nice little house costs out here?"

"No Grandma, that is what a really, really nice estate costs out here." Justin had to smile looking at her still shocked, cute little face he had missed so much.

"At least I don't think so. I haven't been house hunting. I was saving that for Bree. All I'm saying is; don't worry about the cost or money. We have plenty for once in our lives. Find us a nice home that has big hallways and large rooms for Bradley's wheelchair he will be using eventually.

We need five, master bedrooms, or we will have a contractor add them on. We need one for you, Bradley, the nanny one for me and one for Nathan when he comes to visit us. Even if we have to knock out some walls, don't worry, that can be done. I have already told the Realtor what to look for to narrow down your search." Grandma laughed looking at Justin and said, "We sure got spoiled fast didn't we? Yes indeed, we all need our own bedrooms and bathrooms now that we can afford it. What a great day in my life." She chuckled her sweet giggle Justin knew so well and had missed.

"Grandma, I also suggested a good sized yard for Bradley to get him outside of the house as often as possible." Without a pause Grandma replied, "Yes, that is exactly what we need for our boy." They sat at the kitchen table drinking their coffee and discussing house details until the Realtor arrived.

"Grandma, you have the complete freedom of decision making here. Just be sure and get us a nice one. This is no time to be frugal." He winked at Grandma to let her know he was fine and feeling pretty stable again.

"We'll furnish it after we buy it." Justin said as a last bit of information.

"I don't have a problem with the task set before me if you're worried." They both smiled happily, and off his Grandma went with the Realtor.

Grandma was tired of house hunting, and thank God, she had finally found the just right house after three days of hunting. They were living in the luxurious hotel suite, but she knew they needed a home to call their own. After dinner, one evening, when Justin was home, Grandma sat down to relax in her favorite chair. She wanted to talk with Justin and asked him to come sit with her. Justin didn't know quite what to think, because she didn't give him a chance to ask questions. He came over to his Grandma and sat on the floor at her feet. He felt like a child. Actually, he was at this point in his life. He felt no bigger or more mature than one at the moment.

"Justin, what was the cause of your deafness, blindness and hesitation to face your demons and defeat them through God's holy word? You do know better because I taught you better. Let me explain something to you very carefully and as clearly as I can."

"The cruelty of life that has been imposed upon you is from natures form of equalization. You are an unusual athlete and very gifted for a purpose. Your life is almost perfect. The law of averages pronounces the fate becoming each of us to make us stronger and better if only we will allow it. Everything in a person's life can't be perfect; something has to give." Justin wasn't sure he understood, but listened intently because Grandma always made sense.

"You look at your mother. She was beautiful and smart and had a great college career ahead of her that might of turned her into a medical doctor or research expert. She was highly gifted herself. Instead, what did she choose to do? She chose to let evil creep in and cover her in a cloak of darkness until it consumed her. She chased a bad crowd of people to be popular and accepted. She wasn't strong enough to lean on her God or her family, like you are now. I do not want you to be ashamed that you called me to come to you. This is one of the points I'm making my lovely boy." He understood perfectly well now the point. He did have his mother's blood in him. He saw the similarities that could have been.

"The other point is, never again, stop reading your Bible and praying to God for protection, discernment and guidance. If you will listen to me, you will continue to make progress and never be lost again. The Bible is God's word and it keeps you strong. Life *is* going to become more complicated the higher up you move in your career. Your already experiencing the money side of it and more will come. Don't let it ruin you." She pointed her finger in front of him while saying this. He had learned years ago, this was another one of Grandma's tactics for making a very strong point.

"Money has caused many a person to go off the beaten track. They think people are their friends when all they really are is a bunch of head nodding sycophants. They want to be your friend because you're important and they are not. They will allow you over and over to pay their way for them because they're after a free ride. They think this will make them important and gain favor for whatever their personal reasons are, which are usually selfish. There are people who will be so convincing, it would take a jury to decide if they are genuine or not. You don't need anyone but your senses and your gut feelings because that's God leading you." Justin knew all this very well from Grandma's many lessons. He had slipped more than he cared to admit, even to himself.

"Women will swoon over you and throw themselves at you for your money and position. Beautiful women do this because their beauty works to their advantage and they're too lazy to go out and earn a degree or work for a good decent honest living and get a good man the right way. They want a short cut to wealth and fun." Justin was missing Bree again because it had always been about love and family, not money.

"Remember, people in general are good, but they are hidden in your world for now. Because of your fame and fortune, you are a prime target for the wrong crowd. Good people are usually content to be humble and might be intimidated, unaware or unimpressed by you right now. It doesn't mean they don't want better for their families or themselves, it just means they are not out to be your friend because of your money and associations." He had been so busy making his way in baseball lately, he hadn't even thought of good decent people not knowing, caring about, or, being intimidated with him. He smiled at Grandma and shook his head that he understood.

"People in the professional world will be all over you too, because you're up to their status now, and they can use you somehow. Be on guard--always. Let your conscience be your guide. Justin, you have a good head on your shoulders with a lot of common sense to go with it. If you'll pray and be on the alert, God will guide your life and Bradley's life too. When he is older, he will be watching everything you do and you must be very careful for his sake."

Justin understood perfectly well what Grandma was saying because now, he was good enough for Bree's parents since he was a star athlete and making huge sums of money.

They were a prime example of her term 'Up to their status'. They had been trying to make contact with Justin through the Ball Club. The management would never return their call until Justin said to. He hadn't so far. The memory of Bree's death was still on his mind, and was a direct result of their treatment of her and his precious son. They could rot in their drunken, guilt-ridden world. He wanted them to leave him and his son alone.

Grandma continued with her talk and Justin rotated back to reality once again.

"In time, I do believe God will show you another good woman. Now, don't shake your head 'no' at me either. Give it time my boy there's no rush, but everyone needs someone. As handsome as you are and with all you have to offer as a man, I don't doubt for a second God will bring someone special into your life to fill that void when the time is right. Let nature take its course."

Justin was mesmerized with Grandma's words. She always made so much sense of things. He was taken back to his roots with her words. She had always taken time to teach him about life, about himself and about God. He had done the right thing asking her and Bradley to come to him. Stabilization and a comfortable feeling was coming back into his life.

"Bradley needs you right now more than any other person. You have priorities to set straight. There's no need to worry or doubt when your head is in the right place. Be cautious and be diligent, but save the day, and do savor each day, have fun and enjoy life."

Grandma kissed Justin's head and leaned back in her chair. "I'm enjoying being here with you more than I should be, I must admit." She gave him a wink and a smile.

Grandma had always given him wonderful life lessons and he cherished them all.

Life had to progress, and take its natural course. Justin was ready to start moving his life forward and get out of the rut he had put himself in. Things had changed for the better since they had arrived he thought discerningly. They had prayed together a few times and he felt his spiritual strength returning. Strangely, he was beginning to once again move into his mental zone, and he was transfixed on shutting out the agonizing thought of the tragedy that had occurred weeks ago now.

Time was of the essence, as the playoffs were beginning in a few weeks. He had begun his rigorous training. It was self-designed from his years as an athlete in training and his research in medical journals and on-line research. The medical field had been his second choice as a vocation. It seemed so strange to hear how it had been his mothers' first choice until she got caught up in drugs. Grandma had never told him such details before about his mother. He was happy she had died. It meant his Grandma would raise him, and his life was never the same hellhole again.

He stopped in his thoughts and said to his self, "What did you just say?"

For the first time in his entire life, he admitted he was glad his mother had died because she was such a bad drug addict and prostitute. If she hadn't died, God only knows what would have become of him. Living in filth and almost famine. He would have surely had to go out at an early age and started working to support them both, or welfare services would have eventually found out and stepped in and placed him in an orphanage or a foster home. He had heard bad things about the welfare services people and to this day, didn't like the name of it at all.

With Grandma, he had come to a home, not a house. It was clean, in a beautiful neighborhood with great schools he was able to go through.

He had excelled in school academically and athletically and had earned college scholarships in both areas. Justin immediately felt a tremendous inner relief when he allowed himself the permission to admit his deeply hidden feelings, and not feel guilty about them. He really was moving forward. He had a burst of energy and happiness he hadn't felt in a very long time…an eternity, actually.

"Where do broken hearts go?" those words came out of nowhere in particular, they just came out. It's just so hard to forget someone who gave you so much to remember. Justin knew it would take more time to get over Bree's constant presence in his life, but he also knew he would be able to deal with it now.

Chapter 39

After Grandma arrived in Boston, Justin had returned to practice. His teammates and the coaches came up to him one by one and personally gave him a hug, a pat on the back or shook his hand to give him a show of camaraderie. They were happy to see him back.

Justin would never forget how they had all showed up for Bree's funeral as a team. It was one of the most beautiful and meaningful sights he had ever seen in his life. His teammates, Coaches, Mr. Duncan and the entire Red Sox Management, came in beautiful dark suits all holding a red rose for Bree. They had come for him in his time of need and grief. He remembered being proud he was associated with them. He was where he belonged and was so grateful once again.

A couple of weeks passed and Justin's coaches became concerned with his rigorous workout program above and over what the normal practices were. His non-stop workouts and sprints seemed like erratic behavior. They sent Coach Haskins, his outfield coach, to talk to Coach Chambers.

"Sir, we are really concerned with Justin Edge."

Chambers raised his head from reading and raised his eyebrow over his left eye, this meant you had his full attention. We were wondering if it is a good idea to let Justin continue with this arduous work out program he has aside form the team training already established. This guy is working about 17 hours a day. That's not healthy or normal. We were thinking perhaps we should even have a coach's talk with him. We are afraid he might strain himself, or worse yet, kill him self." He was half kidding and half serious.

"Haskins I'm going to tell you something." Said Coach Chambers as he raised himself out of his chair and walked over to the window to look at Justin working like a machine. "If we were to stop Justin from his "personal program" and take him out of his chosen sequence and vision, we would be handing him over on a silver platter, to the pain he is striving to overcome. He has experienced his wife's death not that many weeks ago, and his baby boy's paralysis."

Coach Chambers paused briefly thinking deeply and compassionately while he stared out the window watching the other team members practice as well.

"This is his drug of choice. Some people take anti-depressants. A lot of other people do stronger drugs to escape reality. Some quit on life all together. I say, leave him alone. He is self medicating and he is in a fixed trance. Quite frankly I think it will be to his, and our advantage as a team, as we head for the playoffs and perhaps beyond. If not this year, I expect the next few years will prove me right. We are progressing quicker than I expected considering we came in last place when he joined our ball club." Chambers was reminiscing about the first year Justin came in. "It's been a wonderful change for the better. Leave him be for now. I'll keep a close eye on him, as I want you all to continue doing because you're with him much more than I am. Report in to me daily, okay?"

"Okay, Sir. I tend to see your point as valid. I'll get back with the other coaches now." He said as he turned for the door.

"Thanks, Haskins. I'm glad to see my coaches have a good eye and a good heart. That is a good sign we're working as a team. I have a really good feeling about this ball club. We will never see last place again as long as I'm head coach with the team we are acquiring. Tell the coaches I said that too!" Chambers smiled again as he said those words that sounded so dear in his own head. The playoffs were within reach with this team. The World Series would come. His instincts were telling him so.

The Fielding coach worked harder with Justin than he had earlier in the year. Justin demanded constant batting practices. He was like a crazed man in his lust for more practice and more time consumed practicing.

"Whatever you want, Justin." Said his coach, "Let's do it."

Every day, they fielded, ran and batted until the sun went down and sometimes they used the field lighting. Justin then went in and worked out with weights and got a therapeutic whirlpool before getting a shower and going to bed exhausted. One thing he did do right was his eating regime. He had always been a healthy eater. "Thank goodness." The coaches said to each other as they glanced at Justin every now and then while eating lunch.

"Justin, you are ordered to go home for a few days and relax before the Division playoff's begin. Coach Chambers orders." Said Coach Randy Anderson, his batting coach.

"Ok. Actually, I think I could use some time with my Grandma and Son. I'll enjoy the few days. Thanks."

"You bet. See you back here on Monday at 9:30 a.m." Said a very surprised Coach Anderson. He didn't let Justin see his astonishment however.

"Sounds great coach."

Coach Anderson and Coach Chambers were shocked.

"Why are we shocked?" Asked Coach Chambers. "That boy has been unusual from day one. You would think we would be used to his whatever responses by now. Good Grief. I'm not sure we ever will though." He just breathed deeply and went on about his business.

Chapter 40

"Grandma, I would like for all of us to go on a tour of Boston tomorrow." said Justin as he walked unexpectedly through the doors of their new home Grandma Ruby was trying to get set up for them. She was slow but she was methodical. It helped having a nanny, a housekeeper and a chauffer with a car. She turned around to look at him with disbelief and sheer delight. She walked over to him and gave him an extra big hug. He was going to spend a full day with her and Bradley?

"Justin, we would enjoy that very much. I could use a break myself"

"We are going to have a fantastic free day." Justin knew this would surprise and please Grandma. He owed her this and he owed it to himself.

With raised eyebrows and a huge smile, she said, "I'm thrilled with this news. I've got everything pretty well taken care of, I think I can take time off." She gave Justin a wink and another smile showing her true feelings of happiness.

"Let's go out for lunch, tour, shop and dinner. Make it a day to remember, I say. If Bradley gets too tired, they can bring him home. You and I will keep our heels clicking!"

"I say, okay and I'm all in." Justin loved her eagerness to be with him. "It's going to be like the days of high school, Grandma only we have a car." They both laughed at his comment.

"Yes, it will be, won't it, my boy!" Grandma's sparkling eyes showed her happiness.

"Grandma you have this place looking wonderful. It looks like a home and not a house. I can hardly wait to be living here every day with you all again after the season is over. Traveling during the season is hard and lonely at times, yet it's comforting to know you're here with Bradley." Justin often talked with his Grandmother on a very comfortable and complimentary level.

"I'm going to spend this off season with you and Bradley! Maybe Nathan can even come and spend a little of his vacation time with us this year." He said as he popped a pistachio in his mouth from the bowl on the kitchen table.

"Oh, Justin! We will be looking forward to all of that!" Said a very excited sounding Grandma at the mention of having her three favorite men with her.

"Besides, I think Nathan will really appreciate staying close to you, He honestly looks at you as his brother. He truly loves Bradley. That is really sweet of you."

I love him, Grandma. I want Bradley to know his mothers' brother is his Uncle Nathan. She adored him and they were so very close. I just hope we can all keep that memory and relationship alive."

"I'm sure we can, with a little bit of effort, my boy." Grandma looked over the house she had put together still thinking of a full family living here. She had put so much effort into the furnishings based on this hope.

"I realize I wasn't in the mood for a vacation prior to now, but things have changed and settled down for me. Everything was different, strange and unfamiliar for me. Someone at my age has a hard time adjusting, Justin. But I'm 'all good' now. I wanted to find the perfect home for us. It's been fun decorating with no budget." She laughed and had the biggest smile on her face as she described her thoughts with words.

"Do you know how much fun I had being driven around in a limousine and looking at houses that cost more money than I've ever thought about in my life?"

"You gave me the thrill ride of a lifetime, and it hasn't stopped my boy!" Laughing the ole Grandma laugh, she was shaking her head as in thought. This pleased Justin to watch her be so happy and laughing. He had to laugh with her she was just too fun and infectious.

"Well, you have the check book. Whenever you want to shop, call up that limo driver of yours and trot off. I think you should do that more often anyway." He pointed his finger in front of her now and she took it and kissed it, smiling harder than ever at Justin.

"I just might do that this week, because I need a new wardrobe for the winter. I'm not used to winter!" Giving him a wink.

"I hope you do, Grandma."

"Oh, one more thing, Justin. I've asked Nathan to find a Realtor for me and put my house up for sale, lock stock and barrel. Everything I needed, I brought with me, or he has shipped to me. I've bought all new stuff anyway since leaving Montgomery. Nothing left there but old junk. I felt it was time to let them all go." She lifted her eyebrows and gave her big eye look he loved. He knew Grandma was back to her old self again.

"I'm excited you're doing this. We have a beautiful home and what we need, we'll get. Thank you my precious Grandma!" Ruby just gave him her priceless wink and smile and said, "No, thank you, my boy! You have no idea how much money I have spent and had no reservations about doing so." Justin had to laugh now because his Grandmother was being a comic. He did know what she spent, and it was nothing compared to what she thought she was spending. She tithed to their old church in Montgomery, Alabama and that was perfect with him. They had been, and still were such an important part of their life he wouldn't have it any other way.

"Grandma, we have more money than we can spend in our lifetimes. Let's give it a good go though, what do you say?"

"Well, I've been trying, Justin!" Raised eyebrows again. Both of them headed for the limousine laughing. It had been awaiting them with Bradley already secured and sitting with the nanny. This was going to be a glorious day and they both knew it.

They had a normal life once again. Grandma Ruby was always in the middle of the cheering and waving her red pompom she took to every single game to support Justin in her very own designated chair over the Red Sox dugout.

This way, Justin could always look at her when he went out to bat for good luck. Soon, Bradley and Grandma would both be there for his good luck. The seasons were flying by in rapid succession in their quest for the ultimate goal and falling short season after season but not before claiming more and more pennants and awards. They were on the rise and becoming a team that knew each other better and better. Their playing was synchronized and becoming sophisticated. They had been thrust together and now, they felt they were very comfortable with each other. Never, did any player brag, or resent being first string or second string or beyond, because any string could be put into any situation and never miss a beat. It was becoming more incredible with every year. Finally, the time had come. There was nowhere to rise to they hadn't already risen to. No heights to achieve, or hurdles to conquer. It felt right and the air was full of adrenaline flowing throughout the Red Sox team and the city of Boston. The buzz had started, and it had to be right.

Chapter 41

Division Playoff's were at hand. Justin was telling Bradley over the phone from New York where the last of the championship games were being played, how the system worked. He was so smart for a boy almost eight years old now. Justin would forget how old he was because he was so bright and conversant.

"You see son, the playoff berth system in Baseball determines if we go on to play the World Series games, or if we came home for the off season." Justin was about to continue when Bradley blurted out enthusiastically, "I know Dad, I've been reading all about it and we talk about it at school, and Grandma and I pray every night for you and your team to make it. I want to be able to go and miss school."

Justin was amazed, perhaps even in awe, of how well his son knew baseball and what he was telling him. "Well, we will see about the school part son. Most of the games are in the evening." He heard a heavy sigh from Bradley and laughed at his displeasure. When they hung up the phone, he felt so sad for his son that he would never play baseball as much as he truly loved it. Baseball was all Bradley wanted to talk about when he was home with him.

"I have to pry school news out of Bradley to get him off of talking baseball when I'm with home. Poor little guy." Justin whispered to himself. "I'll make it up by playing Special Olympics with him." That cheered his thoughts up significantly.

It had been utterly amazing how the seasons went by so fast and so routinely. It was now a normal to win the division pennant. Fenway Park had so many red and white pennant flags each one displaying the year it was won. The winning pennant meant being the best team in the American League and vying for the World Series. Now days, the teams

A Perfect Match

had to race for a playoff berth. The game of Baseball was ever changing and evolving, that was one constant.

Every year since Bree's death, Justin was playing better and keener. He was becoming an indomitable force that would not stop striving to be better than he already was. She was now a wonderful memory and he looked forward to every day living life to the fullest with his son and Grandma. Nathan came when he could. Life was good with his family, and being with the Red Sox had made it all possible. By now, he was the subject of every ESPN baseball conversation, the newspaper headlines, Sports Illustrated cover many times, and any other form of media that could convince him to interview or advertise for them. Sometimes, the money was too much to pass by for sensible reasons and he would ask Grandma to divide the money between some charities they had chosen together as a family, plus the tithing to their old and to their new church.

He did a few commercials for watches and mostly posed for pictures with their products. The money was just too great to turn down in spite of Justin preferring a private life.

Every year was a progressive year for the Red Sox who had come from last place when they brought Justin to the Red Sox five years ago. In the meanwhile they had traded for a few different quality players such as the not so new now, catcher Montano, while Justin was in Pawtucket and he had turned on the steam every year he had been with them. They nicknamed him as per their tradition, "Hot Pepper."

He was quick, feisty and could burn the ball to anywhere in the field in a split second packed with power and precision. He was an ace and he had a fantastic sense of humor.

The Red Sox brought in a new back up catcher, and a new short stop. Some were trades and some were free agents. The coaches were happy every year they were in the playoff's as they could see tremendous strides happening. Always disappointed not to completely take the playoffs for the World Series, but nonetheless, happy to be there because in years past, they hadn't made it nearly this far.

Justin was now in his fifth year with the Boston Red Sox. They were the wild card for the World Series play off's. He felt confident they were going to the World Series this year!

The fans were more than supportive. People wanting tickets were on a waiting list. Every thing that could be used to support them was at their disposal. The people loved their Boston Red Sox.

There came a day of rejoicing and celebrating when they had won yet another pennant. They were making the usual progress with determined eyes to progress on to so much more though. This was just the first step for the team.

The management was still trading older players and negotiating contracts with agents of players who would fit into the organization and fit in with Justin. He was their key to winning because he interacted with all the players much more so than the pitchers. They were a unit among themselves, striving for perfection and in a tremendous amount of pressure to perform for the team they were deeply a part of.

The many opportunities they had in a playoff as the 2nd best team as a wild card team, and the first best in a wild card and still lost due to pitching errors, or strikeouts were enough to cause the management to focus on the Pitching team and their batting averages. High hopes came last year when they won and advanced only to lose in the best-of-five divisional series. The anguish of coming so close they could smell it and let it slip out of their hands like a slippery fish was the worst feeling. The only thing worse would be to be in the World Series and lose it. Justin and his teammates talked about this and rationalized that when they finally got to the World Series, they were going to win it! "Hopefully", they would interject afterwards with a laugh. The guys did not want to feel the agony of a World Series defeat after having made it to the series. They couldn't accept that defeat and wouldn't.

Justin didn't see or feel any negatives when the Red Sox Management announced that they had just signed a new fantastic pitcher that they had recently added to the already strong pitching team. This gave them some depth to hold out, in any big hunt as they chased the World Series!

"A whale was bagged today guys. Bought outright by Mr. Duncan as a free agent. A super pitcher, supposed to be the best free agent in the league and Duncan went after him. He always gets what he sets his mind on. His name is Willie Steamalik. He has a nickname already too. "The

A Perfect Match

Locomotive" because he had a whole lot of steam, a whole lot of power, and a whole lot of drive." Steamalik sounded excellent by those standards. The guys laughed but they wanted it to be true and not just steam. They laughed at their own euphemism. They knew they would like Steamalik because the management only selected men who fit the criteria of the guys who were there already. They thought of everything in the corporate office. They even had everyone go to the corporate psychologist, so they knew players would be a good fit.

These trades by upper management felt good inside for some reason to Justin. He was excited with the latest new pitcher, Steamalik. He would be a great addition to the team of already superb pitchers they currently had.

With the depth and quality of pitchers they now had, each one had a reputation of imposing sheer terror when they were on the mound. It's a mind game out there for these guys too. Each of them could bat, relieve each other at a moments notice, and never miss a beat. Adding one more pitcher with a reputation that preceded him was the shot in the arm they needed.

This made the pitching team a well-oiled steamroller. Pun intended. Justin laughed at his own humor. This had been part of the strategy the guys had mentally been preparing for and physically working harder towards. A third of the battle was mental preparation and now here it was, done to perfection, at least it was in Justin's mind. He watched everyone like a hawk and he knew what he saw. Steamalik was everything they had said he was. He seemed even better working with a superb team like the Red Sox.

The Red Sox players were working harder and they were developing a systematic stride between them where they could read each other's body language or just instinctually know what play was needed to get results. A slight nod was the affirmation they were on target.

They were striving harder every year to be better at facing the opposing teams who were the competition. They were becoming tougher and tougher, more famous, and in the news every day. The media and public attention was focusing on them and the other teams knew they were the ones to beat if there were any hope for their team to be contenders for any championship, much more, the World Series. Odds makers in Las Vegas were in a slump because the Red Sox were the favorite. They were trying to adjust the spread and still get bets in the early season.

"Everyone says Boston is the team to beat. We are the best. We just need to get over that hump of losing the playoff's for the World Series. If it arises this year, we'll kick it down. We've done a pretty darn good job of it so far too." Said Head Coach Chambers in a team meeting.

"This coming year men, is looking to be very promising as the year we make it to the World Series." Justin was counting on it, and setting his mind, gaze, and focus toward it. He was like Mr. Duncan. Once he set his mind on something, nothing got in his way. He just needed the team to feel the same way. They all did,100%.

Chapter 42

Justin really had no measurement, or realization of time, other than day and night, because he buried himself in constant games, practice and workouts, and traveling to out of town games, end of a season, start of a new one. There were no deviations. He maintained the same structure and the same drive inside of him that he started each season with.

The games and roster were grueling and he felt peace inside of him being so busy he couldn't think of anything but baseball, the next traveling game, Grandma and Bradley. He called them every night before they went to bed. They were at every home game and he was home with them any time he could be.

Nathan went up four times a year to Boston so he could see Grandma and Bradley, each time he made the arrangements to coordinate while traveling with his job. He yearned to see them and to check on them.

He had finally had enough and accepted a job in Boston because they were all there, and he felt they were really the only family he had left, that he cared to call family anyway. Nathan valued the love they kept for him after his sister's passing and he returned that love with all his heart and soul. He needed to be with them to keep his sanity and sense of being, anyway.

"What a great 'brother' you are Nathan." Said Justin.

"On the contrary," he said. "You have filled the void for the family I never really had, and the only one I did have, we lost together in one fleeting moment. I was afraid you would not want me around anymore to remind you of our loss. You have brought me into your family and have treated me like a real brother." Nathan said.

"I too yearned for a family all of my life, Nathan. You have helped to fill that void." They both enjoyed this unusually tender moment that would probably never be repeated again.

"Well, Bree was all the family I had. Therefore, the debt of gratitude is on my part." His voice broke.

"Ok, I'll accept that." Justin quickly said to Nathan. He didn't want him to feel embarrassed for choking up. He knew the feeling all too well.

"Hey Nathan how about you live with us and help Grandma around the house while I'm gone this season, and be that great Uncle for Bradley? You're moving up here anyway. I did ask you before if you remember when we first bought the house, but you had just begun your internship and couldn't break the stride toward your doctoral. I have waited patiently bro. Best part is, you're not in a serious relationship anymore, and the timing is perfect. You would really be doing us the favor and Grandma has so much more energy when you're around!" An exaggerated smile spread across Nathan's face, showing his pearly white teeth, as he called them.

"Since you put it that way, deal!" Nathan replied. He accepted so fast it was as if he had been waiting for the offer. This pleased Justin to no end.

"I want to pay rent though."

"If you dare try, I'll kick you out of the house!"

"Dang! I haven't even moved in yet. That's just too kind and generous, Justin." Nathan said appreciatively. "But, I'll tell you what…. just because of brotherly love, I will make up for it with the kind of care you know, I know how to give… eating all of Grandma's cooking and playing with Bradley." By now, a large grin was spreading across his face. "I am man enough to do this job!"

Justin pretended to drive a jab to Nathan's side, and the two hugged and laughed.

Justin couldn't be happier and neither could the rest of the family when they heard the wonderful news.

The holidays came and the previous year had ended with the promise of the new, Season right around the corner. The entire team was waiting and anticipating great things to come. The team had grown close and they knew each other's thoughts and quirks. As a team they had the talent, they had the heart and they had the coaches to achieve the pennant, the playoff's and the World Series they had watched for too many years slip through their fingers over trite and meaningless mistakes. They all felt it stronger. It had to be this year. No faltering guys they all agreed together.

No World Series screw up's! The made the agreement as a team pact in a circle, all hands in.

This year was a whole new ball game. Justin had taken the therapeutic time to get his house in order and spend as much time with Grandma and Bradley as he could. It grounded him in his soul. He was able to get his head on straighter, he personally felt, and now it was time to roar like a lion pouncing on its prey, this coming Spring Training and forward.

He worked out in Boston through the off-season to be around his family, he wouldn't leave them again. The holidays were very important for Bradley, and Justin intended to make sure it was a pure family joy and made it a tradition especially now that Nathan was here, never knowing how long that would last before he found the right woman and got serious. Justin was the head of the family when he was home, so he would take the bull by the horns and get it going with all the festive qualities he could come up with, sometimes with the help of other teams wives telling him what he could do. It worked for him and the family. Everyone was always excited to see what he came up with every year and every holiday.

"Hey Bradley, would you like to play some catch with Uncle Nathan and I before we eat Thanksgiving dinner?" Grandma insisted on doing most of the cooking even though Justin hired a cook and housecleaner to be on staff every day to help. She did let them do all of the cleaning however. "I'm nobody's fool, my boy." Eyes twinkling. They even do some prep work for me I've taught them my secrets so they can help me. Her eyebrow raised.

"You bet I would, Dad! I love baseball as much as you do. I just wish I could have been a ball player some day. Grandma Ruby told me God has something else in store for me and I won't know until I get there. Do you think she's right?" Justin bent down and looked intently into his eyes and said, "Grandma Ruby is ALWAYS right, son." Bradley smiled, as did Nathan and outside they went to play catch. They did talk about playing Special Olympics Baseball and Bradley was so excited and yelled a huge Wahoo in agreement.

Justin had given Bradley his old fielding mitt and wasn't going to give him his new one until Christmas as a surprise.

"Dad, I carry this to everyone of your games in hopes of catching a foul ball or a tip off. I always am alert just like you told me to be, so I can protect Grandma. Those balls have yet to come near us."

"You never know Bradley, when you least expect one, there it will be! Never take your eyes off of the ball no matter how many games go by. Keep your glove on. A major players rule." Justin would make sure a ball got to him this during these next games. A talk he would have with the guys, and they would make it happen. "I will, Dad. I'll always protect Grandma no matter what." I love that son of mine more than life. Justin just glowed when he looked at Bradley. Grandma has raised another fine young man.

They played for an hour and Bradley did remarkably well catching the balls tossed to him in his wheel chair. He couldn't catch with his crutches under his arms.

The three guys laughed and teased each other until Grandma called them in to wash up for dinner. They were starving and could smell the turkey and fixings.

"What a great day this has been, said Bradley as he was about to clean up for bed. He kissed everyone good night and went towards his room on the bottom floor, with his nanny to clean up and wait for everyone to come in his room and tuck him in for the night.

"This is what the holidays mean to me, Dad, all of us being together. Thanks for being here. Thank you, Uncle Nathan for being here."

"My pleasure completely, Justin." Replied Nathan. How he loved this nephew of his. He exited the room and began walking to the living room with Grandma Ruby, so Justin could say good night.

"I love you, Son." Justin held him tight for a while and kissed him goodnight. Tomorrow, we'll do whatever you want to do, just no shopping! It's a madhouse out there the day after Thanksgiving."

"No worries there, I don't like shopping. I use your Amazon Prime account." A big twinkle came across Bradley's mischievous eyes.

Nathan had over heard that remark and added, "So do I Justin! It's amazing how quickly I get my stuff." Everyone rolled their eyes over his humorous words and quick wits. It was so nice to have him in the house.

"Night everyone, Happy Thanksgiving! It's been wonderful," Bradley's voice trailing off to sleep.

"Well, Nathan, looks like this is a tradition now, so whatever comes in our lives, we must keep it this way." Justin said with full sincerity.

"I must agree with you, Justin. This was magnificent. How could anyone top this? I'm all in. I'll try and eat just as much every year, that's a promise." They laughed, shook hands, hugged and each went to their own rooms to sleep the turkey dinner off and maybe have some leftovers tomorrow.

Chapter 43

The new season had begun with the pre-season Spring Training games as usual. They went to Florida, and became one of the Grapefruit teams, playing the Grapefruit league games. He always thought that term to be rather unfitting.

The weather would definitely be warmer and it was wonderfully beautiful in the winter, which felt weird and wonderful. Fenway Park South was in Lee County, Florida.

He remembered working out in past winters in Pawtucket trying to make his way into the major league. He was here, and he was well into the major league structure and system now. He never forgot where he came from though, he couldn't – his mind was a computer.

Justin saw the signs indicating JetBlue Park at Fenway South, the Spring Training ballpark of the Boston Red Sox, was very close. As the beautiful team bus turned in he was always in awe of the size and looks of this magnificent stadium. It was almost nicer than Fenway Park only it did not have the history Fenway Park had in Boston. It didn't have the aura Fenway Park had with all the ghosts of the greats roaming around. He didn't believe in ghosts, but it was just magical to be playing where some greats had walked and played before him.

It did however, have many features of Fenway built into it such as the "Green Monster" that featured optimal seating arrangements on top of and behind the wall, as well as a manual scoreboard. That was always amusing to Justin how they managed to keep the nostalgia in the Red Sox stadiums. State of the art, JetBlue Park, had adhered to the regulations imposed on them by the City if they wanted to build their South Stadium in southern Florida. The landscaping was designed to keep the 'environmentally-sustainable' features and vegetation indigenous to the area in any area where vegetation was to be planted.

A Perfect Match

The main ballpark could easily seat and stand a crowd of around 11,000 fans, which included the beautiful and lush burms. The stadium had six practice fields, and other adjoining facilities that housed both the Major and Minor League operations. There was even a rehabilitation center incorporated into the building. If he weren't careful, he could easily lose himself in this monstrosity strolling the grounds and learning every square inch of it as he had for the previous four years.

Justin was now a master in his internal thinking and zoning on pitches. His eyes were trained like the roving eyes of an Eagle in the sky. There wasn't a thing he missed. His powerful mind and quick eye, especially where batting was needed, were what the coaches felt the team would use to make it over the hump and win the Series.

They were optimistic every day this year because they claimed it as their very own. This was the year of the Boston Red Sox were going all the way to the World Series.

"We definitely needed this excellent pitching team to be a fierce and formidable element if we're going to make it to the World Series." The coaches talked to each other the same as the guys talked in their locker rooms.

Early one bright, warm, sunny game day, they just evolved into talking about this team and the odds of making it to the World Series this year. They all agreed that the lead pitcher, Raymond Erskine, nicknamed "Iron Arm" was a tall, good looking and super talented pitcher. He could pitch and hit the ball into the grandstands like it was no effort to do either one. Still, he was beginning to need some backup, or now, up front, help. This was the main reason for the Management, under the leadership of Mr. Duncan, to bring in Willie Steamalik. He was the batter Raymond Erskine was and they shared an instant friendship due to their common grounds of talent and interests. Steamalik was younger and could pitch with the same if not more, feverish pitch Erskine could. He shared the starting position in equal number of games. There was no problem with egos on this Red Sox team. This is why the coaches knew they were destined for great things. Everything was perfectly in place now.

The third string, but equally talented pitcher, Bo Blythe, nicknamed, "The Blower." Fourth String Pitcher, Donny Deacon, nicknamed, "The

Preacher." These great Pitchers were just to be on the safe side with a pitching team second to none in the entire nation.

Management brought in these three pitchers of superb quality for relief in the World Series. They had privately talked about this among themselves for the future of the teams pitching staff and how imperative it was to have depth in the pitchers team.

Duncan was doing everything up big and right, dealing now for the future. He was in tune with his coaching staff and ball players, feeling the same gnawing dream that could very well be a reality – they were on their way to the World Series this year.

The team and coaches were doing everything humanly possible to hone the players and Duncan was doing everything in his power to help them get to where they all wanted to be with no glitches this go round. The World Series was serious business and definitely on their docket for this year. He wanted it as badly as the team and the coaches did.

"I intend to help my men bring home to their beloved Boston, the "Commissioners Trophy!"

"Our team has some mighty great batters as a result of all this maneuvering." Exclaimed a thrilled Justin to Pike, his good friend who presided over 1st Base as if it were his best girl. Jeff Pike was a dedicated, smart, decent and hard working ball player. That's what Justin respected about him the most. He wasn't there for glory or just the money, he really loved being in Boston and playing for the Red Sox, something Justin could totally relate to. Pike had come up from Pawtucket with Justin and the two had been best of friends since Pawtucket.

"Ya know something, Justin. I think we have finally assembled the perfect Boston "Dream Team." Thanks to upper management, and Coach Chambers for knowing exactly what was needed to assemble this group of highly skilled professionals will put us over the top."

"I agree, Pike. I'm amazed at the new talent coming in and blending in with us as if they've been here as long as we have. That's professional ball players for you. They blend because they love the game and they want to win. Actually, that's the epitome of a professional ball club. Mr. Duncan will do whatever needs to be done to execute the arrangements. He profiles players to make sure they are a fit with the rest of the team too."

A Perfect Match

"How well I know that one." Said Pike. He is one shrewd businessman as we both know."

Pike pondered in good faith what Justin just said. He too had good feelings about the ball club's future. They went their separate ways as they always did after their early morning talks for the day's practice and plays.

Justin was watching the first, second and third baseman, short stop and out fielders. He thought they were already masters of perfection, but he could see where they were gaining in their mastery of the positions and all possible scenarios. They constantly strived to be better and better, with the prodding of Coach Chambers, the ever present, and ever full of gusto, Drill Sergeant on the field. His team of specialized coaches marched to the same beat Coach Chambers did.

They guys respected Coach Chambers so much, they would have had to draw straws if he ever needed a kidney. Thank God he didn't, they might have backed out if he really and truly ever did. Justin laughed to himself over his warped sense of humor.

Justin was taking a visual overview of the whole team, assessing the potential of every player and every talent in the pool of players. He was in reality, assessing their chances at the World Series this year against the players he had watched in videos of recent games. He had grown to be a very talented baseball player himself. He was so full of maturity, and his brain and skills developing in unison at such a rapid rate. His brain processed things and facts at a record speed with complete accuracy. His body followed the reactions and instinctual commands as transmitted subconsciously or consciously.

This was also the year Justin instinctually knew he could beat Babe Ruth's record. It had to be in the same number of games as the Babe made them in. To top off a year that would be remembered forever, if all went the way he envisioned it. Allowing for a few flaws here and there, his calculations and assessments were going to go down in the baseball annals and this team's memory would live in perpetuity.

This is why every player and every bit of talent was constantly on his mind. If ever it was going to be done, it had to be done in this year because everything and every person stood in their place for a reason, and they were perfectionists. Anything less would be defeating to their spunk and vision, and it would ruin any chances of future hopes. This was not an option he wanted to barter with.

Justin decided the time had come, and it was the right time to ask the Team for help in his quest to beat the Babe's Homerun Record, and before the season began would be best. He had the vision and it was too strong to ignore. The time was now and they would spring out of the starting gates with a heavy thrust, building nothing but momentum as they ran the race to the Championship.

They all knew Justin wanted to defeat the Babe's record, he was the only one in the leagues who could do it first of all, but they just hadn't heard it from his lips when he suspected he would do it, or that he needed their help and involvement.

Justin approached Coach Chambers while he was in his office after lunch and in between practice.

"Coach Chambers."

"Yes, Justin." He said as he looked up surprised to see Justin here and not on the field.

"I know this is different from the normal evening meeting docket, but no one has ever labeled me normal. Do you think it would it be possible for me to talk to the guys this evening for about ten minutes?"

"You're right about the normal part, but what would you want to talk about, Justin?" He said looking up and over his glasses with a half smile.

"It's about my goal to break the home run record of Babe Ruth this season. I'd like to explain my goal and my reasoning to the guys. I want to personally ask them to help me reach this goal. Then I want to ask them to be unwavering in a unified and unquenchable thirst to win the World Series. One year, two titles for Boston Red Sox, This Year, Coach." Justin still looking at Coach Chambers, and Coach Chambers still looking at Justin with his full attention, made Justin continue.

We are a very able, and sophisticated team. We are also a very tight team. I feel that by doing this in front of you and the coaches, it would make more of a commitment and an impact. Thoughts?" Justin waited for Coach Chambers to speak. He had been mesmerized by Justin's forthrightness and direct talk.

"That's so impressive and practical, in my humble and honest opinion, Justin. I'll turn the meeting over to you for your heart-to-heart talk with the guys. You bet I will!"

Chambers was thinking internally as he spoke, "It will be great for the guys, and for you to share your dream and your goal with them. It is just as important for them as it is for you to share yourself and your thoughts of the team winning the World Series together. This is powerful! You will be asking them to be as big of a part of all this and a bit more… the World Series. As for your personal goal of defeating the Babe's homerun record in the same number of games, this is excellent. They will be a part of it by helping you. History will once again be made in Boston and in Fenway Park. Outstanding!" Chambers mind was in overdrive now.

"Thanks, Coach, there's a lot of heartfelt talk going on here, and it means a lot to me you care and you listened to me. I'm so serious about this drive inside of me it often keeps me awake at night. I need to share it and get if off my chest, then go forward as a team."

"Yes indeed, Justin. I'm so doggone proud of you right now, or should I say again? Heck, the guys are already proud of you just for what you have done in the past. This will seal the bond you men share and the coaches will be in on it too. This is a very memorable moment for me as a coach, Justin."

"Thank you, Sir. I respect you and all of them very much."

"I can see that, Justin. Very clearly."

That evening during the team meeting, Coach Chambers went over stats and scores of the players for their scrimmages, as normal and then set the stage for Justin by lighting up the energy of the room. The evening team meeting in the clubroom began to fill every space with unusual energy and fiery sparks coming from Coach Chamber's mouth. He had the same train of thought Justin did, and wanted every man in the room to have the same powerful thoughts and a "no fail attitude" they had. Everyone was feeling the same shift in momentum, so his demeanor was not a surprise to the men. They were already in the zone.

"Men, we are definitely coming upon this year like cannon balls out of a cannon." Clearly, providence is raising her head at every turn. Coach Chambers was using some of the same phrases the men had used several days before while talking at lunch. They wondered if he had over heard them talking. "Time has flown by and all of our efforts are paying off in rapid-fire succession." Chambers looked around the room and all eyes were on him, this was a great sign. He continued.

"Men, this is what we've been working toward for so many years. It should come as no surprise to you that we are now continuous champions of the American League, and we shall be again this year! We must stay focused and not let ourselves become over confident. Never. Never. Never, let your guard down. Every member plays at peak performance, and nothing less. That's what got us here where we are today. We are a team to be feared, as the media states so accurately everyday. That's what will carry us over the mountain peak. We will go in quietly and then tear the house down…you know what I'm saying here? We are horses headed for the barn this year, and our barn sits just behind the Commissioners Trophy! Everyone in agreement?" He let them cheer and whistle and woo-hoo until they let it quiet down on their own. It was a moment of fun, and necessary to make sure everybody felt the energy and urgency.

"We leave in a couple of days to head back to Boston for the beginning of OUR season. We claim it, we want it and it shall be ours for the taking. Upon these thoughts, I would like to tell you. I have something extra special tonight to present to you. Your fellow teammate, Justin, would like to say a few words to all of you."

Justin walked briskly up to the front and started right in as if he were taking his position on the field to play. The same enthusiasm the guys had seen a hundred times before.

"You know guys, As Mr. Duncan said in the beginning of the season, we can do anything, and accomplish anything, if we set our minds to it, and he guaranteed us that we have the full support of the Red Sox Management behind us in our endeavors for greatness. Well…I've set my heart, soul and mind on a particular goal, and that is to beat Babe Ruth's Home run record of 60 homeruns, in the same number of 154 games he set the record in."

"Yeah, Baby." Said voices from the men in all directions of the room. "You can do it if anyone can, Justin."

"I wholeheartedly feel I can do this. It will add a precious stone to our particular Ball Club by beating the Babe's record, and winning the World Series all in one year. This entire team will go down in history forever, because we are going to take the World Series…Right?" His teammates instantly responded with, "Yes, we want it and we are going after it like dogs in a meat factory." Said a voice from the back, probably Erskine's. Clapping and cheering filled the room like men on a unified mission. They liked what they were hearing. It's what they had been working so hard for. Their march had begun.

"Guys, I'm going after the Babe's record with the same tenacity."

The men were quiet at first at the realization this could really happen. After they had gained their senses, they erupted into cheering in agreement and an enormous amount of noise. They believed once Justin said he was going to do something, he did it. It wasn't so bizarre to hear.

"You all know very well I had a hard year about five or so years ago. You all kept my spirits up when I didn't know if I could put one foot in front of the other just to get myself to a practice. Don't think for one moment, I'll ever forget your spirit of friendship, loving support, understanding, patience and kindness toward me. I will never forget how you stood by me in my weakest moments and never gave up on me, even when I had about given up on myself." Justin stopped for a couple of seconds to compose himself because for some reason, he was a bit emotional.

He quickly began again, "I'm asking you to stand that same way with me again in this quest to beat 'The Babe' homerun record. Babe Ruth was known as the Home Run King and the Sultan of Swat, the Sultan of Slide, etc., because of that 1927 season. He was and is still a legend because of his mighty, proficient and powerful swing. Babe is still known to this day as one of the greatest baseball players of all time, and he did what no man before him or after him has been able to do without steroids or drugs, until hopefully, now." Justin had just let the team know he was all natural and clean in his quest.

"He hit 60 homeruns in one single season, of 154 games. I may offend some die hard fans, but think what this will do for us and the Red Sox Ball Club forever!" Being so proud of their Ball Club, this was most meaningful to all.

"Well guys, 'The Legend' is about to share that title with a virtual unknown coming out to play ball this year in Fenway Park Stadium. I'm not a carouser, a showboat or a drinker, I'm just a plain ole, boring guy from Alabama who wants to win and win big. I desire to beat that record for our team's reputation for all of history. I'm asking you guys to stand with me, support me and encourage me as you did five years ago for a different reason this time. It involves all of us and I wouldn't have it any other way. We will always be known as a 'legend team' in the Fenway Park of hero's. If that's good for you guys, it's good for me. Otherwise, there is no glory or spark in a lonely title. I want to do this for you as much as with you. I want it for my son too, guys. I need you to be with me because I'm no good alone. Ask my Grandmother!" He laughed so hard after he said that because he sounded so vulnerable and like a grandma's boy. Everyone enjoyed his remark and the shared laugh session.

"I'm usually a private kind of guy as you all know, and you have no idea how graceless and shy I feel right now to even talk like this in front of this room.

I believe it's this kind of boldness, honesty and fortitude that will make us what and who we are destined to ultimately be, and that is World Series Champions!"

He had the biggest smile the guys had seen in four or five years. It felt good to see him like this. They became more energized and wildly full of pep.

He couldn't keep the noise level down. The guys were celebrating and agreeing to back him up all the way and then on to the World Series. He thanked them and then turned the meeting back over to Coach Chambers. Enough had been said and the guys were with him in full harmony.

Coach Chambers said, "We've all grown close and we've all looked after each other's backs. Let's keep it up men and please indulge me as I say; Let's do this for all the right reasons as a ball club and as a team! I'm depending on you too. I'm asking you as my players, let's do this." Another thought came quickly to chambers,

"We owe this to ourselves and to Mr. Duncan for believing in us. He has been more than happy in making our team the finest in the nation. This didn't come cheap to him – remember this! He has a huge stake and belief in us. Keep kicking my butt, and I'll keep kicking your butt's." A resounding 'Yes' filled the meeting room that Wednesday evening, during the 7p.m. weekly team meeting. They wanted this and they wanted it badly.

A Perfect Match

"We have you covered Justin," shouted Pike, with Erskine and Steamalik." They were quick to encourage him. Then the whole team chimed in agreement and was completely geared to win.

Their star homerun king had just given them the Gladiator speech of all speeches. Coming from a teammate such as Justin, and the Coach finishing it up for him, they were ready to go into battle and come out victorious. Besides, he was due his reward for all he had been through and still kept up his game for them the year he lost his wife, and his son was crippled. Their memories were just as long as Justin's.

The bond these men had developed came through so many of life's twists, defeats and heartaches they shared together. This was the residue of something extraordinary. Very few teams ever have the opportunity to experience such a blended life. It bordered on a fairy tale as strange as it was. Yet it was as real as a delicious juicy steak.

Coach Chambers dismissed the team and said, "Let's get some rest and get back out there tomorrow and kick some booty around."

Cheering with the noise of an over crowded Las Vegas nightclub, they filled the meeting room with thunderous noises of joy. The moments were more monumental than Coach Chambers could remember in a very long time, if ever.

The men were jazzed, amped and ready to play to their full potential, he was as happy as a kid on Christmas morning.

"These players truly are a tribute to the men who devote their lives to the sport of Baseball." Said Coach Chambers to Coach Bricket and the other coaches, as the men left the meeting room with more verve and vigor than he had seen in quite sometime.

"We are on our way to the World Series. We just took the first major step, tonight." They all agreed and went out very happy, optimistic men.

"That Justin can really fire up the guys, with very little effort." Said Pawtucket Coach, Bricket.

"Never saw anyone like him, in all my years. Maybe he is the 'Babe' reincarnated." Quipped Coach Chambers.

"Do you believe in reincarnation, Coach?" Asked Coach Bricket

Coach Chambers just gave him a side-glance and rolled his eyes.

The last day of practice, and Spring Training games came to an end in Florida. Coach Chambers gathered the men around him on the field and said there would be no evening meeting. We leave tomorrow morning so let's get some good rest tonight and get ourselves on that bus in the morning heading for Boston. Sweet home, Boston." Coach Chambers seemed like he was homesick, but he was really eager to get back to the Boston fans and Fenway Field.

"We'll be on our discussed mission tomorrow, the next day, and the next day, full steam ahead until we have what we want." Coach Chambers paused to think and then continued, "We have a lot riding on each and every one of you. I couldn't be more proud of a team as I am of you men." Stopping and looking down at his feet, then back up at the men as they looked back at him, no more words were necessary.

"Yes Sir!" They all said, and off they went to shower, pack and eat before getting to bed for the early morning bus ride to the airport. They were homeward bound for Boston, sweet Boston. Justin was so eager to see his son and Grandma, Nathan too.

Chapter 44

"The Red Sox are the team to beat. They are gaining in momentum and they are moving like a steamroller. They are leveling and flattening every team they have come up against. Could they really be this forceful? Can they be taken down off their pedestal?" News broadcasters were bombarding the airwaves with rhetoric and much to do about everything. They needed to build the hype for every game and eventually culminating with the World Series. It's what they did every year, year round. They were masters of hyperbole!

All season Justin Edge was bringing in men on base, and he was hitting homerun after homerun. Sometimes the pitchers would try to walk him and Coach Chambers would put him in as a pinch hitter with bases loaded when and where it counted and Justin never disappointed. The Red Sox strategies were flawless and their desire was unquenchable. Writers and announcers were going to town writing about them in every newspaper and periodical across the country.

Justin would never allow himself to be the front cover feature because he felt it would take him off course. He let the owner, Mr. Duncan be his front cover guy or Coach Chambers. This pleased both men that he wasn't a glory hog, and they were happy to do the job. Inside, they were humbled by Justin's meekness, in spite of the tremendous fame that had come to him.

Mr. Duncan said, "As the Bible says, don't mistake his meekness for weakness. Justin Edge is a mighty man. Maybe he is our David who slays Giants." Duncan winked at the reporter and turned on his heels, the interview was over that quick.

After the meeting, Justin hung around to talk to Coach Chambers for a minute.

"What's on your mind, Justin?" The two of them had a very close connection and friendship of which both men fully valued and respected. It was very special to know someone covered your back, when you did nothing to work for it, except to give them a reason to trust you unconditionally.

"Nature takes care of those of like minds and spirits, and keeps them together so they can be of kindred spirit." Grandma would always say.

"Coach, I just wanted to thank you for everything and how you care for all of us as if we are your family."

"Justin, you're supporting my inner feelings. I can't hardly sleep or eat, planning and executing the precise plays and imagining different tweaks for the team. I know we are on our way, look at the way we have started the season!" Coach Chambers believed in providence. If another one agreed with him of whom he had tremendous trust in, it had to be so. This is why he and Justin enjoyed a little conversation every once in a while. They were of like minds in their quest for the gold.

"We have assembled the perfect team to get the not so long ago, 'Mission Impossible' team, made into the 'Mission Possible' Dream Team." He chuckled slightly.

"That's one way of saying it, Coach."

"I wonder if any of my quotes will go down in history like Vince Lombardi's have?" They both laughed and walked out of the clubroom. "I'm sure they will, Coach. Probably even make a book from all of them!" They laughed some more, and it felt great.

"Coach, I haven't taken a vacation in five years due to wanting and waiting for this year to come." Chambers noticed Justin's instant change in demeanor and attitude and gave him his full attention.

"When my wife died, and my son was crippled, I lost all incentive to take any vacations, or leave this ballclub and practicing. I instead chose to do nothing but baseball and I gave it my all, you know that. There was no need anyway since my son has been in constant therapy, and my Grandma didn't want to travel due to moving and settling into a strange city and setting up a home all at the same time and at her age. They seem to both be very happy and in a routine that makes them comfortable. I'm happy working out, practicing and keeping my eyes focused on the goal."

Coach Chambers didn't quite know where Justin was headed with this conversation so he just continued listening. Justin was pouring his heart out for a reason to his friend.

"Coach, this is the year! I'm reiterating what we discussed in Florida just because I like to stay focused and talk about it with someone other than my Grandmother. Justin stared at Coach Chambers whose eyes were wide as saucers but his face was beaming and about to burst into laughter. Upon seeing his expression, Justin burst into laughter and so did Coach Chambers who couldn't hold it back anymore.

"Sure, come in anytime, "still laughing and hardly able to get the words out. "I love to talk to you, Justin."

"See you later, Coach." Tilting his ball cap to the coach and walking away laughing himself." Coach is such a great guy.

"You are one special kind of player, and a super special kind of man. There are a lot of hopes and plans riding on you young man. Keep laughing, it reduces stress."

Chapter 45

"I feel we are ready for the World Series, Grandma. I've watched the team grow and mature. We have melded together as no other team in both leagues that I know of. I know what I see, and I see a finely tuned and well-oiled machine. What I saw in Florida blew me away." Justin was looking at a movie reel in his mind when he was telling Grandma about Florida Spring Training and games. She knew that look so well and she knew his mind and how it worked even better.

"I truly believe we are going to the World Series this year. My teammates feel it as strongly as I do. The coaches are in heaven walking around watching us practice, watching our abilities and faults in games. They are fine tuning all of us to perfection. Coach Chambers admitted it to me himself, he feels it as strongly as I do. The coaches are equally as confident, and that is no off-the-cuff, spur-of-the-moment statement either.

"I have never felt better about my personal abilities and I'm not burdened down with the heavy memory of Bree any more. I'll never quit loving her, but thank God, life has gone forward just as you said it would. I am truly ready and I know my teammates are too." Grandma could feel Justin's relief and immense pressure off his mind just by the way he was talking.

"I know you are too, my boy. I want to see you all win the pennant again for yourselves, and then, take home the Commissioners Trophy by winning the World Series for this great city of Boston! I have come to love this city and the people just as you thought I would. I'm proud to call Boston my home."

"There's no lack of support in Boston is there, Grandma?"

"No sir, I must agree with you on that fact. The people of Boston are an amazing fan base. There is a lot of perseverance and faith, friendship and humor from my observations, son. There is the best of everything in these people. It is a big, complex world of good and bad. Never doubt, it's the good that counts the most." Grandma Ruby was a rock solid woman full of great thoughts and wisdom. Justin often quoted her in his rare interviews because it made him sound smarter, especially when he didn't feel like talking.

"By-the-way, Bradley is one of the most loyal and vocal fans you have besides me! I tell you, sometimes my ears are still ringing an hour after the game from his cheering you all on to victory and how excited he gets over any little play that goes in your favor." Laughing her little giggle again made Justin smile. She loved Bradley as much as she had loved Justin while raising him. It felt so good to be back home.

Justin and Pike were having a pre-practice chat one morning after they had done a jog around the field a few times. Justin began to explain to Pike, his thoughts.

"Our vision is similar to the way light is diffused. Take an ordinary light from a reading lamp. Properly directed and focused, there is virtually nothing that it cannot shed light on for you to read.

But if it's light is dissipated and spread out too far, it isn't as good. Let's take it a step further and imagine a laser focused on a target. There is no end to what it can accomplish. The results would be mind blowing if you've ever studied lasers, Pike.

I feel like we are lasers! If we keep our minds totally focused as a team, and don't even think about spreading our focus outside of our 'at -the-moment-target'. Our "optics" will not dissipate out of focus, and we'll hit the goal simply because the theory of vision come from objects casting off copies of themselves and are captured by the eye. If we see it in our mind's eye, we will achieve it in reality! We will be unbeatable, unstoppable, and unmovable in our focus to win. We will become the laser light I just explained to you. I feel that is the line of sight we should be focusing on this year."

"You totally make things into an understandable and attainable visual, Justin. That is the most perfect example you just gave and I think you should share it with the rest of the guys. You make perfect sense, and you really put things into perspective, Instead of thinking it, you put it into words. Nice! Well done my man."

This was one of the reasons why Pike enjoyed Justin's friendship so much. They shared many such quiet times and intellectual talks.

"No horse ever went anywhere with its trainer until it was trained and guided. Niagara Falls never produced electricity and power until it was harnessed. I too, believe we have direction, we are disciplined, Pike. We are talented and we are focused. We play as a team, and we share the same desire, and that is to win! We are a tight bunch of men, and nothing is going to get in our way this year. We are like horses headed for the barn!"

"I couldn't agree with you more on that one, Justin. I'm tired of reading about others accomplishments. It's time we read about our own!" Pike was as serious as he could be. He too, felt the momentum shifting in their favor. After talking with Justin he felt that he could climb Mt. Kilimanjaro!

They did a hearty high five and went out to intensively practice like they were trying out for the World Series every day of this new season. The excitement and focus spread rapidly again through the whole team and they were confident they were going to make it happen this year. The burning desire was too hot and unquenchable. It was the only thing they could talk about over and over and over. They would have felt like a bunch of gossiping women if it had been over any other subject except the World Series. They couldn't talk about anything else…tunnel vision and total focus. "We shall rise to the occasion men!" Said the Catcher, Buddy Montaño.

The games progressed as speed and performance records were made and broken. Only one major goal of the season had not been achieved, just yet anyway.

Justin Edge was on target to defeat the indomitable homerun batting record of the inexpugnable Babe Ruth. This record had to be defeated in Justin's mind, in the same number of games that Babe Ruth played. He wanted to beat it by at least one home run, even a miraculous two if possible. His teammates were behind him all the way and the thought was never out of any of their minds. Neither was the goal of winning the World Series this year. It was a do or die feeling they all adopted. No longer a much dreamed of goal. It was the here and now.

Chapter 46

Coach Chambers was so proud to report to Mr. Duncan the teams focus and determination to win the World Series this year! "It's all they can talk about, Sir. They are the most determined team I've coached in my career."

"You think they are going to do it Chambers?" Asked a pensive Mr. Duncan

"I have no doubt about it, Sir. This is the most talented and ego free team we have ever assembled and I've had the privilege of coaching. The men listen intently, they are all extremely intelligent and athletically superior to teams I've coached in the past. Sometimes, I have to pinch myself to make sure I'm not dreaming. You have made sure of their superiority I might add, Sir." Duncan smiled and walked around his desk to sit down and savor the thought of the most productive year in a very long time. "Yes, I have Coach. Yes, I have!" Pursing his lips and smiling to one side as a proud father holding back too many compliments so he didn't spoil the momentum.

"What they set their minds on as a team, they accomplish as a team. You understand that motive better than most professionals Mr. Duncan. You have set the standards and the men are fashioned after your credo. Besides, it's not beyond their capacity or abilities and they are finely tuned to the point of being indestructible, super stars. They are the most formidable team in both leagues right now. I'm in awe daily with what I see Mr. Duncan. I can't wait to get to the field every day to watch them in motion and how they interact without a spoken word. I would like to invite you out to see first hand, and let the men see you there watching their actions and cohesiveness.

I have no doubt you've been by "stealthily" a few times if I know you, and I think I do, Sir!" Mr. Duncan was listening and finally nodded an affirmative motion with his head while in deep thought. To what,

Chambers had no idea. He had said so many things he couldn't remember what specific answer Duncan was nodding to. No matter, Mr. Duncan was a deep thinking man so there was absolutely nothing to worry about with this genius at the helm.

"Mr. Duncan, the media has made it a daily goal to smother us with photos, interviews and camera crews as I've never seen before. They are pounding on our back doors for interviews at six o'clock in the morning. We have had to limit their hours and numbers. They have become pesky flies and its' become a double-edged sword. We need them. We don't need them, type of thing.

I see it on a daily basis and that is just compounding the confirmation of what we already know. It's like reading tealeaves or being a psychic, or better yet, Nostradamus predicting this phenomenal occurrence centuries ago.

It is so real and surreal at the same time. I feel I'm floating at times. Our men are seeing the invisible as if it were already materialized and that makes them focused beyond any set backs that could creep in.

These guys are prepared for anything, good or negative and they never look over their shoulders unless something or somebody tries to come at them like a pack of wolves, and then these men will crush them and turn them into whimpering puppies."

Chambers was beyond positive in his persuasive description of his team. He was fully committed to them and their goal, so much so, Mr. Duncan had never seen this new improved, energized Coach Chambers before. Duncan liked this new Coach Chambers. He was just as focused and highly polished, gleaming with anticipation and expectation as his ball players were. He looked younger and thinner as if he had a new image of pride and self esteem. It was a classy new look that was very becoming for the head Coach of the soon to be World Champion Red Sox.

The best part Mr. Duncan, Justin Edge is planning on putting the frosting on the cake by beating the Babe's home run record in the same amount of games with no steroids, drugs, or asterisk's affixed next to his name." Duncan leaned forward in his chair and looked at Chambers for the first time with his mouth wide open. "What did you just say? Did I hear you correctly, Chambers?"

Duncan was about to do a back flip. "Yes Sir! He wants it clean, honest, untainted and doubt free for the sake of the Red Sox reputation. He asked the team personally in a team meeting to help him. That really says something! This man has raised the bar for our confidence and performance levels. We are a "First Class" rocking team on the move with asphalt rollers that can flatten anything in its way. I don't know what else to add, Sir or, how else to say it. I'm in the middle of a world of emotions with these men. I am emotional and full of a father's pride for the sons you only dream of or see in movies. Difference is…they are the real deal Mr. Duncan." Chambers stopped because he really was working himself up emotionally, something so au contraire to his personality. He was literally swelling with pride and admiration for these men who were pressing as none he had ever coached before.

This news pleased Mr. Duncan to the moon and back. Duncan's thinking was clicking away. Ten steps ahead of Coach Chambers in his thinking process, he was lost in thought.

Duncan was going to give them all the moral and financial support he could to make it happen for this fine group of outstanding athletes. If they wanted it this bad, God knew he certainly did. This was the checkered flag he had waited for. All systems were a go now.

"Chambers! I am going to give you and the men everything in my power to make it happen if the men and all your coaches believe this is the year. We will go down as one of the greatest teams in all of history and I do know how to work the history books! I have made history before, so I see no reason to suppress it now. Agreed?" As if he needed Coaches affirmation, but they were a team and teams share dreams.

"Agreed and agreed, Mr. Duncan…you are so right in your thinking… no turning back…we are fully committed. If anything turns sour, it won't be by our doings."

"Well…let's make sure that isn't an issue Coach. Focus and effort, focus and effort, makes for a winning atmosphere."

Duncan could taste it now. "We have to give it our all. I will alert the upper management to be on constant alertness and standby for immediate requests. My daughter works closely with me and decisions will be made expediently." He said rubbing his chin thinking intently.

"Is there anything you need, Chambers? Is there anything the men need? If there is anything that needs attention, you will let me know personally and immediately, okay?"

"You have my word, Sir."

"I will address the men tomorrow over a light lunch." Duncan announced to Chambers.

Mr. Duncan was all smiles the rest of the day. Making plans and strategies was what he did best and his full attention was completely focused on the goal.

"A thousand mile journey all begins with the first step. And, this is the first step to our long journey." See you tomorrow Chambers. Don't be late with our men. I'm all in and my time is valuable so let's make it happen."

Chambers was exhilarated and scurried back to the practice field.

Mr. Duncan informed his secretary, "Velma, I shall be out of the office tomorrow because I would like you to schedule a very nice and light catered lunch for the Ball club at the field tomorrow, with tents for shade, fans and tons of fine healthy food." He paused to think.

Oh yes, and Call Coach Chambers and let him know of the plans are for around 12:30. I'll give a short talk and they can get back to practice, tents down etc."

Velma knew exactly what to do and that's why Mr. Duncan relied on her more than any other member in his staff when he wanted an event carried out to precision.

He wanted to speak to the men. He was going to be with them every step of this journey and he wanted them to know it. He was the owner of the team and he was their Fairy God Father! Mr. Duncan laughed at his self-described, description of himself. Shazaam! I love fabulous competition and then striking the opponents down after we have toyed with them for a bit.

The next morning Duncan was on the field by 10am. He watched with binoculars, had his filming crew covering each squad's practice for his personal viewing later, and then it was time for the lunch and short speech of encouragement and letting them know he was with them to the end.

A Perfect Match

"Men, today is the beginning of a brand new year. Every day is the beginning of another step toward our goal as a team to take the World Series Championship.

We've already shown four years in a row we can win the division. Let's prove to ourselves, our fans, and to the great city of Boston, heck, let's show it to the world, we can do this. We'll stagger the world with our determination our focus and our abilities. All professional Baseball Clubs have talents and abilities, but it takes really wise, courageous and confident men to say we will undertake and achieve our vision. What we are doing is taking a pledge to out perform all the other teams in both Leagues of baseball and that is quite an undertaking, no doubt about it. It is the Red Sox turn this year, here and now. We are the most feared and respected team out there even if some of the Diva's won't admit it. They fear us! They will not make fools of the Red Sox I swear on my Scottish heritage." He stood tall and with his head held high upon that statement.

"I personally feel this is the best and most professional team we have had for many years. To do anything less would be merely a job and not a vocation, and you've given the signal this is not just a job. I appreciate you so much that I take full pleasure in you as individuals and as a team that has melded and bonded together into a battle machine that cannot be stopped. We are the newly discovered and highly hidden discovery, much like the splitting of the atom. We are powerful and will not be displaying too much in public. We will take them by surprise because you are humble and gentlemen. I know! We'll do it one game at a time, all the way to the World Series! You men clearly recognize there is no happiness in quitting on ourselves, or each other therefore, we shall not cheat ourselves out of the victory we so much deserve. The victories shall come and never shall we allow the enemy of doubt to enter through these gates. We will toss any bum out of Fenway Park who tries to snatch victory out of our clutches." This statement of using the word "bum" drew a lot of chuckles and clapping, as he had hoped it would.

"We are as nature intended us to be, fighters for the height of our calling." Mr. Duncan felt so emotional he had to pause.

"I want this as badly as you do my fellow teammates." He stopped and gave a moment of reflection for everyone, so they could absorb the realness and finality of their desired achievement.

"This is close and personal to each and every one of us. I wish to ask you all with all the sincerity I have inside of me to help Justin achieve his goal of beating the Babe's homerun record. Let's encourage him and help him in anyway we can. This shall be the year of the Red Sox that will be written in the athletic history books."

The men were listening and absorbing every word he said and feeling the words down deep. He was more than honored to be among these men. They were champions, and gladiators and they were in awe Mr. Duncan looked upon them this way.

"I'm willing to do whatever needs to be done to fully support your united efforts and decisions. Whatever I have in my power to do for you, I promise I will stand with you. I am your humble servant." He bowed his head to the men in their honor, and put his right fist over his heart, he was a Royal Scotsman through and through.

The men were quite surprised and humbled. They stood up and clapped for Mr. Duncan out of extreme respect. They then, let him continue. "As the owner of the prestigious Boston Red Sox Baseball Club, I am so proud of each and every one of you. I am also so excited to be on this trip with you! I stand here proudly and salute each and every one of you, as this is surely your hour, your day and your season. Your positive attitude will cause this year to be your ultimate triumph! Thank you gentlemen, with all my heart and the Boston Red Sox Management's as well. Lifting his glass of water he said,

"I would like to quote Emerson as a toast to you, and then allow you to go back to what you do best." He began with his favorite memorized quote,

"What a new face, courage puts on everything! A determined man, by his very attitude and the tone of his voice, puts a stop to defeat and begins to conquer."

Duncan paused for a moment and then resumed to add emphasis.

"This being our decision and goal, we strive to achieve it this very day. So, I say 'here, here'." An old Bostonian Cheer from the Revolutionary era.

The men all raised their glass water bottles for the occasion and clinked a toast of good cheer and let the hearty cheers of 'here, here' and 'huzzah' agreements be heard far and wide. They were true Bostonians today, and they were truly Boston Red Sox in their hearts and souls.

Chapter 47

It was another beautiful summer, afternoon. The Red Sox were playing another game that was going so well in Boston's favor. Grandma told Bradley, who was growing up to be a beautiful young boy, like his dad. She told him how she remembered all so well the many games she had gone to when his Dad was a young boy himself. These were very fond memories she loved to share with Bradley every time she thought of something new. Bradley loved hearing about his Dad as a young boy.

"Bradley, I'm the official Cheerleader and you're the official outfielder, just like your dad, only on our side of the outfield." Grandma Ruby shook her pompom so hard it almost fell apart, but she wasn't worried, she had more at home.

Bradley carried his baseball glove with him to every game. It was the one his Dad had given him for his last birthday. He would get a new one when he turned 14. So far, he had been able to catch 5 fly balls and some foul balls. A batting practice ball that was specifically thrown to him looking like a mistaken batted ball even found its way into his mitt. "Bradley told his Dad one day, how right he was when he had told him, 'when you least expect the balls they will come.' I've been protecting Grandma in every game now, and I haven't taken my eye's off of the balls once."

"See!" Justin said, "I told you, when you least expect it, they would start coming your way. I know a couple things about a couple of things." Winking at Grandma, when Bradley wasn't looking. She just smiled back at both of them as a proud Grandma would. Bradley was jubilant he was finally, "protecting" Grandma and catching some balls to add to his collection.

Chapter 48

Time and people, are the true remedies for any difficulty in life.

I can say this without any reservations and from first hand knowledge. There were special people who came into my life, and time eventually even took some of them away. Time eventually took the sting and pain inside of me away, but not their memories.

There were days when I didn't know if I could function as a human being or not.

Oddly, and thankfully, a little strength came to me each day, thanks to a God who cares and watches over me. He sent people into my life, who held me together during those times. Eventually all that was left were faded memories. There was no more pain to rip my soul apart, and no more tears to cry when I let my memories come to surface, faced them and let them fade in the sunshine of real life.

I think about a comment made in the Science Fiction movie Star Trek by Captain Kirk, and I don't think I could say it better.

"Would we truly be human without our flaws? A flawed human is worthwhile because these things we carry with us are the things that make us who we are. If we lose them, then we lose ourselves. I don't want my pain taken away. I need my pain. I'll add my own thoughts to this; my pain has made me who I am today, a much stronger, and much more human, human being. I have known true love and have had sincere love given to me. Now, it's my turn to give love back, and to take care of my loved ones. It's my turn to teach people about love and how love conquers all things.

"A thousand times we die in our lifetime. We crumble, shred, break and rip apart a layer at a time until all the layers of illusion and disillusion are

stripped away and then one day all that is left is the truth of who we really are and what we really are supposed to be and what we are supposed to do in life.

We didn't come into this world with a warrantee that said, "Guaranteed not to wear, tear, shed or show grass stains!"

He knew this would make the people laugh so he inserted it intentionally in all of this hard to talk about memories. A nice shocker and laugh for everyone. When the crowd slowly quieted again, Justin began again where he left off.

I have had to learn this truth the long and hard way through the school of hard knocks. No one teaches you this in school of any level because it's supposed to be personally designed. It's a hard pill to swallow, but one that has to be taken no matter who you are.

You see, life teaches us many lessons, but the one most important, is to stay true to what is set before you. Do that which needs to be done each day and the work you began in the fog, you will continue in the sunlight."

The fans loved Justin's plainspoken, meaningful take on life. They applauded his successful effort to make sense out of life's biases. The crowd raved over this man who had risen from the ashes of ruin into the golden boy of Baseball. They listened intently. They felt his pain. They paused to contemplate his points about life. Who could ask for more

Game #154, Fenway Park, Boston, MA.

"To be, or not to be: that is the question." - *William Shakespeare*

Chapter 49

Boston was enjoying the last vestige of beautiful and sunny days before fall and winter set in. The beautiful weather was beckoning the people to enjoy a variety of activities outdoors. Faneuil Hall was bustling. The North End couldn't keep up with the pizza orders. The pubs were packed with friends meeting and chatting. The rowing boats, sculling boats and sailboats were in the Boston Harbor. The dragon boat competitions were in full force. It was indeed a beautiful day.

There was plenty of time for fun before the 7:30 PM Baseball Game on the television sports network. They took their Sports teams serious in Boston and this was another installment of the New York Yankees versus the Boston Red Sox at Fenway Park. Had Justin had 59 or better yet 60 homeruns, it would have been one of the most watched sporting events across the United States.

Most of America was waiting for the World Series Games, or, the homerun number 60 Justin seemed to be destined for. The majority of baseball fans across the nation were unaware that "The Babe" initially played for the Boston Red Sox. Most only knew him as a New York Yankees player and that his most recent challenger was some young kid from Boston. That same kid would be playing against the Yankee's tonight in game #154 with 58 homeruns to his record.

Justin had gotten to the Boston clubhouse early to avoid the onslaught of sports writers. He knew they would try to intercept him to ask an endless series of questions that had been asked and answered ad infinitum. They would also try to catch his coaches, some of the other players, and if they could, the Boston Red Sox front office people. Even Ruby and Bradley would be a target for the cadre of vultures trying to catch a story any way possible.

Today Ruby and Bradley arrived at Fenway Park long after Justin had made his way clandestinely to the safety of the Boston Clubhouse where the clubhouse manager and other clubhouse employees greeted him warmly.

Justin said goodbye earlier that day to Ruby and Bradley with his head focused on his goal. This was the day he had dreamed of and it had to be.

The game began at the TV-appointed contractual time, and Justin was unavailable to meet with any TV or radio broadcasters. In a way, even though he constantly fantasized about the record, there was a large part of him that wished today would be over irrespective of how it all ended. He wanted the victory. He could almost taste it. He was nervous and full of anxiety. He reasoned to himself this is normal to any baseball player chasing a record.

The Yankees got one run in the top of the first inning as the Boston pitcher threw a slider that did not slide and the last time anyone saw the ball it was heading over the Green Monster as Clay Baker began his homerun trot around the bases. Nobody ever said the Yankees were not going to score runs during this beautiful Baseball evening in New England.

The Yankees finished the inning with no further damage that was echoed by the first two Boston batters who struck out on fastballs served up by the Yankee pitcher.

Justin was the 3rd batter up in the first inning and he peeked over to the 2 seats by the Boston Dugout that were always occupied by Bradley and Ruby. The sight of his two family members had a very comforting effect on him. Whatever happened at the ballpark in front of millions of people either in the stands, or gazing at their TV sets didn't affect him as much as his family did. He had been deprived of these feelings early in his life, so he cherished them now.

Bradley sat beside Ruby as always and when Ruby looked over at him as Justin stepped into the batter's box, Bradley whispered, "watch this, I'm expecting a homerun, Grandma." Bradley was intently watching and didn't even deflect his gaze over to grandma as he said these words to her.

A Perfect Match

The first pitch, as Justin expected, was a fastball. Instincts, focus and talent took over, and his bat met the rotating 4-seamer on the "sweet spot" and it was gone in a flash also over the Green Monster.

Some said it was still rising when it departed the ballpark. "I told you, I told you, Grandma!" Shouted an over zealous Bradley. "My Dad can do it, if anyone can."

As Justin circled the bases, a few of the Yankee infielders, but certainly not the pitcher, gave Justin a wink and a smile — they would not mind seeing history made today themselves as they could always brag to their grandchildren that they were there when the great Babe Ruth's record fell.

As Justin touched home plate with #59 jogging toward the dugout, he gave a wink to Ruby and Bradley as he touched home plate and went into the dugout after the team was pumped for his sake. The game remained tied at the bottom of the 7th inning.

The last of the innings were quickly approaching, thank God, because for some reason, the pendulum was swinging the other way all of a sudden.

The players on both teams were beginning to feel the effects of being so tightly wound up in this game. They were fighting with all they had to each do their utmost best. Games like these caused all players to dig deep for that extra something they didn't know they had, and it made it exceedingly difficult on both sides of the field to conquer.

"Winning isn't everything, it's the 'ONLY thing." Coach Chambers had said in the pre-game locker room talk.

"I know it was coined and immortalized by football legend, Vince Lombardi, but it's applicable for baseball too."

In real time now, Coach Chambers, Coach Bricket, the batting coaches, the pitching coaches, all of the other coaches for the bases and outfielders were performing at peak energy levels because the adrenaline was running high. They were ahead more than they were behind in the innings until this last inning. "Oh God! How could this have happened?"

Coach Chambers was just leaning on the wall of the dugout as he watched the game dwindle down to the other teams favor.

"Coach Bricket! Our guys were out performing the Yankee's and our coaches seemed to be coaching more efficiently and had better strategies. We were keeping ahead of the curves the Yankee's have thrown at us all night with their pranks and tricks, but we slipped and now the bases are loaded. Dammit!" Exclaimed a very frustrated Coach Chambers.

"I think the stress of wanting it so badly is affecting their performance. Maybe we should call them in quickly for a little earth-to-players, talk." Not a perfect solution, but it was better than doing nothing." Chambers was all-nerves, right now.

"We do have Justin coming up next to bat, Coach. Shall we wait and see how he does before we call them all in? It's your call coach, but Justin seems to be having a perfect game so far. Actually, the only one on the team who is!"

"Yeah, I've noticed that myself. If we call him in he might get off focus and it would be my fault. He seems so cock sure and relaxed. I'm as nervous as a long tailed cat in a room full of rocking chairs!" Coach Chambers put another stick of gum in his mouth.

"Let him go. It's his record to beat tonight, and he is going after it like a dog in a meat factory! He only has one more home run to go and those cowards are going to try and keep it away from him. I hate them right now!" Said a very upset Coach Chambers.

"The Yankee's are intentionally trying to stop him from achieving the record breaker home run. The total disregard for the game of baseball and the outright low-class of it all makes me want to kick dirt in the other Coaches face for signaling the call to walk Justin. I just saw the sign given because Justin is on deck. I say we let him go up to bat. He's been preparing for this night, for one full year now. I can't bear it if it doesn't happen for him after all he's had to go through. I just don't think I can take it."

Coach Chambers was running both hands through his hair and massaging his head.

"We still have two innings to go and I'm a wreck, don't tell that to anyone else or I'll fire your ass, you hear me?"

"You got it sir." said Coach Bricket, somewhat entertained by Coach Chambers, and relieved for Justin's sake.

Coach Chambers didn't want to disturb Justin's momentum in any way. Justin was in a zone of his own making right now. "If it ain't broke, don't fix it." he muttered to himself about the 10th time.

"Justin entered the batting area again with 2 outs. The same pitcher was on the mound and Justin was almost sure he would see no fastballs having placed the last one far away into the Boston night. He worked the count to 3 balls and 2 strikes knowing that this Yankee pitcher was not giving in to him and would probably prefer to walk him and not allow his homerun #60 on his watch. This was not a gold star it was humiliation as a pitcher.

Justin steadied himself for the next pitch. The 2nd fastball with what seemed to have super-sonic speed, came at him, and without the slightest of hesitation, Justin made the ultimate connection he had envisioned many times. The ball was seen clearly by the fans sitting on top of the green Monster, as it made its way well out of Fenway Park, and into the star filled night. The fact of the matter was, Justin slammed the ball out of the park and was well on his way to breaking the Babe's record having now tied the score.

The pitcher's skill, talent and bravado could not stop Justin's unusual, quick reflexes that allowed him to tie the great Babe's record in 154 games. All on national TV in front of the home crowd against the New York Yankee's.

Bradley and Ruby were standing in front of their seats.

Justin, going around the bases again in a homerun trot, not only had Justin savored the adoration of the fans, but he also had thoughts about Bree and hoped that somewhere, somehow, she was aware of this very special achievement.

Somehow luck had now changed in his favor. The record was tied and to think, Justin still had perhaps, 2 at bats left to go.

His next plate appearance was at the end of the 9th inning. There certainly was magic in the air as Justin again strode to the plate – it would not be the only thing in the air, however.

With 2 outs, Justin entered the batter's box. The New York manager called a time out and walked out to the pitcher's mound. He talked to his 2 hit pitcher who on any other night, and under any other circumstance he would have let him continue with his own pitching style. This was not any other night. This was a monumental night for both teams, and Justin Edge was up to bat!

The manager left his pitcher in and Justin was sure that he would not see any good pitches to hit, but no one was giving up and certainly no fan, at Fenway or home in front of the TV was turning away.

Justin had surmised correctly; he was not getting anything to hit. The manager had given the instructions to his pitcher. The count was now ball 3 and no strikes. Justin was unsure if he would get up later in this game, so he swung at the next 2 pitches that were in the dirt making it a 3 and 2 count. The next 2 pitches were outside but he swung anyway, fouling them off to maintain the 3-2 count. Right now, Justin wasn't sure of the pitcher's intentions but he did know the pitcher was the one tiring and most importantly, running out of luck.

The 8th pitch he saw was coming over the inside corner, maybe too inside and it could be called ball 4, or the Umpire could call it a strike. It could be a close call and one that might just belong to the umpire, but not tonight.

"I'm not taking the chance." His instincts were highly tuned and he was too defiant to put trust in an unknown Umpire to call his destiny.

Justin swung and made contact the way he had seen Mickey Mantle swing inside out on an inside pitch in the 1960 World series in Game #2 in Pittsburgh.

Although Mantle was batting from the right side of the plate, the ball sailed over the exit gate 406 feet away in right center field on a laser-like line. Few right-handed batters could do a feat such as this, but one of the few was Justin Edge. He was no ordinary baseball player!

The ball did not rise much as it arced away from home plate in a hurry defying gravity heading toward right center field. Anyone who knows anything about Boston and Ted Williams knew that the left-handed Williams had hoisted a line drive into the right field stands that hit a fan occupying a seat 520 feet from home plate. No right-hander had ever done this and it would not occur today in that same pattern – but no matter.

The center fielder and right fielder both converged at the right center field wall. The center fielder made the call to catch the ball as the right fielder (the Babe's old position) backed off to avoid a collision with the center fielder – this gave him the best view in the Park! As the center fielder timed his leap perfectly in front of the wall, the line drive refused to alter its trajectory as its speed was still close to what it was when it came off Justin's bat.

Yes, the ball was caught, but by a Red Sox fan who brought his own glove to the ballpark! Now a 13 year old held the most famous, perhaps even priceless, baseball in all of Baseball history. He and the ball were well protected in the stands by his father who kept his arms around the boy. The Red Sox security had rehearsed for this moment to protect the #61 homerun ball. The ball was in the glove of a young man as well as in the record book. It had been achieved and successfully done in 154 games! Negotiations for that ball would definitely be followed up later.

Chapter 50

As Justin slammed the baseball out of the park and into what seemed to be outer orbit, he knew he had the achieved his coveted goal. Breaking the iconic Babe Ruth's home run record. Everyone who was anyone affiliated with the teams or the Babe were there to see history made before their very eyes.

The Major League Baseball Commissioner, the Yankee Brass, the Red Sox Brass, the Babe's grand-daughter and those witnessing this manifestation happen on national TV. Ruby and Justin were both standing and cheering as they awaited a most triumphant trot around the bases by Justin for the 3rd time today. This did not occur immediately however.

Justin ran to the seats occupied by Ruby and Bradley and motioned for Bradley to come to him. As he did, his father gently lifted him and his crutches, off of the bleachers and onto his shoulders. Although Bradley would never play baseball at any level, today he was circling the bases in a Major League Ball Park, in front of the entire world of Baseball. The fans at home, the fans at Fenway Park, the Commissioner of Baseball, every dignitary of any substance who was there, and all on his Dad's very broad, strong shoulders.

As the crowd caught on, they responded with an avalanche of thunderous applause which seemed like rolling thunder that wouldn't stop. The wonderful sound of unbridled cheering soon eclipsed that of a 747 taking off at nearby Logan Airport.

Justin did not think twice about what the Commissioner would say about this scenario that never had been seen before. He knew it was the right thing to do and could not have cared less if it cost him a huge fine. As he started the home run trot with Bradley on his shoulders and his arms around Justin's leg braces, a very spontaneous thing happened.

The 3 outfielders came into the infield from the outfield and the catcher ran up to the pitcher's mound. As Justin and Bradley made their way past

A Perfect Match

the Red Sox 1st base coach, he jumped into the air and high-fived Bradley as did the Red Sox 3rd base coach after the Yankee infield and outfield all did the same as Justin and Bradley slowly circled the bases – it was a sight that had never been seen before and probably never would be again.

The Yankees players were standing outside of their dugout for a full view and even the pitcher and catcher were caught up in this historic moment nodding and giving Justin thumbs-up. History had taken its' course. The Yankee pitcher told his catcher on the pitching mound standing with him, "No man was going to stop the inevitable. Providence had spoken. I accept it as a man and an athlete what has just happened here today."

The catcher patted him on the back and said, "We all do! It's something not just anyone could achieve. Justin Edge is like no other player in either league. Because it had to be you standing here today, is actually a good thing in reality. Your name will always be in the record books. Not mine, not any of the others, just yours. That's a tribute in itself, really. The plan was established in the heavens way before today so, not you, or any other pitcher, was going to stop it from happening. Personally speaking, I'm enjoying it."

They both watched Justin with an inner pride not to be spoken.

Needless to say, Justin's Red Sox teammates and coaches were all gathered at home plate awaiting his arrival with his most precious cargo. They high-fived Justin and Bradley before Justin gently sat him back down in his seat with his crutches. He gave his Grandma a huge hug she so deserved.

He went over to "Babe Ruth's" granddaughter and said, "I am the most humbled man in Baseball right now to be in the same ball field and ranking as your grandfather. I can only tell you, I will never forget this day and this moment in time!" Babe Ruth's granddaughter smiled at Justin and said, "I know he would be proud of such a remarkable and decent human being such as yourself, receiving this honor. I have followed you myself young man." She said with the biggest smile across her face. She had inherited a tinge of her grandfather's smile, he noticed.

Go on in life and hold on dearly to this day, my dear young man. We too, are very proud of you. What a fine example of a human being, and extraordinary baseball player you are for young people, fans everywhere, and America's game of baseball." She kissed Justin's cheek and patted his face gently with all the grace and dignity of a queen.

He would forever hold this in his heart and memory. So would the world. The sound of camera's clicking was unbelievable as "The Babe's" granddaughter kissed Justin on his cheek!

After this game was won 8 to 5, by the Red Sox, the media first seized upon the Commissioner and asked him and his assistant if they were going to let this game and homerun stand as it involved a civilian taking the field in the midst of a sanctioned major league Baseball game.

At first the commissioner did not understand the question and his lack of understanding was explained by the fact that although he watched everything that happened on the field intently and wildly applauded as did every other Baseball fan, he and his assistant failed to notice the presence of Bradley or any other civilian on the field. This was just one of the many reasons why Mr. Bridgers would go on to be the Commissioner of Baseball for many years to come. A very bright man who gave America's game of Baseball another bright, gold star that day.

"Therefore, Baseball's official ruling is that this game is in the books as an 8 to 5 Boston Red Sox win over the New York Yankees with 3 solo home runs being struck by one Justine Edge. This day marks his 59th, 60th and 61st home runs of the season.

Case closed and onward with the season!" Carefully, and appropriately chosen words from a very wise commissioner!

Justin made it a point to sincerely thank his teammates for helping him to capture this victory. He reminded them of the talk he had with them at the beginning of the play off games.

"You all held firm with me, and I know without every single one of you, I would have never accomplished this task, and I dedicate this victory to you all, my team-mates! I thank you from the depths of my heart for being here for me the whole distance."

His voice cracked so Coach Chambers stepped in and was the first to high five Justin. "We knew you would do this Justin. That's why we hung tight with you. Everyone kept on even when the going got tough at times. You were our man to do the job and we wanted to be with your heroic and historical accomplishment. Right Guy's?"

He looked at everyone and in unison the voices all rang out, "That's right, Coach! You're our man, Justin!"

Justin's best baseball buddy, First baseman, Jeff Pike who had been with him since the minor leagues, was the first to come up after Coach Chambers. He gave Justin a huge hug and said with the biggest and proudest smile, "I knew you'd be the one, Justin. I just knew it!"

Thanks Jeff, that means a lot to me. You probably know me better than anyone here except Coach Chambers of course."

"You bet I do, and I'm so proud of you." They shook hands again and paused as if to let each other know subliminally their true friendship mattered.

Chapter 52

The games roared and grinded on until the Boston Red Sox had clenched the American League Pennant. They were on their way to the World Series. The celebratory moment was fierce but quick because now they only had a few weeks to get ready. They spent every moment together as a team, practicing, strategizing and going over their counterpart's qualities and weaknesses. Knowing full well the Los Angeles Dodgers were doing the same.

The Boston Red Sox had already been given the Home Team Advantage by winning the All Star Games. They knew this was not just some fortuitous circumstance. It had come by hard work, and determination of a combined team effort.

The game design is a 2-3-2 game format. The first two games would be in Boston. The fans loved this, as did the players.

"Grandma, have you still been sending Mr. Willie Johnson Christmas cards?" Asked Justin out of the blue one day.

"Why yes, I have been Justin. He wrote once about a few years ago and told me he was following you and you were becoming the baseball star you had told him you were going to become. I didn't show it to you because I didn't want to bring up any bad memories." Said Grandma.

"You've always been my protector, Grandma. I'm fine, really. You made sure I was and so did God. I'm overwhelmed and grateful for everything. So much so, I wanted to invite Mr. Johnson to the first game of the World Series in Boston, but I didn't know if he was still alive, not to be sounding negative, but one never knows."

"I will write to him and ask him if he would like to be invited as your guest for your first game of the World Series. That is just so honorable of you my dear boy. I'm excited to get that letter off. After all, he was the first to hear from your own mouth that you would be a baseball star." They both laughed.

"Let me know when and what you hear, okay?"

"I sure will, Justin, just as soon as I hear back. I would call him but I don't have his phone number and I'm no good at the computer research stuff, you know that."

"No worries, Grandma. I just never wanted to forget the people that were important to me or helped me.

There is one other fellow I'm going to invite, and his name is José Gallegos from Pawtucket. He is the Head Grounds man who let me practice that first winter, remember him?"

"Oh, honey! I sure do. That would be wonderful if those two men could come. You take care of José and I'll take care of Mr. Johnson."

"Deal!" Justin kissed his Grandma on the cheeks and was out the door heading for the practice field and on his cell phone calling José.

For some time now, Justin had been studying the Los Angeles Dodgers coaches and specifically, their best pitcher and their 2nd and 3rd best pitchers with equal diligence in case something happened to the first pitcher and he had to face off with the 2nd and 3rd best pitchers. He instinctively knew the first two pitchers were some of the best in the leagues and he would be facing off squarely with these men in the World Series now.

Any pitcher after those, he was not worried about, because every team always saved their best pitchers for him. The other pitchers for the Dodgers were new to the Majors and he already memorized and knew what their thinking and pitching patterns were from their game videos. Their strategies were still simple and uncomplicated.

He felt honored, and even chuckled a bit at the display of fear and respect over one batter. One Sports Commentator said on the TV sports network, "Since Justin Edge as a batter, is an inveterate home run hitter, he is positively and unarguably, a superior player and juggernaut capable of defeating any opposing player one-on-one. I wouldn't want to have to face off with him as a pitcher!"

"That Batter is me…Justin Edge. Who would of though such a thing five years ago except Grandma and Bree?" He chuckled to himself at all of the clamor and commotion over him.

"Who would originate such rumors over plain ole me with talents and skills given to me only by God himself?" He mused in his usual humble mannerism, walking the field as he did often.

"Hi Grandma, how is everything?" Justin asked as he walked through the door of his beloved home.

"Honey, I just heard back from Mr. Johnson and he couldn't believe you remembered him and was inviting him to your first game of the World Series." Said Grandma.

"He is alive then. That's good news so far."

"He is and he's delighted to be accepting your generous and thoughtful offer. He said he had the biggest smile on his face reading my letter, and didn't think he had ever smiled like that in his entire life! Doesn't that just make you feel so good inside? It sure did to me when I read his letter."

"Yes, Grandma, it makes me feel extremely good to be able to give back to this man. My fellow José is coming with his wife. I'm so excited they can all make it." Justin was truly happy to be able to do this.

"Grandma, will you call my travel agent and make all the travel and hotel arrangements for Mr. Johnson and the Gonzales'? I especially want to give Willie a royal treatment. First class round trip air tickets, transportation to and from both his home in Alabama to the airport, and from the airport to his hotel in Boston Pick one of the best hotels in Boston with full limousine service at his disposal, food tab, and some spending cash in an envelope waiting in his hotel room for him." Justin was beaming at the thought of doing something so nice and memorable for Willie. As for José and his wife, Mr. Duncan already has him coming. He told me Mr. Duncan said it was for the special favor he did for me a long time ago."

"My goodness, Mr. Duncan remembers everything too." Said a very surprised Grandma.

"Indeed he does, Grandma. He's a very special man. I'm going to spend some time with Bradley before dinner."

"Oh that will be so fun and wonderful. I'll take good care of everything. Don't worry about any of it. Will you be able to see him once, while he is here so I can let him know? He sent his phone number too. I'll ask the travel agent to call him and explain all the details because I'm no good at all that stuff. Just shopping now!" They both laughed at Grandma's sense of humor.

"Sure, that would be great, and yes, I'll invite him to the players room, before the game for a brief visit. Please tell him I apologize in advance, but my time is not my own right now. Tell him one more thing please Grandma."

"Sure, honey what?"

"Tell him I never forgot anything."

"I will my boy, I will. You are a wonderfully made young man and so kind. I love you and I'm so proud of you."

Chapter 53

Justin went to the film room and began playing the videos he had watched during the playoffs, to see if he had missed anything regarding the Dodgers coaches, pitchers, catchers, and other players. He was a perfectionist and this was to his benefit. He was well prepared, but his greatest attribute was that he never stopped over thinking and analyzing his opponents.

Justin studied the entire Dodger team, Coaches and management. He studied their play style. He researched to see if each team member had a particular buddy, or system they personally played. He watched to see how well they played together as a team. He had a photographic memory and retained it all, stored it away for a later use and was feeling better and better about the World Series, the epitome of evolvement and achievement. To bring home the Commissioners Trophy had been one of Grandma's demands. Justin laughed to himself as he thought of that feisty little woman and how she usually got what she wanted when he had it in his power to do such. It pleased him greatly and he smiled.

This was how he spent his evenings after the day's practices, before the World Series. Sometimes another teammate would come in and watch the videos with him for their own personal information and they would have discussions. Hours were poured into this project. He wanted to know their coach's style and their personal traits, because the traits always rub off on their players, by force, or by osmosis, sometimes unnoticed to the untrained eye.

Justin's eyes raced to watch all the details of each pitcher. He was never dissatisfied with his assessments of the plays or the players.

He had learned their body traits, such as flinching muscles, what veins were protruding before a crucial moment, as all players do. Eyes darting to the left or right side before another particular play, or, a fake out coming on, like an out of bounds pitch intended to walk him. He was used to this play and he despised it. It kept him from utilizing his God given abilities and what a waste to walk someone like himself. He considered it a terrible waste of a pitcher's talents as well, to not exert himself. He believed they should at least, give it their all to try and strike out a player like him. To Justin, that was the worse of baseball crimes for a top-notch professional pitcher. Oh well, I'll worry about that part when it happens. He knew full well it would because it always happened in crucial plays.

"Just being prepared for everything." He knew he was talking out loud to himself and smiled. It just always made more of an impact when he verbalized it.

Justin was confident and felt strongly that he had memorized all facets and details pertaining to the pitchers. Any traits, qualities, or changes that were telling and/or revealing of every pitching movement was detailed in his mind. All of these great pitchers would be facing him in every one of the games in this race for the World Series victory.

"I'm ready. Come and try to get me." He said out loud again.

He stretched, did some leg lunges and continued his thoughts about the pitchers. He could never just sit and think, He was a multi tasking kind of energetic player.

The pitchers for the Los Angeles Dodgers were great pitchers and he could like them, after the Red Sox grasped the World Series Championship they so yearned for.

There was no time for chitchat, friendships or unfocused thinking right now. He came to defeat them, not to make friends with them.

Never before had he seen or been part of such a huge ordeal as the World Series. There were microphones being shoved in his face at every turn. Fans knew him as if they were best of friends. The media were everywhere. They were on top of the players like flies to fly paper. The spirit and spunk in the air was the fun part. It was full of verve and vigor as never before felt. Justin liked all of it, except being isolated from Bradley, Grandma and Nathan. It had to be for now, and for a very good reason. The players wanted to win the World Series, and whatever it took, they were committed to giving.

"Ok, time to go out to the field and get ready for the game." Announced Coach Bricket over the intercom in the breakfast room. The team had a great early morning warm-up for a few hours and will do a light one again for a couple of hours before the game just to stay limber and mentally into the game.

"It's Showtime Gang!" Justin said to them as they walked through the tunnel and out onto the field. "Hip, Hip, Hurray!" Said most of them who had heard him say it. "You bet it is guys, and it's our night."

Justin felt the prophetic feeling deep down inside of him and his body began to start pumping adrenaline out a little bit at a time. It seemed to get him kick-started and primed for every big night's event. This was his normal beginning of every game only this particular game needed some extra energy. He knew he had it in him because he was the master of his body and it's functions. He was fashioned and created for all of this, Grandma had told him so.

Chapter 54

First Game of The World Series

"Hello Baseball fans across the nation. Tom Hathaway and Mike Brooks here as your announcers for the 'First' game of the World Series."

"Yes Tom, and what a match-up of teams we have for this World Series. I do believe it's one of the best two teams to meet for the Championship out of all the match ups that could have been. I don't say that every year, and I'm backing that statement up by the numbers of people that are showing up in groves in traditional fan wear, per team. It is promising to be a very exciting and a very competitive series."

"Exactly what the fans love, Mike. Stiff competition brings a lot of emotions into the ballpark. Every year it's a whole new ball game for the World Series. You may think you know your team, but the World Series has a special éclat. That's what makes the World Series. Championship so darn fun, and entertaining." Said Tom.

Tom Hathaway now began giving the background of how both teams arrived here in the World Series games.

"At the end of the regular season, three divisional winners, ranked 2,3, and each according to their perspective win loss records, and the wild card team, ranking in 4th place and now makes it four teams competing, go through a process of elimination, to determine who wins the traditional, permanent pennant to fly over their stadium. It is well known, the oldest field in Baseball, the Boston's Fenway Park, has the most red and white pennants flying over their stadium than any other team. They've added five in the last five years straight." Mike added, that's the most historic Baseball field in America folks."

"Yes it certainly is Mike. And from that point, each league, the American, and the National League, has one team from each league who emerges to meet each other for a best-of-seven series to see who will be the new National Champion in the World Series. The home team advantage is predetermined in an All Start game several months before the end of the season. A controversial system to this day, but that's how it's been done and is still done for now.

"The American League's winner is the Boston Red Sox. They are going to face off with the winner of the National League's champion, the Los Angeles Dodgers.

They will compete for the Grand Finale, the Crème de la crème of all baseball Championships…the World Series beginning right here in Boston's Fenway Park, Stadium." He said, in a low, slow, but modulated voice.

Tom was a superior announcer, so full of vocal inflections at just the right time.

He was also excellent in reciting the history and details of baseball. He knew every player and their number, what year they played and for who. He could recite years and dates when something took place as easily as an adult could recite the alphabet. It was indelibly ingrained in his computerized mind. It was no wonder he was the World Series Announcer for so many years.

"In the World Series a pitcher is a mighty important part of the road to the Championships. Said Mike Brooks. "I think that speaks volumes for the pitchers in both ball clubs."

"Indeed it does Mike. And the fans are in for a real treat with tonight's pitchers who are both vying for the winning game tonight." Said Tom with a festive voice, to liven up the pre-show talk points.

"The Lead off pitcher tonight for the Los Angeles Dodgers will be Manning Princeton, a four-year veteran with the Dodgers. As is traditional for the Dodgers they keep one pitcher in until about the 8th or 9th inning before they bring in another relief pitcher. It all depends how the game is faring with that team. They bring in a relief pitcher due to a huge lead, or they bring in a relief pitcher to give the lead off pitcher a reprieve. Tonight it will be Wilbert Lincoln."

A Perfect Match

"Tonight's lead off pitcher for the Boston Red Sox will be Willie "The Locomotive" Steamalik. The new pitcher brought in this year from Atlanta, and has been a riveting force to reckon with, obviously, they're here in the World Series championship playoffs. I love the sound of that mans powerful nickname already.

His relief pitcher tonight, will be the former lead pitcher, Raymond Erskine. Erskine still in his prime, has been a proven and dominating force leading the Red Sox to this championship. The last five years have been kind to him with a tremendous amount of power in that pitching arm he has. The Red Sox, and the Dodgers, have accumulated a magnificent pitching team.

What an all-star line up we have for the first game, no matter how you look at it. This will be a "fireworks" show of power from the pitchers mound tonight, Mike!"

"I think the Red Sox are hoping to jump out of the starting gate with a bang, and no one can do it better than the guy with all the steam power." He said with a little laugh.

"You've got that right Tom," said Brooks. "No doubt the Dodgers are hoping to do the same thing only better than the Red Sox tonight. Both teams look like Rottweiler's. Look at the energy bustling about the dugouts and in the pitchers box. It's all a matter of time now folks."

The two teams are standing ready on the baselines for the National Anthem. We will be listening to the National Anthem being sung by the Marine Corp band and choir." Announced Tom Hathaway.

America was ready for the games to begin.

After the clapping and cheering died down, the President of the United States, threw out the first pitch as was tradition ever since William Howard Taft threw the first ball in Washington, D.C.'s Griffith Stadium in 1910.

The greatest baseball announcers of all time, Vin Scully gave the announcement to "Play Ball." His retirement came after giving 65 years of announcing baseball games.

"That was the voice of "Vin Scully," ladies and gentlemen, boys and girls! This is one of Baseball's finest moments to hear one of the most famous national icons that ever graced the broadcast booth. Baseball fans of America heard about the games of times past, play-by-play and blow-by-blow from this man's voice. We are most privileged to have him here tonight. Thank you Mr. Scully." Tom Hathaway grew up listening to Vin Scully and here he is in his place now.

"The Dodgers have won the coin toss and are up to bat first." Tom and Mike dictated the games every move and maneuver so the fans listening felt as if they were there in person."

"The Dodgers have been unable to get to a single base hit here in the first inning." Denoted Tom Hathaway.

Boston Red Sox Second baseman, Bobby McFinch, sprang his thumb by catching a fly ball in the 2nd inning of the game. The coaches wanted him to be taken out of the game and sent to the hospital for x-rays. They needed to know if it was broken or not. They were taking no chances on one single player through this championship.

Destiny was still on their side. McFinch's thumb was just severely sprung. Nothing a splint, a tight bandage, and a couple of ibuprofen couldn't help. Oh yes, a great baseball glove too.

As expected, McFinch was still extremely upset to be taken out of the game because it had just begun. "I'll be back in a few minutes." McFinch said as he was being walked out of the baseball field with the team medic.

The same fly ball that had inflicted McFinch's, 'fluke injury' was thrown into the pitcher who threw it to the catcher. The catcher, Buddy Montaño, threw it while acting as if it were a hot potato into the crowd as a joke that he didn't want it around. Everyone laughed at his antics. The young man with a baseball glove on the 5th row back, who caught the ball, didn't feel it was one bit unlucky! He was happier than a pig in mud with his new trophy.

"The home fans are loving these Red Sox players, Mike. They are loaded with talent and personality. Nothing like interacting with the crowd to please the fans."

"These guys are acting like they are already winners. Well actually, they are. They defeated quite a few teams in a very long season to be here, and that in itself is a conquest of great magnitude. Personally speaking, I think they're feeling the same way this evening. They look like they are loose and upbeat with a mighty show of confidence. This trait alone, has a great deal to do with being a super power. They know their talents, it shows in everything they do, Tom."

A Perfect Match

"Indeed they do, Mike."

"Tom, if you look over at the Dodgers, they are looking mighty fierce. They are all in a huddle with their coaches probably discussing individual strategies and signals." Mike Brooks was pretty observant and usually right on target in his summations.

Bobby McFinch was listening to the game on the radio in the hospital, as the staff and Doctor on call conducted their routine exams and x-rays. They were listening to the game with him, play-by-play with the announcers.

The Doctor on staff felt Bobby's intense disappointment and began to try to cheer him up just in case the finger was broken, with a story his Dad had told him when he broke a finger playing baseball in Junior High School.

"You know, my Dad told me a story about a baseball player by the name of Clem Labine. He was with the Brooklyn Dodgers. Known throughout the baseball world as a pitcher who could throw one of the best and meanest curves in the game. When Clem was a young boy, in Lincoln, Rhode Island, he broke his index finger on his right hand. Set incorrectly, it healed with a permanent crook. Clem thought at first this would end his dream of a baseball career, but he kept practicing throwing, and his crooked finger helped him develop the weird spin on the ball that won countless ball games for the Brooklyn Dodgers.

I don't know why this story came to my mind other than your thumb and the World Series made me think of my Dad telling me that story when I had my accident. It made me feel better just knowing other men in baseball history had their share of hard knocks and gut wrenching moments. Hope it helps you in some small way too."

"Actually, your care and story go well together. I do feel better. I want you to know, I'll thank you as I go to my position on second base in a bit and probably every night of the series, just remember that, hey Doc?" They shared a laugh.

Off he went back to the Stadium a few blocks away to resume his position in the game, but instead his relief 2nd baseman, Stanley McGuire, was staying in for now. He was doing a great job. Coach Chambers wanted his hand in perfect condition for the future games.

The whole game went smoothly and in Boston's constant favor. The outstanding Boston pitcher, Steamalik, would then strike out the next batter up if the previous batter had made a hit to first base. The Boston Red Sox won Game One, 6 to 0.

"Steamalik pitched an exceptional game tonight and no Dodger player was able to sneak a base hit out of him. Only one fly ball, caught by a Red Sox Center out fielder, Justin Edge. The entire Dodger team seemed to be in outer space instead of Fenway Park." Hathaway began the summations for his ending talk show.

Coach Chambers was proud of their performance tonight and thought the tiny flaws he saw were miniscule in comparison to the highlights. "All in all, you did a splendid job tonight." He told them in the locker room after the game.

Coach Chambers had talked with Mr. Duncan after the game and was happy to inform the team that Mr. Duncan was beyond happy. He said, "They were making his dream a reality and his life a joy." He also said, "Give me three more! Just three more! Those were his exact words." Said Coach Chambers smiling a huge smile.

The entire Red Sox team cheered and all said, "They want what Mr. Duncan wants, and just as much as he wants it."

"Ok,'" Said Coach Chambers, "Lets prepare for tomorrow night's game. A repeat is within reach with the talent we have on this team. I'm proud of you all. I'm super proud of your performance tonight. You looked like professionals all the way to the end! Have a good nights rest and let's do it again tomorrow."

Chapter 55

Game 2 Of The World Series

Game 2 of the World Series was an upset as the Boston Red Sox hit an unexpected speed bump and lost game number two, at home in the "promised land" in Fenway Park. This hurt their feelings badly and faintly demoralized their spirits.

The news buzz on television and the headlines of the newspapers read, *"Where Were The Red Sox Last Night?"*

The men conversed among themselves asking, "How much more could we have embarrassed ourselves, Mr. Duncan, and our Coaches? The men were mindlessly sitting and trying to regroup in the airport waiting room awaiting their flight to Los Angeles.

The biggest news written that really got under their skin came from the LA Times newspaper. "Justin Edge was the only player able to get a hit, get on base and steal 2nd base, but with no other help or reward. No homeruns on the board. It was a huge disappointment and very uneventful for the team and the fans of Boston. The fans and the ball player's thought the game would never end as they kept looking at the same score on the oversized, Green Monster that read; Home 0, Visitor 2. The only bright side was the beer, food and sports item sales. They went through the roof, and the vendors and they were at least happy." Morton Herman, the LA Times sports writer.

"The writer of this story is a prick." Said 3rd string pitcher, Bo Blythe. "We all worked our butt's off to win this game, but the Dodgers wouldn't go down! Herman could have written it with more class and less bias!"

The meeting in the locker room last night after the game, was so brief, the men were shocked. Coach Chambers was disappointed, upset and tired. He had given it his all during the game as he knew he had to in order to keep the guys moving, the coaches in peak attention and all to end in a dismal loss.

"I just want to go home and go to bed. I figure tomorrow will be a new day. I expect to see a whole new game in Los Angeles. Good night men." Were his only words.

The men all said good night and left their separate ways hoping they could go to sleep tonight. It would be a very long flight tomorrow. What would the newspapers be writing tonight? What would their fans be thinking of them? What would the management be feeling at this point? Everyone had been let down and the guys were as remorseful as they could humanly be.

"Shake it off, guys." Came Justin's voice through the executive waiting area of the airport as he walked briskly up to them. Los Angeles is coming up and we need to refocus our attention to that field and the upcoming games. Last night is past history now, and we are not going to repeat it." Justin knew they had to shift gears and go forward. What was done was done.

"We have to figure out who did what wrong and who was not there to cover or help when needed. We need to think about what we individually did to a lesser degree. We have enough flight time to figure things out and let's do it guys!" Justin immediately walked over and grabbed a couple of yogurts and an orange to eat while they waited a few more minutes before boarding the plane. This set their thinking into a different zone and helped to deflect the down feelings they had. Figuring things out was their specialty.

"Game 3, is the first game in Los Angeles that's coming up tomorrow night and Coach Chambers isn't even in the waiting room this morning. The other coaches all are." Stated a surprised Bo Blythe.

The assistant coaches told the guys, "We will have a meeting on the plane today during the flight to Los Angeles. Coach Chambers was too upset last night to talk and he respects you guys too much to talk like he felt last night. That statement spoke volumes!"

The guys felt even worse now. They began to talk among themselves in low tones, strategizing about what went wrong last night and how to counter attack it. They boarded the plane and continued their analyzing procedures.

Ray Erskine was the first to lead off. "Guys, we silenced a 47,000 plus crowd last night during the first round, in our own home stadium and in front of our own home town fans. That was the result of our pitiful playing. We clumsily lost our focus after the first home run in the first inning from their first baseman. We shoved our heads up our butts and freaked out because they went ahead of us. Absolutely unacceptable performance, from World Series championship contenders. We are NOT pretenders, we ARE contenders!"

Erskine was finished so Justin began next. "It has taken us five long hard fought years, to get to this point, and we must stay strong. Let's follow our strategy routine that got us here. Keep watching each other out there. Look for signs from Steamalik, Erskine, Montaño or me, and see what we are saying about a pitcher or a batter with our hand signals. We have some insights the coaches don't have because we are closer to them. Don't tell them I said that or I'll kill you, or they'll kill me first!"

No one was laughing because they knew these guys were serious and essentially the leaders of the team outside of the Coaches and Management.

Coach Chambers, ironically, said close to the same thing on the plane to Los Angeles as Steamalik, Montaño and Justin had said in the waiting room for the flight, but with some additional off of the normal strategy on tonight's game, regarding the coaches, pitchers, fielders, etc.

The plane touched down five and a half hours later and the guys were off to the field in the busses waiting for them. First, they would grab a bite to eat, and then practice for a while. They needed to get a feel of the Dodger Stadium at 1000 Elysian Park Ave, Los Angeles, CA 90012. They would get some practice workouts in and do some personal training to be prepared for the next days game.

"Dodger Stadium is the third oldest baseball park in Major League History," Coach Chambers explained to them on the flight, mostly for the new team player's benefit. Dodger stadium had an aura about it the guys needed to be aware of, and overcome. In the same way the Dodger's had overcome the fear of Fenway Park and it's overwhelming history.

"There will be a short team meeting tonight in the hotel meeting room, and then I expect you to get a good nights rest for a better game tomorrow evening. Everyone on the same page with me here?" Everyone agreed of course.

The men had new and energized, expectations for a great game, as they filed into the stadium. The fans filled the seats and walkways with the same eagerness for the game to start. The grass area was full and the fans spirits were high for the Dodgers. That was to be expected since the Red Sox were on the Dodgers home turf tonight…and it was quite evident.

Tom Hathaway and Mike Brooks were their usual jovial selves while announcing their pre-game show. It was their job to stay enthusiastic and full of ample energy to keep the fans interested and make the games fun for the listeners on television and radio. They would be announcing in Los Angeles, California for three nights so they needed to continue to be professional, neutral and remain known as the masters of hyperbole. These two announcers were masters at their trade, so that would be no problem for them.

Hathaway and Brooks always had a large listening audience for their pre-game and post-game talk shows. Their interviewers on the field were always trying to get the Coaches and some of the players in front of a camera when they could get to them.

"Tom, the Boston pitchers are doing a great job of striking out the Dodger batters as they come up to bat. There is no denying this impressive feature of the Red Sox Team."

"I see that too Mike, but what is happening when the Red Sox come up to bat? They are completely out of sync and look like a different team when they are the at bat team, for some reason tonight. What is the deal?" Asked Mike of Tom as they usually conversed this way during a game.

"In spite of this Red Sox major flaw, they have still been able to stop a possible runaway game with the Dodgers who are operating like a well oiled machine, especially when they're in the outfield. It makes no sense to me either Mike." Said a confused Tom Hathaway.

"As I see it, Tom, the Red Sox were able to hold and stop the Dodgers, but not enough to dig them out of the hole they are in and on to a victory tonight. This was a close game and even came close to being exciting a couple of times. However, no runaway scoring and no big action highlights to speak of other than, Boston has lost 4-2, to the Los Angeles Dodgers on their first night in Dodger Stadium. This has to be humiliating and ultra disappointing as a team."

"Yes, it is definitely a Dodger victory tonight Mike."

"Well fans, we never know what the World Series games will bring us, but we do know, it's never the same thing. "Mike Brooks and Tom Hathaway here and we are signing off for the evening. We now turn you over to the interviewers on the field and let's see if we can get some answers from the Red Sox about tonight's loss. I'm sure they are a very disappointed team right now. We'll also be talking to the players and coaches of the Dodgers who are hoping to cap this series off with a sweep. It may be a bit premature thinking, but at least they are thinking positive!" Mike and Tom chuckled just a bit.

"Hathaway and Brooks here saying good night, and we will see you tomorrow evening. We will be here in Dodger Stadium for two more nights and that means the fans from out of town can enjoy some beach and sun time, eating and some great shopping as well as sightseeing! Good night everyone."

All the Red Sox coaches, except Chambers were meeting together privately, and were discussing why the players just couldn't seem to get their momentum together.

Coach Bricket began with his thoughts first.

"They lost to the Dodgers twice now and on the Dodgers home turf, 4-2. The men seem to feel desperate and are losing their self-confidence to win this series, or worse yet, pull it out. It seems as if the men are becoming more and more silent and are losing focus. They drop balls. The balls are slipping through their gloves, and through their legs. They have bumped into each other on fly balls a couple of times and embarrassed themselves. They are becoming a bumbled mess we don't recognize. These are little league mistakes."

Third Base Coach, Curtis Baker said, "The only runs in, that counted on the scoreboard, were because Mark Louden, made a good connecting hit that enabled him to get to 3rd base and Justin batted them both in with a home run. That was about the complete summation of a very long embarrassing game we all wanted out of as badly as anyone did."

After their microphones were turned off and their work was done on the set, Tom Hathaway asked Mike Brooks, "What do you think of the Red Sox at this point?"

Mike said without a hesitation, "I think they are stinking up the place, and are an embarrassment to their fans, and management. I wish I knew what their problem was. I hope to high heaven this changes tomorrow night. This World Series might end soon and that cuts a lot of revenue out for all involved. The money is made in the full seven games. Put that aside, and it boils down to, why don't they have the fire in the belly to win? Why are they messing up so badly? What is missing here? We need them on a full team press to build the excitement up. It's a bear doing all the work by ourselves up here!" Brooks seemed a little more than miffed tonight.

"Well said, my friend. I agree with you on everything. I hate to see them go down in defeat so quickly. I too struggle to keep the game alive for the fans. I guess the Dodgers are the more advanced professionals again and the Red Sox will just have to wait for another day. Perhaps they are overwhelmed to be in the World Series. This team has never come close to this. The Dodgers have." Tom shook his head as if in disbelief. The two men walked down the steps in silence to their transportation waiting for them to take them to their hotel.

Meanwhile as the Red Sox were heading for the after game meeting a few of the players were talking as they walked to the meeting room. One of them said, "Tomorrow night's Los Angeles starting pitcher is Bruce Princeton. He is tough, rude and insufferable. Their second relief pitcher, Wilbert Lincoln is just plain tough. What great things to look forward to -- the after game meeting with Coach Chambers, and then two more great pitchers from the Dodgers team tomorrow night! Disgusting." The other players just groaned. Their self-esteem had fallen so bad they were already dreading the next game.

Chambers was in the meeting room waiting for them. He did not look happy. When he began talking, they knew he wasn't happy.

"Who wants to go home?"

The men looked at each other, not fully understanding his comment.

"The performances you have been giving after the first game are down right embarrassing and far below what is expected of Red Sox professional Baseball players.

So, I ask you again, who wants to go home? Some of you definitely don't want to be here playing baseball! You are acting like sissy's out there on their home field, giving up these games half-hearted, little feeling, no determination or even a faint focus. So, I say, go home!" Chambers walked around the room looking at each player one by one.

"I am watching you," He yelled at them pointing his finger in their faces.

This was the first time Justin and a few others had ever heard Chambers raise his voice this loud in a meeting. Chills of resentment went up and down their spines. He must be tired or out of his wits, under extreme pressure in his job, something is wrong, Justin felt. This is not the coach Chambers I know. He would never scream and yell at us like this under any circumstance.

"It's not like we're doing it on purpose, coach." Said the third baseman, Mack Zimmerman. His face was red with anger and frustration. "We fought hard to get here and we are still fighting out there. You see us. Don't tell me you don't feel our pain, and don't scream at us as if we are children! Quite frankly, I want to be here and I want to win as badly as the rest of the men here, but if you want to send me home, then by god do it!" Frustration and tempers were peaking from all the strain and stress.

Chambers knew enough had been said after Zimmerman's comment and didn't want to destroy the team's ego completely.

He turned his anger over to his coaches and said, "You all had better get with it!" He then turned and walked out the meeting room.

The men sat there dumbfounded, humiliated and deeply disturbed. They knew they were letting everyone down but it certainly wasn't because they wanted to.

Willie Steamalik said to the guys still sitting there, "We have got to get ourselves together and work on our basics then work up to some real crafty handiwork. By the way, Zimmerman, Amen for standing up for what we are all working for!" The men applauded Zimmerman. He stood up for the whole team and that took a ton of guts and stamina to say what he did to the Head Coach, and not get sent home!

"Look guys, I'll apologize tomorrow for being out of line to coach Chambers. I respect him more than I do just about anyone, but I was just coming out of the heat of one of my worst battles and my big mouth let out my internal pain. If I'm in pain, I know you guys are too. We are a team! End of story." They applauded him again. "We are a team," they all said in a united affirmation.

Coach Chambers heard every bit of this discussion as he was standing outside of the room. No one knew he was there, they thought he had gone to his room. God, he loved these guys! He trotted off to his transportation to get to his hotel room and get some sleep.

Erskine and Steamalik, said they would pair up with the other pitchers for some intense practice and critiquing. The outfielders would work with each other. The Basemen would work on throwing along with eye and hand coordination, and everything else they all knew to do, but obviously, were not doing correctly, or, they would not be in this predicament they're in.

"Then, we all do batting practice!" All hands went in for a big huzzah. Tired and worn out, off to the busses and to bed they went

Chapter 56

Game 4 of World Series. 2nd night in Dodger Stadium

"Hello Fans of the Los Angeles Dodgers and fans of the Boston Red Sox and all others in between, who are tuned in tonight because you love baseball. We are certainly glad you're here with us and we will do our best to make it a most enjoyable evening for you." Said an energetic Tom Hathaway with his partner, Mike Brooks. "They had already discussed ramping up the energy on their part to keep the game as interesting as possible because the Red Sox definitely were not helping them out in this area.

"We call it as we see it and we are the one's high up in the press box with all the faxes, ear microphones and binoculars. We are the guys who have the best and quickest information at our fingertips, all for your benefit. In other words, we give it our all for you the fans.

We want to particularly thank our camera crew along with our on the field interviewers because they do a stellar job for us all. Even our sports writers are in full force to give it all to you as it unfolds as quickly and clearly as it is played."

"The people of Los Angeles and surrounding areas have shown their love of baseball and it has been wonderful to be a part of here on the West Coast. We have been showing some clips from fans in various pubs and public places across the city. The fans have gathered every night of the series to watch with other fans and are more excited with every game thinking their Dodgers are going to take the Series. Dedicated Fans, Mike!"

"Yes, and I've enjoyed seeing them myself." Said Mike.

"California Dreamin' is still alive and well."

As Usual, Tom Hathaway gave the word. "We have the Play Ball signal. Here we go fans."

The game dragged on with no score on the board up to the sixth inning. The Dodgers pitcher, Ralph Broderick, threw Justin Edge a low curve ball pitch that should have been a ball, but Justin swung at it anyway. He swung at it so hard it made the sound of a bullwhip with the bat cracking the ball out of the park. The ball sailed out over the fence and Justin had his homerun for the Red Sox. The guys were standing and waiting for him to cross home plate. Spirits were lifted.

During a station break, Tom asked Mike, "What do you think of this game so far?"

"Another quasi-drag." Said Mike to Tom as he covered his microphone.

"Yes, but are you noticing something different tonight?" Mike shook his head yes as they were back on the air. Boston had three strikeouts and one homerun. The teams have now switched sides as we enter the bottom of the 7th inning.

Tom got so excited for the first time in tonight's game he let out a quick, bellowing announcement, "Folks, the Dodger's center fielder has just hit a home run with another man on base and the score is now Dodgers 2, Red Sox 1." He looked at Mike and smiled because there was at least something to announce about. Mike laughed at him.

"We have hit the last out in the Top of the 9th inning and that's all we have for this evening. A hard fought game that was a real nail biter as it ended up. Both teams were fighting for their lives here! Two very professional and highly talented Ball Clubs dueling it out for the Championship title and both teams nearly ended with a no score. Which, would have gone into overtime. The Los Angeles Dodgers take tonight's game by one run in the 9th inning. We'll return for our post game show after a brief station break." Said Tom Hathaway.

Mike Brooks couldn't help himself it just popped out of his mouth. "How does it feel to be such a liar? This game a real 'Nail Biter'?" Both men laughed so hard they had tears in their eyes.

Hathaway said, "thanks for that laugh, this is how we keep ourselves pumped up for the announcing, you joker you!" both laughed again. "And, were back." Hathaway said quickly into his mic.

"I'll bet the two Dodger batters are heroes in the Dodger locker room tonight. The whole team are heroes again tonight on their home turf. They won this game through team effort."

"Oh, no doubt about it Mike." Tom Hathaway continued, "The top of the 9th inning was the highlight of the game by an unexpected, and quirky hit from the Dodger's catcher, Johnny Cook. A brawny man, with quick reflexes, he came up to bat at the top of the 9th and gave a stellar performance. Cook physically walloped the ball over the back wall of the field and it went into the stands and was caught by a very happy fan. This game had a very interesting ending!"

Mike Brooks asked off the cuff in wonderment, "Will our people be interviewing Cook tonight so we can hear from him how he feels about being the hero of tonight's game?

"Let's cut in with Jenny Kerns and see if she is able to get a few words from Cook. I'm curious too, Mike."

"Jenny Kern's here, Tom and Mike, and I do have Johnny Cook here with me for a few words before he heads into the locker room." Handing the mike over to Johnny, she asked him if he would share his feelings and thoughts of his performance with the people listening.

"Boston's pitcher, Erskine, gave me a fastball pitch that broke only slightly as it came across the home plate. I just so happened to smack it in the right place at the right time and saved the night from going into a loss, or overtime. It was really a great feeling for me to keep my team on top in this series. I felt the bat hit the ball with strength, and I knew I had at least a two, maybe a three base hit out of it, but when I saw the ball take to the stands like a bird in flight, I went crazy inside. The rush a player feels when he knows he's done something like this is amazing. Tonight, was a very lucky night and I'm so happy to be a contributor for my team to win this game tonight."

"Thank you Johnny Cook for your time and words. Congratulations and best of luck tomorrow night which could very well be the last night of the series." Jenny was thinking presumptuously. "Signing off for the night, this is Jenny Kerns. Back to you guys now, Tom and Mike."

"There you have it folks, comments from a very happy Dodger Catcher, Johnny Cook.

On the other side of the coin, Coach Chambers was pretty somber and focused. The interview time was short and sweet and to the point.

"We lost. We lost by less than the last two games, but we lost. We have to figure out what we need to do to win tomorrow night's game." Chambers was not in a mood to say much.

"Better luck to you and your team for tomorrow nights game, Coach and until then, back to the drawing board, huh?"

"For sure. We don't want to be out of the World Series tomorrow night. Tomorrow is do or die trying."

"Well put and very honest. Thanks Coach Chambers." Said a very savvy Tom Hathaway.

"Mike, if I didn't know better, I'd bet you Coach Chambers is going to bring a different ball club onto the field tomorrow night. The 'die trying' comment was the tale of the tape for me. What do you take of it?"

"I feel, he had better bring on a different team or it's going to be a really frustrating long ride home to Boston with zero wins in Los Angeles."

"Fair enough my friend. Honestly stated." Replied Tom.

"Having said that, I'll say this now…join us tomorrow night for Game 5 of the World Series, the last game here in Los Angeles

Signing off and we'll see you tomorrow night for the determining game if we are done, or if we go to Boston. Good night everyone."

Tom was more than relieved this game was history now. He actually felt sorry for the Red Sox humiliating themselves like they were and knowing they were better than this. He had really hoped and expected a very competitive World Series between these two teams. It just didn't look like it was in the cards at this point. He hoped he was wrong, being the eternal optimist that he was.

The dreaded team meeting after the game was not at all what the players were expecting thanks to Justin and the two pitchers - Steamalik and Erskine. They had already ran to the front of the room and began their speeches as Coach Chambers came huffing and puffing late into the meeting room due to his interview. The men had immediately begun taking over the meeting by talking as fast as each was able in their own turn. No hesitation between the three who were talking in case Coach tried to yell at them again and take their steam out. Even if he tried, they were prepared to keep the talking going. What the heck, it was the last chance they had to make a difference. They were determined tonight, to keep that from happening!

"Guys! Did you see firsthand how we held them back tonight? This is what we were working on today in our strategies and workouts." Said a hyped Justin. We knew what their plays were before they knew them. We stopped them! We just didn't stop the last 'grand-stand' hit, which was a fluke, and the catcher said so himself in so many words.

Coach Chambers was both shocked and impressed with the start of the meeting without him, not to mention the control and leadership these men were displaying all without him.

"We can do this! Tomorrow is the night we win." Said Erskine. "We are going to turn the tide of events. The pendulum is going to swing the opposite direction tomorrow night.

Steamalik was so hyped he chimed in with the instructions, "We are going to do the same tactics, strategies and practices we did today, only with more determination and focus tomorrow. Everyone got it?"

Everyone stood and high fived each other and the noise level was deafening with the sound of determination, cheering and jazzing each other up.

Coach Chambers looked at all of them half smiled, shook his head and turned around to begin walking to his awaiting car. He was thinking to himself, I have never in my career had a team take over one of my meetings. I would have never allowed it, but this team is different. This is definitely a first. What a fine display of take-charge leaders those guys were tonight. The team was intently listening to their fellow teammates as their leaders. How could he be angry with them for pumping each other up after the dismal failures they have suffered so severely this series. He chuckled to himself. He couldn't wait for tomorrow night's game after this infamous, courageous and impromptu talk tonight in his meeting room, with his team. He shook his head and smiled. "Unbelievable." He said to himself.

Chapter 57

After Game 4 of the World Series, and the 2nd game in Los Angeles, the L.A. newspaper headlines read:

"Another day. Another loss."

"Essentially, the game was not worth mentioning." The subtitles read on the newspapers about last night's game. "The 2nd game in Los Angeles playing the series of series and the Red Sox are dirty sox already."

The Boston Red Sox lost 2 to 1 and the only run in was a fluke homerun by Justin Edge due to an underpowered ball from the Dodger pitcher, Ralph Broderick who was pitching with a tired arm. Edge must be the only one of the Red Sox players who showed up for the game last night. When the guys read that article, they were devastated and embarrassed for themselves, and everybody they represented. They were angry with the writer for irresponsible journalism and wanted to break his computer over his head for lying about Broderick's tired arm.

The Newspaper Headlines across the city of Los Angeles stunk, as did their treatment of the Red Sox team as a whole.

"Boston Implodes in Game 4."

Said another newspaper headline. The brilliant television analysts and over thinkers were so down on the Red Sox team as a whole. The guys had to make a pact to not listen or read the negative stuff anymore, but instead, gather together and regenerate as they had the day before. "More tenacity today," they all yelled, clapped, jumped in the air belly shoving each other and genuinely pumping each other up.

"Those ungrateful, scumbag journalists. We let them on the field, talk to their worthless hides and this is the gratitude we get? Qué lastima!" Said Boston catcher, Buddy Montaño. He was the best catcher in the league by anybody's standards.

A Perfect Match

"Big deal, we had the home field advantage. What good did it do for us in Boston?" Groused, Boston catcher, Buddy Montaño.

"Here we are in Los Angeles, California and now the Dodgers have the home field advantage. They cleaned our clocks three times already. They called our sox dirty too! I'm so angry over that unnecessary slap in the face. Imagine what Mr. Duncan thinks. We don't change our socks." He had the men smiling at his lack of understanding the pun of the writers euphemism.

"I realize that is not unusual for World Series games, but I wanted to win both games at home, and then win at least one or two games here in LA! I know I sound like an irritating scratched record, but my mom called me this morning and chewed me out for loosing and I'm feeling really grumpy. I can't back talk her or she would come out here and kick my butt. More than it's been kicked already."

Montaño's personality was the type that even when he was as serious as he could be, he was funny. The men enjoyed a quick laugh during a very stressful situation.

Justin spoke to the players and the assistant coaches as they arrived to the Dodger Stadium practice fields. "Guys we have to get over this weird and abnormal feeling of being losers because we are not losers. We wouldn't be here if we were losers." Everyone agreed completely. Justin again, made sense of things, and he usually made everyone feel better too! He was their guiding light most of the time.

"You are so right man. This has got to end right now!" Said an easily energized Buddy Montaño.

Everyone else fell into step heartily agreeing that it ended right now. "Ok, everyone back to their personal locations on the field, and carry your deepest, most elevated concentration efforts with you." Justin was more determined and intense this morning and it was catching on fast. The scattering began and they didn't walk, they ran this time. Same strategy as yesterday guys, he yelled back once more as he was running outfield.

That very night, before going to bed, Justin decided to watch the recent Dodger game films of the games they had played in this series.

"Strictly business, and everything personal." Justin said after he was finished with the very last of the videos and putting them away in their proper jacket covers.

"There's no room for being over confident or over anxious, but Justin now knew every player and coach on the Dodger team like an open book. He would share their quirks to look for with the other teammates tomorrow." He headed to his bed so he could get some sleep before an early rise for practice. Fielding practice usually started anywhere from 5 to 8 hours before game time. The teams had to be there anyway, so might as well make the best use of time. Justin would have the guys walk the field and bases, dugouts and bleachers with him again, because he wanted them to feel like they owned the place!

He gently slid into bed. "It was always good to go to bed with a smile on your face, so you would wake up with a smile on your face. It makes everything better. Let's see if it works as Grandma says." Justin mumbled to himself while drifting off to sleep.

Chapter 58

Game 5 of World Series, 3rd night at Dodger Stadium

Game time came and the place was abuzz as usual with reporters, analysts, media and TV crews all setting up and conducting their testing of various equipment. He chose to stay away from them and focus on his game plan. He didn't really feel like being around people right now other than his teammates, and focusing on tonight's game. "It is this important to not lose my focus by any one or any thing."

Game time was coming soon, so Tom and Mike were busy giving the last four series games statistics and pre-game talk as usual.

"Hello loyal fans, Tom Hathaway again with my colleague and partner Mike Brooks. We are hoping for a very high energy and entertaining game tonight as we always do with both teams fighting it out for the championship title."

"If the Dodgers win, the Series is over. If they lose, the games shifts to Boston with a day in between for travel. Mike, I love World Series baseball games in a different way, and I'm not quite ready for these games to end are you? I do apologize in advance to you die-hard Dodger fans who want to clench the title and have it over and done with!" Tom said in a courteous 'after' comment.

Both announcers agreed and laughed about how much they loved these games. "The tension is high folks. Both teams are looking good, and we know you all are ready rock and roll. These two tremendously matched teams are locking horns and going for the sweet feeling of victory. The stress and expectations have to be off the charts right now."

"Okay Folks, there was our Play ball signal. And We're off!" Said Tom it as if he were announcing horse racing.

"It's going to be a barn burner tonight Mike, I feel it in these old bones of mine. I just hope it's not the flu I'm feeling!"

"Oh my gosh! What a thing to say as I sit right next to you. You contagious, antique!" Both men laughed and were ready to announce the game as they saw it unfold.

"The Boston Red Sox are having a tough series and they are hoping for a change of events tonight, as their Head Coach Chambers was telling our staff earlier today from the practice field. They have been up early and working in the war room as they call it. They have been out on the field for their regular workouts and as an extra addition to their normal routine, they are inner team practicing and "tweaking" as they call it." Said Tom.

Mike Brooks inserted, "These men are professional ball players and they take it very serious. They can take being defeated, just not in succession like this – when their hearts and eyes were set on the trophy."

"I can relate to that comment." Tom said earnestly. "It's hard in any situation to feel like you're letting others down, especially when it is expected of you to do better. No denying how close they were to it either." Yep, that's what hurts," agreed Mike.

Tom announced, "We have a Play Ball signal now folks. Here we go – 'Game 5' in Los Angeles."

"One-by-one, the Boston pitchers have struck out the Dodger batters as they come up to bat. When the ball has been hit, they have all been air balls and caught by one of the ball players. This saves the pitchers arm and makes us realize their luck isn't so magnified tonight, Tom."

Mike offered a logical explanation, "Looks like the pendulum may be swinging the other way for the law of averages to be in effect. I believe in that ya know? It's nature and it's natural." Mike was talking with his shoulders up to his neck and his hands out.

"You know Mike, I must say, I do too." Tom said as he looked over his shoulder to Mike.

"It is incredulous, and normal, if that makes any sense, that we have no score on the board yet, and it is the bottom of the fifth inning. This is not that strange that neither team has a run in at this point of the game. It has been the normal for a few past games due to the talent on both teams."

"Folks," Tom Hathaway said meticulously.

"This game has been a challenge of the wits and the physical abilities of two extremely talented teams. It has been so tight the Red Sox had to squeak by to get that last batter on base. Pitcher Bo Blythe managed to swing and make contact sending the ball out to left field and making it to 2nd base. He was a little more than just lucky. He hit a grounder that went through the legs of the Short Stop but was stopped by the left out fielder and he quickly threw it in but not before Blyth made it to 2nd base. He's a speed demon tonight. He ran like a road runner in the open prairie."

Mike broke in. "The Red Sox seem to be giving it more power and prowess than they had the last three nights. Maybe I'm saying that because they are the first to score tonight, but that's the way I'm seeing it from up here."

"Justin Edge is up to bat and he has three fouls and 1 strike so far. The next pitch is a fast curve that looked low and out to me but it didn't seem to matter to him because it's going over the back wall right now. Edge is doing his curtain call trot around the bases. He is a very happy ball player tonight, being met by a very happy team at the Red Sox dugout. One or two homeruns can mean a game win with these two teams."

"The score is Boston 2 and the Dodgers 0. The way these two teams have been scoring low this series, this might be the final score, Mike."

"Right you are, Tom. I've seen enough of this match-up to know, it's anyone's game."

"The Boston Red Sox are blowing the covers off of the balls being pitched to them." Said a mystified but relieved Tom Hathaway. "It feels great to have some activity to report," he said to Mike as he covered his microphone. He rolled his eyes and blew his breath out for relief.

Earlier in the day Justin instructed and explained to the whole team and the coaches how to effectively defeat the Dodgers from what he had gleaned from the game films he had watched. "Here is what to look for in these pitchers."

He physically showed them each pitcher's traits, movements, anything and everything he recalled from the videos he spent half the night watching.

"These are the telling features and body movements as to the pitch the guys would be receiving 95% of the time. If it gives you one second to adjust, it's worth it. The rest is up to your professional abilities to hit the balls and hit them with all your might. Not an easy feat I know, but just do it any way!" He said seriously.

"You basemen will do these things with the Dodger's basemen regarding the runners." He had diagrams in hand and verbalized his information to expedite the passage of information for his teammates' sake. Use your gut feeling with your wits tonight. Our future depends on each other, guys." Every man knew what he had to do. Every man was intent and all ears when Justin explained everything he observed. They knew he was the king of awareness. They didn't have his extra quick eye for the fastballs, but they each swore, they were going to give it everything they had tonight to save their quest for the championship and their pride! The next thing they had to do was stop the Dodger's when they were up to bat.

"Stay alert in case they get a hit." Justin said. However, the Red Sox pitchers each said they could hold the Dodgers to a minimum, no matter who was pitching. The Coaches and the men were one in thought from this moment in time, forward. They were focused on winning this game tonight. So far, all of Justin's strategies and information the guys heard earlier, were working!

The Red Sox players were getting on base and making it to home plate. When Justin came up to bat, it was just the way they all liked it – bases loaded. They needed a homerun because the Dodgers were on their heels and the score was lingering at Dodgers 3, Red Sox 4 on the scoreboard. It was in Boston's favor tonight. This was the highest the score had been the entire series.

Justin did his deed. He blew out a homerun clear over the left fence and into the crowds. The scrambling for the ball was something to see, as packed as the seats were in Dodger Stadium. They went ahead with a score of 8 to 3. They were able to hold the Dodgers for their last at bat to no hits. The Pitchers did their duty, much to the chagrin of the Dodgers. The Red Sox with the help of the entire team and Coaches had pulled game five out with an impressive, and unexpected victory. They were headed home to Boston for Game Six. Some of the players had tears of joy in their eyes and some of the others were cheering so hard, they made themselves hoarse. Justin took it all in and cherished the win with his teammates in his silent and relieved way.

A Perfect Match

"We're going home guys!" With those words, he too, had tears of joy in his eyes.

"What a game and what a Win! The Boston Red Sox did an amazing turn around and flawlessly won tonight's game 5 in Los Angeles. The final score was 8 to 3 Red Sox win. We are on our way to Boston Folks. This Series is nowhere near over. We have two wins for Boston and three wins for the Dodgers. Wow! See you in Boston at Fenway Field. This is Tom Hathaway with my partner Mike Brooks signing off until Friday in Boston."

"Unplug me guys." Said Mike, I'm so happy I have to stand up and get the blood flowing in my legs again. I sat on the edge of my chair all night. That was a fabulous come back by Boston!"

Everyone agreed heartily, and all the people in the media box were more talkative than normal, as they began folding equipment up for the move to Boston.

Chapter 59

Early the next morning, the team was up and assembled for breakfast together. They were leaving for Boston and every man was eager and ready, coaches included.

They would hit the runway of Boston's Logan Airport, in the early afternoon, so they decided to do some light warm ups, batting, pitching and running practices for a couple of hours before leaving. Then, they would take it easy and stay in the locker room and cafeteria area inside of Fenway Park. The traffic would be a non-negotiable, bumper-to-bumper affair for the next two days as cars filed into the parking lots and parking areas that were charging an exorbitant fee to park for the evening of the game. It was nothing unusual for Boston. What made it more amusing was how quickly the people adapted to the frenzy as being normal and exciting. It was required the players all stay at Fenway tonight for the game tomorrow, and stay together. No media, or newspaper people inside to screw things up today.

Security was setting up monitors. The police were using the police dogs to sweep every inch of the stadium for any possible bombs, drugs, or anything else unusual for tonight's game. Tables were set up to inspect bags, and lockers were set up for larger items. Nothing out of the ordinary would be allowed in. Extreme caution. This was Boston Red Sox territory and they expected a winning team to be returning to them.

Delivery trucks were parked bumper to bumper waiting for their turn to unload, beer, hot dogs, beverages, peanuts, ice cream, bathroom cleaners, you name it, and it was going on.

Justin was entranced and amazed over the hustle and bustle of the day's games whether he was in Boston, or in Los Angeles. He shook his head, smiled and went back to softly working out for the big game tonight.

He was especially happy to be home and would be able to talk to his son and Grandma more easily. They would be at the game tomorrow night instead of watching it on TV. Everything felt great. He knew he would have a great night's sleep in Boston where his home and his family were.

The next morning Coach Bricket announced, "Coach Chambers would like to say a few words before we go out for tonight's game, men." They assembled in the meeting room.

"Men, we have come a long way from the start of the season and I wanted to thank you for all of your hard work. Your commitment to be the best of the best has been nothing short of astounding. We have had fair share of "downers" in these championship games, but you men fought hard, and brought us back here. I believe in you with all my heart. I believe without a doubt, you will all go down in history as one of the greatest teams in Boston Red Sox history. I thank the coaches. You men have shown them respect, and in return they have given their respect to you. That is a beautiful thing to see.

I have a good feeling about tonight's game, and I have butterflies in my stomach from being excited. I don't have a crystal ball to tell me what will happen, but I think it's going to be fantastic. We are all so darned proud of you, and we won't be one bit shocked when you win tonight and tomorrow night and bring home the Commissioner's Trophy!" Everyone erupted into shouts of cheering and joyful noises of all kinds.

"We've had a fabulous year, let's end it fabulous. Now, Mr. Duncan is giving you a surprise visit and wants to say a few words."

"Hey, alright! Yeah!" The men were so happy to have their owner with them.

Mr. Duncan came from behind a locker where he had been listening to the coach and the players. He stayed tucked away so they would be natural and he could enjoy the realness of the moment without intimidating them by being there.

"Fellas, you came up through the ranks the same way this old Scotsman did. By hard work, raw determination and confidence in your abilities. No one can tell me different. You're the most special team in baseball today. The Red Sox Management was informed months ago, that we were going to win this World Series this year. You remember our luncheon commitment? I do and there's no reason to change our minds now." Duncan was reminding them in case they were in a state of mental derailment or nervousness.

"You have had some pretty tough days in this past year, and particularly in some of these World Series Games. LA especially. They were trying to kill you and take it by a sweep. Somehow, you all managed each time to regroup and bring it on home. I know I was there with you. I was at every game in Los Angeles and not one time was I embarrassed of you. Not once! I want you to know I'm proud of you at all times because you gave it your all. You wanted it! That means everything – to want it! Duncan paused for the emotions of happiness and cheering to subside.

"I have to commend you for your strength and stature. Who else could have done what you guys have done? No one! I appreciate you more than words can express because I see your love for the Boston Red Sox Ball Club. It's more than clear you're proud to be a part of. For all of this, I thank you from the bottom of my heart!" Duncan put his hand over his heart.

"When this is over, and when you've brought home the Commissioners trophy, I'm going to throw the biggest party for you Boston has ever seen. I swear on my Scottish heritage. I will be one very proud man to make my promise good. Go out and have fun. Remember the history of Fenway Park Stadium. Remember the national hero's that were here before you, and be proud because you're one of them now too! God Bless you tonight and all my well wishes are with every single one of you! I'll see you from the top of the 600 Club with the other top office managers who send their congratulations and appreciation so they could be here for tonight's game." He Clapped his hands hard and said, "Let's play ball, men!"

Cheers of happiness ensued. The guys were relaxed and ready to go, just waiting for time to dress and go out and do their normal routine of mixed practices before the big game began.

"I can hear the people in the bleachers from here, said the second baseman, Bobby McFinch as they were in the locker room about ready to head out to the field. The players listened and shook their heads in agreement.

"There's no better sound than the calling of the Boston Red Sox fans to get ourselves out there and play ball." Said Short Stop Ricky Roubidoux.

"Let's go give them what they're out there waiting for guys," said "The Locomotive" Willie Steamalik, Lead Pitcher for Boston and surely headed for the Cy Young Award for the American League, beyond a shadow of a doubt. Tonight he would be the finisher in the ball game. Raymond Erskine would be the lead off Pitcher.

Boston Pitcher, Raymond Erskine known as "Iron Arm," high fived all the players, charging them up, and made the guys whistle and holler with happiness as they trotted out to the dugout through their familiar long tunnel. "Stay mentally tough and positive guys. We can do this, we're home!" He yelled one last comment of zeal.

Chapter 60

"Good Evening, America!" Said Tom Hathaway, the lead announcer through the World Series. Tom had demonstrated a standard of accuracy and reliability, with a distinctive style of play-by-play announcing. He was a born natural to announce the World Series. He had a love for the game that had earned him the respect and reputation he so deserved. He wasn't talented enough to play baseball, but that love for baseball propelled him into the announcing field. He knew from the first day on the job this was his passion and would be his legacy. He quickly worked his way up to announcing Major League Baseball games and eventually was added, the World Series. One way or another, he was associated with the game he loved dearly.

He and his partner, Mike Brooks were narrating highlights and Stats of the World Series games as the teams were warming up just like they always did.

"Raymond Erskin, also known as 'Iron Arm', is an ace for the Red Sox pitchers. He was a dominating force in last night's game as the starting pitcher and Bo Blythe came in as the relief pitcher. He is a veteran pitcher of the Red Sox and quite leader in skills and personality." Mike Brooks added

Tonight's lead off pitcher will be "Willie "the Locomotive" Steamalika. The newest pitcher on the team signed on this last year." They continued with the lineup and the stats they always gave in their pre-show talks.

Justin couldn't help but allow himself a rare one-minute to himself. Here he is. The kid out of no-where, and from no one essentially, at least from the time of his birth to Grandma, then came Bree and Bradley into his life. He felt so blessed at this moment.

A Perfect Match

As he looked around the dugout, some of the coaches and teammates were biting their nails, rearranging their hair and replacing their ball caps, as if it mattered. Some men were checking over their equipment one more time. Others, were eating sunflower seeds and spitting the hulls out as if he were a human hulling machine. Most of the men were chomping on gum at a fast pace. One guy was praying on his knees in the corner. Another guy popping his knuckles. Another man was standing stoic just looking into the stands. Everybody seemed as if they were each performing some sort of personal apotropaic ritual before the game. He found them all amusing and wonderful. Justin observed it all profoundly as he felt in his soul it was divine providence. Destiny was in this stadium tonight, calling his and his teammates names out as winners. Calling a strong demand for action with a very clear message of what action was needed to win this championship.

He didn't understand how he knew some things so clearly, and at other times, things were a blur. He just took it at its' meaning; God is in control.

Justin looked across the stadium and to his surprise, saw the hugest banners he had ever seen in his life stretched out across the Bleachers and the Bottom boards below the first row stadium seating. They had printed on them:

"We Have The Competitive Edge."

"Just-an Edge, That's all we need!"

"Double Edged batter."

There were a many other smaller ones, but these caught his eyes as he was taking a moment before the start of the game to take it all in as best he could. He never wanted to forget today.

The game went in the Red Sox favor from start to finish. Each man guarded his base and his position. They watched the batters, the pitchers, the coaches and went by their gut feelings for action. The Red Sox managed to barrage the Dodgers with wits, athletic ability and endurance. The playing abilities were astounding. The Red Sox were over the top in peak performance. Their time had come. The fans were hysterical, they were crying, cheering and hugging each other. Some came in Suits straight from work and others came in casual clothing. It didn't matter, Boston had shown up for the games.

The Red Sox pitchers were holding the Dodgers back and not allowing a base hit. The basemen were getting them out if a stray ball came their way. Outfielders were catching fly balls and the entire park was filled with music of winning, and winning big. The final score was inching up to Boston 8 homeruns with Justin's homerun with two men on base, and each player was able to hit the balls even from the "dread pirate," Dodger lead pitcher, Wilbert Lincoln. He didn't even make them blink in fear. The Dodgers were trailing with only 4 runs on the board. The tide had turned.

"That's the game tonight baseball fans across America. Coming to you live from Boston's famous Fenway Park. The Red Sox have clenched tonight's game with a score of 8 to 4." Said Tom. "What an exciting turn of events this Series has turned into. It's anyone's game and victory tomorrow, Mike."

"Let's go down to the field and see if our people can interview some of the players and coaches." Said Mike.

"Sounds good, Mike and we'll see you wonderful fans tomorrow night for the last and final game of the series. This is turning into an incredible World Series battle."

Tom Hathaway turned off the microphone, made sure all sound machines were off and asked Mike, "What do you think will happen?"

"Man, I don't know. The way the Red Sox have come back with a complete and untarnished vengeance, I think they could very well be the champs. But then, look how they came back, what's to keep the Dodgers from doing the same thing? What are your thoughts? You're the 'Brainiac' in baseball, Tom."

"I'm telling you, Mike, I have a feeling tonight and tomorrow night are it. My gut is telling me, Justin Edge is on a mission, the pitchers are on the mission with him and the whole team is right there with them. They are the tightest team I believe I've ever seen in baseball history."

Tom continued thinking then began again with, "The Red Sox are extraordinary, think about it. No tempers flaring. No personal jealousies, no gossiping behind the backs of other players. They have this Three Musketeer's attitude like, 'All for one, and one for all,' type thing going on. I'm amazed out of my mind. I have watched them, talked with them and Justin Edge has made a difference in the team's thinking. He's like the "Alpha dog" theory. Their participation and eye on the goal has been motivating and moving. There is such a noticeable element in this ball club's attitude, such as rarely seen if ever. I've never known such camaraderie, as this team possesses. Even the owner, Mr. Duncan is behind them all the way. He is acting like a proud Papa of his little guys. They want for nothing because they have his complete respect and heart. They talk with him, include him in everything and visa versa. He is truly the Father of the men when they are in the Red Sox organization at least. The Coaches are dedicated. The Red Sox organization has put four maybe five years, into some serious creation to pull together a team like this. It's been a picture perfect creation. The pitchers are the best in the league as a unit. They are tight and supportive of each other…amazingly intertwined in the same think tank. If only all teams and players could be so fortunate, we would see a different breed of ball clubs and great mentors for our youth who have morals and scruples. As my mother would say, if wishes were horses, beggars would ride. For whatever that completely means, it sounds applicable at this particular moment." They enjoyed a last laugh together for the night.

Tom and Mike were overjoyed with the new results they were experiencing and seeing firsthand.

"Thanks Tom for always making things sound sensible." Said Mike as they got out of their limousine and went inside the hotel.

"I thank you, Mike, for listening to this old codger. See you tomorrow. Good Night." Each man was exhausted from all the talk and activity. They departed for their hotel, to do some homework for the next and last night's championship game.

Unbeknownst to Justin, he would not see the start of the next game.

Chapter 61

There is a unique and unmatched beauty in a selfless nature. There are few people who go through life choosing to put others first, but Grandma Ruby was one of those few. She was preparing dinner for Bradley so everything would be ready for him when he got home from school and they could get themselves to the ball park for tonight's determining game she knew the Red Sox and her boy were going to cinch. Something wasn't feeling right in her chest, and then it worsened.

Ruby had managed to call the ambulance that had taken her to the emergency unit of the hospital. She wasn't sure if she was having a heart attack a stroke, or heartburn. All she knew was something was horribly painful in her chest. Her explanation to the paramedic on the phone was, "it's as if elephants are stepping on my chest." She barely made the phone call and swallowed two aspirin, opened the front door and collapsed in front of it.

The next thing she knew she was in an ambulance with an oxygen mask over her face. That's when the paramedic asked her quick questions so he could phone ahead to the hospital and brief them on the incoming patient.

The housekeeper, Wanda, called Nathan and Justin's cell phone. Nathan answered and asked what hospital they were taking Ruby to. She said, "to Massachusetts General Hospital." Wanda then left a message for Justin because he was in morning practice. Once he got the message, he informed Coach Chambers of the present situation with his grandmother. He was as nervous and emotionally shook as Coach Chambers had ever seen him. Justin began to display a near hysterical facet of emotions. This concerned Chambers deeply. He had gotten used to seeing only the intense and competitive side of Justin. Chambers had seen Justin emotionless, stoic and unable to function after his wife's death, and never wanted to see that side again. He quickly told Justin, "by all means, get to the hospital."

A Perfect Match

When he arrived at his Grandma's room, her hospital bed was connected to a lot of equipment. This set up shocked him for a second upon the realization that her condition was very serious. His Grandma seemed to have needles stuck in her body everywhere. Some with drip systems on a tall rack. There was the faint sound of electronic monitoring equipment, beeping, pinging and other rumbling sounds going on behind her bed that were undistinguishable.

Justin pulled up a chair so he could sit down beside her and hold her hand. She tried to make light of the situation seeing his tormented and frightened looking face. She said, "Gee, do you think they have any larger garden hoses they could stick in my arm?"

This made him slightly smile to hear her speak, even if it were ever so faint.

The renowned heart specialist, Dr. Crescent, had been writing down his notes as Justin arrived and was now about to leave his Grandma's room. The Doctor asked to speak to Justin privately. "Justin, your grandmother is deteriorating fast and I want to be completely upfront with you. We always hope for the best, but sometimes we have to expect the worst. In this case the later is more probable."

"Dr. Cres", Justin stopped as he was choked up.

"Your grandmother is in critical condition, Justin, and has lost 80% of her heart's ability to function properly. With her age, and the damage, there is a very strong chance she would never make it through a heart surgery. That is out of the question at this point. I strongly suggest you call in your family and any close friends for your grandmother's last hours. I'm sad to say it so bluntly, but son, in my profession, I would rather tell you the truthful facts rather than give you some stimulating comment, only to let you down later. Without the reality of the situation some people go into shock. Please forgive my strong bedside manner, but it is best for the family to have time to say good-bye and accept it as life's natural course."

The heart specialist had just told Justin, to prepare for his last moments with his Grandmother. This fact registered with Justin quickly. His Grandma was in the hospital bed weak and pale from the after effects of a severe heart attack that has left only about 20% of her heart functioning. Time was critical. Justin heard his Grandma speaking to him.

"Justin my boy, I've given all I have to give in this life to you and Bradley. It seems the time has come for me to hand over the reins to you. You have been the head of this family for quite a while now, I just didn't want to let you know." Grandma smiled ever so slightly, her eyes had one more twinkle left in them.

"You are the sole leader and caretaker of this little family now. Carry on and do just what you have been doing, because it's all been good." Grandma gave a faint chirp of breath meant to be a chuckle, with a slim smile.

"Grandma, how can I ever take your place? The love you've given to me. the time you've given to teach and nurture every one of us you love. How can I ever do that? It's not my gift." He kissed her little hand so gently.

"You just do it honey. Kind of like your drive to excel in baseball. You use the same instinctive action. It's God given my boy. Trust your instincts and just do it."

Ruby was struggling to breathe but wanted to tell Justin one more thing before she went to meet her beloved Lord God, and her loved ones who had left this earth years ago.

"Whatever happens with me, good or bad, you get yourself to this last game and fight like the champion you are, and I raised you to be. I'll know what the outcome is either way. You do this for me. You do this for Bradley. Most of all, do it for yourself. Do you hear me, m-y b-o-y?" struggling to finish her statement. She paused and caught her breath then continued.

"Do it because of my love for you, my complete devotion to you. It's been our life's goal. One we have shared together, and now you're here. You win this World Ser," She couldn't finish her sentence. Justin heard, but wouldn't accept her asking him to leave her in the hospital and go to the game.

She was struggling harder to breathe, so Justin rang the bell signaling for the nurses to come promptly. The head nurse came running in.

She saw Ruby struggling, Justin white as a ghost, so she quickly called for the ventilator machine to be brought in hopes it would help her to breath easier.

"We need to get oxygen into her lungs, help eliminate more carbon dioxide and ease her breathing until she is able to breath better on her own, Justin. It doesn't allow her to talk, so please understand. We are also going to give her some medication to help her forget this unpleasant situation, but it will cause her to be sleepy."

Justin knew this was the final moments of his grandmother's life. A huge part of his life was slipping away. He couldn't watch her suffer if there were any way around it. The Ventilator was only prolonging the inevitable – death. He hated that word.

"I'll be watching the screen and when my grandmother is completely on the respirator's breathing function, that is when I understand what must be done. But until then, please let me hold on to her as long as I can."

"Absolutely!" The head nurse quickly responded. "We will be in and out of the room very often. She then offered, "would you like for the hospital chaplain to come in?"

'Yes, that would be nice. I'm also calling her minister right now, but until he gets here, it would be nice to have his presence." Ruby's former minister and his wife had come in from Alabama for the World Series. Ruby had asked them to come to see Justin in his first World Series game. He was so thankful they were in Boston right now.

Justin called the limousine company he used for his son and his Grandma every day. "Herb, Justin here. I'm in the 'Massachusetts General Hospital' with my Grandma. I need you to pick up Bradley from school and get him over here ASAP. You're on file with them, just get here with Bradley quickly, please."

"You bet I will Justin." We'll be there as quickly as we can. This is serious isn't it?" Herb knew Justin never asked for appointments like this with an ASAP attached.

"Yeah, it is Herb. I just hope you make it here with Bradley before," Justin's voice cracked and he stopped.

"No worries my man, I'll take care of it." Herb disconnected his cell phone fast, then called Bradley's school. "Hello, this is Herb Chester, of Boston Limousine calling to request that Bradley Edge be ready for my immediate arrival. There is an emergency in his family and I'll be there in five minutes to sign him out." The receptionist knew Herb well and said she would do it immediately. She didn't even ask any questions.

Justin began to cry slightly as he took his Grandma's little withered hand in his big hand. She had used those hands to do so many things for him, and for Bradley. It was almost unbearable for him to see. Would Bradley be ok seeing this?

About thirty minutes had passed when he heard the door knock gently. It was the head nurse. "Bradley and his chauffer are here, what would you like to do?"

"I would like to come out and tell Bradley first please. Thank you for the notice before letting him in." Justin maintained his courteous mannerism.

"Absolutely, Mr. Edge."

"Dad!" there was urgency in Bradley's voice.

"Son, your Grandma's life is ending. I wanted to tell you before you go in and see her. We need to be strong for her sake right now, ok?"

Shaking his head yes, Bradley softly let out an "Ok, I will Dad."

"The hospital staff had to place her on a ventilator machine because she wasn't breathing well enough to get oxygen into her lungs and body. What you'll be seeing is Grandma sleeping because she is on strong medication. Do you think you can handle it?

"I can, Dad. I'm not a stranger to sickness, or to death. I'll be ok. I want to be with her, and not let her be alone." Bradley sounded so mature and grown up. It knocked Justin back a bit. "I think he's taking this much better than I thought he would. I'm the one who isn't taking it very well." Justin thought to himself.

"Our minister and his wife, from Grandma's Alabama church just arrived and are in there with Grandma right now, so she's not entirely alone. We'll go on in now son."

Justin turned to Herb who had been standing by silently the whole time.

"Thanks Herb. Could you just stand by? I may need you to take Bradley home. His uncle will be there with him through the night if this lasts that long. I'll keep you posted, ok?"

"Anything you need, Justin, anything." Herb headed to place the car in a more suitable long term parking area, yet still close to the entry doors for quick access.

"Dad, you have the World Series game to attend tonight." Bradley suddenly remembered.

"I've called into Coach Chambers already and told him I'm not leaving my Grandma until she is gone, or better. I don't care about anything but us right now son, and being with the most important woman in my life. She molded, shaped and loved me into what I am today. The same goes for you, Bradley. Where would you have been without her in your younger life? She has been our mother for a lot of years now. I'm just giving some of my love back to her... that's all." Justin was still rambling on when Bradley cut in, "but Dad! this has been the dream you and Grandma have waited for your whole lives...to win the World Series. I don't think Grandma Ruby would approve at all if you missed this opportunity. You've got to go! I'll be here." Just thinking of leaving this little lady like this was tormenting him.

The Doctor came in, and touched Justin's shoulder.

"Hi Justin. I wanted to let you know your Grandma will be waking up soon because her medication will be wearing thin and it will be a good time to talk to her, but don't expect a reply."

"That would be nice to talk to her one more time. It will be different for her not to reply though." A little wisp of a chuckle could have made its way out with a bit more energy, but that was the best Justin could do.

"We will be outside the door ready to give her medication for pain relief, after you have visited for a few minutes."

"Thank you. Dr. Crescent."

Justin and Bradley and Reverend Matthews all sat around Grandma Ruby's bed talking softly to each other. About 20 minutes had passed since the Doctor had left the room when Grandma Ruby's eyes slowly began to open. She was still groggy, but came into reality very slowly. Her eyes jerked wide open with concern when she saw Justin there.

"Grandma, I'm not leaving you!" Justin knew exactly what her expression meant.

Her eyes were all telling again when she rolled them and then narrowed them looking at him. He knew that look. He had seen it all of his life in pressing times to let him know she meant business.

"See Dad, Grandma wants you at that game!" Bradley saw it.

"You show respect son, I'm not leaving Grandma."

Grandma Ruby looked at Justin with pleading eyes and then turned them towards the door without moving her head. She did it three times.

Justin saw it and he knew what she was insinuating. He whispered into his Grandma's ear,

"IF, I go, it's all for you, and only for you. Do you understand that?" Grandma winked one eye at Justin in approval and acceptance.

"I love you Grandma with all of my heart and I always will. Do you hear me?"

She let her eyes look happy and closed them, opened them and closed them to signify a yes answer.

"In all sincerity, how can I do this Reverend Matthews?" Justin looking for any reason for them to tell him not to go, instead they said, "you had better get going, or your Grandma will be very upset."

No sooner had they said this than the monitor on the screen let out a high pitched alert sound indicating her heart had stopped beating completely but the respirator was still functioning. The nurses were in the room immediately, resetting the machine and looking at Justin. Bradley and Reverend Matthews were against the wall and out of the way.

Justin walked over to Grandma Ruby and kissed her forehead. He looked at Bradley and then over to Reverend Matthews through tear filled eyes. "Reverend, will you please take care of everything from here?"

Reverend Matthews nodded his head and affirmed, "yes I would be honored to, Justin." Justin walked out of the room and didn't look back. He was at peace, but it was so hard to let go. The void was already setting in, and the hurt was indescribably harsh. He walked down the long corridor to find his car with tears rolling down his cheeks.

Chapter 62

"This will be the Seventh and final game tonight of the World Series fans across the land. We will have a new champion tonight after a long and hard fought battle." Tom Hathaway began his broadcasting as soon as they were switched on air.

"As the very famous football coach, Vince Lombardi once said, 'I firmly believe that any man's finest hour, the greatest fulfillment of all that he holds dear, is the moment when he has worked his heart out in a good cause and lies exhausted on the field of battle – victorious'." Mike Brooks said, "I love baseball, and I loved the Green Bay Packers, football Legend, Vince Lombardi. I feel his statement is most appropriate for tonight's final World Series game.

Fans of Baseball, tonight you are in the company and care, of the two most excitable and best sounding announcers on television and radio. A title bestowed upon us by our very selves of course. Who better to judge us than us? I'm Tom Hathaway and my partner is Mike Brooks. We're coming to you live from Boston's Fenway Park Stadium in historic downtown Boston.

This City is more than amazing. We can't help but be in the middle of history and tradition, no matter where we set our feet. However, for the next few hours, our feet are firmly planted here in the press box. We're not going anywhere until this game is over and tonight's winner has been determined. If it is another game like last night, we are in for another historical moment in this already monumental city full of history."

"This is a spectacular evening for every baseball fan across the world. The projected viewing audience tonight is somewhere around 32 million. It's the largest viewing audience in history." Tom was being fed this information through his headset as he began his pre-game talking show.

"Folks, there are magic moments in the hours and minutes before a World Series game begins. By that I mean the passion and anticipation of the fans. Who will win the game is the first question of course. Who will be the MVP? The excitement of the game as it unfolds is the ultimate in curiosity, nervousness and excitement. The fans across the city have been interviewed today and they are all optimistic and full of anticipation. They love their Red Sox!"

Mike Brooks broke in and said, "although baseball is proudly called 'the national pass-time game', it is also a game of extremely talented men who know even the easiest of games are highly complicated. They just make it look easy. After every game has ended, they begin to see tomorrow's game. There is no taking their minds off the game or the competition they will be facing. In high hopes of repeating the last two nights winning streaks, the Boston Red Sox are on the field working in mixed forms and doing some stretching in preparation for the game about to start. The starting pitcher for tonight's game will be Willie "The Locomotive" Steamalik.

Tom added, "The Los Angeles Dodgers are also in their element doing their normal formations and pitching practice in their bullpen. Their starting pitcher tonight will be the formidable and fearsome, Manning Princeton. Some of the players are talking with their specialized coaches and the moments are ticking away before the start of the game." After a brief commercial break, they were back on the air.

"You know Tom, I find the rich history surrounding the Red Sox very interesting. It's as much a part of baseball and Fenway Park as it is to Boston itself." Mike was in deep thought of Fenway's history.

"For instance, It goes way back to the year of 1920, when the owner of the Red Sox at the time was Harry Herbert Frazee. He needed the $125,000 he received from the Yankee's for the sale of George Herman better known as "Babe Ruth" to finance a Broadway show he wanted to produce.

"I don't think he loved baseball as much as he did Broadway." Interjected Tom.

"I don't either Tom. After that dreadful deal, the 'Curse of the Bambino' was a superstition surrounding the failure of the Boston Red Sox to win a World Series for an 86-year period." Mike had more to add to his story.

"That was, until their first baseman Doug Mientkiewicz caught the final out of the 2004 World Series. The fans went crazy yelling, "the curse has now been reversed"' That precious and historical day changed the

A Perfect Match

misfortune of the Boston Red Sox forever. But, the fierce rivalry between the Red Sox and the Yankee's remained, and exists, until this very day because the Babe helped take the previously lackadaisical Yankees on to become one of the most successful ball clubs in North America. They were so bad, they shared a field with the New York Giants baseball team. After Babe Ruth, they were financially able to build Yankee Stadium. It opened in 1923 and to this day is referred to as 'The House that Ruth built'."

"That was a delightful slice of history, Mike. Thank you!"

"Here we are now…the Red Sox defeated the Yankee's for their place in this World Series. It was against the Yankees that Justin Edge broke The Babe's actual home run record in the same number of games. Ironic isn't it?" Tom loved baseball trivia as much as Mike did.

"Consider that while the Red Sox had Babe Ruth, they were one of the most successful and formidable professional ball club franchises in the nation. They had also amassed five World Series titles. When he was gone they went into a downward spiral. I tend to believe in the Curse of the Bambino myself." Said Mike.

"That goes to show you Mike, the city does have the ghosts of their legends walking among us!" Tom didn't laugh as usual while thinking of this bit of trivia.

"You do have to wonder about some things at times." Mike said as he too went into a deep and serious train of thought.

"I know you don't have to walk on the moon to know it exists, and you don't have to question the science of gravitational pull which causes the rise and fall of the oceans tides. I don't have to question that many wonders and phenomenal occurrences have been going on for as long as man has been around. This is what makes life so grand! I enjoy folklore, like discovering superstitions, reading history and love baseball. I'm an all around kind of guy, Mike."

"Yes, it does make life a wonderful display of human complications and discoveries. That's why I'm looking forward to a fun filled night. I'm having a good time already just being here talking with you, Tom. I'm eager to see how this evening's game turns out more than anything right now."

"One thing is greatly bothering me, Mike. Justin Edge is not at the ball field tonight nor is he on the roster." Exclaimed Tom with a definite air of shock in his voice.

"What on earth is up with that?" Said a befuddled Mike Brooks, in a very quick response to Tom.

"I have no idea. We haven't heard a word about this so far. We'll try to find out folks, what is happening, because something is definitely wrong with this picture." Said Tom who was absolutely mystified by now.

"Folks, this Series is hanging in the balance scales and it could tilt either way. Both teams are equally wanting to win tonight and take the trophy home."

Now talking faster and more up beat, the two announcers finished their statistics of the previous games.

"Alright, the time is here folks, we have the play ball signal. It's time to fasten your seat belts and get this game going." Said a very excited Tom Hathaway the "Play Ball" announcement was always his highlight comment.

"The home field advantage is definitely a factor in most games, but not with these two teams. Both teams are out for blood tonight. It's a full moon tonight too ya' know, Tom!"

"I had thought about that myself, Mike. A full moon has powerful effects on everything from the ocean tides, to people's attitudes and temperaments.

Wow! I hadn't thought of all the 'other stuff' when I made that 'illustrious' comment. I'm really intuitive tonight -- watch out folks, I may read the plays before they happen."

"Don't believe him fans of all ages and in all places! He's hallucinating." Joked Mike Brooks.

"That's okay, our time for action has arrived. Looks like the teams are more than ready for tonight's game." Tom Hathaway announced in his usual pensive voice.

"The Dodgers are first up to bat with Kendrick Waters, their right fielder, leading them off and facing the ever so intimidating, Willie the "Locomotive" Steamalik, of the Boston Red Sox. Steamalik has yet to let a batter get a homerun off of him in the Playoff's or this World Series. Yes, sir! He is a new addition to the Red Sox Ball Club and another impressive

Boston pitcher among the group. The teams in past playoff games said he is a foreboding opponent to be respected and feared. The Red Sox have truly succeeded in accumulating some of the best athletes in baseball this past four years. It was their plan as stated, in their press conferences when the season began. No surprises here, Mike."

"Steamalik has succeeded in striking out Martin Larson. This is the first out in the bottom of the 1st inning with a score of 0 to 0. Next batter up is Ronald Meckler, the Dodgers Center Outfielder. This man is known for his fast running speed and powerful arms. The Dodgers probably have their fingers crossed with this man to just get on base. From there, he is the Flash."

"As in the DC Comics, Flash?" Brooks asked.

"Exactly!" Tom said, half chuckling that one off. The thought still weighing heavy on his mind…what happened with Justin Edge?

"Oh my! He has hit the ball and it's headed to far right field bouncing its way to the hands of Boston's Right Out Fielder, Mark Lewis. He's throwing the ball in to stop him on 2nd base." The telling in his voice was one of great anticipation for the man on base.

"Next batter up is Dodger's Bentley Briggs, relief catcher. He let the first three pitches go by him. The umpire has called two balls, and one strike. He is taking his time to gather his thoughts and shake off the shock of not being on base yet. Briggs is now taking his stance inside the batters square and readying himself for the next pitch. "Thar she blow's! Right past him and over the center of the plate without a single attempt to swing at it. The radar gun showed a 98 MPH ball I'm being told in my earpiece. He didn't have a quick enough eye to see that one coming folks. I don't know of many who would. That was a scorcher pitch from Willie Steamalik and right over center plate. The next pitch was exactly the same and Briggs now has three strikes in a row. Great job, by Steamalik. That man definitely has his head in the game tonight

"This crowd is going wild over this refined Red Sox Team. They have finally come home and it looks like they have shown up for this World Series game back at home. Their fans support and love them. You know this has got to help the guys in their efforts to give that extra chunk of what they have inside of them." Tom was talking so fast and loud, his partner, knew he was thoroughly in this game head, heart and soul, as he was himself. However, Mike was keenly aware something was wrong and couldn't shake it.

Princeton was true to form. He was an excellent pitcher for the Dodgers and managed to keep the Red Sox in check through several innings with zero runs batted in. He struck the batters out in succession and they changed positions on the field again. Score held at 4 to 0, Dodger's favor, and it was now the bottom of the fourth inning.

The Red Sox were up to bat and Boston's 2nd baseman, Jeff Pike was up to bat first. He swung at the ball hitting it over center plate. It did a few clumsy bounces before the center outfielder finally caught it and threw it into the pitcher. He had managed to get on base and so happy to not get struck out by the beast…Princeton. Next up to bat was Red Sox Left Fielder, Wayne Daniels. He had powerful arms and legs and a lot of hope riding on his abilities to hit the ball tonight. First pitch, strike. Second pitch strike. Third pitch…homerun! The Boston fans were elated and going crazy with relief. They now had a score of two runs on the board. Pandemonium broke out in the Red Sox bleachers. Score: 5 to 2 Dodgers favor and the bottom of the 4th inning.

Princeton was so aggravated he allowed the homerun on his watch he struck out the next three batters out with a one, two three strikes and you're out attitude. The teams were changing positions on the field. The Dodgers would be up to bat in the top of the 5th inning.

The Red Sox were starting to sweat it out without Justin in the game and wondering what had happened to him. They needed him. Where was he? Coach Chambers wasn't telling them anything. For a very good reason he felt inside.

During a station break, Mike told Tom, "It's just coming in, Tom, Justin's Grandmother was in the hospital and just passed away 15 minutes ago. The Boston Coaches knew he was at the hospital with her and wouldn't be in, so they didn't put him on the line up. No wonder."

"Oh NO! That's terrible news." Said Tom with a painful frown on his face.

"I feel so bad for Justin. He had been such a vital part of this whole team being in the World Series. This team has come this far and now to miss the last game, inconceivable. This is just horrible news." Tom was visibly upset.

"I know." Said a very solemn Mike. "Very sad news. You should let the fans know when we come back on the air."

"Okay, I will. This is going to be tough on them. Kind of like it is on us." Tom was very melancholy for the moment.

"Ladies and gentlemen, what a sad day today, for Justin Edge. We just received word his Grandmother who raised him, has passed away this evening about forty-five minutes ago. This explains clearly why he wasn't seen on the field for opening ceremonies, playing with the Red Sox, or on the roster. Our deepest condolences go out to Mr. Edge and to his son Bradley whose chair is also empty tonight next to his Grandmother's. This is a very sad day for the Edge family, and his extended family, the Boston Red Sox. Our deepest condolences to all."

Immediately the sounds of deep groans and sympathetic tones were coming from the fans in the stadium. They were disappointed that Justin Edge would not be playing tonight. They were so looking forward to seeing their hero play in this last game of the World Series and helping to win it.

The news stations were abuzz on television all over the news regarding Justin Edge. It was a blow to the world of baseball. Justin Edge missing game seven. He was nowhere to be seen participating in the 'World Series that he had worked so hard to get to.

"Folks, these last four innings have been a hard mountain to climb for the Red Sox Ball Club. But who knows what will happen in the next up coming innings to come. That's the traits of baseball, it's full of surprises. During a station break, Tom and Mike discussed the reversal of momentum the Red Sox had at the beginning of the game and how they had slid so badly.

"Well perhaps it's a mental thing, Tom. They are a very tight ball club and their fellow teammate, Justin Edge is not here with them to win game seven he has been a very instrumental part in helping to get this team here. Top that off with losing the woman who raised him and his son and attended every single one of his games. That would affect anyone in my opinion. Remember, this same team was with him when he lost his wife and his son was crippled too. This compounds their sorrow. They are professionals…I'm sure they will shake it off somehow, someway."

"I'm in agreement with you there, Mike."

"We are beginning the top of the 5th inning and the Dodgers will be first up to bat. The Dodgers managed to swing and get one base hits, over and over. This had allowed them enough leverage to put three more homeruns on the board. Finally, with three outs, the bottom of the 5th inning came and the Red Sox had another chance to get some runs on the board.

Princeton was able to send fast, curve balls past the Red Sox who were definitely freaking out over the low score, plus…one of their top player's was suffering from the death of his grandmother they all knew so well. They were almost out of the game, mentally with their attitudes, and seemed to be losing their physical stamina. The Dodgers sent them back to their dug out for the change of positions and into the top of the 6th inning. The score was now 8 to 2 Dodgers favor.

The Dodgers wanted to knock out the Red Sox momentum and regain it for themselves by winning this Championship game tonight. It looked as if the current streak was in their favor. They were feeling quite confident that the deed was about done, especially with Justin Edge being out of the game. A bit of jovial celebration had begun a little early in anticipation of their victory.

The Dodgers first and second batters had been struck out by Steamalik with three straight strikeouts. The third batter up was Kendrick Waters, the Dodgers right outfielder. The pitches were released and Kendrick was standing at the batters box with 2 foul balls and 2 strikes.

Steamalik gave it everything he had as he released the ball and struck him out for the third strike and third out. "Thank God!" Said Steamalik… and the rest of the team as well!"

"Steamalik is definitely holding the Red Sox team together tonight, Mike. He is doing a superb job pitching in a loosing battle, one would assume by the scoreboard. He is not a quitter, quite evident. The Red Sox team is being lead by a true Spartan of baseball. Kudos to Willie Steamalik, for showing true leadership and a never give up attitude." Said Tom Hathaway with full sincerity.

The teams are changing positions and the Dodgers will be up to bat in the top of the 7th inning now.

During the time it took for the teams to switch sides a sudden rush of cheering and fan fare was sweeping through the stadium. The nose level was rising for no apparent reason that the announcers could see at the moment.

"What is going on to make the crowd go into a frenzy like this?" Asked Tom, half thinking and half announcing.

Chapter 63

The Security Guards looked at each other completely startled!

There it was again, the sound. A faint metallic click and a thud, a metallic click and a thud, each making their own distinct sound the two men knew so well. The unexpected, familiar sound of Bradley's braces and crutches pounding the concrete of the long corridor as he was making his way from the entrance door of Fenway Park stadium to the end of the ever so long corridor to his seat above the dugout.

They both looked and all they could see was the dark silhouette of legs, crutches and braces attached to shoes due to the curvature of the slanting hallway. They didn't need to see his full body or face. They knew instantly who it was, and by his mere presence they each let out a cheerful yell as they looked at each other again.

Yes! It was Bradley coming down the corridor as he had done so many times in the past with the sound of his crutches making the thud sound and the leg braces making the clicking sound with each step he took making the sound over and over as fast as he could carry himself. He was making his way down the long corridor to go to his usual seat, but without Grandma Ruby at his side this time. Herb had left him off at the tunnel entrance and went to park the car.

Their hearts jumped and they hollered at the top of their lungs to him, "we're coming Bradley, we're coming son, hold on." It was the most beautiful sight and sound they had seen all day!

They ran to greet Bradley and help him on down and into his seat as if he were a fragile prince tonight. They were laughing and hugging the boy and patting his shoulders. Instantly, they lifted him up as if their arms were a chair and whisked him up as they carried him to the entrance of the seating area to hurry the walk. The men knew he was the 'other half' of the man now in the dugout after hearing the clamorous and ear-splitting noise coming from the stadium.

Tom Hathaway had to yell into the microphone to be heard. "Can you believe it? Justin Edge is here at the stadium and in the Red Sox Dugout supporting his team? His Son, Bradley was just seated in his usual seat, with the vacant seat of his grandmother's, filled by his Uncle. My God, what a beautiful sight" Tom sounded like they were his very own family.

"What Justin Edge must be feeling is incomprehensible." Said Mike Brooks. "But here he is, nonetheless. I just don't have the words to express the feelings for this team right now. It is one of the rarest and most enigmatic of events to occur outside of the earthquake in San Francisco in 1989!"

"Great analogy, Mike." Said Tom, "I think you just summed it up the best. This is certainly earth shattering!"

"Justin Edge has made an impact by just being here. The fans are covering their hearts and some are saying they're singing 'Amazing Grace' over in Left Field where he been playing. If this can't help ease a little in his grief, nothing in the world will. It's making it difficult for me to speak at this moment!" Said Tom.

"This is truly the epitome of human kindness we are witnessing here tonight. I don't think I've ever seen anything like this in all my years of broadcasting." Said Mike to help cover Tom's unexpected show of emotions during announcing in any game.

"Folks, they have stopped the game momentarily due to the over powering noise. No one can hear a thing. We'll take a brief station break."

"Justin Edge is a very much loved and respected human being and a prime player of rare qualities, Tom. Just listen as the crowd. They're still reeling and roaring from the excitement and shock of only seeing Edge in the dugout. My Gosh, I am stunned by the show of affection myself."

Mike let the fans listen for about 20 seconds to get the full effect of what it was sounding like in the stadium at that very moment. It was ear shattering to say the least.

Coach Chambers came over to Justin immediately and gave him a huge fatherly hug. He was stunned and so happy to see him. The same sentiments were shared by all of the team when they saw him walk into the dugout.

"Justin I'm so sorry about your Grandmother."

"She went fast and painless, Sir. That's they way she would have wanted it to be. She also demanded I be at this game tonight before she went out." Justin barely got it out.

"Justin I'm going to put you in as a pinch hitter for Steamalik, next time we're up to bat. We're in a desperate situation and we've got to do something to pull it out. Do you think you can handle it, son? Are you up to it?"

Coach Chambers instinctually knew Justin could pull it out if anyone could, even in his time of personal crisis.

"I'm ready any time you say, Coach. That's why I'm here and not at the hospital." Justin meant every word of it and Coach Chambers knew it. He silently sighed a breath of relief and went over to the other coaches to make the changes on the paperwork final.

Justin immediately began to transport his emotions with intense concentration. His diligent training of setting his brain into a different zone was out of extreme necessity, especially now, and he needed it to be. Justin had been unaware of what had been going on around him in the stadium until now. Shocked and humbled, he looked around and couldn't believe what he was seeing and hearing. Once he had settled and he heard what was going on in the Stadium. He remembered Grandma telling him once to honor these people for their admiration and support for him. He would for her sake again tonight.

The crowd was cheering him on. He stepped up to the opening of the dugout and looked over all the seating areas in the stadium. The Cheers erupted even louder, if that were possible, once the fans saw him come out of the dugout.

Justin took off his ball cap and placed it over his heart as he faced the fans. It was his signal of thanking them. He placed his ball cap back on his head. He tapped his heart lightly with his open palm, and pointed to the crowds in different sections, letting them all know he appreciated them, and loved them. They went for the gestures, and he owned them! They loved him. He was Boston's Golden boy.

Mr. Duncan, in the owners box, had tears running down his face and was trying to wipe them off with his handkerchief and not doing a very good job of hiding his emotions. This was his team and Justin had once again gone above and beyond words. This was an incredible moment in his life seeing this young man once again performing when others would not have.

This noise level is unbelievable. He smiled with pursed lips as he was thinking about all of this to himself. "Little do they know how badly I need them all tonight! Time to give them something back now. Grandma…you had better be watching!"

Tom came back on with all the spunk and energy he was known for in the world of announcing. "Okay, baseball fans all over the world, we have a signal to play ball now. Folks we're back in the 7th inning and the Boston Red Sox are trailing the Los Angeles Dodgers by 6 runs. The score now is Dodgers 8 and the Red Sox 2."

Mike Brooks, said into the microphone, "Justin Edge's teammates are sure happy he is here with them tonight."

"Heck, I'm thrilled he's here!" Said Tom. A super smile accompanied his comment.

"The fact he showed up tonight shows tremendous support to this home town of Boston, and to his teammates, as demonstrated with what we have just witnessed. What a guy and what a team! That's Boston for you! First responders. What an appropriate name to this day."

Before Justin came out of the Dugout he first said a silent and brief prayer as he was taught by Grandma to do. He had grown to realize the peace of doing this before anything of importance. "Be with me Lord and prepare the way. Thank you, and Amen."

Willie Steamalik held the Dodgers from making any homeruns and struck them all out pretty quickly with his 95 - 98 MPH fastballs. He was in a hurry and had new spunk in his pitching. He was all business and out for blood now that Justin was back and the team was complete.

"This is the bottom of the 7th Inning, the Red Sox are up to bat, folks. This is show time again! I'm Tom Hathaway and my partner is Mike Brooks. We're waiting to see the tale of the tape as the Red Sox try to regain their momentum."

"The Red Sox have managed to get two men on bases and show time is definitely coming up folks. Justin Edge has been put in as a pinch hitter for the pitcher, Willie Steamalik. Can you believe this Mike?"

"I sure can, knowing Justin Edge as I do. I am also betting the coaches are saving Steamalik's pitching arm. Wonderfully, quick thinking on the coaching staff's part."

Justin came trotting out of the dug out, waited for his chance to go up to the batting square and face the pitcher. He wasn't worried one bit. He was quite calm and very self-assured. This scared the coaches on both teams and they wanted to just faint, each for different reasons.

Justin knew his son, and he knew instinctively that his son would be seated just above him in his usual seat, and he knew there would be a vacant seat next to him. He dreaded looking up, but he would be strong no matter what the circumstances were. He was the man of the house. There were no women left.

He chose to feel that somehow, Grandma Ruby and Bree were watching. This comforted him in a welcomed way. He didn't want to see the empty chair but he had to do the traditional wave to his son. His son would be there like the faithful, wonderful son he was. When he looked up and waved, his jaw dropped open and a smile spread across his face.

Nathan was sitting next to Bradley! They were both grinning broadly. Nathan and Bradley waved, and gave him thumbs up signs. His heart jumped for joy just seeing them both there.

"Thank you, Nathan!" He lip synched, and hoped he could read his lips. He seemed to because a huge smile spread across his face and he gave Justin a two thumbs-up sign.

"Thank you God for letting Nathan be there. Bradley and I both needed him."

The huge banners, the fanfare, the chance of a World Series victory were within reach of this one game tonight. His adrenaline began pumping faster. Justin was getting his head fully into the game and the players he would be matching up against.

Tom said over the microphone, "As if things couldn't get any stranger, or better, I should probably say, Justin Edge is up to bat as the pinch hitter for tonight's pitcher, Steamalik. Justin Edge, is a remarkable man! The Red Sox have a runner on second and third base. Call me crazy, but it seems like the Red Sox are back in this game." I don't think I'm making this up either, Mike. I call it as I see it."

"Right you are. What else could it be?" Said Mike shrugging his shoulders and sounding as concentrated and baffled as Tom.

"Edge is in as pinch hitter. The crowd is roaring again, Mike! This is without a doubt one of the most abnormal and exciting World Series Games in history."

"Oh my! Yes it is and yes they are." Said Mike. "I can't say as I blame them either. This is a shot in the arm of some good stuff. I'm as waffling as you are with all I'm seeing here tonight. Never have I seen such a twist of events in a World Series Game or a regular game for that matter. Never."

"Mike, you and I have some of the best seats in the ballpark and we're not giving them up! We are strapped in and not even a bolt cutter could pry us loose! We are hanging on tight because this game is going to be as exciting as a boat rocking in the turbulent ocean." They both laughed freely.

"Justin Edge is facing off with the Dodgers impressive Pitcher, Manning Preston. It looks like Edge is really ready for the pitch. Look at his poised body and concentration, Mike." Tom Hathaway was so excited he about slipped off the edge of his chair while announcing. He caught himself but not before Mike saw him and they both began laughing so hard they had to cover their mics.

Coach Chambers nervously placed his ball cap back on his head and silently said to Justin, "let 'er rip son!" Justin never heard him. He never heard the crowd cheering so loudly the media couldn't talk over them. He only heard his blood pumping and his heart beating inside of his body.

Justin's focus was on the game. Within milliseconds he had closed his eyes and gone deep down into himself, bringing up the details of each pitcher, and coach, for this team. He had perfected this technique, it was his and he owned his body. His body owned his mind and it was subject to the owner's instructions. He had accomplished his meditative state of mind over matter with great training and practice. He was into his own personal zone where he dwelt in the middle of it. He shut all minor thoughts out into a black area of his mind. He allowed the personal traits of each man to surface from his subconscious mind into his functioning minds eye. He was now ready for any and all calculated and premeditated actions to take place. All this was done within seconds once he called on it to surface. He walked to the batters box and took his stance.

When he reached this state, all he heard was the whisking sound of the ball as it was pitched to him and the sound of his wood bat hitting the outer leather part of the baseball. He could even hear the sound of the rubber in the middle of the ball instantaneously converging inside when his bat made contact with the ball. Everything else was shut out.

Justin had studied and knew the makings of a baseball, as well as a mechanic knows how to build a car engine. The seams on the ball are raised stitching that act like wings of a bird when hit and can cause the ball to fly or swerve on its way out of the park, especially if it caught some wind. He knew all the pitches of any significance and those without significance, intended to walk a player such as him.

Each pitch was determined by a mutual agreement between the catcher and the pitcher using a hand signals. The pitcher was focusing on the catcher in every pitch hoping his ball would fly past the batter and safely into the catchers' mitt. Justin knew their signs for every pitch from watching and memorizing, game films. The pitcher and catcher usually decided jointly, if it were going to be a curveball, slider, sinker, cutter, four-seamed fastball or a two-seamed fastball. They took their instructions from the pitching coach on the field. Heads nodded no and yes to try and confuse ordinary players. Justin was not ordinary.

It didn't matter to Justin. He just wanted a piece of the ball kissing his bat.

"Oh yes, and the pitch is coming. It's a low fast dropping, curve ball. Justin let it go by. He's waiting for pitch number two now. Waiting for it again with deep concentration, wow! it was snapped so fast I'm not sure I caught it. The ball is heading out towards the right outfield and it looks like it could be…no… wait…It IS over the bleachers and heading for the parking lot." Yelled Tom Hathaway.

"The Red Sox just got themselves some help with a home run batted left handed by Justin Edge. Princeton tried to switch Edge up with his left handed pitch but got a shock, Justin is a switch hitter! What a gift of showmanship. Princeton the Dodger pitcher has had the advantage up until Justin Edge showed up. It all happened so fast I didn't even see the ball pitched, Mike."

"I know! I had to watch the catcher and the umpire and wait for the people on the field to confirm it was a 97 MPH fast pitch myself. It was a little low, but still over the plate. Justin's foot just touched home plate, and we have a new score folks; 8 to 6, still Dodgers favor in the Bottom of the 7th Inning." Announced Mike's overly excited voice over the microphone.

"The Red Sox are only trailing by three runs now. The pendulum is swinging in the opposite direction one might say." Said Tom Hathaway.

"Due to the unforeseen circumstances of Justin Edge not being in the game until the seventh inning, and considering why, this game is an all out fight to the finish with his new arrival and the Red Sox new energized actions." Said Mike.

"I'm seeing it the same way you're seeing it Mike." The Red Sox have had a shot of adrenaline and seemed to have found a can of 'whup-em'. I'm wondering how this is going to turn out as it's anyone's game now!" Excitement was in the air and was even overtaking the two men in the press box.

The balls had been pitched and now bases were loaded for the Red Sox.

"Justin Edge is up to bat in his regular spot on the roster now. Red Sox have Marty McQueen on Second base by means of a stealth steal. Bobby McFinch on third base, who hasn't been able to move since he got there. Boston shortstop, Ricky Roubidoux, just got on first base. This crowd is not even trying to contain their zeal at seeing Edge up to bat again. Things are beginning to happen. Doors are hanging on different hinges, the pressure cooker is steaming." Tom always had a new line for the television and radio guest's interest.

"Bases are loaded and the situation is serious here, Mike."

"Things are looking up as Edge moves onto the batters box. Oh man! There goes the pitching coaches to the mound." Said Mike in a hollow voice not knowing what to expect at this moment of the game.

"Oh Yes they are and I can't say as I blame them." The Dodger coaches walked out to the pitchers mound and discussed the situation with the pitcher. They were determined to walk Justin and give them a run on the scoreboard, but block a potential homerun that would ruin the chance of winning for now anyway.

Chapter 64

"Tom, look at the focus on the Princeton's face and the focus on Justin's face. I'm seeing and sensing some strange vibes going on between these two men." Mike could see their faces too, and read them just as well. They were staring at each other even with the coaches out on the mound.

The coaches had gone out and talked to Princeton. They fully warned him. "Do not allow Edge to touch that ball. Do you understand this directive fully?"

Princeton gave a yes reply; even though he hated the demand. He knew he could strike Edge out because his talents in pitching were equal to Edge's batting abilities. They were just acting too conservative and scared. He resented being treated like a lesser talented pitcher than what he was.

This embarrassed Princeton because they insinuated they didn't have the faith in his abilities. His ego was as big as his reputation. He had gotten them into the World Series, now they wanted to put a harness on him. What a way to show gratitude to your star pitcher who would no doubt receive the MVP award for the Series. "Braying Jackass's," he said softly as they left the mound. "Whatever you geniuses say. You're the men with the power over the plays."

The coaches despised his arrogance, and they had heard every word the hot shot said. They just hoped his ego didn't over-ride their instructions. He was a great player, huge on ego, and short on obedience. "That over confidence is probably what makes him great," said the Dodgers head coach, Bernie Brown, as they stepped back into the Dug out. "I still don't trust that guy." Brown said.

Justin had learned through watching the World Series videos. The Dodger's star pitcher, Manning Princeton, was a talented athlete but also very egotistical. He didn't like to be told how to play and was overall, not a great team player. Justin was a bit surprised and hadn't expected that because of how well his own team played together. He knew not all teams were like the Red Sox. He now knew even better, how to play Princeton like a violin.

Princeton began by throwing the first ball outside of the batters square and laughing at Justin. It was growing more apparent the coach's intentions were to walk him. This had to be their only rationale besides his egotistical personality, for complying with his coaches.

Princeton had to make a sport of it to supply his ego with something he could identify with. In his mind doing this foolish stunt in front of the millions of people who were watching this game, made him look inept and not Edge. Therefore, he mocked Justin to make himself feel better.

Princeton was walking around the pitchers mound taking his time. He enjoyed the attention and being the star on the TV screen. This gave Justin the added seconds to do a thorough study of his body language and he knew beyond a shadow of a doubt, another outside of the batters box pitch was coming. He also saw the aggravation in his facial muscles. Princeton was disgraced and livid. This was all good to Justin.

Suddenly, something over came Justin. The very thought of this egotistical jerk throwing him another ball out of the batters square, so as to intentionally walk him, would destroy his chance of a home run hit. This could cause his team to lose the last game of the World Series. This instantaneous thought caused jolts of electricity to run through him. This was just so shallow, deceitful and wrong. Princeton was mocking the situation, and Justin. That was just wrong! He didn't care about looking like a hero, or a fool. He cared about playing ball and winning. He cared about his team! This was do, or die time for him.

His blood was running through his veins at a super and abnormal speed now. His Id was systematically taking over his mind by his own will allowing it to do so. He was letting the super ego part of the psychological apparatus, succumb to his present psychological needs. It was working in coordination with his conscious mind, but Justin was still in full control. He needed this part of his brain, the Id, to be conscious and active because of its non-negotiation functions, and its fully instinctual impulses operating at its' full capacity. His Id was projecting images he knew were correct and more powerful than his own mind. Justin let it take over intentionally, physically and emotionally. He was now in too deep to stop it and didn't want to. Justin was now using it to his full advantage.

Justin, or rather his Id, yelled at Princeton, "You have no confidence in your pitching abilities and neither do your coaches. What in the hell are you doing in the majors, you little pussy?"

He had never used language like this before…it was definitely his Id in control and he enjoyed it momentarily.

Justin respected human beings, just not this one tonight! In the heat of battle, he called it all fair. Justin didn't have an ego problem. He had an inner drive to achieve. His whole team had a desire to win. There was more ingenuity and imagination going on here than this snot-nosed fribble could ever understand.

There's a big difference between the two. One was physically and emotionally in control, the other was playing superstar games for the crowd. The Fop was out for himself and Justin was going for the gold for the team. He and the Dodger's coaches both knew it! They were yelling at their pitcher to stay on tract. He ignored them. His ego had taken over.

Justin was David and they were Goliath. He had his stones to throw and he would. That very thought deeply concerned the LA Dodgers coaches who were not concealing their emotions any better than Coach Chambers was.

Justin's son was here and he wanted to win this World Series for his son, so he could see his Grandma was right in making him come to the game. They had talked about it and planned it together to win this series. Now this piece of flippant garbage was mocking him and depriving him of all that was good. "I shall overcome this." Justin said to himself and prayed that God heard him too.

"I can hit that ball straight down your bulging lips and grinning mouth, if you'll only throw it to me you little organ grinder's monkey!"

He yelled again. "You're a good little simpleton, now give me what I want. A good or bad pitch, just pitch to me you boring and pretentious, mental midget!" With these words, Princeton seemed to have steam coming out of his nostrils and his ears.

Justin was yelling again. He wasn't about to let up and give Princeton time to think on his own. "Keep it coming you little engine that could. I'll have you so far off your game you'll think you're playing miniature golf, you stupid buffoon."

Justin kept it coming until Princeton would give him a pitch. "Not tonight, you little leaguer, and not with this batter." Justin yelled at him again. "You little punk. I read you like a bad book; quickly, and then toss you in the trashcan."

It was definitely something in what Justin had said. The next pitch was going to be straight at him. Princeton was going to hit him on purpose to hurt him and hopefully, take him out of the game. It was going to have a ton of fury and power propelling it. Justin was reading the split second signs in Princeton's definitive movements and his personal tell tale signs of his body. Princeton ground his jaws. Then he shifted the weight of his feet as he did his wind up. There it was! His left foot dug into the dirt and twisted. It was like a bull digging in to charge the matador. All in split seconds. Justin knew every detail of this pitcher and the goofball didn't even know it.

Justin's adrenaline was pumping harder than it ever had, and he was deep in the super competitive zone he could place himself in at any time. This next series of moves required all the skill and care Justin had in him.

He felt as if he was in a time-lapse machine and time was moving slower than normal and perhaps in his mind that was running faster than the pitchers pitches were.

While he went through his final microsecond mental activities, he carefully guided every movement with planned, regulated precision and accuracy. Justin concentrated deeply. His knees were slightly bent and he leaned in just a bit so he had bounce and room to make any adjustments. He searched for that "feel good" place to grip on the bat. He pulled the bat up to his right shoulder with his left arm up and just below his eyes all while he was watching the Princeton's body parts for more of his body signals he knew all so well. He finally steadied his gaze on the red and furious eyes of the pitcher. It was as if time were standing still.

Princeton wanted to knock him out of the game, but that wasn't going to happen from this dim wit, Justin said to himself.

"One of my favorite pitches you dumb Dahjah!" He intentionally mocked the word to mock and agitate Princeton further. He wanted the pitch his way and he was going to get it.

In no more than a split second he saw the release of the ball, he knew exactly where it would be hit on his bat and went after it like a Jaguar chasing it's dinner. The cracking sound of the bat hitting the ball could be heard for miles.

Justin watched for a split second and he knew he had it. So did his teammates, so did the Dodgers and so did the jackass on the mound. The guys on the bases knew it too. The home crowd saw it and threw their hats, towels, son's and popcorn into the air. The guys on the bases began to run around the bases as fast as they could to get to home plate and allow Justin to have the reigning show. He deserved it and they were honored to give it up for him. Justin did his "curtain call" trot around the bases the noise level rose so high nothing could be heard. He had come back to normal and heard them.

Justin waved to the fans as he strode by each section. He tipped the brim of his ball cap as he passed Mr. Duncan's owners box, and he saw him standing and clapping for him. He tapped his heart in a show of appreciation and emotion for the fan's love for him, even though his heart still hurt. He had made it to home plate where the entire team and coaches were waiting for his arrival. There was clapping, cheering and hugging on Justin for his beautiful homer. With a return to reality, this would be an exploding star memory Justin would never forget. It was nuclear!

Now he was exhausted from all the mental depth he had drawn out from within himself. He was giving it all he had left in him as if he were running on fumes. No gas left.

This is how it sounded from the announcers view. "Oh yes, no doubt! And the pitch is coming. It's a low curve ball and Justin let it go by. He's waiting for pitch number two now. As Justine continues his plate appearance, his concentration is immense and he works the count to 2 balls and 1 strike. It looks like Justin Edge is yelling at the Pitcher. Can anyone make out what he is saying? We can't hear a thing with the noise up here. The Dodger Pitcher is looking mighty hostile. Whatever is going on down there is pretty intense. This eternal wait will soon be over and the tell of the tape will soon be known." Reported Tom.

"The next pitch has been released with never before known fury and it is followed by an unmistaken sound of wood meeting the fastest of fastballs, with the meanest of mean sounding wood hitting leather. We could hear it from the ground crew's sound system. My gosh, folks, this is out of the park mercy going on here." Said Mike.

"The beautiful white sphere is heading out towards right field and it looks like it could… No…Wait… It IS, over the bleachers. The Red Sox, with the help of Justin Edge, have gone ahead by one run in this mystical, magical and mesmerizing 7th game of the World Series and they did it in a hurry." Tom Hathaway was literally yelling over the microphone, so as to be heard above the loud and deafening roar of the fans that sounded like twenty freight trains passing through the stadium.

"I'm telling you folks the noise in Fenway Stadium is physically, ear-piercing. The flavor and aura of baseball is hanging thick in the air making us all realize, this IS what Baseball is about. This game tonight, is what makes Baseball America's favorite pastime sport! God Bless you Justin for making it extra special tonight!"

"Tom I'm telling you, even I had to watch the catcher, and the umpire and wait for the people on the field to confirm that it was indeed a 97 MPH fast pitch. Can you believe that? Speed, place of pitched ball, and weather are no restraints on Justin Edge. When this man is focused, there is no breaking down his concentration level. The Red Sox have rallied ahead in tonight's game folks, with a brand new score of 8 to 9."

Tom spoke up quickly. "There is another time out, so I'll use this moment to give you all a bit of baseball trivia since we're in the Boston Red Sox Fenway Park.

It was in 1916 that then, Red Sox player Babe Ruth, pitched a 14 inning complete game against the Brooklyn Robins in Game 2 of the World Series against the opposing pitcher, Sherry Smith. The whole game came down to a walk, sacrifice bunt and a single score to win the game. What a nail biter that had to have been. I say all that to say this; I feel the same nervousness and tense feelings here tonight in the very same place of so long ago. Traditions run long and famous here in Fenway Park, Mike.

Chapter 65

"The Dodgers are replacing manning Princeton with their Veteran, lead pitcher, Wilbert Lincoln, here in the Bottom of the 8th inning." I saw some of Lincoln's pitches in the bullpen earlier, and they were quite impressive I must say." Tom was complimenting the Dodgers new pitcher. He knew they had him in for the heavy weight, Justin Edge who was now there.

"Desperate times call for desperate measures. Both teams here tonight have had to make such desperate adjustments as we have seen a few times already tonight." Said Mike.

"Boston Left out fielder, Wayne Daniels, is up to bat for the Red Sox. He is all over that batters square, taking some practice swings, and he's ready for the pitch." Tom was on the edge of his seat watching these next plays.

"Would you look at that folks, the ball is heading straight out to mid field bouncing its way towards the outfield and stopping short of the back wall. It bounced back and Johnny McGuire missed it and is running back for the ball. He's got it now and he's throwing his weight behind it and making it to the pitcher…. too late. Daniels the speed burner, has made it all the way to third base and his coach stopped him there. Great call." Said Tom.

"Schmaltz follows with a line drive and is safe on first." Announced Brooks.

Tom again, began the sequence of events taking place. "Next up to bat for the Red Sox is one of their relief catcher's, Albert Zachary. Another trade the Red Sox did over the off-season in revamping their weak spots on the team. I'm anxious to see what he can do even though this is his first year."

"This Red Sox team is really giving us a lot of firsts, and the fans are seemingly quite pleased."

"Lincoln has released the ball, and Zachary has hit a ground ball that flew past the pitcher and the short stop and into the right out field where it was stopped and sent in field. It was enough to get Schmaltz to second base; but Zachary is called out at first base! Man, that was close."

"Next batter up is Boston's 1st baseman, Jeff Pike. He just landed a hit that got him safely to first base. The right outfielder dropped the ball, quickly recovered it, but not soon enough.

"We have the next Red Sox batter-up, Boston's main catcher, Buddy Montaño walking over to home plate. This man has got the muscle in his arms and legs, to hit the ball to the moon. He looks ready for his part of history to be recorded. We are in the bottom of the 8th inning. Buddy swings and makes connection. The ball is sailing almost into the stands. Oh! It fell just a bit short. Nonetheless, he helped the Red Sox to make two more home runs and he is on second base. That makes for a lead of three runs by none other than the magnificent Red Sox Catcher, Buddy Montaño.

"We are in the bottom of the 8th inning now. What is your take of the game at this moment Mike?" Tom asked him.

"I think the Los Angeles pitchers are doing a fabulous job there's no denying that. But with what just occurred, I have a gut feeling they are putting a lot of pressure on themselves right now because they know this turned into a whole new ball game. The men in the Dodgers dugout are standing, and are very serious looking. Something we haven't seen in a few games. They were relaxed and self-assured of their victories. Tonight they were celebrating early, and now they are biting their nails." Mike breathed a heavy sigh. You never celebrate early, Tom.

"Right now, the pitchers on both teams have to keep clear heads and think calmly. Things have become very tense in these final innings. Every man up to bat is going to be one isolated piece of critical mass. By that I mean, the chain reaction of happenings that are caused from action or lack of action… hits or no hits. This game could still go either way tonight. I don't discount a thing. Nothing is etched in stone. I sure do wish I had a crystal ball that really worked. Not a real good answer, but this is unlike any other game so far. They're all different and this one is no different!.

That's my thoughts anyway, Tom. Do I sound like Dizzy Dean yet?" They both chuckled.

"Actually, yes you do. I'm seeing what you're saying and agreeing with you, so what does that say about me?" Both men laughed again. It felt great to be announcing a real baseball game as it was unfolding with all kinds of unforeseen events.

"Folks, we are in the bottom of the 8th inning and looking at an often and quickly changing game squarely in the face. These two teams are fighting tooth and nail for the championship in this last game. Neither team is giving up." Tom was in motion announcing again.

"Up to bat now for Boston is Mack Zimmerman, the third baseman. He has a powerful arm for throwing, powerful legs for grounding and ultra quick reflexes. Right now he has three balls and no strikes. Here comes another pitch. It was a fast curve ball and Zimmerman smacked it hard and it's caught fair in the outfield. The Dodger outfielder has quickly sent the ball to third base where Schmaltz is called out. The second base umpire called Pike safe as he slid into third base. That was a close one, Mike."

"Boston has Pike on third base only. The next player up is Justin Edge."

"We can tell from the noise level of the fans. Besides, Justin Edge is always the go to guy for these tense situations. I actually believe he loves it like this. He thrives on tense moments. I do believe that." Said Mike.

"As always, Justin runs to the batters square and does a few practice swings and readies himself for the pitch. He watches everything the pitcher does very methodically." Tom loved giving a blow-by-blow description of how Justin played and moved.

"He is a very intriguing young man. Not another player out there like him." he announced his thoughts over the microphone.

"Edge is watching the pitcher most intently, not moving his body one inch. There goes the pitch and it's an outside curve ball. Edge didn't even flinch. He sees the ball before it arrives to him, I think."

"Ok, we have a lightening-fast pitch straight over the plate and Edge met it with the crack of the bat with that familiar home run sound. Sure enough folks, there she goes flying over the Green Monster and Mr. Duncan, Red Sox owner is watching it with his neck craning to see it fly by. It could be looked at as a tribute to Mr. Duncan if we let our minds run wild. It was right over his owners box. That was one powerful and amazing hit, Mike." Tom sounded proud and amazed.

"Justin brings his fellow teammate on in and he just touched home plate himself. The score is now in the Red Sox favor with a score of Boston 11 and Dodgers 8 at the bottom of the 8th inning.

What a privilege to watch an athlete like Justin Edge bat. He is definitely Boston's boy! They love that young man." Tom gave his thoughts out freely.

"There's no arguing that one, Tom." They both were talking freely now. The game was about cinched by Boston.

Chapter 66

"We are now at the top of the 9th inning as the Red Sox have been struck out. The Dodgers have one last chance at bat to win this very tight championship they previously thought they had in the bag. How the tides shift ay' Mike?"

"And how!" It's mindboggling.

"We have a mighty fine batter up first with the Dodgers, center fielder, Marvin Meckler. He has arms of massive muscle and legs of steel.

Red Sox relief Pitcher, Raymond (Iron Arm) Erskine is at the mound. All the Red Sox are in position and awaiting the pitch to see where Meckler hits it.

Erskine winds up and releases the pitch and Meckler got a line drive off and made it just in the nick of time to first base. The intensity may be rising here. Mike."

"I feel it too, Tom. If we feel it, imagine what the Dodgers are feeling on the field. Sometimes a three run lead is not enough as evidenced in this game tonight." Mike was still not settled comfortably with the game just yet. He was still on his toes in announcing.

"Second Pitch is to Dodger Catcher, Bentley Briggs. The pitch is released. Briggs swings and makes it to first base safely, and Meckler is on second base." Tom is also very serious in his announcing as the tension is mounting in this last inning.

"Briggs is a mighty happy man right now. Needless to say, the Dodgers need every man to count in their 'up to bat' participation right now." Mike interjected.

"We have two men on base and a great batter coming up, Dodgers short stop, Andy Billman. He is waiting anxiously, and finally the pitch is released. Billman pops it a good one folks. It looks like it is headed all the way out for left field. The left out fielder, Justin Edge, has just caught the high, fly ball after it came down straight into his glove." Tom said as it unfolded.

"Oh My Gosh!" Tom yelled into the microphone to over yell the fans, "Edge has thrown the ball all the way in to the catcher, Buddy Montaño, at home plate. Montaño caught it straightway in his glove and immediately swung out over to his left side to touch Meckler before he came near home plate. Within a split second he sent the ball off again to Boston's third baseman, Mack Zimmerman where Briggs is headed and he's out! Say's the Umpire! A triple play and three outs all in one svelte play."

"Holy smokes if you got 'em!" Said Hathaway in a moment of non-thinking talk. He was watching the game and talking faster than he was thinking about what to say. The fans probably couldn't hear him anyway with the decibels being so loud in the field right now. They were talking anyway just in case the TV or radio fans could hear them.

After a few minutes the sounds subsided a bit and they continued with their broadcasting.

"Fans, Tom Hathaway here with my best mate, Mike Brooks. I want to make a very commending statement right now. The Catcher, Buddy Montaño, did all of this fancy work and may have even tied a previous record with what we witnessed here tonight. Montano was waiting and watching, expecting the ball to come to him. He knew where every single runner was positioned on the field. All in split seconds, he made the decisions to stop the man running to home base, and then send the ball to third base so he took the chance for a triple play and it worked! Justin Edge caught the ball, threw it all the way from center outfield into the catcher. From there, the rest is in the playbooks now."

"My Gosh, it worked people!" Tom was going into convulsions with this kind of baseball playing going on in front of him. "This is what Coaches, players and fans dream of, and we are seeing it right here tonight folks. This is the epitome of professional baseball at it's finest. I'm so glad to be alive and witness this game, I think I need a drink and we'll do a little celebrating later. If you're up to it that is, Mike."

"Oh, I'm up to it pal. I need it after this game." Said Mike.

"The definition of professional Baseball was just encapsulated in this last play that will go down as one of the greatest in history. I wonder what famous name it will be given, Tom?"

"I hope a mighty fine one, and one that's easy to remember." That's funny, but so true.

"Hey, Tom." Brooks still had to yell. "Report just in, the Radar gun on Justin's throw was 98MPH and Montaño's throw to third base was recorded as 98 mph. That, my baseball friends just tied with the long standing record of Steve Yeager's same ball throw and speed from a semi-crouched position over 35 years ago. Amazing performance, just simply amazing!"

"What on earth?" Bellowed Tom. "There isn't a man alive who can run faster than what those two men threw out there on the field seconds ago." Tom was just hoping the people could hear him over the roar of the stadium. This game would be replayed tomorrow anyway.

"This was a play of epic proportions and we are some of the luckiest people in the world to have seen this in person!" Mike was deliriously happy, as was Tom. The fans were still yelling themselves, as their own testament to their happiness.

"That's the Game! The Boston Red Sox are the new National Baseball Champions!

They were literally shouting over the microphones in order to be heard above the press box celebrating and the crowd going wild with joy, pride and happy to be Red Sox fans right now. They had the feeling it was not going to stop for quite a while either. The noise of the stadium was heard for miles outside of its' walls. The whole city was now yelling and cheering to add to this thunderous eruption of joy encompassing the mighty game of Baseball!" Brooks interjected hopefully, over the noise of the crowd.

"Folks, this game is now history. What a joy to be a part of this, especially from Mike's and my perspective." Tom was reeling in this high-energy moment.

"Tom said, simply put, Justin Edge is the best ball player I've seen in my lifetime."

Mike said in return, "There is not an ounce of argument coming from my mouth on that one. We're bragging folks. We weren't old enough to see the previous greats. We lie sometimes too." Laughter was so easy now.

"Oh! What a night! Oh, my goodness, what a night Folks!"

Tom and Mike both were in the middle of the frolic and merriment because they just witnessed one of the most tremendous, World Series games of a lifetime. They let their professional guards down without noticing, by joining in the epic gaiety going on in the press box. Bottles of Champagne were popping open, confetti was everywhere and they were revealing their involvement in the games, the announcing, the stress and now the celebration. Being the World Series announcers made them a huge part of it automatically.

"Great games are hard to come by, Tom. I'm having the time of my life being stuck up here watching everything still happening on the field. It's mayhem down there. The people are happy and uncontrollable. What a sight to see from our perch."

They would certainly be in the history books, as the announcers for this game.

"What a world we live in, hey Mike," Tom asked.

"Oh man!" Exclaimed Mike. "What a wonderful world it is tonight. I feel like I'm Louis Armstrong singing What a Wonderful World. I could just jump in the middle of all this if I weren't plugged into so many electrical units!" They both laughed fervently.

"This will be a night to remember for the rest of our lives."

"It sure will be Mike!"

Mr. Duncan in the Owners Box was yelling for his Red Sox team, and jumping up and down hysterically. There was no doubt he was jubilant and so proud of them. He had finally obtained his dream... A World Series Victory.

Duncan gave it just a few minutes with his guests in his private skybox with his friends, family and media. He excused himself, and then went running down the stairs towards the field. The security detail was clearing his path to his players on the field in front of their dug out. He wouldn't have missed being in the dirt and in the middle of this celebration party, for all the Whiskey in Scotland!

Portable stages and microphone had been quickly set up for the Commissioner of Baseball to present Boston with their Championship Trophy. Mr. Duncan was standing at the base of the awards stage with his team players and coaches. The inner management, his wife and his two daughters were also at his side.

The awards and speeches would be given soon. No one was leaving the stadium and the noise level was still clamoring as loud as ever, so no since in screaming over them.

The Team was in high spirits and still celebrating among themselves for tonight's long awaited and hard fought victory. Everyone was together. Management, players, coaches, and Mr. Duncan because that was the kind of organization Mr. Duncan ran.

The guys reminded Mr. Duncan about the biggest party Boston had ever seen, and he simply laughed and replied, "You just wait!"

They said back to him in unison, "Huzzah!"

Chapter 67

"Last, but certainly not the least, I thank God for a long and illustrious career with one of the most renowned Baseball Clubs in Baseball history, the Boston Red Sox." Justin was beaming now as he was completing his reminiscing from his beginning days through the last days of his career with the Boston Red Sox.

My biggest surprise came when I discovered the other side of the owner of the Boston Red Sox. I had a front row seat view to what a kind and well-meaning man Mr. Durie Duncan was and still is.

There was not a soul alive who could be tougher, better at negotiating, more stubborn, a flaring temper or a fierce force to contend with, when he needed to be, than Mr. Duncan. I had the honor of seeing both sides of the honorable Mr. Durie Duncan, and quite frankly I loved both sides of him because you could lean on that man. You could trust him for his word. His word was his honor. You didn't have to wonder if he was sincere and meant what he said, and you didn't have to doubt if he liked you or not, because he told you either way. The crowd chuckled and Mr. Duncan sitting in his front row seat appreciated and then laughed at the kind and funny words Justin spoke about him.

"I Thank God for my team mates throughout my career. They were all 'Alexander the Greats,' to me. They were noble. They were professional, and they were full of heart and soul. Some of them were downright... filthy, obnoxious and horrible creatures, pranksters, comedians and horse thieves." Justin paused for effect and let the crowd enjoy their hearty laugh, allowing them to see his humorous side once more.

"They made me laugh too... sometimes, when I needed it the most." Shaking his head in a yes manner he said, "We were a Team!"

The people stood and applauded these spoken words. The fans still loved Justin Edge and the team he played with. These people could not have made it more evident than they did today.

"*I have had the most blessed career I could have ever dreamed of and I thank all of you for letting me a part of the Boston Red Sox my entire career. And a very special thank you, to Mr. Duncan!*"

He tipped his hat to the man sitting in the front row who was older, but still wonderful and he still loved that man.

Chapter 68

In less than two minutes the technical men had bright, portable lights set up by the cameramen for the upcoming interviews.

The energy was alive everywhere, fans were not leaving. They were still running on adrenaline and relishing the spectacular nights game. The game that made their team the new World Series Champions. The entire Red Sox Team was determined to savor the night's victory as long as they could too.

"Here on the Field with us, we have Willie Steamalik, also nicknamed, 'The Locomotive'. Your team has just won the World Series Championship Willie, and what a contribution you have been to the Red Sox Team. You are to be the recipient of the Cy Young award, Congratulations on that achievement! Now, what would you quickly like to say so we don't keep you from your team, celebrating and the awards ceremony?"

They quickly put the microphone up to Willie's face.

"If there truly were anything to attribute it to, it would be the desire and mental prowess we all put ourselves through this year as we went all in for the race to win this Championship. We played smart, we worked out smart, we ate a lot, I mean, we ate smart and we tried to rest smart." Steamalik smiled after his comment. He was definitely in high spirits. His sense of humor was back.

"We actually believe in each other. We trust our individual abilities to make one whole team, which is highly unusual in most ball clubs. No one is superior in our club. We were in this as a team to win. We made the pact and stood firm with our coaches and the owner, Mr. Duncan. What you said is true, we are a very unusual but highly disciplined Ball Club, and we have been given a very unusual and blessed victory tonight!"

"Words of wisdom, Willie, no wonder they call you the "Locomotive," your reputation precedes you. Happy celebrating. A huge congratulations on your "Cy Young" award, and thank you for your time."

"Thank you, Sir, and I'm deeply honored to be receiving the award. I'm a very happy Red Sox Baseball Team player tonight!" He answered graciously because he knew his owner would expect this of him; and because it came natural.

They were interviewing Erskine now and were hoping to interview Justin Edge next. The people were searching frantically in the crowd for Edge and Coach Chambers.

"Justin, the sports announcers are looking for an interview with you."

"Coach Chambers, I'm not a showman like the pitchers are. Can't they just interview them?"

"You're the MVP, Justin and you just beat Babe Ruth's Home Run Record earlier this season in this very field and in front of these devoted fans. You have achieved a life long dream of yours. You have to go out there for an interview for your sake, your son's sake, your Granma's sake, the team's sake and Mr. Duncan's sake. I would say that's quite a few great reasons to go out there and sing like Tweety-bird, Justin."

"Please ask them not to ask me about my Grandma, Coach."

"You can count on me, son. Now get your self out there with me." Justin felt such a fatherly bond with Coach Chambers right now. In fact, he almost wanted to cry and wouldn't allow himself to. This was a beautiful feeling he had never experienced before.

Coach Chambers went out with Justin following him. After a few seconds with the announcers he called Justin over into the camera's view.

"Justin, you essentially had a magnificent World Series even when your team lost games. While in Los Angeles, you owned that field, you owned the pitchers on the mound. You commanded the ball to go where you wanted it to go when you were up to bat. I mean, this is how it looked. You were playing the ball! You are an amazing athlete."

"Thank you."

This should come as no surprise to you, Justin, but the fans are marveling what a similarity you are to the Babe.

You commanded the ball, pitchers, and plays. What in the world was going on in your head?" Asked the interviewer.

"Movies." Justin replied.

"Movies? How do you mean?"

"I have watched these pitchers and know some of their tactics. (He didn't want to give away his professional secrets). I just watched, and because I could see their moves and the direction the ball was coming, I relied on the bat and ball to connect and do their thing. Give me home runs. We needed them and I was lucky enough to get them at the right time."

"That sounds so easy and surreal," said the interviewer, "but we know it isn't. How can this be possible as the game defies such actions?"

"I guess I'm a maverick with a lucky charm."

"Now that doesn't sound as savant as I know you are." Heckled the interviewer as he gave out a slight laugh. He was annoying Justin with his haughty attitude. Coach Chambers was about to yank him out of this disrespectful interview. He was Justin's protector tonight, but Justin began to come on strong on his own. He backed away to watch for just a bit more.

"Okay…first of all, I'm praising God for everything he has done for me and made me into. The rest of the compliments go to the entire Boston Red Sox Ball Club, plain and simple." Justin said this looking the interviewer straight in the eyes and never blinking. He was rather intimidating up close thought the interviewer. He's big, muscular, and extremely intense. The interviewer never interrupted or asked another rapid-fire question. Justin proceeded.

"The nexus of my thoughts are connected and centered around what I've been blessed with. Abilities beyond my explanations and I am playing baseball with an extraordinarily talented ball club. It's full of the best players, coaches, management, workers in unnoticed jobs, and an incredible owner who has backed us up every step of the way.

I have a personal creed I live by and that is to be as good of a person as I can be. I want to be an outstanding athlete for the Red Sox and I want to be a great father to my son. My happiness depends on my purpose in what I am and what I do. I am honored to be where I am tonight. I'm grateful for every day of my life and for the son and brother-in-law that I have here tonight with me in spite of my personal circumstances." Coach Chambers about fainted when he heard Justin bring up his personal life. He knew he was annoyed and hurting at this point, but he was doing a usual Justin Edge, perfect performance as no one else could.

His Interview totally fit in place. It fit in so well, he didn't even realize it at the time. He was letting the people share his life and pain with him. This was meaning more to the fans than he would realize for weeks to come. He was in a fog, but the people would grow to love this ball payer more than his wildest dreams would ever imagine because of his sincerity and openness. The noise level had even come down so they could hear what he was saying. The fans wanted to know more about him and he didn't realize he just let them see more into his person and further devotion to the Red Sox and Boston fans.

"I do believe as a team, we have been able to display in this series all of these factors working together as a team. All the Red Sox players did their jobs and played their positions extremely well. We ended up winning this very intense and hard fought, championship through blood, sweat…and tears." Justin wanted to give credit where credit was due.

"I will tell you with full sincerity, the Boston Red Sox, as an entire organization, won this World Series and every other title bestowed upon us because of who and what we are as a team. The owner, Mr. Duncan treats everyone of us as a gentleman and expects us to behave and act like civilized gentlemen on and off the field. The rest falls into place when you act like a decent man.

The management is a vital part of the operation and communications. They stay in touch as no other organization I have heard of. Nothing is left for chance. Everything is scrutinized and agreed upon by all. It's a wonderful organization and a perfect place for me to be in my life."

He was finished. He quit talking completely and stood up to leave.

"Thank you for your time, Justin, Congratulations to the whole team and please promise to be a guest on our show when all the celebrations are over." The interviewer was trying to pin him into a television interview as he was walking away.

Tom Hathaway jolted into the conversation via headphones, as Justin was taking off the headset and leaving. Tom quickly said, "One question for an old man in the announcers booth, if you will please Justin."

"Of course, Sir."

"I know it's too soon to ask, but I'm going to ask anyway. Do you have any words regarding plans for next year? We are just so darn curious up here.

"Yes, as a matter-of-fact I do, Sir." Said Justin

"Misoneism." It's the best word to start our next years strategy with!" Everyone laughed and Justin finally smiled slightly with his lips pursed. It was the best he could do.

Tom Said, "Not a bad way to forecast the next year in very few words, so typical of Justin Edge."

"As the old saying goes from my favorite Coach, Mr Chambers, If it ain't broke, don't fix it."

"Justin, what you did out there tonight and through this whole series was almost incomprehensible. If we hadn't seen it with our own eyes, I doubt seriously anyone could have described the flawless plays you made that were dramatic and heroic. I would chance to call it Drama in poetic motion, that's the best I can describe it. As a baseball fan it was beautiful and jaw dropping to see. This is what baseball is all about. Expecting the unexpected. We thank you and the rest of the team for such a beautiful and dramatic night for game 7 of the World Series!"

Justin had nothing to add to the comment, so he just nodded his head, shrugged his shoulders and smiled.

"It will be a celebrated occasion for some time and many years to come after, no doubt. Congratulations on your MVP, your place in history and winning the World Series Championship. Those are some bragging rights for a very humble man who wouldn't even let him self be placed on the front cover of a newspaper or a magazine this season. Is it that you're just so humble, or is it that you prefer to be invisible, Justin?" Asked the interviewer.

"Neither." Said Justin. "I just want to play baseball and do it well for everyone it matters to."

"You're a kind man, Justin, and you are in ours and all of Boston's hearts tonight."

"Thank you, Sir."

He winced back a choke, and left the interview station with Coach Chambers at his side. Coach Chambers said, "I couldn't tell them in the press box not to say anything personal, Justin."

"They were fine, Coach. Thank you for standing with me tonight. It really means a lot to me."

"You're my boy, Justin. I'll always be there for you."

"Justin looked at Coach Chambers and said that's what my Grandma called me, and always said to me!"

Coach Chambers was speechless for the first time in his life.

"Tom Hathaway here, and The Boston Red Sox team have succeeded in bringing home the Commissioners trophy to Boston. Durie Duncan, owner of the Boston Red Sox, is one ecstatic and happy man tonight receiving the World Series Trophy."

"This is one happy city tonight, Tom. What a joyous night this must be for all of Boston. Their team has added another World Series trophy to the infamous Fenway Park Stadium."

Chapter 69

The Los Angeles' Coach interview came after the guys were in their locker room. He stayed behind and on the field as it was expected of him to say a few words.

"Hello, this is Bill Alexander here, with the Coach of the Los Angeles Dodgers, Coach Bernie Brown. We'll make it short Coach because we know you have a long flight back home tonight. It's understandable that you and your team, are extremely disappointed to of come so far and then miss the mark by one game. Can you tell us where you think you failed to reach the mark? Where the turning point was, anything that stuck out to you a something to work on next season?" Asked Bill.

The interviewers never know when to stop with one question, was his first thought, but dare not say it, even in his miserable state of mind.

"We played against a very organized and tough ball team tonight, no doubt about it. As the signs around here say, Boston has the 'Competitive Edge', Justin Edge. He deserves to be the MVP of this series. He also deserves to be called another legend of Fenway Field Stadium Park."

The LA Coach paused for a moment and then said,

"There were 25 players on the Los Angeles Dodgers team tonight.

There were 24 players on the Boston Red Sox Team.

Then, there was Justin Edge who plays in a league all of his own."

"End of Story."

"Thank you for your time and comments Coach. We appreciate you and a great World Series the Dodgers Organization gave us all. Safe travels too."

"Thank you, as well."

I know they are an extremely disappointed, Dodgers Ball Club tonight. Our Best thoughts go with them all." Said Mike Brooks, from the Press Box.

Chapter 70

"I was one of the members of the team that won the First World Series with the Boston Red Sox after a 15 year dry spell. Those moments were the epitome of what a professional ball club should be like.

We knew our own team and we knew our competition. We knew where everyone was on the field at all times. The almost inexpressible joy we shared as a team made us kings of the field that last night of the World Series, and together, for one memorable night, we were the "Boston Red Sox Home Run Kings and World Series Champions."

It's not something that I can easily be put into words how much it all meant to me, but by being selected to have my name placed in this monument with all the other Baseball greats, I don't think I have to say very much. It speaks for its self.

One very important topic I do have to mention is my son, Bradley. You see he has been at my side since he was born. He has been with me in good times and in bad times, in happy times, and in sad times. He was with me when I beat the Babe's Home Run Record and he was with me on my shoulders as we trotted around the baseball field after the winning homerun that allowed me the distinguished honor of beating Babe Ruth's Homerun record that stood for so many years undisturbed. He is with me here today, for the honor of a lifetime. Yet another honor we shall share together.

Bradley, just take it at my word, how much you have redeemed me as a person.

This is for both of us son!"

He lifted the plaque up in the air and pointed to Bradley, while looking into his son's face he saw tears running down his cheeks.

I am a very proud, humble and thankful man today, as I am able to once again, represent the Boston Red Sox in accepting this induction into the

Baseball Hall of Fame as none other than a Boston Red Sox Player my whole career.

Thank you from the depths of my heart. God Bless you all, and you too, Mr. Duncan."

Justin winked at Mr. Duncan and he responded with a nod of his head and a tip of his hat to Justin Edge, his pride and joy to this day.

"Yes indeed, It all had to start somewhere. My story started a long, long time ago.

Ever since, I've lived happily ever after."

Epilogue

Justin and Bradley were far removed from Boston, World Series, Baseball, fans, reality, their own home and reality, or any forced semblance of normal life and order. He had finally taken advantage of the "other part" of his original contract with Mr. Duncan and he was in the Caribbean with Justin on Mr. Duncan's yacht.

The Baseball season had ended in a what Justin called "poetry in motion." He had beaten Babe Ruth's Home run record in the same number of games early in the play off games. The Boston Red Sox had won the World Series. They were enjoying Mr. Duncan's yacht and Nathan was with them, but was in town so they could be alone.

The two of them were fishing off the swim platform deck at the aft of the ship with their feet and legs dangling in the warm water, while soaking up the warm, 'vitamin D' of the Caribbean sun, on Mr. Duncan's yacht and enjoying each other's company. The talk was jovial and light, the mood very relaxing. Nothing much about anything except the beautiful surroundings and what a great day it was seemed to be the highlight topic of their day. Justin and Bradley were always so relaxed with each other and Justin talked more to Bradley than he did to just about anyone, other than Nathan, of course. How could you not talk to chatty Nathan.

"I'm really happy you finally took Mr. Duncan up on his offer Dad. This is something I'll remember forever and ever." Bradley told his Dad with a broad smile across his face. The look on his face made Justin melt with the love he had for this son who was his joy and love. Bradley was the sole owner of his affections and he loved him so very much. What a lucky person I am to have such a wonderful son Justin was thinking to himself. Then Nathan's voice popped in and broke his thoughts up.

"Hi guys!" It was Nathan and he was back from town. "I thought I would grab a fishing rod and give you two some pointers on fishing seeing there are no fish in the live well as of yet."

"Uncle Nathan, we're not as much concerned about fishing as much as we were worried you wouldn't find your way home in time for lunch, teased Bradley."

"Oh, man! Nothing to fear there! This yacht stands out from all points of town, you'll see on from the pictures I took all around the Island when I upload the pictures to our computer at home. Besides, I'm sure that was really a big concern for the two of you sun worshipers." They all smiled.

More sun, more light talk and thoughts of what the Chef was preparing for lunch.

"Talk about lunch! My dear men, I am here at your service and apparently at the perfect time, with lunch in hand." Han's said in his beautiful Swiss accent and his lovely head Stewardess, Tristen. Justin had figured out the puzzle. She was the "other daughter" of Mr. Duncan. He had seen her with him at the World Series acceptance awards and immediately recognized her. Her beauty was hard to miss. He didn't even feel guilty for thinking this or feeling this way. Life goes on.

Tristen was learning the Shipping and yacht business from the bottom up as her sister had done with the Red Sox Ball Club. He had the utmost of respect for her secretiveness that she still didn't think he knew. She was beautiful and well poised. He knew she would be a tremendous success, especially learning from her doting and intellectual father, who tried in front of people, to keep it all business.

In spite of it being an all business atmosphere, there was the little flirtation message she would send his way now and then. It was mutually well received. First time in years Justin had a tingle in his stomach. It felt great. Maybe another week on the yacht, or a dinner in Boston would be in the horizon. That was, if Mr. Duncan approved first! Justin was always the gentleman and would ask first if there were a chance she would accept his invitation. Somehow, he felt she would.

The other wait staff came in quickly to clear the area and set up the lunch Hans had prepared for them. Tristen professionally and efficiently, directed where to put what, as Hans visited with the guests on board. Justin watched her even more now. Knowing what he knew was like being an unnoticed fly on the wall. He had fun with his little secret. She didn't know that he had it all figured out. Justin wanted to keep her secret safe, for now anyway.

Hans' assistants had the trays of food and beverages that had been prepared picnic style so no one had to move from where they were.

"Hans, you are the greatest and best ever." Said Bradley who was quite hungry and excited with all the extravagant service at their beckon call. The staff was entirely responsive to their slightest request or wish. I think you read minds, Hans,"

Nathan remarked. "Bradley's stomach was beginning to rumble and talk to us."

They all relished the fine compliment and joking in such a relaxed environment that was completely embellished with the beauty of the yacht, the professional yet personable employees who seemed more like friends now than employees of Mr. Duncan.

"To think, all of this to ourselves, with out lifting a feeble finger." Remarked Bradley acting like an aristocrat in the making. Justin and Nathan each threw a grape at him, all of them laughing at the same time.

They had been finished eating for a bit, when the crew came back to clean up the picnic lunch. Justin noticed the loosely done hair up off of Tristan's shoulders with the dark hair and the golden threads weaving in and out of the color, probably from being in the sun and getting sun bleached. Her eyes were blue like the water.

He was busy noticing her slender and shapely petite body in her deck blue shorts and white aquatic shirt with matching hat for the sun no doubt. He hadn't noticed a beautiful woman in a long time and didn't feel a bit guilty about it. Grandma Ruby's words still rang in his ears every now and then… "You'll find another woman to love someday." He didn't know what to think about that just yet, so he wouldn't.

He noticed Tristen looking at him as he looked up. She looked away quickly, but she had been watching him watch her. Justin kept looking at her anyway. He suddenly noticed the shimmering silver hair comb shining in the sun. It was so familiar to him. He knew it was the same insignia as the hair clip worn by Mr. Duncan's other daughter, the President of the Red Sox, Mrs. Tanya Argona. Mr. Duncan must have given those as gifts to his daughters because it was their family crest. They wore them with such pride almost every day. Maybe I'll get one someday. He halfway laughed to himself.

Nathan said, "My eyes are related to my belly. When my belly is full my eyelids come down. The crew smiled politely.

Bradley promptly replied, "You are related to me, Uncle Nathan! I have the same condition, but I can't leave this comfortable place. I'm too comfortable here. He leaned back gently placing his head on the pillow behind his head, with his feet still dangling in the azure blue, clear, lapping, warm water. He was almost asleep.

All of a sudden he jolted straight up with his eyes bugged wide open. This was highly unusual behavior for Bradley.

Nathan and Justin looked at him in surprise, almost with neuroticism, as they said in unison, "what is it Bradley, what's the matter?" His response was shocking.

Dad! I definitely felt something nibble on my left big toe! They all looked at each other in shock and astonishment. Without waiting another second, Justin swooped Bradley up into both of his arms and ran with him to the limousine to take them all to the airport while yelling at Nathan to get their shoes.

They were headed for Boston Medical Hospital. Bradley had feelings in his toes! Tristen was already calling for the corporate helicopter and the corporate jet to get there quickly!

© Barbee Kinnison, 2015

Printed in the United States
By Bookmasters